ALSO BY

AMY SKYLARK FOSTER

When Autumn Leaves

The Rift Uprising

The Rift Frequency

The Rift Coda

THE UNDERVALE

AMY SKYLARK FOSTER

ISBN: 979-8-35097-698-4 (print)
ISBN: 979-8-35097-699-1 (eBook)

*This book is dedicated to
the incredible and formidable women
through luck, fate and magic
have become like family.*

My chosen sisters.

PROLOGUE

The thing that did not yet know what sort of thing it was at all watched them from behind a large oak tree that was shedding its summer skin. The thing knew it was . . . something, though it did not have a name or fingernails or lips or the tiny hairs that should have been standing on end from goosefleshed arms. It did not have arms.

It had no memory of its birth. It had no parents and no idea where it came from. It certainly did not have anything like the gabled house it was looking at or the three girls it was spying on. Pretty girls with dewy skin and a bounce in their step. The three girls did not always smile, but their faces were so open and wide. It was as if a smile was waiting there, tucked behind their jaws, ready to pounce and spread along their teeth at any moment.

With sudden clarity, the thing knew that it must at least have eyes; how else would it be able to watch them? And then the thing thought, *how would I even know what an eye is?* This was a remarkable discovery. The thing had thoughts. It had desires and wants. Though all the thing wanted was to watch these girls . . . relentlessly.

Why this house, and why these girls? The thing was feeling something—something important. But feelings were newborn to the thing—they were floppy and feeble and unable to sit up on their own and declare themselves. The thing went still and tried to focus. What was this thunderstorm thrashing in its belly—this beaten wasp nest that thrummed and kicked in its middle? Why did the thing feel like racing inside the house and bashing one of the girls into a wall over and over again until she could tell it what was true?

The thing collected a word on its tongue the way a tender bud might unfurl itself for the rain. The word was . . . *rage* . . . and then another . . . *hate*, and finally . . . *blame.* The thing watched as the one with the pushed-up sleeves cleaned the lens of a black machine. The thing despised these girls, with heads emptier than its own, which was barely full of nothing.

The thing had only one mission now: it would watch and wait and collect the information that these girls dropped like a trail of breadcrumbs. These clues came in the form of tracksuits and silly movies, in the click and shutter of a camera eye, and in the positions, they slept in.

As the bile and vitriol raced through the amorphous shape of the thing, the thing found that it grew. It wasn't much, just an inch or two, but it was enough to cast a shadow on the grass beside it. Though the thing did not have a mouth to smile, it smiled still, from the inside out. Hatred would be the fuel that made it bigger and smarter. Hate was all the power it needed, and one day the thing would no longer be just a thing but something else. Something that had a name and a memory. Something that could take the slender white necks of these girls and squeeze them so hard that they would cease to be happy, sunny sisters and simply become . . . dead.

Dead *things*.

- 1 -

I am in the backyard this and every morning because I have an uncontrollable itch to shove my fingers in the earth. The soil is solid and firm, and when I am inside it, I feel solid and firm too.

Sometimes I feel like I am only half here.

Sometimes I feel like my body is a collection of feathers that could fly away at any moment.

Is it wrong that I get a kind of morbid glee when I deadhead the flowers? The dense click of my shears as they split off a dying bloom is probably more satisfying to me than it should be. I really like the gardening, but I *love* the payoff. I take pictures, and after I'm done puttering around the garden it reveals something new and beautiful every day.

My first stop is always the shed, where I grab a large trash bin and the rest of the tools I'll need—various spades, a rake, a trowel, and the aforementioned shears. My camera is hanging across my chest and slung over my back. One of these days I am going to break it beyond repair because I treat it like an old sack. Then again, photojournalists take pictures in warzones dodging shrapnel. If I start treating my camera like it's made of glass, I will for sure miss a great shot.

My mother (as she loves to point out) bought me this camera. She's out of town so I don't have to worry about her telling me for the umpteenth time how my camera belongs in its well-insulated bag. Even if she was home, it was the previous owners of this house that made this glorious garden. My mother rarely steps foot in it.

When the weather is nice, my sisters might help out with basic maintenance, but as soon as the sun disappears, so do they. Ana will watch TV while sketching a design. She might even cut a pattern right on the kitchen table and begin to sew pieces together on our avocado-colored machine that has been in the family since before our mother was born. Ana can and will do many things at once.

Since Etta is the chef in the family, the vegetable patch in the garden is hers, although she tends to it without pleasure. She enjoys the spoils, but she complains out loud (to herself? Me? The Garden Gods?) every single time she pulls a weed. For the most part, the three of us are house cats.

Besides the vegetable garden, there are four more formal boxes—two are filled with spectacular roses with names that always make me smile: Duchesse du Brabant, Papa Hemeray, Marchesa Boccella, Sweet Peg, and my favorite, The Undervale, a rose the color of a creamsicle sunset.

One other box has violet and plum-colored hydrangeas, and the last one is for annuals. At the bottom of these boxes is a healthy crop of wildflowers that require just the right amount of weeding. If I pull up too many, it will lose all sense of abandon.

Beyond them is a long full stretch of grass surrounded by massive oaks and maples. The grass ends abruptly where our property butts up against a dense thicket of woodland.

The first thing I do this morning, as always, is bury my fingers in the ground. I let the dirt collect in my nail beds. I wiggle and push until the earth chills my entire hand. A great sigh of pleasure escapes my throat.

When that is done, I bounce down to the grass and rake the leaves into a pile. There are surprisingly few given the season and the wind, which is gusty enough to make my nose cold.

Eventually, I look down at my progress. There are claw marks in the grass and a few brilliant crimson leaves scattered between the gauges. I stare thoughtfully at the earth. The turf has been sliced cleanly, disemboweled almost, and the scarlet foliage is like a mix of blood and tissue. I frame the tableau in my head. I cheat a little and move a couple of the leaves and then pull up my camera and start taking pictures. Mid-snap, I hear a rustling from the hedges leading into the forest. This isn't so unusual. There are all kinds of critters and birds back there, but it's really loud. A chill races up my spine.

Something is not right.

Something is not normal.

I walk slowly to the edge of the property. My black rubber boots catch in the mud where the rain collects, and there is little to no drainage. The backyard tilts ever so slightly on a downward angle and then levels out again at the entrance into the woods. The bushes rustle too frantically to be a rabbit or a squirrel. Could it be a deer? Do does or bucks watch people the way that I feel I'm being watched?

I pick up my right foot so that I can walk forward into the dark thicket. Even as I do this, I know that it's stupid. It is, in fact, epically dumb. It goes against the rules of every horror movie and True Crime TV show there is. But this is *my* house and *my* backyard. I am not going to be stopped by a damn noise. I will my body to move, and I am baffled when I realize that *I can't*. Not even an inch. When I lower my foot, the sound gets louder.

"Hello?" I hate myself for sounding like such a little girl. Much to my relief, no one and nothing answers back. I squint my eyes and stare into the black mouth of the dense forest. My pulse begins to thunder and my face flushes. I whip my head in one quick, deliberate motion. I remind myself to take a breath and be rational. There's no reason to be afraid. I've been playing in these woods since I was a kid. We built forts out there, lost entire days exploring, and brought home countless treasures—bark chips with dried sap that looked like icicles and dozens of smooth-surfaced rocks.

"Hello?" I ask again, and thankfully this time with more gusto. Still, my voice sounds weird outside of my throat, as if it doesn't quite belong to me. The bushes rustle again, and then... I see something, an outline, a shape ... a shadow? I bring up my camera and quickly begin to take photos. It's impossible. How could there be a shadow inside the shadows? The bracken and trees are so thick that it looks like it's a different time of day in there, not quite night, but maybe late evening?

I gingerly back away, my heart slowing down as I do. I want to run to my sisters and tell them ... what exactly? What could I tell them? That I heard something inside the forest? I saw a shadow? They would snort and call me paranoid, and maybe I am. But that doesn't explain the absolute terror I felt or the fact that my body flat out refused to enter the woods.

Whatever it was—my imagination or a wild boar or ... I don't know—I am done for the day. I return my gardening gear and race back inside.

"I made grilled cheese," Etta says as I stomp through the back door, making sure to leave my boots on the mat. "Mozzarella, Jack and a bit of Gouda with just a touch of Tabasco."

I groan. "Why? I don't like cheese," I tell her plainly. It might sound rude after she made lunch for us all, but she knows my tastes.

"Not true," Ana chimes in from the couch. Sure enough, her sketch pad is on her lap and there's some sort of Alaskan wilderness program on the TV. A man with a beard covered in ice is weaving pine needles into what looks like a kind of sweater. "You like white cheese—cheese that doesn't really taste like cheese."

"Like I said ..." Etta is twirling a wooden spoon in her fingers. "Mozzarella."

"You lost me at Gouda, sorry. I need to get into the shower; it's chilly out there and besides, I really want to develop the photos I just took."

"I made food." Etta smacks the wooden spoon on the counter.

"She's been in the kitchen for a while" Ana pipes in, but she's not that invested, I can tell. She is drawing, and mountain man on the TV is doing a weird kind of dance in his tree sweater.

"I appreciate that," I tell my sister earnestly. "But I just *cannot* with the smelly cheese. I'll grab a protein bar, okay?"

Etta cocks her head and narrows her eyes at me. Protein bars are sacrilegious. I might as well have told her I was planning on eating a Twinkie covered in Doritos.

Normally, I might try to reason with Etta or at the very least do a better job at apologizing. I'm too freaked out and cold and curious. So instead, I run up to the bathroom and take a shower that is so hot my skin is bright red when I come out.

I clear the steam off the mirror with my palm. My face is pink and my hair, which in all honesty is my best feature, is russet and copper when dry. Because it's wet, it just looks like a blah brown now and despite the healthy glow from the near boiling water, my eyes look strange and old and wearily exhausted. I give them a squeeze and push my knuckles into my lids as I shake my head. This whole day is going sideways. When I look in the mirror again, my eyes look normal.

I put on a thick cardigan and sweatpants. I throw my wet hair into a bun on to the top of my head just to get the damp off my neck. I grab the protein bar and my bottle of water from the kitchen before Etta can say anything and race down to the basement.

My darkroom is a large narrow space under the stairs meant for storage. While it is only six feet wide, it's almost fourteen feet long. I've even built a ventilation system of sorts made of white tubing that I assembled in serpentine shapes leading out to the basement window. It isn't fancy and it certainly isn't pretty because most of it is reinforced with duct tape, but I give myself credit for not being stupid enough to work with chemicals in an enclosed area.

Even though I take pictures and I could technically call myself an artist, I know that I'm not cool, at least, not like Ana. Ana is tall and willow thin. She is so insanely beautiful that I would probably hate her if I didn't love her so much. She has deep chestnut-colored hair that is bone straight and falls perfectly to the middle of her back in a severe line. Her eyes are a green so bright that there isn't a pretty word—a *natural* word—to describe them. They look radioactive. Ana knows that she is gorgeous but, she doesn't really care. This is what makes her so cool, obviously. I've heard plenty of models and actresses on television claim they don't think about their looks but, they are full of shit. Ana really does not care. She is dreamy and emotional and bored easily. She has seen her face a thousand times. It is no longer interesting to her.

The three of us are artists, but we all approach creativity differently. Etta is precise and meticulous. Ana, of course, is all over the place. I can be spontaneous, sure, but mostly I am diligent and responsible. The way I see it is that I have years to perfect my cool-girl persona and enigmatic artiste vibe, but adolescence is a dangerous business. Kids die all the time—car accidents, drugs, even swimming. I can't afford to be so dumb. Although I'm a triplet- which means that we are all technically 17, I feel like I'm the most maternal (though I'm sure each of my sisters would claim that *they* were). We don't have a bad mom, just an overworked and often absent one.

I click on the red light bulb and begin the process of developing today's film. I let it soak for a minute in the tank and then go through the various processes until the reel is ready to look at. After looking through the loop, I decide to print out two of the photos from the grass and leaves and then another three from the forest.

As I hang the 8 × 10 papers up on a clothes wire to dry, I decide that the photos with the raked grass are actually pretty good.

At first glance, the forest photos don't appear to be as successful. The first two pictures of the woods aren't all that revealing. They're a bit out of focus and don't look like much of anything beyond the dense thicket that I saw.

But . . .

The third and final photo is unmistakable. There *is* a shape there, a long shadow looming above the bracken. It isn't quite like a person, so at least there's that, but still. What is it? It looks like an oblong blob about seven feet high. Even more curious is that inside the shape is a flurry of swirls and fuzzy bits.

My lungs suddenly feel as though they're being squeezed by two invisible hands and a rattled click escapes my clenched teeth as I try to swallow. My throat is like sandpaper. My eyes scan the photo again and again and as I do so, I start rationalizing.

Eventually, I talk myself into believing that it's just an odd shadow from one of the trees or possibly a host of sparrows captured at just the precise moment to make them look like one single object. Even though my breathing is still a bit ragged, and my teeth are kind of stuck to my lips, I surrender. Whatever this photograph has captured is not supernatural or an omen of doom. I simply lack the experience to understand what I am seeing. At least, this is what I am determined to believe.

I hang the paper up and leave the darkroom. It's dinner and Etta has made pasta for me, salad Niçoise for Ana, and quinoa fried chicken for herself. While we eat, Etta goes into detail about how the meals were prepared, which consumes most of our dinner conversation. This is not unusual. Etta is a master of the humble brag.

My sisters notice that I am tense. They know this by the way that I am holding my fork and rounding my shoulders. They also know not to ask about it because I don't like to be pushed. I talk when I'm ready. I share when I have enough detail to defend my position. They let me have my silence and I love them for it.

After dessert, Etta goes upstairs. Etta's room takes up almost the entire third floor. It gets hot in the summer and frigid in the winter. Temperature never seems to bother Etta, so it was an obvious choice for her. Ana and I rarely go up there. It's a nice enough space, but a little too Spartan for my tastes. Even though Etta has an overly large navy sofa, it's impossible for me to ever get really comfortable on it. The walls are painted an icy blue. The bed has a hard wooden headboard and a thick pinstriped indigo comforter. It's not a room for lounging and I suspect Etta has done this on purpose. She needs her space.

Etta isn't like other girls our age and that's okay. In fact, it's great. Of all the families Etta could have been born into, families that wouldn't have understood her eccentricities or odd little ticks, she had been born into this one. At just over five feet tall, Etta is the smallest triplet, though her boobs are the biggest and as Ana is constantly pointing out, her ass looks great in literally anything. She keeps her platinum hair pixie length so that it won't fall in her eyes when she's cooking. Etta doesn't care about romance. She isn't interested in dating boys or girls. Her only friends are Ana and me. She is an opinionated extrovert. She is stubborn and mouthy and equally tender and nurturing. Our house is her domain. Her demands are practical.

Etta doesn't care much about the world outside. I watch her sometimes, trying to connect with a story Ana is telling about one of her boyfriends or girlfriends. Etta's eyes dart back and forth. The way Ana and I exchange our feelings, the way we call out what is simmering underneath our skin never quite seems to land with Etta. I think maybe she doesn't have these kinds of feelings or maybe she does, but they are so much weaker than her passion for cooking or her love for her family that to Etta, they aren't even worth mentioning.

We all retire to our separate spaces. I flop on my bed and the mattress makes a sound like its being punched. I undo my hair and even though it is still wet, it feels good to let it down. My temples relax and I cradle the back of my head in my hands.

The walls are still same ballerina pink of my girlhood although now they are filled top to bottom with my own framed photographs. There is a lot of pink in this room, which I should probably change given my age. Then again, I like pink. I especially like the pink lampshade near my bed that casts a soft rose glow over the entire space making it warm and cozy. I feel like there are a lot of things I'm supposed to let go of now that I'm older, but I don't think the color of my room has to be one of them. I turn my little TV on and mute the sound while I read. I click the lamp off at 11:56, just like I do every night.

Behind my closed lids, I see the shadow from the photograph, and it makes my stomach lurch. I allow myself a full five minutes to think about it, about all the awful, terrifying things it might be- zombies, mutants, ghosts, the actual Devil, and then I lock down my thoughts, shoving them all the way into the back of my mind. I absolutely refuse to dwell on something so irrational. Life is great. It's my favorite time of year. I have my sisters and my camera and my own darkroom- and, if I'm being honest (and vain) my really great hair. I mentally tussle with the image of the shadow until it's firmly stowed away. I feel my body give and lengthen. And then, I fall into deep asleep.

- 2 -

I am in the backyard this and every morning because I have an uncontrollable itch to shove my fingers in the earth. The soil is solid and firm, and when I am inside it, I feel solid and firm too.

The mid-morning sun is being smothered by a stretch of gray sky. I snip off the head of a brown hydrangea. The stalk cuts cleanly, easily, like it's relieved to be rid of the part of itself that is dying. I stand back and survey my work in this small area. The weeds have been pulled. The soil, rich and loamy, has been turned.

My back is to the woods. I feel something on my neck, an icy finger pressed into the jutting top bone of my spine. I whip around and my camera bangs against my hip.

I get this strange and sudden feeling that I am not safe, which is ridiculous. And the weirdest part is that it's more déjà vu than actual anxiety. Like, I'm remembering something that I have no memory of. I gaze into the forest beyond our yard, and it looks like it always does. The only sound I hear is the trilling of bird song. I shake my head and scratch my eyebrow with the back of my gloved hand. I am spending too much time at home with my sisters and not enough time out in the actual world, having a social life. It's like I'm living inside a Gothic novel.

Still ... for whatever reason, I don't want to be out here anymore. I quickly put all my gardening gear back in the shed and go in through the back door.

Etta, predictably, is in the kitchen. "You've only been out there for like, ten minutes."

"Do you time me?" I ask her as I kick off my boots. "Is that a thing that you do?"

"Well, I'm making brunch, and you know, the food doesn't cook itself. Believe it or not, I arrange things on the weekends so that everything will be ready after you take your shower and Ana's finished at least one pattern-y thing."

"You do?" I ask in genuine surprise.

"Really?" Ana stops all her various activities to stare at Etta.

"Yes." Etta huffs in frustration. "You are both super annoying. And rude. I was going to make grilled cheese, but I thought I would go the extra mile. I'm doing a proper English fry up. Eggs, sausage, fried tomatoes, beans."

My tummy had started grumbling the minute I had walked in and smelled the sausages. "That sounds amazing. Let me help you," I offer, "you know, because you thought I was going to be in the yard longer and I screwed up the timing."

Etta scrunches up her nose. She looks so young sometimes. "No, it's fine. It'll work out."

Both of my sisters look at me and this awkward sort of silence begins to thicken the air. "What?" I ask them.

"You always take a shower after you garden," Ana tells me from the couch. She has turned around to face me and her long, delicate fingers are smoothing the fabric of the sofa.

"Okay, but I wasn't really out there for very long so I think the shower can wait till after Etta's meal, right?"

My sisters just stare at me.

There's a few more seconds of weird silence and then Etta finally speaks. "Yeah," she says with a shrug. "Yeah, of course. We can eat now."

"Wait...." I ask with a grin, "are you guys high?" Because well, Ana does enjoy the occasional joint and Etta doesn't do drugs at all except sugar, but I wouldn't put it past Ana to trick Etta into it with some sort of edible. "It's like your brains are stalled or the Zombie Apocalypse happened when I was in the backyard. Am I missing something?"

"No," Ana assures me. "You just have a routine and I guess we're both used to it."

I can't help but cringe at the thought that I am so predictable. I don't always take a shower at the same time every day. That is literally impossible. We are in school during the week. "Okay, well," I put both my hands out, as if my palms have all the answers. "I'm pretty sure you are both high and that's fine. I don't why you would lie to me about it but *whatever*, let's just eat and you guys can laugh and talk about clowns, or My Little Pony and I will simply enjoy Etta's cooking."

"We aren't high," Ana says emphatically. She's got on hunter-green joggers that she'd embellished with her visible mending over one knee and along a large part of the outside seam on her left hip. Her t-shirt has fallen perfectly down over her shoulder exposing smooth olive skin. I do not know how she makes her pajamas look like they could be on a Paris runway, but she does.

"I don't do that shit, and you know it Lo," Etta says with a sneer. It doesn't matter. I'm already over it and I'm too hungry to care. "But I suppose ... I don't know. Today does feel weird. Heavier? Or maybe lighter? Like it's made of nothing."

I nod my head.

Not high my ass.

"Okay," I concede, because if they want to keep such a stupid thing a secret, there's no point in pushing it.

True to her word, Etta's meal is entirely prepared. And this is strange because if they thought I was going to be longer in the garden and then upstairs, how could she be done with it already? It's too much to think about without caffeine. In the kitchen, I pour myself a big mug of French Pressed coffee and take a plate out of the cabinet. The three of us dance around one another as we put our meal together. This is what it is to be a triplet—the inexplicable knowing, the perfect choreography around each other's bodies. We twist and turn and bend, unconsciously aware of the spaces we are occupying and the places in the room that we are not.

When my plate is full of fluffy scrambled eggs, a crumpet, two pieces of sausage and three small fried tomatoes from Etta's vegetable patch, I take a seat at the table which is halfway in the kitchen. The other half occupies the living room. I sit at the head. Ana and Etta sit beside one another. Ana needs to face the TV. Etta insists on being in the kitchen. She's generally up and down half a dozen times during the meal. When our mom is home, she sits across from my sisters. My mother is totally uninterested in the television, a fact that Ana likens to being uninterested in breathing.

"This is really great, Etta," I tell her after I swallow a forkful of eggs and tomato. Ana has her eyes glued to the TV and I kick her under the table.

"Oh yeah… amazing, like always," Ana says with a genuine smile. Etta preens, which she has every right to do. My bet is that she'll have her own restaurant before she's twenty-five. Ideally it will be within walking distance so that I'll never have to worry about cooking. (I've heard that being an adult is mostly deciding what and where to eat.)

"When's Mom coming home again?" Ana asks like she was reading my mind about us always staying together.

"Tuesday," I tell her. Our mother is a successful entrepreneur and although she has explained her job a bunch of times to me, I still don't really get it.

"Guys," Ana says after swallowing a big gulp. Her face is brighter, and her eyes get wide. Etta immediately sits back in her chair with a wary expression and my eyebrows rise. "I really think you should both consider having some people over tonight. Not like, an actual party, more like a casual hang, you know?"

"Really? Not a real party? That's bullshit," Etta spews icily. "Two people tell two more people and two more after that and then suddenly there are three hundred annoying drunk kids in here, helping themselves to whatever they want from my fridge and then throwing up everywhere except the toilet."

Ana looks at me with wide-eyed expectation. "Sorry," but actually, I'm not sorry at all. "I don't have anything against parties and being social. I just have a problem with the social part happening in this house which has so much of my very expensive camera equipment inside of it. For sure kids are going to go down into my darkroom to bone. And again, all for boning, just not in my own personal space."

"Fine," Ana waves her hands wildly. "*Okay*. But I'm not staying home. *Again*. You guys don't want to be social at home? Fine. Then WE are going out. All of us. We spend too much time holed up in here. People already think we're bonkers."

I take a sip of my coffee and level my gaze at both my sisters. "Okay Ana, where do you want to go to experience this super fun social time?"

Ana drops her hands and looks at me curiously. Her mouth is stuck open, as if her jaw has locked. She was probably expecting an argument from me or at least an excuse. But, if Ana wants to go out so badly, she should. It's better than her skulking around here. If she wants *the three* of us to go out, that's not going to happen. Ana is never going to be able to come up with a place where all of us can have fun because we are just too different. We don't even have any friends in common.

Ana smiles smugly and then she looks . . . stumped. Just as I predicted.

"Forget it," Ana practically growls. "We'll stay home . . . again. But when mom gets back, I am going out next weekend."

"You can go out on your own *tonight*, Ana," I counter. "We'll be fine."

"I know," Ana answers as she stuffs another huge forkful in her mouth which she quickly swallows. "The problem is that I know I wouldn't be able to have any fun. I would feel too guilty that you guys are just sitting here, again, all by yourselves. At least when Mom is home, it's normal. I can be normal. I can go out and have a life and let Mom be worried about how socially maladjusted you both are."

"I'm not maladjusted," I balk. "*I* am going through a really creative phase right now. I don't have time to sit around and listen to people gossip about celebrities as if they know them personally. I don't have the patience to watch immature teenage boys do a bunch of dumb shit just to get attention that will more than likely end up with someone in the hospital and Mom getting sued. But... Etta is pretty maladjusted; I will give you that."

"I'm going to spit in your dinner," Etta responds in a tone so sinister, I know she isn't joking.

"I can make my own—" the doorbell cuts me off mid-sentence.

The three of us momentarily freeze. The bell sounds... *wrong*. As if it has rung inside our chests and bounced off of our ribs.

"Was that the door?" Ana asks. She begins to blink a lot. That is how I know she's nervous.

"Obviously," Etta snaps. It rings again. It's more than that though. It is a clamoring, a thousand bells ringing at once—church bells, bike bells, wind chimes, the welcome bells that whistle when you walk into a store—all happening at the same time inside my head. I stand up quickly and my chair falls on its back behind me startling all three of us.

"You're going to get it?" Ana asks.

"Why wouldn't I get it?" I ask, trying to sound casual. The fact that someone is at the door is no big deal.

Or at least…

It shouldn't be.

"Because—" Ana begins and then breaks off. Logically, rationally, there is no reason why I shouldn't answer the door. But somehow it feels wrong, scary even. I clench my fists.

"All of you are being weirdos," I tell them, because they are, and I am too. This entire day has been off. We're all on edge. I walk briskly to the front of the house and my sisters clamber behind me. I put my hand on the brass knob. I exhale quickly and then pull the door open before paranoia gets the better of me.

"That's a baby," Etta announces.

"Uh, yeah," I say looking backward just so I can roll my eyes at her.

"What's a baby doing on our doorstep?" Etta asks no one in particular because obviously, it's not like we would know if she didn't.

The baby in question is sitting upright in an old-fashioned stroller, what Ana's historical romance novels would call a pram. The child has a head full of strawberry blonde curls, bright green eyes, and skin like Etta's—a perfect, pale alabaster.

"Yay!" The baby claps and giggles.

I take a step forward and Etta stops me by placing a firm hand on my arm. "You can't just bring it inside! It's not ours."

"Are you kidding me? Of course I'm going to bring him or her inside." I shoot Etta a dirty look.

"Why would you do that? It's an actual baby," Etta protests loudly.

"Yes, and it's autumn. What if it starts to rain? You think I should just close the door and hope the baby somehow wheels herself back to her parents?"

I try to move the stroller and Etta blocks me ... again. "It's obviously a mistake," Etta stutters. "Someone will realize and come back for it."

"Okay, well, when they do, *if* they do, these amazing parents who left their baby, know how a doorbell works." Every time I try to get to the baby, Etta stops me. Eventually, Ana has enough. She shoves both of us aside forcefully and grabs the pram while backing it into the house.

"What is wrong with you two?" Ana demands. "You're acting like it's a pervy salesman or a religious...what are they called? I guess they are also salesmen or salespeople...whatever. This is an adorable little baby. It's also proof that both of you are actually maladjusted."

"Wha...But..Tha..." I stutter, unable to even finish a word. It's like she hasn't been watching me for the past three minutes, trying to bring the baby in. Etta was the one who wanted to leave the baby outside.

Because I'm still miffed at her not noticing that I was on her side all along, I sweep the baby up in my arms before Ana can start cooing and singing.

"Hey!" Ana protests, just as I knew she would- she *loves* babies. "I wanted to hold her, or is it a him?" The baby is in a white jumper that looks hand knitted. With deft fingers, I undo the buttons and take a quick peek inside the diaper.

"It's a girl. Now, Ana, if you really want to make yourself useful, there's a little bag underneath the carriage. Pull it out and see if you can't find out any information, like a name or an address."

"Yay!" the baby squeals, and I am swept up in her bright green eyes which are framed by such expansive lashes it's like she's wearing a dozen daddy-longlegs spiders. All of my qualms and worries about that morning evaporate. I bring the baby close and smell her head, that wondrous mix of powder and soap and sweet baby skin.

Ana puts the suitcase on the kitchen table and Etta moves quickly to clear the dishes away. "Okay, there's formula, extra clothes, diapers, a little rubber giraffe. Hey," she says holding up a hunter-green contraption, "there's even a sling thing? What's it called . . . a harness? To carry the baby on your chest?"

"It doesn't matter what it's called," Etta interjects. "*We* are calling the police."

"We absolutely are not," I counter quickly.

"Lo," Etta shakes her head. "Be reasonable. This is a baby. This is someone's baby. She could have been abducted or abandoned."

"I know." I deliberately swing my body and the baby away from my sister. "And that's why we can't. If we call the police, then the baby goes straight to foster care. I don't think anyone would actually steal a baby around here, which probably means that she was abandoned. What if it was just an overwhelmed mom? A post-partem thing? What if it's a neighbor who knew that she would be staying close by? Or even a girl from school? If we involve the police, then someone could be arrested. I think we should just keep her for a while, see if someone comes back for her."

"You have completely lost your mind," Etta declares, even as she quickly moves to the kitchen with the baby's formula and bottles in her hands. "We are not adults. We can't be responsible for the welfare of a mystery baby! Ana? What if something happens to that child when she's in our care? Even if it's not our fault, we'd get the blame."

"Are you planning to drop the baby, Etta? Or spike that bottle with Vodka?" I ask her sarcastically. Etta looks at the bottle in her hand. She blinks hard like she doesn't know how it got there.

"Of course not. *Jesus.* I'm not a monster. But somebody has to make some formula for her, in case she starts wailing." Etta goes about preparing the bottle. She whips the taps up and down in a frenzy and clangs the pot on the stove with unnecessary vigor as she sets the water to boil. "Ana," she says anxiously, leaning both hands against the sink.

"I know you love babies, but come on, we can't just keep her. Not even temporarily. We need to call someone, an actual grown-up person."

"How about Mom?" Ana says suddenly.

"We can't," I jump in quickly. "Mom told us she would be off and on planes all weekend long. Remember?" Ana frowns and a small V forms between her eyes. "Remember?" I goad. "She said she would be unreachable." Ana looks down to the ground, as if the conversation we had with our mother is lying somewhere at her feet, in between the floorboards or in the carpet fibers.

Etta walks around the kitchen island. She holds out the bottle toward me but instead of taking it, I push the baby into Etta's open arms. At first, Etta startles and then I see her body give way and relax as she feels the chunky weight of the baby settle.

"We can't call Mom and we can't call the police," I insist.

"Fine" Etta concedes as she sways back and forth a little. "But we do need to call someone. I don't think you get what a big deal this is."

Ana suddenly looks up. She races toward the kitchen and points at the fridge.

"We could call her!" she says gleefully, tearing a small piece of notepaper from the stainless-steel door.

I quickly snatch the paper from her hands. "Stop!" Ana whines in protest. "Sorry," I rush to tell her. It was rude to rip that paper out of her hands but, actually? I'm not sorry at all. Ana's friends are not reliable people. They can't be trusted to help us with a baby. I can't think of one who'd be sober enough on a weekend to even say the word "baby" properly. I glance at the writing. "I just didn't know what you were talking about," I lie and feel a pang. I don't like lying.

In case of Emergency, call Em 5776294739

"Seriously?" Etta says in genuine shock. "That number has been up there since... I don't know when. I guess when Mom started traveling for work?"

I bite down on my bottom lip. So, it's not one of Ana's friends. Is Etta, right? It *could* have been stuck on the fridge for a while, but I don't recall ever seeing it. Then again, we see things all the time and never really look at them. It's the entire theme of my photographs lately.

Now, I'm *really* curious.

I walk over to the small alcove built into the wall and pick up the phone. "Uggh," I grunt while rolling my eyes. "What is with this thing? Why doesn't Mom get one from this century?"

I look at the number and use the rotary to dial it. I can't help but huff in frustration as the numbers click and whir at a slug's pace around in a circle. "This phone is ridiculous," I tell my absent mother as much as I'm telling my sisters. I put the heavy receiver to my ear. It's so big that we can all hear the ring tone blurt out from the speaker. It rings once, twice, five times and then finally—

"Hello?" an impatient voice clips. The accent is British. The voice is low, sultry.

"Uh, hi? Em?" I ask. There is a slight pause.

"Yes." The voice sounds tentative.

"This is Lo ..."

"Lo? I don't know anyone named Lo. Lo who?"

"Uh, Lo Smith?" I'm not sure why I make this sound like a question. I know my last name. It's just that this woman's voice puts me on edge.

"I don't know anyone named Lo Smith. How did you get this number?"

"Our mom gave it to us. You must be a friend of our mom's? I have two other sisters, Etta and Ana? We're triplets? Anyhow, our mom left this number for us to call you in case of an emergency and well, it's not like, a life-or-death thing, but we have a situation." Now, maybe this woman, this Em, whomever she is, doesn't remember *my* name individually but certainly, she would remember our mom. How many women had triplets?

"Wait, you have two sisters?"

"Yeah, there's three of us and our mom is out of town and—"

Before I can say anything else, Em interrupts me. "If this is who I think it is, you're wearing something pink or red. Probably pink though. Am I right?"

I look down at my dingy robe which in fairness, did used to be pink. "How did you know that?" I eye my sisters who are throwing up their hands and shrugging.

"Tell me, Lo, how old are you three."

"We're seventeen."

At that, Em starts to laugh. She laughs so hard and so long that I have to drop the heavy receiver down to my shoulder.

"I'm sorry," Em tells me breathlessly. "I'm really ..." Em sniffles. Obviously, she had laughed so hard she had actually cried. "Sorry. Yes. Okay. I'll come over. That is, if you're sure I can get in?"

"Why wouldn't you be able to get in? We have a front door like everybody else." I clap back. I'm no longer using my polite voice, but this is a grown-up lady who just laughed in my face for a full two minutes.

And *who was* this woman anyways? Is she really a friend of our mother's? And why on Earth would *this* be the woman our mom thinks we should turn to in case of an emergency?

Em snorts elegantly. "Glad to know some things haven't changed, Lo. Always with the clever comebacks. What's the date today?" I look over to Ana who shakes her head. Etta looks behind her at the kitchen wall where the calendar is, except it isn't there. Weird.

"It's October," I answer confidently, that much I'm certain of. As for the day, I just guess, "the twentieth?" It might be the fifteenth or the seventeenth. Why does this woman care about the date? Does she have some kind of obsession with calendars, or date planners? Is she heavily invested in the Bullet Journal system?

"Don't be so obtuse," Em says meanly. "I'm talking about the actual date. Let's see, okay..." I can hear papers shuffling back and forth. "It's the forty-third of the Patchwork Harvest. And it's Teal Day so your house will be on Pegasus Blvd and Magpie Meadows Lane."

"Excuse me?" My jaw drops. Both of my sisters are staring wide-eyed, exchanging startled looks from the speaker of the mouthpiece back to me and then to each other. Etta's lip is curled up so hard that it looks like it's assaulting her face.

This Em is obviously an insane person, and I don't want her anywhere near here, let alone a defenseless baby. At least she is so crazy that she won't be able to find us. Clearly, she has no idea where our house really is. Etta draws the baby in closer and Ana folds her hands together and clutches them to her chest.

"I'll see you in a few minutes." The line goes dead. I stare at the phone, baffled, as I replace it back on the chunky receiver. The three of us stand there silently. The baby gnaws on the strap of Etta's apron. Ana, who loves babies most of all, has finally gotten fed up and takes the baby out of Etta's arms and sits down with her on the couch. Etta hands her the bottle and Ana coos while directing it to the baby's open mouth.

"Alright well, this Em person, whoever she is, is not part of the plan," I say firmly while cracking my knuckles. "She is not coming." It's a statement, but I think I made it sound more like a plea.

"No way," Etta announces resolutely.

"I mean, Pegasus Blvd? What was that about?" I ask no one in particular.

"Is that a real street even? We live on Rosemont Avenue." Ana says but not with the kind of veracity I'm expecting. It's like she said the name of our street just so we would agree with her. *Validate* her.

"What is a "patchwork harvest"? Is sounds like a fair or something?" I mumble as I begin to pace. "Maybe she isn't even a friend of Mom's. Maybe that number was from the previous owners. It's just like Mom to leave something on there for years."

"Totally." Ana nods her head.

"She is not coming," I repeat, and my sisters agree. We are all nodding our heads vehemently when the doorbell rings.

Again.

- 3 -

I crack the door open but only slightly. Four tapered fingernails the color of ripened blackberries grab at the side of the wood. They push with significant force, and I stumble back. Scrambling, I try and close the door again, but it's too late. Em is inside our house.

It's not like I wanted to open the door; I'm not an idiot. We ignored the bell and the pleas from outside. Eventually, I got worried that there was so much racket one of our neighbors might call the police and then they would take the baby. Which, all things considered, may or may not be for the best, but I still want to give whoever left her some more time to rethink their fateful decision.

Em stands majestically in the hallway. She is a tall woman, over six feet with raven black hair done up in a sophisticated chignon. There's a plum-colored wrap around her wide shoulders and leather pants that are just one shade lighter than the suede black boots that go all the way up past her knees.

"Don't just stand there," she barks disapprovingly as she walks down the hall. "We have work to do. Where are your sisters?" She sweeps past me into the living room. Em stops short when she sees Ana sitting on the couch holding the child.

"What is that?" she demands.

"That is why we called you," I answer coming up behind her. "Someone just left her here. In an old timey carriage, with clothes and diapers. We weren't sure if we should call the police or . . ." I break off, unwilling to say more. Although Em's age is anywhere from thirty-five to forty-five, (making her technically, at least, an adult) she was an absolute lunatic on the phone. I don't like her being here, in our space, in our home. Em's voice makes the hairs on the back of my neck stand at attention.

"Someone just left it here? You don't know who it belongs to?" she demands while narrowing her brown eyes at the child.

"*It* is a her," Ana says quietly. "And no, we don't know whose she is."

"Well," Em takes a deep breath, "that's . . . ironic. And it also explains why you called and why I was finally able to get in here."

"Can you talk like a normal person?" Etta demands abruptly, rudely even. I shoot my sister a look. It's one thing to be snarky on the phone but in real life? The woman is unhinged and now she is in our home.

I have to admit though, there is something about her, something I recognize. I don't know the woman. I'm sure I've never met her. It's strange. It's like Em has featured prominently in a story about all of us that I've been told- but I don't have a memory to go with it. Maybe Mom? Maybe our Mom talked about her without ever using her name?

Em sighs deeply. "I can see this is going to take a while. Bloody curses . . ." Em mumbles to herself as she takes off her wrap with grim determination, revealing a cashmere sweater the same exact color of plum underneath. She sits in one of the dining chairs, though she faces it outward so she can see all of us.

"So, the three of you are all normal teenagers, correct?"

"Obviously," Etta throws out. She is leaning against the counter, unwilling to sit. I decide to take a seat on the back of the couch, placing myself squarely between Ana, the baby, and Em.

"So, what high school do you go to? Can you show me any of your textbooks? Some homework assignments you've done?"

I choke out an annoyed huff. I open my mouth to tell her . . .

Except . . .

Except . . .

I don't have the answer. My mind is completely blank, and all I can hear is the rush of my pulse beating wildly in my ears. The three of us look at one another frantically.

"Uhhh," I begin, but Em cuts me off.

"And you live here, with your mom?"

"Yeah," Ana answers quietly.

"And where is she, then?"

"She's on business," Etta jumps in. Finally, a question we know the answer to. "She's away, on a business trip," Etta reiterates. As if saying it out loud twice proves something.

"What kind of business is she in?"

"What?" Etta asks.

"What does she do? For a living? What kind of job would require her to leave her kids on their own? It must be pretty important," Em says skeptically. The three of us open and close our mouths like fishes plucked from the ocean and laid on a dock flopping around, struggling to breathe. "When was the last time you saw her? When was the last time that any of you remember your mother being right here, in this house?" Em folds her arms and waits for an answer. "Okay. Well... let's try something easier. What is your mother's name?"

I sit up straighter, my eyes darting back and forth. I know it, *of course* I know my own mother's name. It's right on the tip of my tongue.

I clench down angrily on my back molars. This Em woman is doing something to us. She used drugs or hypnosis the moment she walked in here. Except . . . how? Em hadn't sprayed anything in the air or dosed our coffees. She is wearing a watch, a very expensive watch covered in diamonds, and I am pretty sure you need an old-fashioned pocket watch or something pendulous to swing back and forth to hypnotize someone. Em had just pranced right in, acting like she owned the place.

"I can't with the three of you," Em tells us with an exaggerated sigh. "It's pathetic. Truly. So, I'm going to tell you something that will be difficult for you to comprehend. It will shock you but you're young, sort of. You'll adapt, eventually . . . probably." Em exhales one shallow breath before continuing. "You're fairies. We're all fairies."

My sisters and I don't say anything. We just stand there. And stare.

And keep staring.

Eventually, Em clamps her lips together and closes her eyes as if *we're* the ones who are being outrageous and irrational.

"Okay listen," she begins slowly, as if she's talking to the baby in the room and not intelligent and dependable teenagers. "You don't have a mother or a father and neither do I. We weren't born. We were created, before the beginning of time, or perhaps it was at the end of it. There's a lot of nonsense about how one of us is made every time a child laughs but clearly," Em spits, nodding her head in the direction of the baby, "it's a myth. Look at that thing. Like she would be capable of doing *anything* but cry and fill her diaper."

"Hey," Ana says protectively, sheltering the baby from Em's disparaging remarks by lifting an arm and blocking the woman's view.

"Just because we're young doesn't mean we're stupid, or gullible enough to believe that load of bullshit. You sound like you're off your rocker." I'm angry now. Fuming in fact. I can feel my knees shaking.

"Off my rocker?" Em barks with a mean giggle. "Oh yeah, that's totally the kind of language teenagers these days use. Sock Hop anyone? *Groovy*."

"Hey!" I'm about to launch in, but Em stops me with a glare.

It's an *extremely* scary glare.

"Look, I get it. You guys think this is bullshit- that I'm just pulling nonsense, random words out of thin air." Em has just danced right past her rudeness and that look which could and probably has frozen an ice cube. "I promise you; I am not crazy. There's no easy way to say this and I'm not one to sugarcoat things which is why, I'm sure, out of everyone you know, you three chose *me* as your emergency contact. That and the fact that I'm extraordinarily powerful and gifted. So . . . the truth is, all three of you have been cursed."

There is a moment. A beat of absolute stillness. Em's chiseled features remain steadfast. I wrinkle my forehead, wondering how anyone can be so cruel. This woman is not only saying something that is totally and completely bonkers, but she also seems to be enjoying it. She's smirking. It's like a game to her. Em has the audacity to sit here, in my own house and tell me that I'm really a fairy? That my entire life is a lie? That I don't even have a mom and that I'm some sort of victim? No. I refuse to take it.

"If by curse you mean that a beautiful and glamorous Black lady swanned into our home and tried to gaslight us into believing some sort of fantasy so that we . . . I don't know . . . join your cult? Is that it? You're a cult leader with a brainwashing voice?" I am not quite screaming. I know I'm being loud and screechy and now my entire body is shaking with rage. Is our Mom part of this cult? Is this some kind of initiation ceremony? Did she give birth to us for the express purpose of *offering* us to the cult? My mind has gone beyond racing. It's tripping over itself, leaping faster than sound, maybe even faster than light.

And then Ana goes and nods her head! "Actually, that does kind of explain some things. Not the cult stuff. I don't think cult leaders as a general rule dress as well as you do," Ana purrs. Unbelievable! Ana is flirting with Em. "I keep wanting to leave. Just this morning I suggested that we should all go out tonight, but then I got this overwhelming urge to stay put. I don't know why, I just felt like we all had to stay here for some reason. Can't you guys feel it? Like something isn't right?"

"I'll admit that something feels off." Etta, thankfully, is using her most rational tone. "But a curse? No way. Not in a million years. That is absurd. *I* think that we are all suffering from carbon monoxide poisoning. I haven't checked the batteries in the alarms for a really long time. To me, that makes the most sense. And you," Etta says as she points to Em, "are probably just a hallucination, but I will concede that you *are* dressed extremely well for an imaginary person."

I give Em a triumphant smile. Etta's logic is sound. Whatever this stranger is trying to accomplish has failed. I feel great for all of five seconds until I realize that although Em seems to be many things (including and not limited to, having wild delusions of grandeur), she doesn't come across as an actual liar. Which means that Em believes what she is saying. And realistically, though that word seems ill suited to this situation, if we're all having hallucinations, wouldn't we be seeing different things? As impossible as Em's story is, it would be even more impossible for all of us to hallucinate the same exact thing.

I'm going to stick with cult leader, but I decide to play along to get more answers.

"When you say curse, are talking like a fortune teller kind of thing? A gypsy did something to us? Is that what you're trying to say?" I suggest mildly.

"First of all," Em looks up to the sky, "no one uses that word anymore. It's pejorative. And secondly, no, a personage of *Romany* descent did not do this to you. A human could not have done this. You've been in this house for five years, basically reliving the same day over and over again. I tried to get to you—I really did—for six months. I spent at least five minutes every day thinking about your situation. But this house is covered in vines and thorns which again, irony, right?" Em gives us a snide chortle.

Ana sinks down further in the couch. Etta growls sofly and I'm angry. I'm offended. We're kids and we need help, and this woman is messing with us. "Okay well, that's ridiculous on a hundred levels. Even if I did believe that curses existed, which I don't," I begin as my anger continues to build. "How would that even work? There's always food here. We haven't starved. Ana has a new book to read every other day. We get cable. And I go outside all the time."

"To the backyard," Ana points out.

"Ana," I warn.

"Uh, it's magic, so yeah," Em says as if we are all idiots. "The curse weaves itself around the illusion, feeding it, giving it what it needs to stay intact. It's a good curse, and I've thought so from the start, but you know, I've seen better. Personally, I think it's overkill. Turning you all into seventeen-year-olds would have been enough of a curse on its own," Em tries and fails to smother a giggle.

"Very funny," I snarl. "You expect us to believe that's a thing? That people go around cursing innocent girls? Who would even want to do that to us? We aren't bad or evil. What could we possibly have done to deserve such a horrible thing?"

"I don't know. What *have* you done?" Em's lips curl into a sinister smile. "You have no memory of a life before this. Maybe you're all murderers. Maybe someone dropped off that baby as offering so you could eat it."

I take a sharp and audible intake of breath. I can feel the blood draining from my face. I don't like Em's weird fairy cult.

At.

All.

And then Em's stoic face breaks wide open and a mean-spirited laugh bubbles out of her throat. "Oh my God. You should see your-selves. Where's my phone? I should get a picture. This is amazing." Em is now doubled over with laughter, but she really shouldn't be because if *I am* a killer then she is now number one on my hit list. "I'm kidding. It was a joke. I wouldn't take pictures. Probably."

"It wasn't funny," Ana simpered.

"Well, what do you want me to say? I mean yes technically, you've killed people, who hasn't? But *context*, you know? Wars and evil beings and what not. This is not that. It's probably something silly." Em's tone has changed. She has raced through ominous, past the mundane, and now she sounds kind of irritated. "As you can imagine, being immortal can be extremely boring. So, our kind can sometimes be a little dramatic, overly sensitive. Not me obviously," Em offers quickly.

"What do you mean by 'our kind'?" Etta asks suspiciously. "Are you trying to say we're witches or angels or the other thing . . . demons?" Etta's neck muscles flex and the bottom of her mouth dips. "Because we don't have any magical powers. I admit that I am confused. But I would know if I had super powers."

"We aren't witches. Witches are human. And angels are not real. "I've already told you, we're fairies," she says slowly as if the three of us are trying to be ignorant, as if we're only playing at being dumb.

"I heard you the first time and I find it even less believable now," I say with a chuckle because actually, the witch idea isn't nearly as crazy as the fairy one- Hermione Granger, Circe, The Scarlet Witch... "If I'm a fairy where are my wings? Aren't I supposed to live in a flower and drink dew drops and have little shoes with thistle pom poms?"

Em scrunches up her face before letting it relax again. "Well, some faires are like that. It's a lifestyle choice. Which is fine, I'm not one to judge." Em innocently throws up her hands but, she's addressing us in a tone that says she might actually be the Queen of Judging everyone.

I cross my arms and lean back so the edge of the sofa digs into my spine, steadying me. "Okay, so prove it. If we're all fairies who can do magic, only *we* can't do magic because we've been cursed, have at it, Em. Show us what you've got," I goad. At this point, I'm kind of desperate to believe that Em is indeed, delusional. Not that I want someone suffering from a mental health crisis in my house, but the alternative? That we aren't who we think we are? That our lives are a lie and that we are trapped? Not just in this house, but in this world where nothing makes sense, and we can't trust anything we see or feel? I can't even begin to imagine how to navigate that.

I just hope that this woman, whoever she is, will say a bunch of goofy words and then, when nothing happens, we can call the police. The police will take us to a hospital where Em will likely be sectioned, the mystery of our amnesia will be solved, and they can take care of the baby. It's what we should have done from the very beginning. I should have listened to Etta.

Em lets out a long melancholy sigh from her raspberry painted lips. She pulls out a slender black wand from the sleeve of her sweater.

"That is supposed to be magic?" Etta asks indignantly. "That's the worst magic trick I've ever seen."

Em points the wand at the fireplace and then, like *actual* magic, a roaring fire springs to life. The three of us jump back in unison. Stunned. Em quickly draws the wand in a slight semi-circle, and we are no longer in our loungewear. Etta is dressed in a very chic, velvet blue jumpsuit with a co-ordinating silk bomber jacket. Ana is in a jade green sweater dress and high black boots, very similar to Em's. I'm suddenly wearing a camel-colored pencil skirt with a pale chiffon pink blouse. I'm also wearing boots, but mine are soft leather, the color of butternut squash.

We endure a full second of horrified silence and then, Etta lets out a blood curdling scream. She begins to run around the room, smacking at her chest and her thighs, swatting at her new clothes.

"Oh my God! *Oh my God!*" Etta yells.

At this point, Em is once again laughing hysterically. She starts looking around and checking her pockets. "I know I said I wouldn't, but this is too good. Where is my damn phone? I *have* to film this."

"Etta, calm down," I try to say, but my words are locked in my throat. Em isn't crazy and she isn't a liar . . . well, at least about this. Magic is real.

We are fairies.

And we have been cursed.

It makes no sense at all except for the evidence I'm witnessing and then it makes total and complete sense. It should feel like some sort of daydream or nightmare, but it doesn't. It feels real, and somehow, oddly, inescapably, it also feels right.

"Get them off me, get these demon clothes off me NOW! Oh my God!" Etta hollers.

"Yay," the baby says, clapping.

Em points her wand at Etta and Etta freezes mid-freak out. She looks like a wax figure in one of those museums. "Remember how I told you our people were overly dramatic?" Em flutters her eyes and rolls them overly hard. I think she may be talking to me or Ana. Maybe she's just talking to herself. "Etta, if I release you from my hold, are you capable of being calm?" Em asks without an ounce of sympathy. The question is rhetorical obviously, because Etta can't move. After a few seconds, Em's wand dips and Etta is flung forward, catching herself on the back of the couch.

I realize something then, with a sickening kind of clarity, and my stomach drops. "Wait . . ." I begin, running my fingers over my top lip and across my cheek. "So, we don't look like this? This isn't really us?" I'm asking Em, maybe. I'm probably just asking myself or God, or the universe because I suddenly understand that I am not really me. There must have been something in my voice though, some level of fear that Em can't ignore or giggle over.

"No," Em answers with more warmth and kindness than I thought she would have been capable of. "But that's good right? You don't really want to be teenagers, do you?"

"Well, not forever, but now . . . yes . . . ," I rush. "This is who I am. I don't know how to be different." I say with halting finality. "If this isn't my real face or my real body, what do I actually look like?"

Em's eyes wander to the ceiling. Her long black lashes which had looked false but which I now assume are real, well *magically* real, reach up to her eyebrows. "Our natural appearance is ephemeral. We are beings of ethereal light. Which is so boring. It's not like we can actually do anything without arms or feet. Only a few of us live in that state and it's impossible to talk to them. It's like trying to have a conversation with a Magic Eight Ball."

Etta clutches at the couch so hard her knuckles go white. Em's shoulders drop as she tries to explain further. "We've all worn a thousand faces, but it's not as if who we are *inside* does any changing. And with every altered appearance, there is something familiar with each guise. We can recognize one another through the glamor, but don't ask me how that works because I have no idea."

At this point, I'm afraid I might throw up or possibly even pass out. This idea, that my face doesn't entirely belong to me, that I have only borrowed it, like a library book or a friend's sweater, shakes me down to the core. My temples begin to pound; the blood races to my brain where I need it most. I can feel the veins in my neck begin to swell... Unless of course, I don't even have any veins. That's always a possibility too.

I might not be able to wrap my head around the fact that my face is only temporary- but the matronly pencil skirt? *That is* something I can control. "Can you just put us in normal clothes? I look like I'm going for a job interview." The outfit is too much. I can't even take a decent stride. It's not me, or at least, the me I think I am.

"I'm actually good with what I'm wearing," Ana says quickly as she preens at her reflection in one of the windowpanes.

"Like I said, regardless of our appearance, the essence of who we are remains. Ana is the only one of you with any sense of fashion," Em observes while turning Etta's jumpsuit into navy yoga pants and a velour hoodie. I get jeans and a light pink turtleneck, cashmere, of course.

I finger the soft wool of my sweater. This feels like a dream. But there's always a way, even in the very worst nightmares, to turn things around if you're clever enough to change the rules. This revelation gives me an idea, of sorts.

"If you have all these powers, I have to assume they aren't limited to turning us into Career Barbie or Fashionista Barbie."

"Teenage Barbie is Skipper," Ana interjects pointlessly. She's like a magpie, my sister; any shiny new thing and she gets tunnel vision.

"Break the curse," I challenge. If this is a curse, I wanted it broken. If Em is right, and we will always be who we are deep inside, does it really matter what we look like? Especially since, if the theory holds, I can keep the body I'm currently in anyways?

It's not like I inherited my face from my parents. According to Em, I don't have a father or a mother.

Mom

I whisper the word softly. Invoking a feeling of longing, rather than the memory of an actual person. Of all the things Em has told me, the fact that we are motherless is oddly, the easiest to accept. I can't even picture the mother I had been so sure existed only an hour ago.

"I'm afraid I can't do that," Em says, interrupting my thoughts, though she sounds more frustrated than sorry.

"Why not? That wand of yours works okay," Etta sneers as she pulls her hoodie up over her head.

"Because a curse like this has a million interconnected threads," Em points out vehemently. "It would be like asking me to unlock a bank safe when the combination changes every time I turn the dial. The upside is that the curse is, for whatever reason, already breaking down. Now that I've talked to the three of you, my best theory is that it's connected to your memory. The more you remember, the less effective the curse."

"*Great*," I groan. It's one thing to accept that all of this is real, but quite another to be told that it's *our* job to figure out how to undo this curse by remembering something I didn't even believe could be possible when I woke up this morning.

If it was this morning.

My brain is scrambled. I don't know if two weeks ago was two years ago. It's bad enough I can't recall being a fairy—a monumentally epic thing, a thing I can't fathom forgetting—I don't even remember the details of the life I'm living now. And I really do not understand this Em woman. Doesn't she see how helpless we are? Doesn't she care?

Because I'm so damned frustrated, I rush over to Em and grab her wrist. "If you can't zap our memories back into our skulls, how are we supposed to even know where to begin?"

Em's gorgeous face offers up a look of disgust. She peels my fingers away as if they are poison. "Your wands…*obviously*," Em tells me as if that should mean something. "Your wands will provide a great deal of assistance."

"Wait," Ana says, while putting the baby's empty bottle on the table, "are you saying that we are magical beings, but the only way we can do any magic is with a wand? That doesn't make any sense at all."

"*That's* the thing that doesn't make sense?" Etta snarls, but Em just laughs. Her lips spread across her face like a stain.

"Are you actually looking for a logical, reasonable answer to any of this? Don't be so pedestrian, darling. It's beneath you." Em sighs dramatically.

"It's a fair question," I argue, even though I think at this point, she's probably right.

"It is not fair, not at all," Em pounces. "There is no fairness in this world or any other. The wands prevent us from becoming monsters. They keep us in check, reminding us that we owe our magic to a force that is beyond us. Without them, we are powerless."

"You know what, Em?" Etta bites back angrily. "Not only do you speak in some bizarro new age-y cypher code which you obviously know that none of us can understand, you suck at being a fairy godmother."

"*I am not* a fairy godmother," Em says with indignation while brushing an invisible piece of dust off her shoulder. "That job is more your speed. And I am helping. You wouldn't even know about the curse or any of this unless I had told you. I'm sorry if you don't feel like that's enough, but even with all my considerable talent, which is, as I previously mentioned, vast, there's only so much I can do."

"There must be something," I ask frantically, "some kind of a spell that tells us where our wands are?"

"Wands don't work that way," Em scoffs. "However, I can tell you that I believe there is one hidden in this house. Somewhere. I can hear it. Humming. And if the three of you would shut up and listen instead of complaining and whining about the fact that you don't have a Mommy, maybe you could hear it too."

And with that, Em stands regally. She flicks her wand once more and magically folds the wrap around her shoulders in the chicest way possible.

"You're leaving?" Ana asks wide-eyed, the baby clutches at her long hair but Ana doesn't even notice.

"I've done all that I can do here. Find a wand and call me. I can't promise that a single wand will undo the entire curse, but it should help you on your way."

"You should take the baby." Etta scrambles, as we all do, trying to get this stranger—whom none of us actually like (except for Ana maybe, but Ana likes everyone), who has managed to both terrify us and make herself totally indispensable—to stay longer because there is no way we can do this on our own.

Ana purses her lips and tears begin to well in the corners of her eyes. "We may be immortal beings of light, but we don't feel that way," she croaks, her voice breaking mid-sentence. "We feel like kids. And how are we supposed to do anything when we have a baby? Maybe my sisters are right. This baby sure is adorable but maybe you should take her with you."

Em blanches. Her entire face curdles like she might throw up a little bit in her mouth. "Oh God no. I don't do babies. *Ever.* It's a thing," She informs us as she backs away from the baby like the little girl is radioactive. "And no, you can't call the police or child protective services because we're in The Undervale, not the mortal realm. Do you understand that? We police ourselves and there are no fairy children because like I said, we are made, not born. Here in The Undervale, up is down. Sideways is back beyond. Fairies lie for amusement and almost everything is an illusion."

The Undervale. The name of my favorite rose. It could hardly be a coincidence. Not that it matters. The roses outside are just normal flowers ... probably? I don't think they are going to help us. I've gazed at them long enough to know there are no answers written on their sorbet-colored petals.

"Besides," Em says as she curls a single burgundy lip, "I wouldn't be so quick to get rid of that mewling thing. The baby tore a hole just big enough in the fabric of the curse to let me inside. You have an ally. Somewhere." Em begins to walk toward the front door, trailing a hand over frames and books as she goes and then inspecting her fingers for dust that isn't there. "You may well have to trade it for important information. Black Market babies are a valuable commodity in The Undervale, though I can't for the life of me understand why."

"We wouldn't trade her," Ana says with horror. "What's wrong with you?"

Instead of answering, Em sighs so loud that it's almost a groan. Her boots click and clack down the hardwood floor hallway. She puts her hand on the doorknob. "Good luck, ladies. You have my number, but please don't call me to whinge or sob. Intense emotions make me uncomfortable. Also, I'm very busy." And with that, Em throws the door open and walks outside. I watch as she disappeared down the tree-lined street. I take a tentative step forward, thinking it might be a good idea to see where Em is headed. Before I can put a single foot on the doormat, I get a giant, invisible push backward. I land on my bottom, hard, and the door slams shut. Etta races to help me up.

"It'll be okay, Lo," Etta tells me without much conviction, but I appreciate the effort because there are three things I know for sure now: We *are* fairies. We *are* cursed, and we are most decidedly, absolutely and truly, *trapped* in our house.

- 4 -

It only took six minutes for Ana to rig up a mobile for the baby to play with. She strung stuffed stars and crocheted alligators along a bent rod, securing it inside two potted plants. The baby is lying on our living room floor, reaching, laughing—thoroughly unfazed by her circumstance.

We are not faring as well. Ana is drinking a glass of red wine. It came from one of the many bottles that belonged to our imaginary mother. She has filled it to the absolute brim. I let her pour me a drink as well, though my glass is only half as full. Etta sticks with tea that smells like lavender and beets.

We need to have a conversation. We need to talk about this but, none of us wants to start it. No one wants to speak because the words we will use are thorns on our tongues and burrs in our cheeks. The conversation is bound to cause us more pain than we are already in. The table we are seated at, the table we have sat at—apparently for years, enjoying meals and one another's company—has become an ocean. We are anchored miles away from each other in choppy, black waters.

Finally, Ana opens her mouth, probably because she's drained her glass. "I just want to say . . . I need to say . . . that I don't think we are bad. I do not believe this is a punishment."

"You mean, you don't think we murdered anyone," Etta offers. "You don't think we're serial killers or old hags who lure children into the forest with candy to fatten them up for our dinner."

"That actually *would* make us serial killers," Ana spits back. "And no, I don't think so. I think whoever did this is jealous of us, of our closeness, of the fact we are triplets. I think this is someone being petty and mean."

"How do you know that all fairies aren't triplets?" Etta demands.

"Because of Em," Ana responds quickly.

Etta clunks her teacup down on the saucer. Em's name alone is enough to make her hostile. "She didn't tell us anything about herself-apart from how amazing and talented she is. You couldn't possibly know if she has siblings or not."

"Etta," Ana slurs a little and leans towards both of us, "you know food and you know us, but you don't know people. Em wouldn't have been such a miserable meanie if she wasn't so lonely. Pain turns people into monsters. If she had two sisters, I don't think she would have been so awful. If she had more love, she would have been more compassionate."

"Okay drunk, Oprah," Etta sneers. "I really don't give a crap about Em's personal life or her family. Don't you get it? We are *imaginary creatures*—like unicorns or leprechauns—and in The Undervale, they may even be our neighbors," Etta swings a hand over to the window and points to a home out the window, "right over there, a family of leprechaun unicorns could be living beside us. Everything we know about ourselves, and our lives, is a lie. We are prisoners in this house with a baby. And that's worth mentioning, isn't it? A little girl was dumped on our doorstep. And now all of us," Etta twirls her tiny finger in a circle, "including the kid are trapped inside a literal nightmare.

That's the headline, okay, Ana? Not Em's abandonment issues or yours for that matter."

"Don't take this out on me," Ana chokes out, obviously stung. "I'm trying to understand how we got here. This is my way of figuring it out."

Etta snorts. "There *is* no way to figure this out! We're screwed. We have to find our wands and break this curse and get our real lives back. I don't think it matters at all how we got here."

"You're wrong," Ana argues. "It absolutely matters. If we don't know how we got here, then maybe someone will curse us again. Maybe they have already. Maybe this is like the tenth time we've had this exact same conversation."

I take a deep breath and close my eyes. My sisters continue to bicker, but I've momentarily checked out. I imagine that I'm in my happy place- the garden. But then, my chest tightens, and I suddenly feel anxious. I remember the shadow inside a shadow and a thought occurs that fills me with a terror that is paralyzing.

"What is wrong with you?" Etta's screeching drags me back into the moment. "Why are you being so quiet? You're the bossy one! You picked a hell of a time to be mousy, Lo. Ana and I are not going to fix this on our own just so that you can turn around a week from now and tell us how terrible our ideas were. You don't get to opt out. No way."

I gulp and bite my lip. I don't want to tell them, but I have to. "I do have a solution . . . maybe. But I don't think you two will like it," I offer softly.

"Lo," Ana says with a slow smile. "We need to consider everything, even if we don't like it."

"Okay." I look up at the ceiling. I can feel tears beginning to collect in the corners of my eyes. "What if this isn't a curse? I think Em genuinely believes it is. But maybe, she's wrong."

Etta folds her arms and leans back in her chair. "Not a curse. Right. So, being trapped inside this house, inside these bodies with no memories is actually a reward? Tell me, what kind of exceptional deed deserves such an amazing prize?"

"Shush, Etta," Ana warns. "Just let her finish."

"What if all of this," I say as I wave my arms around to illustrate the scope, "is a spell—a magical thing, yes—but a spell designed to *protect* us."

My sisters lock eyes with one another, but they don't speak. "Just, wait here. I want to show you both something."

I race up the stairs and grab the photo I had taken in the woods. It is now hanging on my wall in a frame. I don't allow myself to consider how it got there. I certainly don't remember putting it up. I whip back downstairs and slap it on the table in front of Etta and Ana. "Look," I tell them as I point to the shape. "Yesterday . . . I mean—shit, I think it was yesterday—I took this photo. I sensed something terrible in the woods out back, something evil."

"Evil?" Etta raises an eyebrow. "That's super dramatic, even for you."

"Ignore her." Ana says kindly. "I believe there's evil in the world-all the worlds, I guess. But I don't think people or imaginary creatures or whatever, can be 100% evil, you know? Nothing is that black and white."

I realize that Ana is drunk and likely to go off on one of her tangents, so I interrupt before she can say anymore. "I think someone, or something might be trying to protect us. This could be a spell that is hiding us from whatever bad, scary thing is outside."

"Hmmm, I don't know," Etta ponders. "You're the one who saw it- or *you think* you saw it. And I'm looking at these pictures and all I see is a blurry blob. What I'm trying to say is- and don't get pissed off-but we've never seen this thing you're talking about. And if it is real, again, no offense, then the bad, scary thing knows exactly where we are so . . . there can't be a spell hiding us."

I hadn't considered that. I look down at the photo again and my stomach roils. "Okay, maybe the shadow that I saw and felt knows where we are but can't get inside, just like we can't go outside and maybe, whoever helped us and cast this spell, sent us the baby so we wouldn't be bored. That sort of makes sense. Em did say there was no way she could get to us before and that magic is personal to the caster, so the baby must have come from the person or people who are trying to save us."

"Wait...What? ..." Etta knits her brows. "I don't get it. What are you trying to say?"

"I propose that we do nothing. I think we should stay here and when the coast is clear and that Long Shadow Thingy has been defeated, someone will come and get us and return not only our wands, but our memories too." My eyes are wide, hopeful. Long Shadow Thingy is probably not the best name, it's certainly not the scariest. Maybe just, Longshadow.

Ana looks at the photograph again. Her neck dips low and she squints her eyes. She straightens her back as if her drunkenness had just been an act. She pushes the photo away from her and both my sisters, as if they had rehearsed it, say "*no,*" in unison.

"What do you mean no? We can't just go wandering around fairyland. It's not safe. The only place we're safe is right here. At home. I think we should just let this thing run its course."

"Who are you right now?" Etta demands with a snark. "You want to bury your head in the sand? For like, *a hundred years*, maybe? What is wrong with you?"

"Nothing," I bite back. "And if you felt what I felt back in the woods, you would be thinking the exact same thing."

Ana shakes her head with vigor. "I do see a shape in your picture, and it does look suspicious, menacing even, but Lo, you need to snap out of it. I don't think Em lied to us. This is a curse, not a protection spell."

I stand up and my chair scrapes against the hard wood. The baby gurgles in response. "There is no way for you to know that. We don't remember Em. Were we all best friends? Maybe, but I don't think so. She gives off a vibe like she's an expert on everything and she's always right. But we have to consider that maybe she's wrong. Maybe *she's* part of the problem. Did it occur to either of you that's she's rude because she's actually a really mean person? Ana can play therapist all day long, but Em is…I dunno…shady, and I am sure she knows way more than she is letting on."

"Let's just take Em out of the equation for a minute," Ana says diplomatically. "We are in fairyland. I'm not saying that your experience out in the garden wasn't real but considering where we are, you might be jumping to conclusions. Maybe the shadow was just passing through." Maybe it doesn't have anything to do with our situation at all."

"Seriously?" I tell her with a curled lip. "It so obviously does." There's a creepy shadowy thing right outside and we are physically unable to leave the house's boundaries. I couldn't even step a foot inside the woods. You think that's a coincidence?" My hands are waving wildly now, like I'm conducting my argument. "I am telling you guys that someone—some fairy, a *good* fairy—is trying to keep us safe. Like a real fairy godmother. So, let's just forget about magic and all the rest of it. We stay here and we live our lives- which are pretty great by the way. And now we have a baby to look after. It'll be fun! Besides, this is temporary. We won't be stuck—" My siblings throw me a nasty look. "Okay, stuck is the wrong word. What I mean to say is that this isn't going to last forever. Probably. The protection spell or curse, if that's what you're convinced it is- actually amazing. We have everything we could ever want or need. If we get bored, we can take up a hobby and the house will just provide us with yarn or clay or uhhh … stamps … and even though Em doesn't like babies, she'll probably help us find out where Baby comes from- *if* that's something we want to do. Or we raise her ourselves. I vote for that."

"You have *totally* lost the plot, Lo, wow. Stamps? Really?" Etta says as her chest heaves up all the way to her chin. "More importantly," Etta continues, "There is no world or realm or dimension where the three of us would play damsels in distress and hide away. I do not believe that. If something was out to get us, we would fight. We would go to war. We certainly wouldn't just let someone else take care of the problem while we carry on in a magical house streaming vampire movies and developing photographs that no one is going to see."

Etta's words hit me like a body blow, and I flinch, leaning far away from both my sisters. Ana looks worried. She clasps my hand and pulls me back towards her.

"Lo," Ana prods gently, "you know that Etta is right. We must have an enemy because whether you're mentally in a place to admit it or not, *this is* a curse—it's not protection. You don't protect someone by stripping them of their memories and their freedom, not if you're a good fairy godmother. And we would never back down and let someone fight our battles for us. I may not know exactly who I am, but I know I'm not that—and neither are you."

"You say that now, but when you get close to Longshadow, both of you are going to piss your pants and run straight back here. If we had our memories, we very well might go to war. But we don't. And we don't have any magic in a world where all the rules are based on magic. Think about it logically."

Ana decides to pour another gallon of wine into her glass. "Ha! Logic. That's the word you're going to use? On purpose? Wake up! Look at my outfit! It was made out of *magic* by a beautiful Black Goddess. If you want to sit here and play happy families with the baby, go ahead, but I'm going to figure out what is going on," she declares with triumph.

"Me too," Etta echoes. "I may not have magical abilities, but I can feel . . . something . . . or hear it maybe? Don't you guys?"

"No," I tell her honestly, though I do try to strain my ears. I get nothing.

"It's like a radio playing a song in another room. And I know the song, but I can't quite remember what it is, or what it's called. But it's there, even though it's barely a whisper. And more importantly, I do not want to be anyone's prisoner, no matter how safe or nice the jail is."

I sigh and look away. My sisters have forced my hand. I won't let them brave The Undervale without me and I do not want to be alone in this house for years looking after a baby who was most likely kidnapped.

"Fine. I will help to search for the wand in the house and if we find it, I will go with you to find the other ones. For the record though, I think it's a very bad idea and the only reason I'm agreeing is because I think that baby has a mom and dad out there who are absolutely devastated. I don't really care about the curse or the spell or friggin' Fairyvale. But I do care that we have a defenseless child under our protection, a child that needs to be reunited with her parents- even though admittedly, I would like to keep her."

"So, you're in?" Etta pushes. Ana flutters her eyes and puts the wineglass down.

"Yep," I tell them stiffly.

"Well okay," Ana says, smacking the table so hard that it wobbles. "Let's go be fairies."

- 5 -

It doesn't take us long to get organized—flashlights, rubber gloves, garbage bags. Ana grabs tweezers, though I can't imagine why.

When it comes to the baby, however, that is another story entirely.

The baby has *needs*.

The baby has *requirements*.

"Check again," Etta demands as Ana riffles through the baby's belongings.

"I've checked twice already, Etta," Ana says as her mouth disappears into a thin, frustrated line. "If there was some kind of a name tag on any of these items, I would have seen it. My memory might be screwed up, but my eyes work just fine."

I rock the baby gently. Her jade-colored eyes flutter and her limbs grow heavy. She smells like milk and exhaustion. It's easier for me to deal with the shock of today with the baby in my arms. Now that there is a plan, a way to move forward, Etta has been moving around the house like a turquoise-colored butterfly, gently touching down on one thing, only to flutter away to the next in a matter of seconds.

I still think this is a bad idea. It would be so much easier, *nicer*, to believe that we are under someone's protection. I know this makes me cowardly. I also know that my sisters have a point. It doesn't make them right but...I have to admit, it makes them right-*er*. It is irrational to believe that anyone trying to save us would leave us so defenseless.

"That baby needs a name," Etta states calmly, but I can hear the tension in her voice. "She has to be called something other than she or her."

"How about Jane?" Ana says brightly, "or Audrey or Coco or Esmerelda? Esmerelda is a lovely name."

"We'll call her Baby, for now," I announce, leaving no room for discussion. An argument over names could last all day with us. I pick through Baby's things until I come upon the sling. "Somebody named her and if we start calling her something different...I dunno, it feels wrong. Besides, we would never agree on one we all like and since you're both hell bent on breaking this curse, we should focus on the mysterious singing wand." I can't believe I actually said those words-for many reasons. 1.- they are ridiculous and 2- I don't want to go looking for anything. But my instincts are calling the shots and now my gut is telling me that Baby is not safe. She's already been snatched away and renaming her would only break her parents' hearts (and maybe ours when we have to give her up) even more. "Help me put this thing on and she can sleep on my chest while we look."

Ana swoops in and takes Baby. Etta examines the contraption quickly and then expertly attaches it to me as if she has done it a hundred times, which, maybe she has. Ana lowers Baby gently into the carrier and I use the clips and pulleys to strap her in.

"That is handy. Both my hands are free, and I can still hold her. I think we should begin in the basement and work our way up."

"I hate the basement," Etta complains. "Let's start at the top of the house and work our way down. That way, we might not even have to go down there if we find the wand first."

"I go into the basement every day," I snip, "why are you so scared of it?"

"I am not scared. It smells bad," Etta says defensively. "And I'm sure it's teeming with mold. It makes my allergies act up."

"Hmph," I grunt but before I can say that everything makes Etta's allergies act up, Ana steps in.

"We're starting in the basement because Lo really knows her way around down there." She puts both hands on her hips and narrows her eyes at us. "There is enough going on. Please don't make me referee today. No arguing, okay?"

Bickering with Etta will indeed slow us down but it's not my fault that Etta is so salty. As far as I'm concerned, the sooner we find the wand (or don't), the sooner we'll have some answers and so, Etta and I make a truce—one we both know is only temporary.

We shuffle down the creaky steps into the basement. I start by ripping apart my darkroom. I am not surprised when I don't find a wand. I would have seen a weird magical stick because I spend a lot of time in that room.

After I finish up in there, I help my sisters inspect the rest of the dank basement. Etta and Ana go through boxes of old Christmas and Halloween decorations that look at least fifty years old. I go to a shelf that holds dozens of jars and bottles. I had always assumed they were preservatives of some sort. To be honest, I had sort of forgotten they were there. Now, as I bring each one down to hold up in the weak sunlight pouring through the single window, I can see they are most definitely **not** filled with pickled vegetables or jam.

The wider jars hold dried plants. I unscrew one of the lids and then angle my body away so that Baby can't snatch or inhale whatever is in there. I dare a tentative sniff and it smells bizarrely like wet woolen mittens left to dry on a radiator even though the plant inside looks like a simple evergreen. I scrunch up my nose and replace the lid. I smell all sorts of strange things in the jars, smells that do not fit, like freshly baked brownies and rainstorms and crisp dollar bills. When I examine the liquid bottles more closely, I can see little trails of speckled stars and glowing neon confetti. Some of the jars are not as transparent, but I can feel something solid inside a few of them, something that moves and tilts the bottle in my hands. I quickly put those ones back on the shelf and place my arm protectively around Baby's back. Who knows what kind of disgusting creatures live in there? Besides, if our wands are anything like Em's, the bottles would have to be much bigger.

"You know," I begin as I scan the now upturned but completely inspected basement space. "There's no washer or dryer in here. It never occurred to me. I can't remember doing a single load of laundry, but we always have clean clothes."

My sisters stop in their tracks and look woefully around them. It's true. Not one of us has a memory of sorting, washing, or folding clothes. We have hampers in our rooms and we each agree that every night, our dirty clothes go into them. Do our clothes get magically washed or . . . do we just get new clothes every day? I can't believe I never thought about it. More and more I am beginning to feel foolish for allowing myself to be duped in such an obvious way. If this is a curse—a theory that seems more likely with every minute I spend scrutinizing our living space—it is a vile and wicked thing, not just for what it did to us, but for making us feel so small and stupid.

We make our way reluctantly up the stairs. Etta of course, takes the kitchen. She pulls every single item out of the cupboards neatly and examines not only the spaces they used to occupy but each item itself. She digs her hands inside tins of flour and scrounges around sugar jars.

In the living room area, I open every book and let it fall to the floor with a thud. Baby does not seem to mind the noise in the least. She lets out a giggle every time a tome drops to the ground. The books, some old, some so new they make a near deafening crack when I open them fully, are unknown to me. *The Tailor's Baleful Needle*, *Two Parrots and a Tiger Cub*, *Low Country Cakes and Pies*, *The Duchess's Unsuitable*

Suitor, Photographs from a Half-Lived Life . . . all titles that would appeal to the three of us and all of them wholly unfamiliar, which is of course, unlikely. I had just returned a book to that very shelf three days ago (or what I thought was three days ago; it could have been months or years).

Ana throws cushions, unzips pillows, and gets on her hands and knees to inspect every nook and cranny. We move the furniture around, hoping for a loose floorboard but the search is fruitless.

Baby dozes for a while and then wakes up. I change her and get her another bottle before we head up to the next floor. As the minutes tick by, our panic increases. Etta swears she can hear it, but whatever sound it's making doesn't seem to be helping her at all. How are we supposed to find our other wands in a hostile place like The Undervale when we can't even find the one that is supposed to be right under our noses?

As the search goes on, we take far less care to preserve the house's appearance. We start with what we had always thought was our mother's room, but which is, in point of fact, a neglected linen closet shelving a single threadbare towel and a musty, moth-eaten blanket. We move on to my room, ripping it apart, searching behind each photograph on the wall, and inspecting each pocket of every pair of pants and every jacket that is hanging in the closet.

Ana's room, like herself, is moody and romantic. The walls are a deep Mallard-green, the curtains, drapey and sheer, are emerald. We become whirling dervishes, spinning and flailing, searching for something, anything, out of the ordinary. When no wand is found, we move on to the bathroom and then up to Etta's room, which takes far less time because she has an inherent love of minimalism and can't stand clutter.

In the far-right corner of Etta's room is the access door to the attic. Baby coos happily. The three of us crane our necks to look at the small cutout in the ceiling.

"Well, if it is here, it's got to be up there," I announce pragmatically. "We've looked everywhere else."

"But what if it isn't? What if Em was lying to us?" Etta counters. "She did say that all fairies liked to lie. And maybe part of the curse is to turn me crazy. That could be a thing, right? Like, auditory hallucinations. Maybe I only think I'm hearing that music."

I would give Etta a good shake if Baby wasn't strapped to me. I don't know much, but I do know you don't shake a baby, even when your sister is sort of being a scaredy cat who can't make up her mind.

"You aren't delusional. No way- your cooking is way too good. If *you were* crazy, you would have been putting rat turds or MSG in our food." Ana says pragmatically. "Besides, Em wasn't talking about herself—or maybe she was, but not about something so important. She wouldn't lie if our lives were at stake." Ana sounds like she is trying to convince herself as much as she is the rest of us. The outfit she had insisted Em not change is covered in dust and grime. Her hair, which generally looks as smooth as an oil slick, is disheveled and there's a black mark running across her nose.

"She came to help us," Ana insists, which makes me and Etta groan. "Okay, so she wasn't super helpful, but she did tell us about the curse and everything else. Why would she lie about lying?"

I look out the window. The night has stretched out to its fullest and even though my stomach growls, I don't feel hungry. It's as if my body is on an automatic timer and my belly is the alarm.

I'm starting to think that fairies don't need to eat.

This is not a revelation I will be saying out loud because…. *Etta.*

I look down at Baby and it occurs to me that she should be put to bed properly. I'm no expert on babies, but along with the no shaking rule, I'm fairly sure they need a proper bedtime. It's just after 8:00 p.m., which seems about right. Besides, Baby shouldn't go up into the attic. It's dusty and I don't entirely trust the floor.

"I'm taking Baby to bed," I announce.

"I'll do it," Ana jumps in.

"It's fine," I say protectively. "I've already got her."

On the way to my room, I think about Em and the note on the fridge. It was in my handwriting. I didn't say anything because my sisters didn't seem to notice, but it's been bothering me. There is something visceral about my dislike of Em, something sharp, that makes my shoulders pinch. What would make me go to *her*, for anything? The only conclusion I can come up with is that Em, however disagreeable, is telling the truth, and the other me, the one with memories and magic, trusted her. I can't say exactly why I feel so sure about this. I'm not a psychic or anything. At least, I don't think I am. All I know is that Em is 100% for sure a liar, but she wasn't lying about who we are, and she wasn't being dishonest about this curse that's holding us in its teeth.

- 6 -

I carefully chart a course around the clothes and items that had been pulled to the floor. My left eye twitches several times at the state of my disorganized room. I don't have time to clean it but at the very least, and for Baby, I hastily remake my bed. I change her diaper efficiently and put on a onesie that looks slightly more pajama-like. I set the child down gently in the middle of the bed, surrounded by pillows. When I'm sure she can't roll over to the floor, I give her another bottle.

"Yay," Baby says, though with much less exuberance.

"Yes," I acknowledge. "Yay." I trail a finger down the slope of Baby's tiny nose. Tears well in my eyes and a couple of fat drops clamber down my cheeks. Two tears are hardly anything at all. I should be hysterical, as should my sisters. We should be panicked and crazed. This whole situation is . . . I search for a word. Fantastic comes to mind, but not the good kind of fantastic. The kind that means it's almost too incredible to conceive of, let alone accept. Perhaps Baby has become our anchor. Baby needs us to be focused and clear. We have someone to look after who doesn't care whether or not we are cursed or immortal. And so, for that at least, I'm grateful.

When Baby's eyes close, I go back up to Etta's room. I waste no time yanking on the long, beaded string that releases the hatch. The trap door falls open, along with a wooden ladder that Etta unfolds.

I carefully climb the rungs and reach around in the dark for a switch, praying for a light. I exhale loudly when my fingers stumble across the switch. I flick it on and call for my sisters.

There is not one, but two bare lightbulbs hanging from the ceiling. Without a shade of any sort, the light should be harsh and jarring. But the bulbs are made of pink filament, washing the entire attic with a warm glow. The front of the space closest to us is filled with trunks and steamers, some leather, some metal and some the sort I imagine a soldier might have. They are stacked four or five high on either side of the sloped roof. We get to work immediately, pulling them down and opening them.

The contents are mostly clothes, so it's Ana who's the most impressed. There are tea dresses and top hats, ball gowns and flak jackets. There are corsets and wimples, short shorts and faded jeans covered in patches. The clothing doesn't just span decades but centuries. Had we worn these things? We must have done. It's like we stole the entirety of a property room on a Hollywood studio lot.

A couple of trunks hold mementos and souvenirs. There are dance cards and tickets, postcards and bundles of letters all tied with red satin ribbons. None of these things look yellowed or dog-eared, even though the dates suggest they should be nothing but pulp. They are all in pristine condition, which I can only assume is some sort of magic. At this point, I'm feeling a little conflicted. I suppose I want to find the wand, *but* that would mean that my sisters were definitely right. There is a part of me, selfish and petty, that is hoping that the magic Em had felt in this house was actually just the preservation of these interesting but ultimately useless time capsules. I know it's ridiculous, but I want to go back to believing that the curse isn't real and that we are being protected by an unknown benefactor—someone so powerful that our wands don't matter. Someone that is so magically gifted that Longshadow in the woods wouldn't dare come near us.

When all the trunks had been thoroughly examined and rifled through (and Ana had made a conspicuous pile of things she wanted for herself), the three of us move on to the other side of the room which is empty in the middle save for a faded oval rug. Around that bare space, however, are bookshelves of all colors and sizes. Instead of books though, the shelves hold hundreds of tiny boxes.

"What do you think those are?" Ana asks, holding onto my arm, either out of excitement or trepidation. Some boxes are silver and others gold. Some are jeweled, some painted, and some are carved wood.

"Could it be jewelry? Are they little treasure boxes!?" Ana's voice shakes with wonder.

Excitement it is then.

I take a single box off the shelf. It is small and its edges are just barely contained in my palm. The wood is lacquered and inlaid with mother of pearl. When I inspect it more closely, I can see a bronze winding key. I turn it several times and then open the lid carefully. A tune begins to play as a strong smell of teak fill my nostrils. The box is empty. Ana snatches it hastily away. She turns it over and runs her thumbs over the velvet lining.

"This can't be right," Ana huffs. "Boxes are meant for keeping things in."

Etta ignores her and takes down another box and winds it up. Maybe, because of the mysterious magical humming she's been hearing, my sister is thinking that the music itself is some kind of key? The room fills with tinkling tones, scraps of sonatas and refrains from old songs long forgotten. Ana and I join her. I wind each box, round and round carefully until the mechanism clicks. I'm not sure these boxes can be broken but I don't want to be the one to test that theory.

We take down each one from the shelves, examine it thoroughly, and then place it on an empty space on the floor. There are at least two hundred, and with each one we take, we're sure that it will be the box that holds the much sought after wand. When the shelves are picked clean, I bow my head.

"It isn't here," I say out loud to both of them, or no one, or maybe just to myself. "We've searched everywhere, this entire house."

"Yeah? Well, I think Em knows exactly where the damn thing is. She's probably laughing her ass off in a bath full of milk and rose-scented baby's blood. This is exactly the kind of thing a woman like her would get off on," Etta says angrily. "And now we're stuck here. Forever."

"That was mean Etta, and also weirdly dark," Ana frowns. "Sorry, Lo, but I think we're going to have go outside into the yard," Ana says while she looks directly at me.

"I'm telling you, both of you, that is a terrible idea," I counter.

"But it does make a kind of sense. What if the Longshadow you saw *is* some sort of guard beast or security monster *but*, it's protecting the curse and not us? You know, like...keeping it intact and making sure that we are missing out on our real lives. If the wand is anywhere on the property, it's probably in the place we absolutely don't want to go," Ana argues.

My chest begins to constrict. If she felt what I did back there, Ana would never make that suggestion. She's so casual when she says the word "monster", but she has no idea what it's like to be near one. If her theory is true, now that we have Baby and Em has been to the house, Longshadow is bound to be extra horrifying.

Etta is ignoring the both of us. She has slumped to the ground, turning her entire body into a tiny, navy-colored ball. I sit down next to her and put my hand on her knee. "I know it feels hopeless right now," I begin.

"Hopeless?" Etta spits, looking up at me. Her bottom lip quivers and her blue eyes pool with tears that she seems unable or unwilling to let go of. "I don't feel hopeless! I feel like I'm having an out of body experience, like I fell and hit my head and now I'm probably in a coma. This can't be real or right." Etta tries to take a deep breath in, but it gets caught up in her lungs and escapes in stutters, like a stalled engine turning over and over.

"Don't you even think about quitting on me, Etta Smith," I warn. "We need you. We need the way you think to solve this. Out of the three of us, you have the worst temper."

"Lo!" Ana interjects.

"What I mean is that you're fierce and tenacious. If you give up, what chance do Ana and I have? We'll be trapped here, without any answers. So, before we go outside—to what I'm pretty sure is certain doom—let's make sure the wand is not in this house. We should all have a really good think. Maybe there's a place we've forgotten or a cupboard we didn't fully check out. Where could a magical wand be hiding?"

"Are you serious?" Etta blurts out, along with an oddly maniacal laugh. "You're telling me not to give up on finding a *magic wand*? It's …it's …" Etta stammers, "it's preposterous! I'm starting to think that there *is* no wand. Em was messing with us, or maybe someone else is. Maybe we've been cursed by some pervy fairy guy who kidnapped us and has spent the past God knows how many years spying on us with hundreds of invisible fairy cameras. Now that he knows we're onto him, we're probably going to be killed and chopped up into a hundred little pieces."

Etta begins to cry. Ana and I take a step back. When Ana cries, she wants to be held. When I get teary, I need someone to be there and listen as I talk my way through what I'm feeling. For Etta, breaking down is a defeat. It is failure. She turns away, folding her body in on itself, an elaborate and melancholy piece of origami. She puts her forehead on her knees to stifle her sobs.

When she raises her head up just enough to wipe her eyes, she blanches. I follow her line of sight and see a corner of the shelf glinting. I squint, wondering what exactly I am seeing. And there it is again, the tiniest of gleams, no bigger than the head of an eraser on a pencil. I start to move but Etta beats me to it. She crawls over to the bottom shelf on her hands and knees.

"What is it?" I ask hopefully.

"Shhh," Etta bosses. She sticks her hand all the way back, into the corner. Halfway between the shelf and the floor is a teeny, tiny, mirrored box.

"Well, it's not going to be in there," Ana huffs. "That's barely big enough to fit a thimble, let alone a wand."

Etta ignores her sister. She blows on the top of the box and dust particles go flying. She rubs the surface gently with her thumb. I imagine she's trying to polish off some of the dirt, but the little box remains tarnished and spotted. Etta turns the tiny key no thicker than a sewing needle, and then carefully, she lifts the lid.

The moment that the first comb strikes the metal bead inside, the top pops open and the music box yawns. The opening gets wider and wider. Etta's hand drops as it becomes too heavy for her to carry. All three of us screech in alarm but what unfolds next happens so quickly, it's impossible to process. One minute it was just a small little box and the next it's a gaping mouth. The tines of the music box become teeth made of splintered, termite-riddled floorboards and glinting butcher knives. The entire contraption gets so big that it swallows us whole in one giant gulp.

Ana is screaming. I have my eyes scrunched together. Etta has stopped her simpering and now she's furious.

"It ate us!" she harps angrily. "That stupid little thing just took us prisoner. Doesn't it know we're already trapped?"

The tinny music floating into our ears is slow and warped. It bleeds through the walls of this newest jail just loud enough to make my skin crawl. It isn't any sound I recognize or anything I would ever choose to listen to. It's eerie, dissonant chords remind me of the themes they play in horror movies right before someone gets stabbed, or strangled, or gorily disemboweled.

"Maybe this is good?" I say, trying to sound optimistic over the dastardly song that careens through the walls because one of us has to stay positive. "This is obviously magic. The wand should be here."

Truth be told, I am doubtful about the wand's presence, but I think pulling an "I told you so" right now would be overly mean.

"Really? Why?" Etta argues stubbornly. "For all we know, this is Em's way of overriding the curse and killing us. We could starve to death in here. Or die of asphyxiation!"

I cross my arms and finally open my eyes so that I can shoot my sister a nasty look. "Will you please adjust your attitude, Etta? Seriously. If Em wanted to kill us, I'm pretty sure she would have done so in a spectacularly gruesome way when she was with us. This is terrifying enough on its own. Would you please stop jumping right into worst case scenarios? Your negativity is making the most terrible situation ever, even worse."

Etta grunts and in two short steps gets up into my face, or what would have been my face if Etta had been taller, or I had been shorter. "This is a box. You think there's unlimited oxygen in here? Even if we're only half an inch tall, we still need air! Who's going to find us? Who's even going to look? More to the point, who would curse us and then put the very key to breaking that curse inside the place we're stuck in? I'll tell you—no one! Because that would be dumb and whoever did this to us is many things, but dumb isn't one of them. Isn't it more likely that the crazy supermodel is an Evil Villain, with magical Evil Villain superpowers who wants to kill us?"

I bend down so I can yell in my sister's face. "Why would she even want to do that? Did you see her? She literally has everything!"

"What if she needs to drain us of our powers? For eternal youth or something?" Etta screams back.

"That's it!" Ana says, getting in between us. "I told you, no arguing today, and just because the box ate us doesn't give either one of you permission to break your promise." We both promptly shut our mouths.

A promise is a promise.

"You two are so busy having a go at one another that you haven't even noticed. Look around you!" Ana sweeps her arms wide. "Take it all in. Notice anything familiar?"

I take a step back and for the first time, I survey my surroundings. The walls are not walls at all but rather a complete oval of beveled mirrors, each bevel is about half a foot wide, floor to ceiling. It's odd, but it's nothing compared to what I see when I finally *look*. This place is an exact replica of our living room- there is even half of the dining table- chopped crudely where the other half would have been in the kitchen.

However...

It doesn't take more than a few seconds for me to figure out that this version is a grotesque reflection of where we live.

Instead of the wide and cozy velvet sofa sectional that I had spent hours curled up on, this one is its hideously neglected twin. It's musty and tattered and its color so faded that it's a non-color, not even beige. Most of the stuffing is pulled out of the cushions. Some of the holes were obviously made from tiny moth mouths while others are just giant gapes.

The varnish of the couch's wooden frame has been entirely scratched off. The small claw marks are disgustingly rat sized. The dining chairs are in even worse shape. One seat looks like it has been punched through entirely. Another chair is turned on its side and is missing two legs.

In our living room, our *real* living room, there's a long rectangular ottoman that squats in front of the fireplace. It isn't the most comfortable place to sit, but it works in a pinch to warm our hands and bare feet in front of the fire. Here, the padding of the ottoman is shredded to bits and a foul-smelling cotton batting is spilling out of its center like fat loops of small intestines. Flies hover and buzz around it. Curiously, the fire is blazing, though how that can be possible when there's no chimney is totally bonkers, but it's the least of my concerns.

The coffee table is a wreck- like someone has taken a sledgehammer to it. Just as it is in our actual house, it's long and low and mirrored. The surface on this one is far too cracked to be reflective. And bizarrely, even though it's smashed to bits, I notice one of Etta's teacups. I only recognize that it's one of hers because there's a hand-painted hydrangea bough still intact on a single shard.

A panicky feeling begins to race up my chest. Logically, I know that this is not our house at all. It's some sort of sick puzzle that needs working out. And on this point, finally . . .

I am certain.

At first, I was sure there couldn't be a wand in here, mostly because I didn't want there to be one. I was still clinging to the idea that we were being protected and that our home was a sanctuary. Inside this vile place, the truth is like a knife at my throat. It isn't just that this jeweled box—ignoring space and dimension—is bad or wrong. It is *personal*. This is a horrific mirror image of our home. The curse is obviously designed to rip right into the center of us. It's meant to terrify and intimidate. Maybe Em is in on it, maybe she isn't. It doesn't matter. In this very moment, the who and why is not nearly as important as the how. How do we get out of here with the wand?

I've read enough fairy tales and given the fact that we are actually *in* fairy land, the illogical logic of it is obvious. The wand is hidden somewhere inside this foul magic. And even though my eyes sting with tears and my chest feels like it's being pulled taut by a tourniquet, I know that all three of us will have to really look. At everything. At every disgusting, disturbing item.

On the dining table is an assortment of moldy bread and rotten fruits. There are maggots wriggling gruesomely, writhing around on a plate that holding a few flesh-colored rinds that used to be meat. The smell is awful, and I cover my nose. I crane my neck and see a vast expanse of spider webs. They are so thick and intricate that I can barely even see the ceiling.

"Lo," Etta hisses while yanking on my arm. I swivel my head so I can see Etta's face. My sister is speaking but her mouth isn't moving because her teeth are clenched so hard. Her eyes are wide, and her expression is frozen. "Look in the mirrors."

I slowly turn my neck and see, not myself, but a stranger. I can't help but gasp as I walk closer to the mirrors. Instead of the creepy music, All I can hear is Etta and Ana's whimpers conjoined with my own.

It's a child's face looking back at me. A dark-haired, blue-eyed, little girl. I instinctually put my hand to my cheek and the reflection does the same. When I move my head slightly to left, I catch my image in another bevel of the mirror. This time, the reflection staring back at me is an olive-skinned, severe looking woman in her 50s. In another bevel, I am gray-haired and wearing a red chiffon dress. Every individual piece stuck on the wall shows a different face, but they are all me, moving and gasping and trembling as I do.

"What is this?" I manage to say. My sisters, wrapped up in their own reflections, do not answer. I scan an image of myself as a good-looking young man in a football jersey with overly excellent hair. Had I been him? Had I been all these people? I catch a glimpse of a lovely looking lady in her 30s with the same strawberry blond hair as me, though her features are profoundly different.

And that is when I catch a glimpse of it- Longshadow.
Here.

My eyes widen.

My reflection's eyes widen.

The shadow is just a hint of a thing, a swirling smudge above my head in the mirror. I might not have even seen it all if I hadn't felt it, that same paralyzing fear.

Ana was right after all. It must be attached to the curse. I realize in that moment that I can scream or cry or have a tantrum. I can pee my pants like I almost did the last time I saw it . . . or . . . I can just ignore it. What can a shadow do? It's a trick of the light. It's absence. It's nothing.

I mean, really, what is a shadow compared to a mirror that shows you hundreds of different yous? That's the real horror show. I close my eyes and turn away. I can barely wrap my head around accepting me now, as a weird and awkward, seventeen-year-old girl.

Was I really that brave? I can't imagine being so self-confident that I could change my face and my age and my gender on a whim and still maintain my sense of self so absolutely. But obviously I did, and I was. I realize that I'm going to have to lean on that, we all are . . . if we are going to survive this room. I look up, scanning the ceiling for Longshadow, but it's gone. I would be relieved, but I have a feeling it showed up here just to prove that it could, that it could get to me, *to us*, anytime it wants.

That is a problem, a very big problem, but it will have to wait. This awful room needs to be dealt with first.

"Turn away from them!" I yell to my sisters but it's more of a plea, really. These images, these other us's are seductive and mesmerizing. We could be lost in these strangers for days, possibly even years, searching for a single feature that might be familiar. "Do. Not. Look," I bellow. "It doesn't matter what these mirrors are showing you, real or not. It's a distraction. It's another trap."

Etta and Ana tear their gazes from their reflections. Like me, they are disoriented. Etta's arms are outstretched, as if she is waiting for something solid to slide into them and hold her up. Ana's shoulders are up around her ears. Her eyelids are blinking with such ferocity that her entire face is turning red.

"Is that real? Is that us?" Ana asks breathlessly. "I don't like this. Maybe you were right after all, Lo. We should stay at home and wait. This is too wrong, too terrible. I need to get out. I need to get out right now." Ana's breathing has become ragged. She turns around, as if she has just walked out of a door she can go back through again. I know better. There is no door.

"Ana, calm down," I bark. I want to be more tender with her, but she picked a shitty time to finally side with me. "We will be okay as long as we do not look at those mirrors. I know this is awful and the fact that it looks like our house makes it even worse. This isn't our house though. This is a sick version of it designed specifically to slow us down or even worse, make us break. I'm not going to let that happen. We reasoned this out. It doesn't matter anymore that I wanted to let the curse run its course. I was wrong and both of you were right . . . Ana? Did you hear me? Ana!"

Ana looks at me and I all I can hear is a strange set of breathy grunts falling out of her throat.

"We agreed to look for the wand. And maybe it wasn't the smartest choice but, we all made it. And once we start something, we finish it. That's who we are . . . I think. I'm almost totally positive that is who we are. So, we cannot leave and let this place beat us, okay?"

"No, I'm sorry," Ana says as she begins to cry. She squats on the ground and puts her arms over her head. "I can't do it. Please don't make me."

I inhale deeply from my mouth to avoid the stench. I want to shake my sister or maybe even slap her. I wasn't the one who wanted to play hide-and-seek for the stupid wand and now, somehow, it's become my job to find it.

So typical.

I always end up looking after them and making sure they're okay. Why would we need an actual, living breathing mom when they have me?

I'm their mother.

Then again, sometimes, they are mine.

I take a beat and try to find my center, although inside this filth-ridden, magical beast of a thing, that's a tall order. Ana looks so small and so lost that affection overrides my fury. She's a strong girl but not in this way. She's good at comforting people, but not so great with the unknown, and this is the most unknowable of all the unknowns.

I suppose the room isn't *so* big. If Ana is too overwhelmed, well, it's a good thing there are three of us.

"Fine. Just keep your back to the mirrors and focus on something else, like -design a really complicated dress in your mind. We'll move as fast as we can," I tell her as I squeeze her shoulder. "And don't worry. If there's a way in, there has to be a way out again."

I glance at Etta and all she offers up is a shrug. It's a tricky thing, trying to search an entire room without being hypnotized by magical walls, but that's exactly what we do.

"Hmph," I cluck to myself.

"What?" Etta chimes in quickly. "Do you see something?"

"No," I answer sharply. I'm not mad at Etta; my rage has turned into something else entirely, something seething, hot and white. "This so-called enemy of ours thought that by making all of our things rot and break and go all moldy was going to slow us down ... well ... screw that. This is *our* house. If the wand is here, we're going to find it."

Etta nods her head in brisk agreement. If I tell myself this room won't get the better of me enough times, eventually I'll believe it; I can only hope that eventually comes sooner rather than later.

Etta and I start with the floor. We pull up all the threadbare rugs that are covered in so many mysterious stains that they look more like macabre modern art than carpeting.

After throwing them in a pile, we press our shoes into the spongey wood, feeling for a hidden compartment. We don't have one in our actual home but then again, the floorboards aren't rotted there.

Etta and I get stuck more than a few times, but thankfully, our boots protect our ankles from the splinters and slime of rot. When we reach down, all we can feel is smooth velvet along our finger pads. The lining, presumably, of the music box. I count this as a small blessing, I was expecting several dead things down there. It certainly stinks badly enough, but in this one thing at least, we are spared.

We move on to the furniture. I gag as the smell of rot and mold invades my nose as I rip open what is left of the gutted cushions. Etta turns the chairs and the ottoman over and searches fruitlessly underneath them. We throw the decomposing food plates on the floor and examine the ruins of the decayed meal. Then we turn our attention to the multitude of bookshelves.

Our real living room has more shelf space than wall space where we store hundreds of books and movies. In the music box version of our home, there are hardly any books at all. Instead, there are cobwebs and discolored paper towels and bits of fabric stiff from dirt and fluid. All this empty space on the shelves means there is less to search, but it adds to the room's despair. I can't explain why I feel this absence so acutely. It makes me sad and a bit desperate, like a hungry child who pillages a pantry and finds a half-empty jar of prunes and a can of sardines.

I shake my head resolutely. Now is not the time to waiver. I walk to the few books that are there and give them a once over. The forlorn volumes have their spines ripped open and their bindings are more pulp than paper. The gilded leather is shredded and so faded, that I can't make out a single title. Even so, I tear what's left of them apart. Pages litter the floor beneath us like battered autumn leaves.

I wind my neck in a single direction, hoping that an idea might come to me. There is nowhere else to look. We have searched everywhere.

Then I see Etta staring intensely at the fireplace.

"What?" I ask immediately. "Do you see something?"

"I don't know," Etta answers, though her voice sounds far away. She is mesmerized by the leaping flames.

"We checked the mantle already . . . do you think something could be inside the grate?"

"I don't know," Etta repeats with that same distracted voice. She begins walking toward the fire, but I grab her arm.

"If you see something, just tell me," I practically beg. Etta is off— or maybe she is on—a light switch flicked upward. "Stop," I tell her firmly. "Just wait. The last time you went for something on your own, a music box ate us. So, tell me what you see, and I will get it. *Carefully*."

"The fire is so bright, but the rest of the room has almost no color at all," Etta says softly while keeping her eyes on the flames.

"Okay, okay," I tell her quickly, relieved that we have another venue to investigate. "Before we do anything, we have to put the flames out," I warn while throwing a worried glance inside the roaring pit at the same time. "Alright," I'm talking to myself now. Etta is practically catatonic. Ana is crunched up in a green silken ball. "I can do this. How do I do this? How do I put out a fire that's burning inside of a magical music box that is really the size of a Quarter?" I scratch the back of my neck and sigh. "Put the fire out, Lo. There are obviously no fire extinguishers. I'm not even sure we have one in our real house. So…I need to deprive it of oxygen. Is there even oxygen in here? No. probably not. But I can smother it. That might work."

I begin to rip the fabric completely away from the cushions of the sofa. I glance at Etta who is still transfixed. "Please, *please* stop staring at the magic fire and help me," I plead.

"It's bright, but it's still so cold. It's nothing like the fire at our real house. The flames here are more blue than orange. A fire should be warm," Etta whispers.

"What?"

"It's the wrong color," Etta tells me flatly.

"Blue means it's hotter," I explain as I turn my head away from the dust that explodes in the air when I tear another piece of fabric from the couch. "Or knowing this place, it might mean it's made of garden gnome tears or something."

Etta doesn't respond. She just keeps staring. "Hey!" My voice punches a hole through the silence. I snap my fingers in front of her face. "Hello? Etta? Maybe you could turn down the zombie vibe to like, a three? I need help."

There's still nothing. She looks spooky as hell just staring into the flames, her platinum hair reflecting the silvery ice blue. I continue with the cushions until I've got four large pieces of fabric. I bite at my bottom lip and angle my body away as much as I can. With my neck jutted backwards, I drop one of the pieces of material and kick it inside the grate. I stomp on it quickly with my foot. The flames might look look and feel cold according to Etta, but they are hot; so hot that a few tiny licks of sweat immediately start to bead at my hairline.

I nudge Etta all the way over and decide to throw the entire pile in, to smother it *entirely* with the scraps of brocade. I cough as the smoke from the leaping embers begins to burn at the fabric. "Uggh," I moan in frustration. "This isn't working! The fire is actually eating these massive pieces of fabric. I need water but that means we have to find a way out of here so that we can come back with buckets and bowls filled with water. How many would we need? Five? Ten? ETTA OH MY GOD WILL YOU ANSWER ME?!" I yell into her ear.

Etta's tiny fingers suddenly squeeze my bicep. I stop what I'm doing and look at my sister who smiles faintly. And then, before I can stop her, Etta pitches forward. She plunges her entire arm into the flames.

"Etta!" I scream. "Stop, what are you doing?"

"No, Etta!" Ana comes flying from the other side of the room but it's too late. Etta has her arm inside the blue flames. Her face collapses in sudden agony, but she keeps her arm in there reaching, searching. I try to pull her away, but Etta kicks her small leg out at me.

"It's here, I know it. I can hear it," she tells us grimly.

Etta's mouth freezes in a perfect O. Her eyes widen and then bulge in relief. She snatches her hand away and the three of us are forcibly pitched out of the music box. We roll over and over as if the magical room had spun us up in a rug made of nothing but stars and velvet, unfurling us in one graceful sweep. Etta holds out her hand. It should have been charred flesh but it's just a little pinker than normal, though the sleeve of her hoodie is burned black. Etta looks around the attic, disoriented. Her turquoise eyes are two full moons that narrow when they land on me.

In her fingers is a long, ivory colored wand- although I doubt it's actual ivory because that would be gross- I can't imagine fairies being ivory poachers. Then again, Em...she probably has a coat made of kitten pelts or a purse lined with puppy fur. Or both.

Images flutter down like pictures torn from a magazine and thrown against the wind.

> Red and white checks . . . I count the squares...one, two, three . . . what comes after three?
> Three
> Three
> Mud and silt and springtime.
> Daffodils
> Four . . .

"Flora?" she says softly. And in that moment, I know without a doubt my real name is not Lo Smith. I am Flora. Flora Bloomshade. Ana is Fauna and Etta is really called Merriweather. But that's all I know. Beyond our real names, I can't remember anything beyond those few disconnected fragments that flashed so quickly; I barely had time to figure out what I was seeing.

And although I am certain about the truth of my name, the name does not fit. Not now. Not yet. Inside, I'm still just Lo.

Etta quickly snaps out of her daze. My sisters both blurt out their real names simultaneously, and with enough enthusiasm that they sound like they're trying to win money on a game show.

"Great, we all know our actual names, but do you remember anything else? Anything that is actually useful? Because I can't." I don't bother to mention the scraps of memories that came to me. I'm not even sure if they were memories, or my imagination going extra wild because of that horrendous box.

My sisters answer by way of looking at the floor and then the ceiling. Seems like they can't recall anything other than their real names either. Etta cradles her wand as if it's the most precious thing in the world, as if it's a fragile sliver of glass instead of bone or wood or whatever it is. Etta practically sways with reverence.

We found the wand, and nothing has changed. It's all very anti-climactic really, considering that we had shrunk to the size of ants or . . . maybe the music box had magically teleported us to some night-marish version of our own house in a Through-the-Looking-Glass fairy dimension.

The three of us leave the attic and head for our separate domains. We had spent the entire day and night with one another and we all need our space. Normally, the thought of my little pink room would be comforting, but the music from all those boxes is tumbling around my head like a broken drying machine.

I decide that a cup of herbal tea will settle my thoughts. I put my hand on the banister and take a tentative step forward. My stomach lurches and I come to the unsettling conclusion that I do not want to go down the stairs *at all*. Rationally, I know the place I had just been trapped in was not my house, not really. It was just a trick and a mean one at that. I straighten my spine and clomp down the steps with resolve. I'm not about to let the curse stop me from going anywhere I want in my own bloody house.

When I get to the landing, I stop in my tracks.

We ransacked the living room in our search for the wand and now, seeing the state it is in, I can feel tears pooling at the edges of my eyes. I manage to get my foot to move down a step and then my lungs tie themselves up in a knot. There is nothing rotting here, no cobwebs or mold but it doesn't *feel* right. The music box version of our house had broken a promise that I didn't even know I had made. These walls are my sanctuary; this is my home and now it's tainted.

The only thing I can compare it to would be like finding a dead body in my bed. I could wash the sheets and even buy a new mattress, but every time I would get under the blankets, I would know that something dead had been in that very spot and my sleep would never be the same again.

Unable to face the living room, I slowly climb up the few steps I had managed to take. First, the curse had kept us prisoner in our house and now it has made our prison full of darkness and revolting memories. I'll probably never look at my living room the same way again. My tears would have rolled with real gusto at that point, but fatigue has flattened me like a steamroller. I don't even have it in me to weep.

I go to the bathroom and wash my face and hands. I'm too tired to climb in the shower. As I pat my face dry, I decide that despite her suspect behavior, I will call Em tomorrow. Hopefully, even with her snark, she'll offer us enough helpful information so that we can work out a plan. We have a wand, and my best guess is that we can get out of the house now. There is no way I'm about to test that theory tonight.

The day has overwhelmed me. My arms are stiff, my thoughts are untrustworthy, and the dark is too dark. The night outside looms, crouching over the house like a greedy over-fed child.

I gently climb into the bed, being careful not to wake Baby. I feel a sudden pang of guilt. We had left Baby alone, not on purpose, but alone, nonetheless. I nervously watch her chest to measure its rise and fall. Baby is fast asleep, and I let go of the breath I'd been holding. What if that box hadn't spit us out? What would have happened to Baby? It's such a terrible thought I can't even hold on to it. We have to do better. We have to find a way to make sure Baby won't become a casualty of this curse.

Beyond that, or maybe because of that concern, there is something else besides this new mistrust of my own home that doesn't feel right. I flash again to the photo of Longshadow. I see it in the mirrors inside that terrible jewel box room, there and not there, above the face of a stranger's reflection. Adrenaline starts to thrash in my bloodstream.

It is out there. I know it.

I bolt up out of bed and begin to race around the house. I ignore the panic that bubbles up as I whip by the couch and the fireplace, though it makes me breathless. I squint my eyes so hard that everything becomes a blurry haze. I don't want to look at the house this way. I don't want to see something I can't unsee right before I try to sleep. I manage to check every window. I lock and relock the doors. And I wonder . . . if we can get out now, does that mean that something else can get in?

I go back to bed, my breath ragged and my pulse racing. I nuzzle my face close to Baby's.

"Don't worry," I assure my tiny charge, "whatever happens. We will keep you safe." I promise and I pray that it's a promise I can keep.

- 7 -

Unlike my manic race around the house the night before, this morning I take the stairs furtively. The thought of facing the mess we made is not only giving me a headache, but also squeezing my throat in short little bursts making it kind of hard to breathe.

I know what I see down there is going to remind me of that wretched music box room and I'm positive that no matter how hard we scrub and shine and sweep, our lovely little family room will never be the same again.

Well.

Shit.

The space is absolutely pristine. The counters shimmer, the hardwood floors gleam, the rugs are vacuumed, and the spine of every book is straightened.

The curse has reset and wiped the slate clean.

And this, most of all, is the insidiousness of the damned thing. It needs to make us forget. It wants us to think that everything is just fine. "Nothing to see here!" the curse shouts with beeswax on the cabinets and fluffed up pillows on the couch. "Move along now, go about your day. You're fine. *Everything is just fine.*"

I don't feel fine.

I'm aching to talk about what had happened, but it's as if the curse has dipped into my chest and attached my heart to mouth. I'm sure that every word I'm going to say this morning will be a non-stop litany of frustration and angst. I wouldn't put it past the curse to take a perverse pleasure in collecting my despair. I refuse to give it the satisfaction. I decide that I will talk as little as possible this morning, at least until I'm in a better mood.

Etta is downstairs already. She probably has been for a while. She is quiet too, as she cooks our breakfast. She's got her wand between her teeth to free up her hands. Ana must have grabbed Baby in the night or right after dawn. She isn't much of a morning person, but her affection for Baby has likely overridden that. She dips and rocks her, using Baby as a talisman seems to ward away whatever darkness is lingering from our previous adventure, if adventure is even the right word. It might end up feeling like one eventually, in a few (hundred?) years when we have some perspective. Not now though. Now it's just an ugly thing we endured.

With the help of Etta's good cooking, I manage to calm down. I don't settle; I'm not sure I'll ever truly feel settled again. I find a way to push back the anxiety that's been pulling at my ribs since I woke up, because I realize there's simply too much to do. I can't afford to wallow, none of us can. We have our names, and that's a start. But we have no memory of our life before and we certainly don't have any magic.

It's time to see if we can leave the house.

It's Etta who volunteers to go first, with Baby and the newly liberated wand in her arms. We fight about this. Ana and I think Baby should stay inside. Etta's skin reddens and her eyes glint.

"Baby got in and Baby has got to be the key to getting out," Etta pushes.

"It's too dangerous," I argue. "You should try it alone first, with just your wand."

"Are you trying to be an asshole?" Etta rears. "I feel like you're rubbing it in, the fact that I don't know how to use this. Shut up about my wand!"

"Whoa." My entire body straightens in offense.

"You're being paranoid," Ana tells her lightly, taking Baby out of Etta's arms. "And rude."

"I don't care what you think I'm being," Etta snaps back. "I'm taking that Baby and my wand and I'm going to see if we can get out the door. Give me back the kid."

Ana and I glance at one another. When Etta gets like this, she is stubborn as hell. We could spend all day caught up in this fight. "Why can't you just try it on your own?" I offer meekly.

"Why can't you just trust that I have a gut feeling about this. Baby is the key. Why else would someone drop her off? Who abandons a baby to a bunch of teenagers with amnesia in fairyland?" Etta yelps and without waiting, she lunges toward Ana and peels Baby out of her arms.

"Hey!" Ana barks. "I can't believe you just did that. She's not a doll! We all have to agree. It's not just your decision alone."

"Pfft," Etta huffs. She walks to the door, opens it, and takes a tiny little mouse step. To her credit, she cradles Baby's head, when her bare foot touches the mossy pavement of the porch, she immediately leaps back inside.

Was it the wand? Or Baby? I don't think it matters now.

The important thing is that we are no longer trapped in the house. Even if it's just *one* of Etta's toes that managed to breach the outside world, it still feels like an enormous victory. I flush with relief and declare that it's time to call Em. I stand a little taller, my back is as straight and confident as a prima ballerina when I pick up the phone with marked determination. I dial the number but unsurprisingly, I have to wait for it to ring ten times before I finally get an answer.

"Hello," Em says with a gravelly voice.

"Oh, sorry," I stutter, looking for a clock but then I realize that of course, we don't have one. "Did I wake you up?"

"Of course you woke me up. It's not even 10:00 a.m. Aren't you teenagers? Shouldn't you be sleeping like, fourteen hours a day?" Em retorts.

"We have a baby here. So, I don't think we can sleep in?" The register of my voice goes up, as if I'm asking, which I suppose I am, even though I know that babies don't sleep in.

"Uh huh," Em says levelly, as if the conversation is already boring her.

"So, we found a wand, Merriweather's wand actually."

Silence.

"Did you hear that? I said *we found Merriweather's wand,*" I repeat.

"Yeah great, and?" Em sighs.

"We found a wand and we remembered our real names and all you have to say is, yeah great?" My sisters and I exchange looks of annoyance. In even more unsurprising news, Etta looks the most irritated.

"What do you want? A medal? I told you it was in the house, and you found it right where I said it would be. It's not exactly like you live in a palace. It couldn't have been that hard."

I exhale one long breath with my mouth away from the receiver in an attempt to stay calm. The tactic does not work. "Actually…it *was* hard because it was hiding inside a miniature music box that grew a mouth and ate us and we ended up inside a disgusting room that looked like a nightmare version of our own living room … with maggots! And spiders! And Etta had to stick her hand inside an actual fire to get at it."

Silence. Again.

"Em!" I bark. "Are you listening?"

"Of course I am. I just don't know why you sound so desperate. This is The Undervale. An enchanted music box is pretty tame considering. Although, the fact that it looked like a warped version of your own house is rather telling though, isn't it?"

"What is that supposed to mean?" I practically snarl. "What can it possibly tell us besides the person that cursed us doesn't even want us to feel safe in our own home? That's hardly a revelation."

Etta edges in on the receiver and screams down the phone. "The person who cursed us is a masochist!"

I push my sister away and reclaim sole use of the massive receiver. "Etta," I grunt, "masochists like to hurt themselves. I think you mean a sadist. And that's exactly what this curse maker is. Maybe they thought this punishment wasn't harsh enough. Maybe they figured we were getting too comfortable and so they needed to shake things up a bit—*shake us up*. Because let me assure you, Em, the inside of that box wasn't tame." I know I sound practically hysterical at this point, but I don't care. Em doesn't seem to have an empathetic bone in her body, that is, if we even have bones, which is debatable now that literally anything is on the table. I can't get her to really listen to me. I can't seem to make her care. "It was awful, I'm telling you."

"If you say so. The thing is, I'm confused as to why you're calling *me*," Em declares through a casual yawn. In my mind I see her curled up in black silk sheets with a matching sleep mask perched perfectly on her perfect head.

"Hmmm . . . let me see," I clap back sarcastically. "Could it be that two days ago we didn't even know we were fairies? Or maybe it's because even though we know our names now, we don't remember anything else? Possibly it's the fact that you are literally the only person we know besides each other. No . . . wait. I think I have it . . . I'm pretty sure I'm calling because *your exact words* to us were, 'Call me when you find the wand.'"

Em groans. Then she covers up the phone and says something to someone about getting her a coffee. "Well, I thought you'd remember something more useful than your names. I was hoping that a single wand would be more helpful. I really don't know what you expect me to do. Thank you, Giacomo." There was another silence and then a slurping sound. Em must have gotten her coffee.

"Who's Giacomo?" I ask suspiciously.

"None of your business. Good God, you're nosy. Put Fauna on the phone. She's the only one of you I really like." Her barb stings. Em's hardly my favorite person either but I would never actually say that to her face, or her ear (if we're being technical). The space between my collar bones begins to itch. I think she's making me break out in hives.

"Wow! What a surprise!" I squawk. "*I know* why you like Ana. When she's not under this stupid curse, you probably hang out together and make her wear uncomfortable outfits while you boss her around, which she would let you do because she's a pleaser."

Ana throws me a nasty look. "Hardly," Em says with indifference. "I like her best because she's the most fun and her sex life is almost as fascinating as mine."

Etta tries to take the phone away from me again, but I bat her away and duck around the corner. "Look, just give me a hint. This curse isn't stopping us from leaving the house now. Where should we go? Who can help us with this if you can't? Don't think of it as a favor for me, okay? Do it for Ana."

I can hear a tapping noise. I think it's her nails pecking at something close by. "Ugghhh. Fiiiine," Em relents with such petulance that I just know that her eyes are rolling so hard that they are looking at her actual brain. "Well, first off, I would be very careful not to throw around the F word around in The Undervale."

"What are you talking about? I didn't say . . . wait . . . you mean *favor?*"

"This is a society run by magic. How do think we pay for things around here? Credit Cards? Gold coins? Because I could move my wand a millimeter and fill an entire dump truck with jewels and gems and bouillon. No. We trade, we bargain, *we collect favors*. So, don't use that word and don't promise anything to anyone."

Em's newest revelations make me want to use the *actual* F word. I assumed fairies were nice and did things because they had big hearts. It never occurred to me that our species was so self-serving. Then again, I'm basing all this on books and a few not-so-great movies.

Still, we don't have money and we have nothing to trade (Baby is a hard no despite Em's gross suggestion.) We're going to have to be very creative about how and whom we approach for assistance.

"Honestly?" Em's voice cuts through my inner monologue. "You should go to the library and ask one of those boring librarian fairies for a book on curses. No doubt it'll be the most thrilling thing that any of them have done in centuries. Imagine being created for the sole purpose of magical reading and cataloging? *Nightmare.* They might actually be more pathetic than you three."

Sometimes Em is so mean that her words pinch my kidneys. I can't believe she says the things she does. Out loud.

"Flora," I startle when Em uses my real name. "Get off your ass and do some research…some actual work. I realize that you aren't really seventeen, but I find it oddly suspicious that you've suddenly adopted your generation's worst attributes. No one is going to hand you any answers in this place, so stop expecting that to happen."

I exhale loudly and shake my head. There's something that just doesn't make sense here. I'm not expecting logic of course but just common sense. And common sense tells me…. "Wait, don't we have any friends?" I sputter. "I'm not looking for handouts, *or* favors. I'm looking for guidance, which friends are happy to give … right? I'm not buying this cut-throat Mad Max version of The Undervale you're selling. We must have friends . . . well, maybe not Etta, but Ana for sure. Even you like her."

"I don't know who your friends are," Em pounces. "Am I supposed to keep track of your social circles? I told you; fairies are complicated and vicious, but you're free to believe whatever you want. Either way, go do the work yourself and at the very least keep your secrets as much as you can. Go to the library. Find your own answers."

"I guess the library *is* good idea," I concede, even though I'm certain she's lying to me about our social lives. Maybe she's jealous. Maybe the three of us are the most popular fairies in the whole realm.

Em's tongue clicks off the roof of her mouth. "Don't sound so surprised, Flora. I have a thousand good ideas, literally, every second. It's exhausting. And before you ask, I know where the library is, but I don't have the first clue as to how to explain it to you."

"Okay, well..." I begin amicably, hoping she'll change her mind and at the very least, tell us to go right or left when we walk out the door.

"Good luck," Em cuts me off and phone goes dead. I stand there for a second, the heavy receiver drooping from my wrist.

Every time I communicate with Em, it leaves me feeling like I've run an emotional marathon. She consistently insults me. She belittles me. She plays games; this whole curse thing is obviously amusing her to no end. But she also gives me just enough valuable information to keep me going back.

"So," Etta says sharply, "the library. With a baby. That'll be great."

"I can stay behind," Ana offers.

"No," I rush. "We stick together. We don't separate. Ever. The only advantage that we've got in this place is that we have each other. Baby will just become our human . . . uhh . . . I want to say doll? But no . . . that's wrong. She's our mortal godchild. That's a thing, in books at least. And speaking of books, children go to libraries all the time. That's why they have kid sections." I don't bother to mention that since fairies aren't born, presumably there are no fairy kids. I'm determined to show my sisters as much positivity as I can muster.

"Okay," Etta says, throwing up her hands. "Then we should start getting ready right now. I'll have to make up at least four bottles. Baby needs snacks and a change of clothes." Etta huffs and looks at Baby who is sucking on Ana's shoulder. "It's a good thing you're a cute baby. Otherwise, I'd be really annoyed right now."

"Yay!" Baby claps her hands and squeals.

- 8 -

Thirty minutes later, we're all dressed, and Baby is in her oversized pram. Etta and I had argued about how many layers she needed but Ana swiftly took over as Baby's stylist and that was that.

When it's time to leave, Etta is the first to go. She doesn't look anxious at all. In fact, the only thing she does mutter is about the likelihood of rain. Ana merrily bounds out while pushing the carriage.

It isn't the same for me.

I hover at the door frame and look sharply at the street. There are houses directly across, little cottages, though none nearly as big as our own quirky Queen Anne. I bite at my lip and pick up my foot to walk through. Right away, my pulse starts thrumming and my fingers tingle.

"Come on," Etta bellows.

I swallow, or at least, I try to. Inside, I am discord. I am two opposing states of mind that are scraping up against one another. I want to get away from the house very badly. I haven't been able to shake off the music box room. My bed has become too hard and the sofa too narrow. My back hurts from all the odd angles I have tied myself into in a useless bid to get comfortable. Even my breakfast hadn't tasted right. The French toast had left an odd tang in my mouth, like sour butter. As disagreeable as my house has become, it's still my home. I know it. It's familiar. Whatever is coming next is . . . well . . . who knows? A wander into my own attic *seemed* innocent enough, but because we're in The Undervale, that little jaunt turned out to be a one-way ticket to the PTSD Express. The scope of what we could be facing next pins my toes to the floor.

As if reading my mind, Ana smiles brightly. "It's okay, Lo. I was scared too, but you have to do it. We can't hide in there forever. And you have your camera. Think of it like a photojournalism assignment."

I clutch at the camera hanging from my neck. It was muscle memory. I don't even remember grabbing it. I think about artists and journalists in conflict zones and what they put on the line to make sure the world knows the truth of a thing.

I am also after the truth. I need it. In its own way, photography is like magic too, pulling a single second out of time to preserve it forever. This quiet, tree-lined street is deceptive. It doesn't look like a war zone, but I know how dangerous it is. Even though Em was unreasonably rude on the phone, she was also right. I'm going to have to work to get the answers I want. Maybe my camera can help me. Maybe through its lens I can tweak the focus and frame something real and true. I set my jaw and walk stiffly out the door.

I let go of the breath I was holding and walk out . . . Nothing happens. The bar is so low at this point that I take my easy departure with such gratitude I could do a cartwheel right here on the porch.

I help Ana carry the pram down the front steps. Right away, I notice the weather. It's autumn. I'm sure of it because the tree tops look as though they've been set ablaze. They're all fiery scarlets and luminous yellows. The temperature should be nippy, even though the sky is blue and clear. But…It isn't cold at all; it isn't anything. Why? How? I layer up when I work in the garden. I know it's been chilly back there.

My nose is always running and when I go back inside, my cheeks are pink. The curse. Again.

But now, outside is like a movie set that's been painted and dressed to *look* like fall but is climate-controlled to comfort. I have a sneaking suspicion that a lot of what I'll see today will feel like this. Unreal. Fake. Impossible.

We stand on the sidewalk, looking up and down the street. "Any ideas about which way we should go?" Etta asks curiously.

"Uhh," I mumble, taking in the wide avenue which appears almost endless. "I think we just have to guess."

"That's okay. Baby likes the fresh air," Ana says happily while reaching down to secure her blanket. I turn right and start walking. My sisters fall in step beside me. The pavement stretches like gray taffy to accommodate our width. I wonder if Etta and Ana notice that it has done this. I decide not to point it out. If I start making a habit of all the trippy things we're going to see in The Undervale, I'll get laryngitis.

I have to admit though, it is beautiful. I start snapping photos and each one I line up looks like a postcard. The houses are colorful and quaint, full of character and Old-World charm. There is nothing modern, no sleek lines or concrete. I wonder if all of The Undervale will be such a cliché.

After about ten minutes, I'm both relieved and wary to see another person. The gentleman approaching us is wearing a tweed cap, a red waistcoat, and funny pants that end at his knees, revealing well-defined calves beneath orange argyle socks. Ana glances furtively at Baby, who is now lying down. Hopefully she'll be asleep soon.

"Hello," I say as soon as the man gets close enough to address.

"Hello," he replies, tipping his hat. After surveying us for a second or two, his eyes light up. "Oh, it's you! Oh my, my, what good fortune. I almost didn't go for a walk but then I thought to myself, come on you wastrel, it's the Patchwork Harvest. We only get one of them every seventy-three years. Not that the Walnut Harvest isn't grand, or that the Vulture's Peak Harvest doesn't have its own kind of beauty too . . ." the man trails off.

"Yes, I agree. You know us, right?" I don't mean to phrase this like a question, but I'm suddenly all teeth and wide eyes, like a game show host. I even sweep my hand in an odd, robotic gesture.

"Know you? Well, now," the man says, tilting his long, thin face sideways, "are you having a laugh? Are you trying to prank old Axis Hefferwill?"

"No, no, it's just that we, uhhh, we're experiencing some very minor lapses in memory. No big deal at all," I tell him casually, or at least, I hope I sound casual. Then, I lean in, almost conspiratorially, and say, "There's a bit of a curse thing going on." An odd cackle gurgles out of my mouth and nose. I look at my sisters for some help and they start to laugh too. Ana sounds like a twittering bird and Etta is more of a skipping record.

We are really going to have to work on our improv skills out here.

"Oh," Axis steps back, as if we're all contagious. "Well, er, yes, I did wonder about the house, but I thought perhaps it was one of your art installations, Flora. Your work is always so . . . interesting."

My forced giggling comes to an abrupt halt, and I give the man a narrow look. "You thought I was doing performance art for five years?"

"Has it really been five years?" Axis's eyes pop. They are a rheumy blue, like shaved ice. "Well, to be fair, I wasn't really paying attention. I'm no art critic."

"It's not for everybody," I tell him congenially, but I scratch my neck with both hands to keep it from throwing the little man a dismissive jut. "Could you by any chance, tell us where the library is, from here? From this very spot we are now standing in?" Em's words are ringing in my ears. I need to be specific- like I'm talking to a genie granting a wish.

At first Axis looks confused, then suspicious, then he gets a rather smarmy expression that worries me. Etta, who has been paying close attention to the exchange, steps in. "Don't you even think about sending us on a wild goose chase, Axis Hefferwill, or we'll come back and find you with a curse of our own," she warns, shaking her wand in his direction.

Axis furrows his considerably hirsute brow. "Very well. Straight to the library from here." The man pauses and strokes his pointed chin. "Today we're on Featherington Lane, and the library is in the Village of course, which on a Feastday would mean that it's three turns up and two stretches across. So, you continue walking in this direction. And I assume you're planning to walk properly? You aren't folding your steps?"

"We have a baby. The fresh air is good for her," I tell him as I block his view of the carriage. I have no idea what it means to fold a step, though it's obviously magic. And now that Etta's threatened him, there's no telling what he'll do if he knows that her wand is broken. He might turn us into cockroaches for trying to leverage him or even just for the fun of it. Axis cannot know our sorry state of magic-less.

"A baby you say?" he asks sheepishly. "A human child?"

I don't answer and neither do my sisters. We just glare at him. *Severely.*

"Very well," Axis says sharply. "You continue to walk until you hit Hummingbird Crest, that's just after Pansywood Street. Make a left and then walk until you hit Blushing Begonia Avenue. The library is there today. You won't miss it. It's a big, ramshackle building, yellow limestone, says the word *library* on it," Axis intones cheekily.

"Thank you, Axis, we appreciate it," I say genuinely and then I herd us away quckly. He didn't seem like a particularly dangerous man, but I think it's probably best to interact as little as possible with the residents of The Undervale until we get our memories back.

Once we hit Hummingbird Crest, the views change dramatically. The buildings are no longer residential. I'm assuming this is the Village. I half expect that everything will be as twee as the dwellings we'd passed to get here, but they are drastically different. Yes, there are some quaint little teashops with painted wooden signs. There are also bustling, industrial-looking coffee shops and art galleries with giant stone plinths advertising their names in fat block letters.

There are people milling around too. Lots of people. Some are dressed in long iridescent capes, their hands stuffed in mink muffs. Others are similarly outfitted, the way I always imagined a fairy would look, in layers of chiffon and feathered fascinators. But there are plenty of residents dressed quite normally, in jeans and navy peacoats. And there are even some that look like they've walked right off a fashion runway, in sleek white and ivory suits, powdered faces, and streaks of silver brushed over their eyelids like a mask. Their androgyny is so chic and chiseled, I can't stop staring.

"Did you get a look at the names of some of these businesses?" Etta asks quietly. "Cloaks of Hopes and Miseries, Giant Squid Sandwich Company, Zero Gravity Fitness, and look there," she says pointing to an open double-arched door with wares in neat stacks that glint in the sunlight. "Golden Yarns. You think the yarn is actually made of gold? I can't think that'd be a particularly comfortable sweater."

"Lo!" Ana says so excitedly that her voice practically trembles. "That sign says A+ Dreams- Over a Thousand Expertly Tailored Nighttime Excursions. Could that be real? I know they don't use money here, but maybe we could trade something? Like a meal cooked by Etta? I'd love to have an expertly tailored dream."

"I'm not cooking for some hippie weirdo fairies who like to crawl around in your brain so they can create a perfect nighttime fantasy. I know you want to think everyone wants hugs and rainbows, Ana, but you've got to let that fantasy go. We're in enemy territory here. Stop acting like we're in a theme park and start treating this place like the battlefield it is."

Ana's lower lip begins to tremble, and I could swat Etta for being so aggressive. "Stop being so weird and intense, Ettta," I snap. "We aren't at war. We do *live* in The Undervale, curse or no curse, so it can't be all bad. We just have to be cautious and smart. Besides," I direct my attention to Ana, "even though Etta's a great cook, I don't think a dinner is the kind of thing that you can use for currency around here and we don't have anything else to trade except Baby."

Ana shrugs in agreement, but I can tell she's sulking. Luckily, her attention span is so minuscule, it'll probably take her all of five minutes until she's onto something new. Given that we are in the heart of the Village, there is a lot to distract her. This place is not only overwhelming but also disorienting. Every time I pull up my camera to take a shot, the stucco edges slip, wooden beams ripple, and the painted letters on the signs peel back and forth. It's like I'm not meant to really see the Village, but just get glances- like I'm driving through it instead of walking.

Architecturally, it's all over the place. Some buildings look like they belong in a chocolate box of an English village, while others are like slouching rectangles-the utterly cool stores you'd expect in Lower Manhattan. And then there's an entire stretch of ten buildings on both sides that look like a working-class American Main Street from the 1940's. Some people greet us affectionately as we walk past. Others look indifferent and a few even roll their eyes. Everyone though, takes special notice of Baby in the carriage. I make sure to give each of them a discouraging glare.

Finally, on the very street where Axis promised it would be is the library, and I sigh audibly with relief. Etta pulls open a hammered bronze door belabored with geometric designs. The library is sharp, symmetrical and art deco (or at least I think so, but I'm just relying on photography books). Once we step inside, the décor is made warmer with vivid colors and plush velvet reading chairs just a few feet from the entrance. I look up, tilting my neck all the way to the ceiling.

"Wow," I say out loud with genuine awe. The mural on the dome has captivated all of us- even Baby.

It's not a true night sky above; it's not the silty black of a moonless evening. It's the deep blushing mauve of twilight, those few moments of gray and purple combined before the day rolls over completely. The color is amazing but that's not the incredible part. There are a few visible stars that are actually twinkling, and the moving clouds are real. They majestically puff and roll across the expanse of ceiling.

Etta pulls at my sleeve. I look down and then out at the vast library. Books are expected in a library, obviously. And shelves too. What makes us practically swoon with wonder is that the books are floating across the vast hall and into the various sections- *shelving themselves.*

"Close your mouth, Etta," I tell her, even though I know I'm being a hypocrite. "We have to act like this is all normal, like we've been in here a dozen times."

My sister mumbles something to herself, but she manages to slap a neutral look on her face. Ana is giddy but, I suspect that's pretty much how anyone who knows her would expect her be, so I say nothing. The three of us walk along the marbled floor, our well-worn running shoes are mostly silent, apart from a squeak here and there from the soles. Baby's pram, with its thick, rubber wheels is silent too.

We approached the information desk and standing behind it is a girl who doesn't look much older than we are.

"Hey," I say casually.

"Hello," the girl answers in a deep English accent that sounds much more mature than the bright pink of her hair would suggest.

"We'd like some information," I tell her courteously. The girl looks at us primly and then down at the large, engraved sign that says **Information.** "Right okay, ha," I chuckle, but the girl's mouth remains steadfastly firm. "We're looking for some books on curses. Different types, people who created them, that sort of thing."

That's when the girl gets a rather mean-spirited smile on her face that makes my stomach tense. Once again, Em had lied to me. This librarian isn't thrilled. If anything, she seems perturbed at best and downright ghoulish at worst. Then again, what would a fairy like Em know about libraries? The thought of her handing over a laminated library card to borrow a book is absurd.

"Alright then. Come with me," she says haughtily.

Despite her shocking pink hair, the girl is dressed conservatively in a skirt and piped blazer. She's wearing low heels that smack sharply on the floor beneath her. We follow her past a few fairies sitting in sumptuous citron-colored chairs. The books float inches in front of their faces as they flip the pages with a tiny flick of their wands.

I duck more than a few times to dodge the traveling tomes that float and land neatly into the shelves. The librarian has led us to a large double door that says *Curses, Hexes and Jinxes* written in bold silver script. She looks at the writing and then at us, raising a single perfectly arched fuchsia eyebrow like we are the dumbest trio ever. "Sorry" I say quickly, "it's been a while since I've been here."

The librarian pushes the door open to reveal a room that's about half the size of the massive hall we had just been in. There are a few tables and chairs on the bottom floor, but the shelves themselves are oval, just like the shape of the room and at least fifteen stories high. Four wooden ladders span the height and run on rollers, so that conceivably, you could climb up to reach any book you wanted. But why would anyone here do that? They have magic. The ladders must be decorative. My eyes glaze over shelf upon shelf of more books than I could read in a lifetime- a *human* lifetime. A fairy would have forever to read them but, we don't have forever.

"There must be thousands of books in here," I warble in frustration.

"Well, it's a library so, yes," the girl observes curtly.

"How are they cataloged?" I ask as a tall leather-bound book goes whooshing past my head. "There must be some kind of a system?"

"Oh yes, it's quite modern," the girl purrs while giving us a hard look. "It's this new-fangled way we have of organizing things where we use the last names of authors. It's called the alphabet. It's *revolutionary*."

I suck the air back from my front teeth. I guess the librarian wants to do disdain and judgmental. Fine. I don't just look seventeen, I *feel* seventeen. I can do disdain and judgmental all day long. "I'm confused, isn't this your job? To help people find books? Or maybe you're a just an intern? Or new? Is this your first day?"

"No, *I'm* the one that's confused," the girl shoots back sharply. "You walk in here like we've never met, like Fauna and I didn't spend an entire year together in Corfu. I didn't realize I was so forgettable." She turns to Ana and cocks her head while snapping her arms in a fold. "It's Sidelia, Sidelia Puddlehop. *Hi,* remember me? Once upon a time, you used to say my name twenty times a day."

"Oh sorry!" Ana gasps, stepping forward. "Yeah, we've been cursed so we don't remember anything about being fairies or living here. We didn't even know we were cursed. This lady named Em had to tell us because we've been trapped in our house for five years thinking we were teenagers, and our mom was out of town. Buuuut." Ana sidles up toward the girl. "I'd love to hear all about what we did in Corfu, maybe later? When you get off work you can fill me in?" She bats her eyes while Sidelia just looks at us all, blankly.

"Ana!" Etta hisses but I'm too shocked to even speak. Ana doesn't lie. I don't even think she knows how to lie. She speaks her mind—*whatever* is on her mind—good or bad. But this blurting out our entire situation is going to get us into serious trouble. The worst part is, I don't even think Ana realizes what a disadvantage she's just placed us in.

"Seriously?" Sidelia finally asks. She doesn't zap us or start flying around. She doesn't even pull out her wand, which is a good thing I suppose? I study Sidelia's face. There's nothing evil about it; she doesn't even look angry anymore. If anything, her eyes, a deep hazel with leaping gold flecks, tell me she is wounded. I can only hope that my sister didn't hurt Sidelia so badly that she'll refuse to help us out of spite.

It doesn't matter anyways. Sidelia knows and we don't have the magic to unring that bell.

"Yes, seriously," I tell her in a soft tone that I make sure retains a certain firmness. She might know the truth, but I won't have Sidelia thinking we're pushovers. "We are here, prepared to spend all day reading a bunch of books we probably won't even understand. So yes, this is serious."

"And Em told you this? Em? You mean Maleficent?" Sidelia bites at her bubblegum-colored lip.

"I guess," I admit, rolling the name over and over again on the tip of my tongue. It sparks something, just the vaguest of memories. I flash on a young boy, a blonde girl singing and purple smoke, but the memory scatters when I try to hold it, like an armful of butterflies. "Why? Is there something about Maleficent that we should know?"

"Well, there's a history there. Then again, everyone here has some sort of history with each other but, Fauna assured me that you had squashed that beef. Maybe you have and maybe you haven't. It's not like I would know." The librarian tries and fails to sound indifferent.

"Look, I'm just going to preemptively apologize for anything we say that comes across as offensive, or whatever we do that is not in line with the fairy code, if that's a thing. We're not trying to be rude or mean. If you haven't picked up on it already, we're in over our heads. There must be a book in here," I suggest softly while gesturing toward the shelves, "that could help us. This is a Grade A curse apparently. That makes me think that this curse maker, if that's the right word, I don't even know what they would be called. But it's probably a fairy who would be very well-known for this kind of thing."

"What kind of thing, exactly?" Sidelia probes.

Etta's lips are thin and firm. I can tell she doesn't like the idea of getting into any more specifics. Ana is grinning, while rocking Baby's pram back and forth.

"This would be a someone who's really good at wiping memories and making people relive the same day over and over again." I hope I don't sound desperate, though I probably do. My shirt is sticking to the small of my back, little drops of nervous sweat cling to the fabric.

Sidelia sighs and shakes her head just a little. "First of all, curse maker is not a word. That would be like calling mortals 'breathers' or 'water drinkers.' All fairies have the ability to curse and hex and also to grant wishes and do lovely sorts of magic as well. And, just like humans, there are all sorts of fairies. So, I have to tell you, there aren't textbooks written by curse masters, or makers because again- that's not a thing. The books here aren't manuals. For all intents and purposes, they're biographies- self-important, puffed-up journals that go on for a thousand pages that include hexes and curses and what not. But really, the only thing a fairy needs to accomplish an effective curse is an imagination. And we are, if nothing else, an imaginative lot."

I squeeze my temples with my thumb and index figure. "So, what you're saying is that there is nothing in this entire room that could help us?"

"I'm saying no such thing," the librarian corrects me while smoothing down a flamingo-colored lock. "I'm saying that if you were so inclined, you could read five hundred books in here and discover a thousand commonalities between your curse and many of theirs. And there's a very good chance you would put enough pieces together to reveal the fairy who cursed you. However, it would take a *really* long time."

"Uh huh," I respond with clenched teeth. "Okay well, uhh…Your definition of help and my definition of help is obviously very different. But we have to do *something*." I throw up my hands and blink several times in a row as I study the thousands of books on the shelf. "I guess we just start reading and maybe we'll get lucky."

"Flora, that is ridiculous. You could lose a century in here. And what kind of life is that for a child? I mean, that's some real medieval shit you're talking about. A human child spending all of her days locked in a magical library? *Come on*, just use your wands. Your combined strength should be able to combat any curse, no matter how good it is. I'm not surprised Maleficent didn't tell you that." Sidelia snorts out a sarcastic chuckle. "I bet she's watching you through her ravens, getting a real kick at seeing the three of you stumble all over The Undervale. It's like the best reality television show ever, for a fairy like her."

Ana quickly glances over at Baby. Etta bites her cheek and looks down at the floor. I squint my eyes.

"Wait . . ." Sidelia says with genuine concern on her face. "Maleficent did tell you that you have wands, right? Because if she didn't then, she's definitely up to something,"

"Yes, yes, she absolutely told us," Ana reassures her quickly. "It's just that we lost ours. Well, Lo and I did. Technically. We found Etta's inside a jewelry box that ate us. And it changed our faces. Anyways, yeah, we don't have our wands. And also? Em told us she wasn't strong enough to break the curse."

The color drains from Sidelia's face. She yanks all three of us into a small alcove. Ana manages to grab the carriage, so we don't leave Baby behind. "You lost your wands? How is that even possible?" she whispers frantically.

"How is it possible that I just found out I was a fairy a couple days ago and we've been living in a house that does our laundry and delivers groceries right into our pantry every night when we're sleeping?" I clap back in a tone just above a whisper. "I don't know how any of this is possible. In my mind, I'm a seventeen-year-old girl named Lo Smith. Why don't *you* tell *me* how this is possible, Immortal Librarian!?"

Sidelia taps her top lip with one of her absurdly long fuchsia fingernails. "But you do have one wand, right? Merriweather's?"

Etta pulls the wand out of her inside pocket and shows it to Sidelia. "It doesn't work. Either because I forgot how to use it or maybe because it needs the two other missing wands?"

"Ummm . . . what?" Sidelia asks incredulously.

"I've tried," Etta told her earnestly. "I've pinged it and circled it and wagged it. I've focused really hard at it. It's useless."

"Wait. . . Do you actually believe that all three wands have to be in close proximity to work?" Sidelia looks more confused than ever. "That's ridiculous! You think all four of us were in Corfu? Not bloody likely. You don't actually live together. You're close, obviously. And your situation is rare, being that you're triplets, but it's not unique. All of you have separate lives, separate houses, separate friends. It's a miracle that you managed to live in such close quarters for five years without at least one of you locking the other two in the basement or a closet or something, but I suppose that's part of the curse too. You can't torture someone if they're not around." Sidelia chuckles.

Something breaks loose inside me, mud and rocks and bits of gravel, a collection of tiny landslides.

Sidelia's words burn the moment they leave her mouth.

They fall on the marbled floor in heaps of ash and smoke.

Well, not really, not magically, but it feels like it. It feels like my ears aren't ready to hear them and my brain isn't ready to accept them.

All these years inside the curse, I have known that eventually, life was bound to pull my sisters and me in different directions; but that idea seemed far away. It hovered, but we didn't reach for it, or try to pull it down and inspect the particulars of a life outside our house.

Rationally, I know that I'm not going to college, that I'm not even in high school. But the thought of living alone, of not waking up to Etta's coffee or snuggling on the couch, watching movies with Ana fills me with a sort of dread.

"So why isn't my wand working then?" Etta's demand shakes me out of my own head.

"I'm not a wand expert, so I don't know," Sidelia says anxiously as she looks at the five fairies who are reading at the tables in the room. "But a wand is more machine than anything else, despite its mystical reputation. It siphons off magic from The Undervale and harnesses it according to the will of its user. It must occasionally be recalibrated and maintained, so perhaps, in the room that you described so pedestrianly, Fauna, it lost its balance and needs to be re-tuned."

"I wasn't being pedestrian," Ana jumps in angrily, "and honestly? I'm not even sure what that word means."

Sidelia lazily raises an eyebrow, suggesting that she knows exactly how Ana was being. *From experience.* "Guys, stop," I say impatiently. "Sidelia, could you please tell us where we can go to get the wand fixed?"

"Justy Bluehorn has always taken care of your wands. His shop is … good Lord, where is his shop today?" Sidelia pulls her wand out of a slim holster that's attached to her skirt. It's so compact that I hadn't even noticed it. Sedalia dots the air. A complex and complicated 3D map roars to life in front of our eyes. "Honestly, *I get it,* the streets rearrange themselves at night so that a human would be 'forever lost' in The Undervale. But that plan was conceived when mortals relied on horses for transportation. Now they use satellites to navigate. It takes much more than moving roads to confound a human nowadays. I wish everything would just stay put, you know? It's a friggin' hassle." Sidelia squints and then points to a name, double-checking the location on the map. "Justy Bluehorn's Wands & Ladies Shoe Emporium. Lucky for you all, it's only one street over, on Fogspark Road. Walk up to the next block, take a right, then look for it on the corner."

"Shoes? Wands *and* shoes?" I ask, wondering if I'd heard right.

"Justy is a character, even for one of us," Sidelia says, giving her head a little shake as if she's recalling a specific memory. "But the shoes are divine."

"Right, well, thank you so much," I tell her, and I mean it. I don't think Sidelia would have been anything other than pleasant—at least to me, maybe Ana not so much—if we had reconnected under normal circumstances. I am leaving the library with more than just directions. I've learned something valuable during this exchange. Fairies are going to know who we are, and from now on, all three of us need to be on the same page about how much of our predicament we are willing to share. Maybe Em has enemies everywhere, but I'm not convinced that we do.

In a way, it was easier when we believed everyone in The Undervale was a threat. We could be wary and guarded; lies could easily slide off our tongues because no fairy could be trusted. Now, we have to weigh every exchange and measure every word. We have to read immortal beings who've had thousands of years to practice the art of disassembly. Not every fairy is out to get us, but I'm nowhere near having a reliable system to ferret out the ones who are. I glance at Ana who looks so peaceful and dreamy. Etta looks like she's ready to fight or run. I am wedged between them, pulling the gray out of their fixed perspectives.

"No problem. I hope he can help you," Sidelia says kindly, further proving my point. "Fauna," she says taking Ana's hand in both of hers. "Get in touch when you've sorted this out. I've missed you."

"When this is sorted out?" Ana giggles. She gives Sedalia a quick kiss on the cheek. "I haven't left the house in five years. I might be back in an hour."

- 9 -

Justy Bluehorn's Wands & Ladies Shoe Emporium is in a tall brick building with arched doors and half-shuttered windows that look like a stretch of sleepy eyes. Baby is up from her nap. We had changed her on the walk over and now she's sucking happily on a bottle. I have no experience with babies (that I can remember) but this particular baby seems to be in perpetual high spirits. She never cries, though she does bleat and wriggle when she's hungry or needs her diaper changed.

Etta is steering the stroller and Ana pushes open the large wooden barn-like door. Inside is all exposed brick and metal beams. There are two ornate chandeliers hanging from the high ceiling that are overflowing with sparkling crystals. The light fixtures are dispro-portionately large, like they belong in a grand ballroom and the watt-age they are giving off is so brilliant that my left eye starts to twitch. The floors are poured concrete but covered in silk rugs. Instead of a cozy, cluttered warren of rooms like I was certain it would be, the space is wide and light and airy. If I call out my name, I am sure it will bounce off the walls and echo back to me.

"Sweet, sweet Lord in all the heavens," Ana says as she holds out a trembling hand. On it is a black leather, high-heeled closed-toe shoe.

The straps are held together by bright emerald ribbons and there is no back to it at all. It's like a high-heeled slipper. "Have you ever, in all your life, seen such a gorgeous thing?"

"Are you ... *crying?*" Etta asks incredulously.

"I think I am," she answers while clutching the heel to her bosom. With her free hand, she wipes her eyes.

"Put it down," I scold tepidly. My heart's not really it in it because the shoes *are* incredible. "Be cool."

"You be cool," Ana bites back. "We won't always be like this." My sister is practically breathless, and her knuckles are going white against the black leather. "At some point, we'll get our magic back and I can change my face to look like a famous model or actress and I can go to fashion shows and sit in the front row and the whole world will see these shoes. Everyone will want a pair, but they won't be able to have them because they'll be mine."

"Oh Fauna, my girl. Certain shades of limelight can wreck a girl's complexion," a disembodied voice rings out.

We whip our heads around and there he is. It's possible he could have stepped out from behind a column, but I'm betting magic is involved. "Truman Capote said that, by the way. But of course, you already know that. *Breakfast at Tiffany's* is one of your favorite movies."

"It is?" Ana asks in surprise. I give her a quick pinch. "I mean, yes, of course it is. Totally."

"Haven't seen you ladies in a while. Last thing I heard, your house was covered in vines that tried to take a bite out of anyone who got too close." Justy's hair is so black it shines blue. His eyes are hazel- the color of moss and ancient ferns. He's wearing a plaid shirt and faded jeans. He looks more like a cowboy than a wand specialist, or even a shoemaker, for that matter.

I give him a long, hard gaze and Justy does the same in return. He could have been thirty or fifty, and while I know his appearance is a lie, it's also imposing, like a disappointed father. When he gets closer, I can smell beeswax and something else—citrus and wood, like oranges popping on a campfire.

I search Justy's face for clues: the hint of a grin, the square of his jaw, the lazy way he bats his long, dark lashes. Sidelia said we always bring our wands to him, *and* he knows Ana's favorite movie. I roll my neck until I feel a vertebrae crack.

"Justy," I begin in a firm but earnest tone.

"Flora," he answers simply, but with a voice that's grave enough to make me feel like bolting.

I think we can trust him.

I hope we can trust him.

Anyone who makes such incredible shoes can't be a villain. It would go against the laws of nature, even the supernatural ones.

"We have a bit of a situation," I stutter.

"Is that right?" Justy puts his hands on his hips and rolls back on his heels.

"Yay!" Baby squeals.

"You steal another baby?" he asks non-plussed.

"*Another* baby?" Etta yelps. "Lo, you steal babies." It's statement and not a question, which I really resent. Regardless of my present circumstance, I know myself. I would never take a child unless it was in peril.

"The child was left on our doorstep, which allowed for certain other issues to become clear," I tell him in my most mature voice.

"Stop dancing around it, Flora, and tell me what you need. I got work to do. The shoes only make themselves up to a point."

I double-check with my sisters. Ana vigorously nods her head. Etta shrugs a single shoulder, offering what is clearly a dubious approval. "It's like this . . . " I begin cautiously. "Someone cursed us. They took our memories. We have been in our house for five years, under the impression that we are seventeen-year-olds and our mom is away on business. My wand and Fauna's wand is missing. We found Etta's—or Merriweather's—in the house. Hidden. In the attic . . . sort of."

"And it doesn't work," Etta jumps in. "It's broken. Sidelia from the library said you have always fixed our wands so if that's true, you should be able to make it work again, and if you can't, then we know one or both of you is lying."

Ana steps right in front of Etta, blocking her tiny frame entirely from Justy's view. "I would also like to ask what the deal is with the shoes? Like, I know you don't use money and ummm . . . .is there some sort of bargaining system? Basically, I want these shoes, but I don't have anything to trade right now. Do you accept IOUs or a signed contract where I would promise to come back and negotiate a price?" Etta reaches forward and pinches the back of Ana's arm. "Owww . . ." Ana squeals but Etta is making a fair point. Unfortunately, Ana is too dazzled to grasp it. "Oh *riiiiight*. We will not trade the baby. The baby is totally off the table."

"Ana," I hiss, "stop it with the shoes and the baby. What's wrong with you?"

Ana curls her lip at me. She doesn't say anything, Instead, she holds the shoe up as if it's some kind of sacred holy relic.

Meanwhile, Justy is gawking at us. When we finally stop bickering, he addresses me and me only. "I'm very concerned about the language you're using, Flora. Your present circumstance qualifies as much more than a 'situation.' What in the hell did the three of you do? You don't get a curse like this over nothing, and you can't get by in The Undervale without a wand. You might as well be human."

"I realize that" I snap. Justy lifts his brows. His entire face becomes a silent warning. "Sorry. It's that . . . ummm . . . we're just a little, I don't know . . . we're really . . ."I scramble to find the words, but they don't assemble properly when I try to move them out of my mouth. They're all lopsided and bent the wrong way. Eventually, his posture relaxes, and he gives me a long, sad smile.

"Okay now, it's alright. Everything is going to be just fine," he says, patting me lightly on my shoulder. I can tell that he feels sorry for us, but there is something else there too. Fear maybe? Or disappointment? That we did something so terrible? Or perhaps he thought we were smarter and more powerful, that we should have been able to avoid the curse altogether. Whatever he thinks, he's not sharing it, which is fine with me. We don't need a reprimand over something that's already happened. We need help and if the price for his aid is a presumption that we're pitiful, we'll pay it. Pride is a luxury we can't afford right now.

"Now, you ladies come with me to the Look See Table, and I'll have a gander at Etta's wand."

We follow him past all the lovely shoes that make Ana quiver and gasp. We walk under a chandelier and over two more rugs. Finally, we arrive at an expansive block of a table, at least fifteen feet long. It's made of a light-colored shellacked wood and polished so finely that I can see my reflection when I look down on it. Justy gestures for us to sit and we do, on three stainless steel barstools which are just comfortable enough to make sure that we can take a load off but not so comfortable that we're likely to overstay our welcome.

Justy pulls his own wand out of a leather holster that's attached to his belt buckle. He gives the wand two flicks and a spin. A large glass bottle appears with a narrow neck. It's filled with an amber-colored liquid streaked with silver flecks. We eye Justy's bartending skills carefully. I want to ask what exactly he intends to ply us with, but I don't want to come across as rude. Instead, I decide to try some innocent intelligence gathering.

"I know this is a weird question. but could you maybe tell me, tell us, where we actually live? Is it here in The Undervale or do we just visit? I must sound so silly, but Sidelia the librarian, she said we have separate lives," I ask cautiously as four crystal tumblers float up to the table.

"All fairies live in The Undervale, but most of us have a life in the mortal realm too; it keeps things interesting. When you're in The Undervale, all of you share a house, though it doesn't usually look the way it does now. The curse has certainly had its way with your home. It's been downsized . . . significantly." Justy points his wand at each glass, and they fill with finely crushed ice. "In the mortal realm, Fauna lives in Los Angeles. She's had a lot of professions over the years, but currently, I believe she's writing plays or maybe costume design? Probably both. She was thinking of relocating to New York."

"I was?" Ana says in disbelief. "I am?" More shock, but I'm not that surprised. All Ana ever seems to do is read, watch TV, and sketch.

"Now Merriweather, last I heard, you were running a restaurant in Bend, Oregon. Went there once, a real pretty place underneath a grove of Ponderosa pines. You told me you were thinking of expanding."

"Hmm," Etta says with a nod of her head and the briefest of smiles. She is warming to Justy. It's no surprise she's a professional cook in the mortal realm- in *any* realm. I think of my platinum-haired sister as chef right now and it never occurred to me that she would be anything else.

"And you, Flora, you live in Avening, which is a small town on an island in British Columbia. It's close to The Undervale; there are even sections of their land that bleed into ours. And because of that fact, it has a lot of interesting residents, a lot of fairies, me included. The human population there is much more enlightened than humans usually are. You're an artist. You change the medium up every half century or so. Currently, you're in a photography phase, which I suppose the curse couldn't get rid of." Justy nods at my chest and I nervously look down.

My camera. I'd been so caught up in our mission that I hadn't taken a photo of this incredible place. I pick up the camera and bring the viewer to my eye. "You mind?" I ask hopefully.

"Go ahead," Justy tells me warmly. I begin to snap pictures of the bar, the floating bottle that's putting the finishing touches on our cocktails, and Justy himself, though he always manages to maneuver himself in such a way that I can only get his hand in the frame, or the blur of his plaid shirt.

I lower the camera thoughtfully. "Do we have fairy jobs? Like, do we do anything as fairies that might have made us a target for the curse? It didn't occur to me that fairies would have magical specialties, but now that I've seen even this much of The Undervale, I realize that fairies do things, *specific* things like capturing dreams and fixing wands."

"You really don't remember anything?" Justy asks. A small V forms between his eyebrows. I shake my head desolately. He looks up from his work, all the way up to the ceiling, conjuring perhaps an answer that will satisfy what he must believe is my utter naiveté.

He begins slowly, rolling out his observations like an ancient Ferris wheel.

"Let's see now . . . all of us fairies are created with a purpose. Some of us help control the weather and the seasons. Some are muses, and some are guardians—of knowledge, of time, of the darkness that seeps into The Undervale from the human realm. I myself was created to ensure that the vehicles of our magic—our wands—run efficiently."

"Yeah, but what do we do?" Ana asks so rudely that I give her a harmless little kick.

Justy honors us with a lopsided grin. "There is such a thing as a fairy godmother, or father. They grant wishes of a sort, giving humans the chance to live up to their potential. Along those lines, you might be wondering why we bother with mortals at all, and there is no one-size-fits-all answer for that. In my opinion? I think we are fascinated by their passion and their brutality and the finger snap of time they are given on earth to experience and process both. Some humans are broken, not because they're evil or lazy or dumb. Sometimes they break because they were born too fragile or to a circumstance that even the strongest among them would crack under. You three are the collectors of the hopeless. Prayers are flung out to heavens, and you gather up the ones the universe doesn't catch. You don't just change lives, you save them. And that's the reason I can't imagine why anyone who would want to curse you. Or what you could have done to make one of us so angry. It's not like you, any of you. The Bloomshade sisters are well-liked and respected in this community."

I think about this for a moment. Can I see myself as a collector of broken people? I am drawn to things that don't fit, to objects that are discarded and discounted but those are items, not human beings. Can it be true? I want to believe it is. I want to believe very badly that I save lives, and that The Undervale, for all its craziness, has a purpose.

Etta doesn't seem to care a bit about this part. She's too practical for reflection and more concerned with our protection. "What about Maleficent?" Etta asks sharply. "When Baby was abandoned on our doorstep, she was the only person we reached out to because hers was the only number we had to call. She's very mean. Everything we do annoys her." My sister leans forward across the table so she can lower her voice. "I don't trust her."

We all look expectedly at Justy who, much to my disappointment, shrugs his shoulders with indifference. "Well now, Maleficent is a very beautiful and complicated lady. Her purpose, her job, so to speak, is to scorch the Earth. Which sounds brutal but it's necessary to make way for new life to flourish. With mortals being so careless, it seems that wildfires get worse every year. Maleficent's services are no longer required very often. But it's something she used to do very well, perhaps too well." Justy laughs then, a barking chuckle that escapes his lips. "Sure, she had her Dark Night of the Soul; we all have one eventually. Fauna, you had yours just over thirty years ago and it was Maleficent and your sisters who brought you back. I don't think she would have done this to you."

"But it's not impossible," I wonder.

"Nothing is impossible in The Undervale," Justy tells us reluctantly. "Here you go." Justy pushes a cocktail toward me.

"What is it?" I stare at the drink like it might reach up and swallow me instead of the other way round.

"Your favorite— Waning Moonshine with two drops of Huckleberry syrup," he tells me with a broad grin.

"Is there alcohol in it?"

Justy frowned. "Damn right. We've been drinking this since Jesus was a carpenter."

"*Was* Jesus really a carpenter?" I can't help but ask.

"No politics or religion. Those are the rules here at the Emporium." Justy leans over the table, the suede patches on his flannel shirt rest casually on the shellacked wood. "You do know that you're not really teenagers? You can have a drink."

Ana shrugs, picks up the glass and takes a giant gulp. "Ana!" I squawk disapprovingly, but my sister is either ignoring me or doesn't care. It's probably both. "We can't get drunk. We have Baby." I may not have ten thousand years of wisdom at my disposal but I'm certain that booze and babysitting are a dangerous combination. Ana rolls her eyes and takes another swig.

Typical.

"How about you give me your wand, Etta, so that I can have a look." Justy holds out his arm. His fingers are thick and callused, a workman's hands. Justy doesn't look like a fairy. In fact, with his battered boots and scruffy face, he couldn't be more different than the fairies you see in storybooks. I wonder how long it's going to take for reality to sink in. How am I ever going to get a handle on a place that's like going backward through a magic castle, a haunted house, and a carnival ride all at the same time?

Etta reluctantly passes her wand to Justy, and he takes it in his palm. Etta's lips are pursed hard enough to drain the pink out of them. I know she hates this but thankfully, logic has overridden her paranoia. What use is a wand that doesn't work?

First, Justy feels the length of it and then he brings it up to his eye, pointing it forward, presumably to check that it's level. He reaches beneath his desk and brings up a battered toolbox with a slim wooden handle. He picks through it until he comes across the item he's looking for, a tiny hexagonal magnifying glass that he fits into his eye socket neatly. Justy maneuvers the wand underneath a bright light that's clipped to the side of the table.

After giving the instrument a thorough inspection, he retrieves yet another item from the toolbox. This time, it's a golden tuning fork, with rods as slender as embroidery needles. He taps the wand lightly and then brings it up to his ear with his eyes closed. Justy turns his head thoughtfully and mutters something underneath his breath.

Finally, he slips the wand into a small hole that has been bored into the center of a teacup-sized crystal prism. He gives the prism a whirl and it begins to spin around the room, throwing rainbows on the walls. I stare in fascination as Justy's eyes track the wand's spinning. Etta has leaned over to watch the proceedings to such a degree that she's practically on top of the table. Ana is swaying with the drink in her hand.

"Merriweather," Justy says kindly as he hands the wand back to her. "I have good news and bad news."

"Just tell me," Etta interrupts brusquely.

"Your wand is most definitely not broken." Justy seems unbothered by Etta's agitation. His voice is warm, gentle even. We sit inside a couple seconds of collective silence.

"Well, that's great news," I announce, hoping my enthusiasm doesn't sound too forced. Etta remains perfectly still, staring shrewdly at Justy. "Etta," I goad, "isn't that great?"

"What's the bad news?" Etta asks grimly, ignoring my optimism. Cheerleading for my sister is getting exhausting.

"It isn't broken, but it is . . . sleeping. No two wands are truly connected. Each one was formed for a particular fairy and that fairy alone. However, in the case of you three, your wands—while not technically connected to one another—share a sort of link. Think of them like a song in three parts. Any one of you can sing a single part and the melody would sound beautiful but sing together, in harmony, and the melody comes alive."

"I don't understand," Etta says bitterly. She takes a look at the sweating, untouched glass of Waning Moonshine and in one swift motion, picks it up and drains it. She bangs the tumbler down on the table. "Can you just tell me why my wand isn't working? Without any metaphors or fancy language?"

Justy sighs but he does offer her a shallow grin. "Yes, Merriweather, I can do that. Whoever cursed you was smart enough to steal your wands and place a curse on them as well. I think it's a kind of dampening hex, which not only hides the wands but makes them inert. Now," Justy moves the empty glass away from Etta and looks at her intently, "here's where there's more good news. Had someone done this to three other random fairies who weren't triplets, you would need to find the individual who cursed you to actually break the curse. But, because your wands are linked, I believe all you need to do is recover the other two wands and all three will wake up, so to speak, and the curse will be lifted." Justy frowns for just a split second before adding, "Probably . . . I'm theorizing because this is such a unique situation, but it's been my experience that there isn't very much in this world or any other that can beat the power of your three wands together."

"Really?" I begin, because in that moment, my optimism has slammed right into a brick wall. "Then, you know, I have to wonder, if our wands are so strong, who would have the power to take them from us? You make it all sound very elementary, but whoever did this was strong enough, magically or otherwise, to wrestle our wands away from us in the first place."

"Huh," Justy concedes. "Yes. There is that. I'm sorry, I really am. You three appear to be in dire need of answers but unfortunately, I don't have the right kind of magic to give them to you. There is a shadow lingering, around the lot of you." My heart skips a beat.

Longshadow.

Does Justy's magic allow him to see it? Before I get a chance to ask, he continues, "It's a kind of bubble that's preventing me from reading your magic or your past. But an Oracle should be able to see through it."

No. He isn't talking about Longshadow. It's something else, some other machination of the curse. I realize that I am gripping the table. Hard.

"An Oracle ... is that a person?" I'm not going to take anything for granted in The Undervale. For all I know, the Oracle could be a floating Ouija board or a bearded parrot.

"Well, they aren't human people; they're fairies—irksome, pretentious fairies who use language as leverage. They talk in riddles, but they don't have to; they could just say what they see. Instead, they speak in metaphors and rhymes," Justy tells us with grim disdain.

"So, we just walk up to an Oracle and ask if they have any information that can help us?" I wonder out loud.

"Hardly." Justy moves around the table and stands in front of us, with his hands knitted together. "For every need, there is an Oracle. There's the Oracle of Weeping Leaves, the Oracle of Gathering Storms, of Wandering Thistles ... you three need the Oracle of a

Thousand Eyes. She should be able to see where your wands are. If she's feeling generous, she may even tell you."

"Wait." I hold up a single finger skeptically. "What would a Wandering Thistle do?"

"You've got to stop being so literal, Flora," Justy scolds.

"Sorry." My voice lifts along with my shoulders. "Every time we tell someone about our curse, it puts us at risk. Now you're suggesting we go see an Oracle who sounds like an asshole and who probably won't help us anyways. There's gotta be another way."

Justy's chest heaves and his jaw moves up and down, like he's chewing on something.

He's frustrated.

Join the club, Fairy Man, I think to myself.

"There is no other way. Not that I can think of," Justy tells me in a pinched voice. "If a curse could be torn as easily as a piece of tin foil, it wouldn't much of a curse."

"So, you're saying that we don't have a choice?"

"Of course you have a choice," Justy offers. "You don't have to do anything. You can go back to your home and wait out the curse. That's an option."

"It's really not," Ana slurs.

"It is actually," Justy argues. "You're not trapped in there anymore. You may not have your memories but worst case? A century goes by, and you'll make friends and talk to your neighbors and live like humans in The Undervale. It might even be amusing."

"We have a child here, see?" I point to Baby.

Justy's shoulder momentarily connects to his ear. "Well, eventually *she'll die*. In the meantime, she'll have fun growing up here. It'll be fine."

I am so tempted to contradict him. I want to tell him that I thought this was a great solution at first too, but it won't work. I also want to argue that raising an infant only to see her grow old and die would be heartbreaking, not to mention that she's been stolen and that her parents are probably frantic. But I don't bother. It's not that he's bad or even indifferent; Justy doesn't get it. He's nowhere near getting it. He can sympathize, but he has no real empathy for our situation, and I think possibly, probably, all fairies are going to be like this. They're immortal. They're magical. The idea of being confused or powerless is incomprehensible.

"I think we need to break the curse, so staying home, waiting a hundred years . . . that doesn't seem like the right thing to do. We'll take our chances with the Oracle."

"Agreed" Etta buds in. "I hate it, but this is the best option out of an infinite number of shittier ones. I can't make sure my wand doesn't get stolen again unless I wake it up. So, where is this mysterious talking fortune cookie, exactly?"

"In the mortal realm."

"Okay." Etta whips up, her tiny body bouncing lithely from her chair, "Open a door, sing a song, do a thing. We should go right now."

"No," Justy tells us plainly.

"What do you mean no?" Etta demands.

I stand up and gently tug on Etta's sleeve. She's itiching for a fight which is both dumb and rude. We need as many allies as possible here, and today has been a lot already. I could use some downtime before facing whatever this Oracle thing is.

"I mean just that . . . no. I've given you all the direction and help that I feel comfortable giving. You were right when you said that whoever cursed you must be extraordinarily powerful. I don't want to get any more involved than I already am. Advice is one thing, transportation is another. I can't afford to end up in this place for five years, alone, believing that I'm seventeen years old. I've got work to do."

"You're really not going to help us?" Ana asks, her green eyes widening in alarm, and I feel that same alarm too. I know that rationally, I'm not a child but I feel like a girl, and it seems so odd, to ask an adult for help and then being denied.

It's also kind of funny that this big, strapping powerful fairy is afraid. Because that is what his reluctance comes down to—fear. Justy Bluehorn—immortal being, expert cobbler, big as a lumberjack fairy—is gun-shy about a curse that us teenage girls have been navigating, maybe not perfectly but plowing through, nonetheless. And we have a human baby to look after while we do it.

"Unfortunately, no, but each of you can take a pair of shoes. Any pair that you wish," Justy says, all smiles now, though the twinkle in gone from his eyes and his movements seem stilted. His arms jerk forwards awkwardly until they find their way into his pockets.

"Yes, I'm going to do that, absolutely totally thank you," Ana tells him as she slides off her chair. "I'm also going to take Etta's pair. She can't appreciate any of your work because they aren't clogs. Sorry, Etta." My tiny sister curls her lip. Thankfully, before they get into a drunken brawl, Justy offers a solution.

"Take as many as you want. They'll fit you magically the moment you put them on. But like I said, got a lot of work to do so it's time for you to get going." Justy pushes us toward the shoes which are conveniently located near the exit to his Emporium.

I had gotten what I needed out of Justy—answers about our wands and the name of an Oracle. If he's too chicken to take us there himself, that's fine.

"Thank you for the shoes and the advice," I tell him sincerely. Ana is already whipping around the display shelves like a girl possessed. Etta sneakily puts a pair of sensible wedge sneakers in Baby's pram. "You know where Em lives, right? You wouldn't mind folding the steps we need to take us *there*." I don't phrase this as a question. Justy gives me a sly smile. "I sure do. Maleficent is the one to help you with the Oracle, because she's already so involved, you see?"

"Yes, *I do see*. And I'll make sure to tell Em every single thing that happened here today. I'll relay each and every word of our conversation, so she'll know how much you helped us." Justy's smile collapses. He blinks twice. I managed to call him out while sounding like I was praising him. I'm getting pretty good at this passive-aggressive fairy thing.

"Great," the cobbler tells me with a stiff jaw.

Ana was wrong. Justy does make clogs and I grab a pair in a gorgeous shade of tomato red off of a Lucite box in one graceful swoop as we walk by. I hold them close to my chest like a trophy as Justy ushers me towards the door.

- 10 -

Justy takes a furtive look in both directions down the street. His paranoia is real, though in my opinion, over the top. I have a giant Longshadow following me and I don't creep around every corner like a cat with its back arched.

Justy draws his wand in several concentric circles.

Folding a step is like collecting the world. It's like closing the streets, the houses, the sharp-edged scarlet Japanese Maples, and all the people in their woolen sweaters and silken coats into a giant accordion. We are all swept up in the wispy bellows of Justy's magical creation. It seems in that moment as if everything that might be living and a few things that were most likely not alive at all (like the sidewalks and the swaying metal shop signs) are taking in a giant breath.

And then the spell expands in a single humming wheeze. The vista stretches like taffy and turns upside down again and again. When the pulling apart stops, I grip the sides of Baby's carriage. Baby is quite amused by the entire process. She's in a fit of giggles now. Etta, on the other hand, is so pale that her skin takes on the pallor of an iceberg.

We find ourselves in a neighborhood quite unlike our own. Instead of the cute and charming little cottages and primly painted Victorian homes I've naturally associated with The Undervale, this neighborhood is much more modern, with flat-topped ranchers that remind me of the iconic architecture I'd seen in books on Palm Springs. It isn't just the houses that are different here, it's the weather. Actually, it's not even just the weather; it's the landscape itself. The houses fit effortlessly into the environment because it appears that in this part of The Undervale, autumn doesn't exist. I think there's only one searing and brutal season in Em's neighborhood, and according to the dry gravel, the abundance of succulents, and the flat blue sky, this is the desert. Without even thinking, I put my camera up to my eye and snap off a few shots. There's one cactus in particular that seems to be bowing ever so slightly. I change the shutter speed a fraction and manually adjust the focus as I let the shutter go.

Ana peels off her sweater and begins stripping Baby down straight away. Etta undoes her coat and I do the same. Where are we? How many steps did Justy have to fold to get us to an entirely different eco system? And who in their right mind wouldn't want to experience autumn? Autumn is the best season of all.

The three of us stand in front of large pavers that wind their way up to a bright yellow door. The house is long and white and narrow. It spirals cross an emerald green lawn like a society lady's delicate fingers. On either side of the massive door are two tall concrete screens of a sort, though they are painted the same color as the house and shaped with Moorish cutouts.

Em is so unpredictable; I don't know how she's going to react to us showing up here unannounced. She's as likely to offer us a refreshing drink as she is to slam the door in our faces. I don't even want to think about how we'll get to the mortal realm if Em withholds her help.

The gold knocker is shaped like a dragon. Its carved tongue is meant to bang against the door. I swallow hard and lift it up and down against the gold bar adamantly. The door opens swiftly but it's not Em who answers. Instead, it's a rapturously handsome man with lustrous brown hair that sweeps across his tan brow. His deep, chestnut-colored eyes glaze over us with a look that manages to convey both amusement and disdain.

I suddenly remember my conversation with Em that morning. "Giacomo?" I ask hopefully.

"Yes." His voice is honey. It pours from his throat. Ana immediately pushes me out of the way.

"Hello," she purrs, while shaking out her bun. Mahogany hair spills down her shoulders like rippling silk. "Is Maleficent home? We are very good friends of hers." Ana leans in closer, possibly to get a look inside, also possibly to smell him.

I'm pretty sure she's still drunk.

"She is not home at present," he tells us, completely unimpressed by Ana's attempt at beguilement. Giacomo goes to close the door, but Ana stops him before he can. If Em can walk into our house without an invitation, then Ana probably figures it's only fair that we can do the same. She pushes the slick yellow door open and steps inside before Giacomo can utter a word. I follow with the pram and Etta skulks in.

Giacomo raises an elegant eyebrow. "I told you that Mistress is not at home."

"Mistress?" I sputter. "Does she make you call her that?"

Giacomo cocks his head and looks balefully at me. I don't think this gorgeous man is a fairy, not that he couldn't pass for one but there is a fixedness to him, a solidity that the other fairies I've met don't have. It's far more likely that Em had fancied him a century or so ago and trapped him here. "Look, we need to speak to her urgently and we're prepared to wait, right here in the hall if necessary." I avoid looking directly at him. He's so gorgeous that he's making my palms sweat.

"This is not a hall. This is a foyyyyeeer." Giacomo drags out the vowels as if my sisters and I couldn't possibly understand the distinction. He gives a singular huff and then herds us into the kitchen, where according to him, we can't damage or stain anything.

Etta's eyes grow wide when she sees the gleaming marble surfaces and the double ovens. There's a restaurant-grade stove and a fridge with glass doors. Each item inside is perfectly stacked and organized by color rather than usefulness. Giacomo begrudgingly makes us a pot of (admittedly delicious) tea and warns us to stay put in the breakfast nook.

Hours pass. The sun goes down. We trot Baby along from lap to lap, amusing her with peek-a-boo and tickles. Etta feeds her some strained carrots that she had miraculously found the time to make from scratch at home. I have no idea when she would have done this, probably at the crack of dawn when the rest of us had been fast asleep. My tiny triplet is a morning person. In a of couple hours, Etta will become a cranky, irrational, and exhausted liability.

We feed Baby a bottle and put her down for bed in the pram, covering the opening with a thin blanket. We don't speak because we're overwhelmed and anxious, a combination that makes our words overly loud. We are equally worried about waking Baby and incurring Giacomo's snobbish wrath.

The desert is hot and crisp. Although it's dark outside, I am not so concerned about Longshadow here. I don't think it followed us and I don't think this climate would suit it. It's illogical, but I am sure Longshadow prefers the other part of The Undervale, where it's Autumn and the winds whip up the dying leaves in circles. I think Longshadow prefers the damp moss of the forest and the jagged edges of fallen logs where spiders make their homes. Longshadow would be too exposed here. There is no cover and Maleficent would be no kind of host.

Although she does not enter through the front door (because we would have heard her), Em finally comes home. I catch scraps of words floating between Giacomo and his Mistress and none of them are particularly welcoming or pleasant.

Em breezes through to the kitchen and stands there, her glorious hair rolling down all the way past her torso to her navel, while her brown eyes narrow in a look that is thankfully, more intrigued than annoyed.

"You're like refugees, the lot of you," Em declares, placing her hands upon her narrow hips. "And probably starving no doubt. Come along." She beckons us with a single pointed nail that's sharp enough to look downright scary. Ana furtively glances at Baby sleeping in the pram. "For Heaven's sake," Em says, her voice rising with irritation. "Leave it here. No one is going to steal it from my very own kitchen, and Giacomo hates children. He won't go near it."

We get up and follow Em, who's donning a chic black pantsuit, into the main living area of the house. Unsurprisingly—to me anyway—it's completely devoid of sentimentality. It looks like it's been styled for a glossy magazine shoot. There's a massive television in the sunken living room but apart from that, there is nothing about the space that feels like it's from this century.

Em guides us to a long, sleek wooden table with chartreuse chairs. The chandelier hanging from the ceiling is all bronze sticks and round bulbs. It reminds me of drawings from chemistry textbooks. But then I shake my head. No. I wouldn't have seen chemical compounds in textbooks. Why would a fairy ever read a textbook? We're all probably just born knowing this stuff. I wonder suddenly what it would be like, to know everything.

Em sweeps the table with her wand and in a flash, there's not only a full dinner service set for four, but there's also an actual meal in the form of delicate servings of filet mignon and slender French fries. Inside a wooden bowl with a gold rim there is a colorful salad. I can smell the earthy beets from where I'm standing.

"Sit, sit," Em orders and then she barks, "Giacomo! Four martinis. You prefer yours dry, isn't that right, Fauna?"

"Well, I, uhh," Ana stammers. She clears her throat and sits up a little straighter. "I want to say that I've already had a lot to drink today but . . . I also want to say yes."

"If I have a drink," Etta begins, "I'm gonna pass out right here on the table. I'm so tired."

Em looks at me with a single eyebrow raised. We've come here for help, not fun. And I trust Maleficent about as far as I can throw her, which would be not far at all because she's a majestic six feet tall.

"Well, one of us has to stay lucid because we have a baby and we're trapped inside a nightmare fairytale land village that is also somehow Palm Springs, so no. Thank you," I explain.

Em grips both her hands on the table and groans. "This curse is such a buzzkill. *Fine.*" The wand dips again and two glasses of ice water appear. "Just the two martinis, Giacomo, for Fauna and me," Em bellows.

"Why don't you just wave your wand again?" The way magic works here is so confusing. I think it's safe to say that Em enjoys ordering people around. But she's also impatient and having her servant boyfriend make drinks by hand seems . . . I don't know . . . inefficient?

"Well, magic can only do so much. Giacomo mixes the most divine drinks, brews perfect coffee, and he has this way of washing the sheets so that they come out smelling like sunshine. He's a mortal and I have *no idea* how he manages these things."

"So, he's your slave basically," Etta grumbles.

"Absolutely not!" Em exclaims with a voice so pinched it's clear that she's offended. "He gets paid in *actual* money and also in eternal youth. Believe me," Em whispers as she leans in, "he's well satisfied."

Gross, I think to myself.

Em begins to pick at her steak, and I cut myself a piece that's so tender it splits like butter. I pop it in my mouth and quickly begin to tear into the rest. I hadn't realized how hungry I had been until the food hit my stomach.

Our host taps her long nails on the table restlessly as she watches us eat. The staccato beat of her fingers is a reminder that we are in the presence of a very powerful being who has made it quite clear that her generosity has limits. As intimidating as Em is though, I hold fast and take my time. If I show her any weakness, she'll sniff it out and pounce, and grind whatever is left of our confidence down into the wood grain of her oversized dining table.

We need Maleficent's help to get to the mortal realm, but we also need some answers that will help inform our behavior once we get there *and* how to proceed once we get back. I'm not sure I could ever really trust Em, but the beef Sidelia alluded to has me worried. I don't really want to know what happened but, my instincts tell me that I *need* to know. I need to gauge how deep our connection runs before we accept any more of her help or advice. It's not that I won't take it- of course I will but, my gut is also telling me that I also need some context.

I sit up a little straighter in my chair. I elongate my neck until the muscles in it thrum. I may not feel particularly valiant, but I know how to act like I do.

"We went to the library today, like you suggested, and we met a fairy there who said that we had a history with you," I say boldly after taking a sip of water. "What happened?"

Em immediately rolls her eyes. "Sidelia, no doubt. She's so opinionated and such a gossip."

"Really?" Ana observes thoughtfully, "she didn't seem that way to me. She didn't say much actually, just that the four of us had history. I think we're all just curious about what that means."

Em waves her hand and looks away as if the history in question is a fly that needs swatting. "Leave it. It was a long time ago. Things were different back then."

"Maybe," I concede. "But I'd still like to know what happened. Just for context . . ." I trail off. I'm not sure if this is the right tactic. Em is being evasive. Deliberately. I'm also aware that if I push too hard, Em might not help us. She may even make things worse.

"That's a roundabout way of saying you don't trust me." Her tone is low and serious with a barely audible pulse of danger mixed in with her observation like a hidden track on a record.

"You haven't exactly been transparent about well, *some* things," I try to explain gently.

Em makes a fist and lightly smacks it on the table in a dramatic gesture. "That's because if I told you everything, your adolescent brains would explode. Despite your inexplicable distrust of me—*me*, the person who positively flew to your house the moment you called—I want you to break this curse. And if I had told you the entire truth about The Undervale, about its terrors and nightmares, you wouldn't have left your house. You would be cowering there still."

Ana audibly gulps and the three of us exchange worried glances. Giacomo arrives and places two chilled martinis in front of Em and my sister.

"Well, thank you, I guess?" I manage. Maleficent isn't willing to be truthful with us. Fine. She has her reasons. But we have no leverage here. The only thing we can offer of any value is our humility.

I lean back in my chair and bow my head.

"Listen, I get it, Em, the way we are now? It must be really frustrating for you. I don't blame you one bit for being annoyed as hell. Please try to see this situation from our point of view." I begin to fiddle with the placemat anxiously. "We don't remember … *anything*. You're the only connection to our real lives that we have, so it's important that we know more about our friendship. If we're going to get through this, we need to feel like we aren't alone and that we do have a history here, even if we've forgotten it."

Em sucks her teeth before draining her glass in one long gulp. "Excellent, Giacomo. You might as well keep them coming." She stares at each of us and shakes her resplendent mane of hair. "Oh Flora, *come on*," Em's lips purse. "We aren't participating in some crystal-filled, New Age talking stick retreat for mortals. Enough with the feelings. I don't think I have any . . . or maybe I have like, *two*, three max. You want to know what happened between us and you want to know why people say my name in the particular way that they do. Stop trying to appeal to my better angels. I told you; angels are not a real thing."

"I know. It's so sad," Ana says and then she makes an odd sort of noise, a soft disappointed sigh. I grit my molars. Why my sister would want to add another supernatural being into the mix is beyond me.

Quite suddenly, Em throws up her hands in surrender.

"Fine. Okay. I'll tell you. But please, try to put a lid on your bourgeois attitudes. I don't need the commentary and this all happened centuries ago. It's all in the past and also . . . some of the details might have escaped me or they're just too boring to remember," she begins. "Anyways . . . there was this king. He was ridiculous, probably because he was inbred. Well, definitely because he was inbred. And because he was so stupid, he was an awful ruler. He was totally oblivious to the fact that his people were starving, and I don't mean metaphorically. I mean literally, skin and bones in every village. But he was so clueless and gauche that he wore a jeweled ring on every one of his fat fingers. You understand? He was that sort of man."

We nod our heads. I can picture him immediately, rotund, short with a wiry goatee speckled with days-old food.

"And his wife! She was insufferable. She had a horse face. I'm not being hyperbolic; she had a face and head that was the same size, same length as a horse. And even there I'm being generous because I've seen more attractive mares. You get the picture. She was hideous in a world where a woman's looks were pretty much the only thing she had to offer. Thank God she was a princess, or she would have never gotten married.

Anyhow, this woman, unbelievably, got it into her head that I wanted to get with her husband . . . *sexually*. Ha!" Em laughed then, a genuine, throaty chuckle. "Gross. Never. I don't know why or how she could believe such a thing because I would rather have intimate relations with a goat. But I suppose *I am* a giver. I'm really generous and people often misinterpret that."

I reach over to Etta who's sitting right next to me and squeeze her thigh. It takes some focus, but I do not react. I know I have to let Em run with her story uninterrupted.

"In those days, things were very different," Em explains. "Humans and fairies interacted a lot more than they do now because back then, mortals were dumber. Well, maybe not dumber, simpler? More superstitious? Anyways, this queen—the Horse Queen—went out of her way to exclude me from everything. She would throw parties and the sole purpose of the party was to make sure I knew that I wasn't invited. I know you think I'm being overly sensitive," Maleficent says to me and me alone, as if my sisters aren't even there.

"No," I rush to tell her. "Not at all." Not because I think she isn't capable of getting offended at the drop of a hat; I know she is, but because I'm having a hard time following this story of hers, let alone the players.

"You see, I know for a fact, the Horse Queen got off on excluding me because when they finally had a child—and this is after years of trying mind you—they had a girl."

Em looks at the three of us expectantly. She lifts her eyebrows with real drama, like the arch in them is sharp enough to pull us up to where she is coming from.

My sisters and I remain silent and Em's body falls. She shakes her head and takes another drink.

"Okay . . . let me explain. In those days, having a girl was like having a cat or a really nice outfit—pretty, but ultimately useless. I mean, did they actually expect me to believe they were going to throw the biggest, most lavish and extravagant event in the history of the kingdom for a daughter? Not in a million years. It would be like having a party because you got a new bucket or . . . I don't know . . . a chair. Actually no, some of those chairs back then were really amazing. Very sturdy. The queen only made it into such an event so she could invite everyone we knew, except *me*. She was a snake."

"I'm confused," Ana puts a single finger on her chin. "If you didn't like them, why did you even care?"

Em's face freezes and her painted lips gape. "Because it was rude. And offensive."

"It hurt your feelings." This is a statement. I'm not asking Em. What would be the point? I want her to know that we're smarter than we look and more intuitive than she is giving us credit for.

Maleficent drains the rest of her drink and bangs the base of the glass on the wood. "I wasn't hurt. I'm not you. I'm not a teenage girl. I don't get hurt. I was *insulted* because I'm an extremely powerful, magical being and she was a horse-faced queen. Okay?"

"Uhh huh." I try to keep the sarcasm from my response but it's clear from Em's reaction that I can't. "Let me guess, we were invited to this banger, right?"

Maleficent's lashes bat in bursts like morse code as she looks to the ceiling. "The three of you had taken up residence in the kingdom. I tried to warn you. I told you it was pointless, but you were determined to get the king and queen to do better by their subjects. You actually thought that you could change their minds, convince those two that non-royal humans weren't just flesh sacks meant for getting them things. I told you again and again that they were terrible rulers and eventually they would just die—problem solved. You didn't want to wait. You felt bad for their subjects. And you know what? *Mea culpa.*" At this, Em throws up her hands like a criminal. "I was frustrated—at them, at you three. And so, even though I wasn't invited, I went to the party, okay? And yes, I admit that I did want to make the queen feel extra bad about herself by looking resplendent and beautiful, which I can admit now was a little petty. But it wasn't big-time petty because she was *terrible* and ugly."

"Once I arrived, and I saw the three of you laughing and having fun ... I just ... I don't know," Em trails off.

"It hurt your feelings," I say again, although this time, Etta is the one to squeeze my thigh.

"Stop saying that!" Em booms. The golden flecks in her eyes begin to leap and darken into a smoldering purple. "I wasn't crying into the punch bowl. Who do you think I am? I had just assumed, as any friend would by the way, that in solidarity, you would decline the invite. How foolish of me rely on eons of friendship. Not only were you there, but you were bestowing magical gifts on the little brat! First, it was beauty and then it was the gift of song, which still baffles me to this day. I mean, why? It's not like she could have had a singing career. She couldn't have gone on tour. You could have turned her into Beyoncé and at the end of the day, she would have been a brood mare like every other woman back then. I just felt nauseated by the entire spectacle. And before you could give her the great gift of embroidery or some other nonsense, I stepped in ... and I suppose ... well ... I tried to kill the baby but like, just a little bit."

Our shock stills the air. The silence is slick. It leaves a sticky film behind our ears and on our tongues. The three of us instinctively look to the kitchen where Baby is hopefully still sleeping safe and sound.

Finally, even at the risk of incurring Em's considerable ire, I had to say, "You tried to kill a baby?"

Maleficent sucks in her cheeks and her right foot starts swinging wildly over her crossed knee. "I knew you would get hung up on that part, but you have no idea. I wish you could remember. She was *such* an annoying baby."

"All babies are kind of annoying!" Ana exclaims in a rush. "But they're also really cute and innocent. Em! She was just a newborn."

"Look, it's not like I was going to kill her right away- that's what I meant by a little bit…It was supposed to happen when she was sixteen. No one was thinking straight; everyone was really heated. It was a very dramatic and intense situation."

"Because you made it dramatic and intense," Etta argues.

Maleficent cocks her head. "Fair point but if you had just taken a beat—all three of you—you would have realized that I was just letting off some steam. I was trying to prove something. Prove that they were awful and dumb and not worth an ounce of your magic."

"So, killing her when she was sixteen is somehow better? Like, that makes everything okay?" Etta is practically shaking, though I'm not sure if it's from fright or fury. "You get that *we're* seventeen? Or at least we think we're seventeen!"

"Oh please," Em says meanly. "You three are hardly innocents. We were all young once … well, maybe not young, but new. And when we were new, we were wild and brazen. Morality is a human construct."

"No," I object firmly. "Morality is morality. Ethics are ethics and murder is murder, regardless of species."

Maleficent doesn't waste any time to correct me. "A couple hundred years ago, humans had slaves; they thought that was moral."

"Yeah, but you kiiiiind of have a slave right now," Ana interrupts. She's trying to focus on Em with one eye. The other is scrunched closed. I'm pretty sure she's drunk again.

"Giacomo is not a slave!" For the first time, Em looks flustered. I think Ana hit a nerve. "That isn't even the point. The point is mortals keep changing the rules. They have no standards. In one century, it's totally acceptable to rape your wife. The next century, you go to jail for it. Ethics are malleable in that realm. Which means that they aren't really ethics; they're just convenient rules that change on a whim."

Em expands. Her arms spread out and take hold of the edges of the table. She looks like a magnificent sculpture, demanding attention without words, commanding awe by the perfectly triangular space she is occupying. "You need to broaden those flimsy little minds of yours," Maleficent warns. "You are not human. Stop trying to fit all of this," Maleficent moves, breaking the spell of her stillness by sweeping her hands gracefully out and across "this story, this place, The Undervale—into a mortal box. It won't fit."

"If fitting in here was as easy as occupying a different head space, don't you think we would have done that by now?" I protest. "What we think doesn't even matter. You're sitting there all regal and imposing, trying to justify killing a baby—sorry, a teenage girl. But. you can't. And I bet we had a problem with it back then too, right? That's where the beef started? That's where the 'history' between us comes in?"

Em's cheekbones appear to grow higher, sharper, as if her face itself is a kind of weapon. Leave it to Maleficent to try to kill a child and then shrug it off as a matter of interpretation.

"We could go round and round debating semantics," Em says ruthlessly which makes Etta snort. Loudly. "The whole thing was all bark and no bite. If you had your memories and you were your true selves, you would get it. Even when I cursed the baby, I never thought it would actually happen. The plan hinged on the teen pricking her finger on a spinning wheel. You see how absurd that it is right? She was a princess. She wouldn't have come within a hundred yards of a spindle. The image just popped into my head, probably because you three *crusading feminists* gave her beauty and a good singing voice. I mean, if you had given her something useful like intelligence, wit, resilience, excellent health, I wouldn't have been so archaic about it."

"So, it's our fault?" Etta asks sharply. I nudge her with my elbow. We all need to be thinking about our approach. Etta's tone is furious. Em seems to be okay with us making an observation. She'll even go so far as allowing us to disagree but, she's not going to stand for a verbal attack. Etta needs to take a breath because killer or not, we still need her help.

"It's no one's fault, Merriweather. Things just escalated so quickly. You couldn't break my curse, obviously, but for some unknown reason, perhaps to prove a point of your own. Or, it could have been that I did all this, well . . . I'm going to be honest here- but stay focused on the important part of this tale, okay? At the time this was going on, I was in the form of a dragon. A very, very big dragon. You three combined your super wands and altered the curse so that if she pricked her finger, the entire kingdom would fall asleep for a hundred years. Which, no offense, wasn't the smartest solution but as a I said, tensions were running high, and we weren't really thinking."

"You were a dragon?" Ana asks almost rapturously. "Wait . . . You could talk as a dragon?"

Em shoots her a condescending look and moves on. "Everyone was screaming, and the queen kept fainting and her useless husband peed his britches, which was, I admit, an absolute highlight. I was in a dark place I admit. But all anyone had to do was say to the princess, 'Hey, don't touch a spinning wheel!' A logical countermeasure, right, Flora?"

"I suppose." I'm racing through Em's version of events, wondering if I've missed something, wondering if the fix could have been that simple.

"Well, the three of you lost all sense of reason. Again, yes, I was a dragon and yes, I set a few things on fire, it's true. Queen Horse Face was sure I was going to kill the baby because she was too stupid to understand how curses worked. And so, she gave you the child, further proving my point about girls, by the way, and then you three . . . you actually took her! You raised her in some one-room shack in the middle of nowhere and lived like mortals. Who even does that? It was spiteful, that's what it was. You knew you couldn't actually hide from me, but you tried. Or maybe you weren't trying, maybe you were just deliberately giving me the cold shoulder. Whatever it was, it was dumb as hell. You had to pee outside. In the bushes! You had to poop outside too with raccoons and insects. All to try and convince this mortal baby that you were her *human* aunties. What a joke."

"If fairies and humans were friendly back then, why did we pretend to be mortal?" Ana asks. She is befuddled, from the booze and Em's story. Our host's words chased their own tails. Em wasn't making a lot of sense.

"After the party, there was a lot of lively discourse about magic. Fairies were banned from the kingdom." Em's shrugs churlishly. "Boo hoo, right? I mean, if we wanted to take over the entire world, we could have. But that would have been a lot of boring work for nothing. It would be like becoming Empress of the Rats or Queen of Kitchen Stools. We let them believe they had some measure of control because we are *very* benevolent."

"So, was it about the baby, or was it about you?" I ask sincerely. "I can't imagine years of living in a shack just to piss you off."

"It was totally about me." Em fans her fingers out across her chest. "You're all so stubborn. Remember, a decade to us is like nothing, a blink of an eye. And unlike now, you knew you were fairies. I'm sure you cheated. Probably when it came to bathing." Em leans back in her chair and shakes her head solemnly. "It was such a bizarre thing to do. Especially since you knew me well enough to know that after I calmed down, I would have lost interest. Actually, I probably would have forgotten about it entirely. But somehow, you committed yourselves to raising a child, without magic of any sort. I dunno, maybe it was some kind of game for you guys. Like a personal challenge, the way humans do endurance marathons or marriage. And then of course, the whole thing blew up in your faces because these particular humans were the absolute worst."

"What do you mean?" I ask earnestly, pushing the plate of food away from me ever so slightly.

"Well, I did check in on you three now and again. I didn't feel responsible, you understand, but I did have a certain awareness that the events at the party unfolded partly because of my temper, which I felt…what is less than guilty?"

"Bad?" Etta offers.

"No. What is less than bad?" Em has her lips puckered, as if she could kiss the word she is looking for

"Forget it," I offer. "You felt something, and it led to you looking in on us from time to time. Please continue."

"Right, okay, I did stay away. But I sent my ravens to you and had them report back just to make sure you three weren't mummified or wearing clothes made entirely of hemp. You all did everything you could to raise that child to be a good person—a kind and responsible girl. She didn't know who she was, but you knew. You knew that one day, she would return to her parents and become a proper princess. But again, those gifts you gave her . . . I don't know what you expected would happen. She was a rotten, ungrateful girl. All she ever did was look at her reflection and sing, *constantly*. It was intolerable, even for my birds and that's really saying something. Have you ever heard an unkindness of ravens communicate with each other? It's deafening."

"So, you were spying on us?" Etta is gripping her steak knife. Em is totally oblivious. She doesn't even bother to answer my sister. She just keeps talking. "And then what does your precious princess do? She turns sixteen and goes for a tumble in the hay with the very first boy she meets. The very first one!! And of course, she gets knocked up. It's not like you didn't teach her about birth control. She wasn't ignorant. The kicker of it was, that she got pregnant on purpose! She thought the boy was losing interest in her, which of course he was, because even her considerable beauty couldn't override how annoying she was.

Well, the three of you finally had enough. You marched her right back up to the palace with the boy, a *farmer* no less. And instead of facing a consequence for such irresponsible behavior, the King and Queen rewarded your little orphan. They made her lover a Prince and gave him a sizable section of their kingdom. Those two weren't about to lose face and admit that their daughter was both wanton and an idiot. The worst of it was, they blamed you three! And then they had the audacity to *banish* you. After all you did and all you sacrificed. The absolute gall of it." Em's cheeks begin to flare with two deep rose spots. Even though this had all happened centuries ago, clearly the experience still has the capacity to, if not enrage, then at the very least unnerve her. Em claims that this was all in the past. I don't have a past, or at least, one that I remember, but I don't think that this is the kind of thing a person can just dismiss or let go of. This story has everything—jealousy, revenge, magic, curses, beautiful princesses, evil queens . . . *a dragon.*

"So, your curse never even happened?" I ask wide-eyed, eager to hear the end of the tale.

"Well, that's the gag." Em drains another martini glass. Giacomo appears out of seemingly nowhere with a fresh drink. "That's the very best part! You told her the truth about her parentage the very moment she informed you of her pregnancy. You warned her about the curse and begged her not to go near a spindle. Well, Princess Eye Roll took one look at the ginormous castle and was absolutely furious that she had grown up in a hovel and not in the palace as was her royal right. Maybe it was the hormones or possibly it was because she was a stubborn, willful girl who thought she was too good for curses. Nonetheless, she stomped right down to the servant's quarters and pricked her finger. *On purpose.* What an asshole. They all fell asleep for a hundred years. Their people rejoiced to be rid of such terrible rulers. And when they woke up again, well, time had marched on. The king collapsed not long after because no one thought he was anointed by God so much anymore. I think his ego actually killed him. The Princess became a Queen and because karma can be a delicious thing, she had fourteen children in a row. Most of them died, of course, and not even your magic was any sort of match for breeding habits like those. She looked sixty by the time she was thirty. It was just delightful, still brings a smile to my face. Their son, though, he was a pretty decent ruler, probably because he wasn't as inbred as the rest of them." Em leans back in her chair and sighs happily.

"That is ... quite a story," I say in amazement. "And after all this happened, how long did it take for us to patch things up?"

"About five minutes?" Em says brightly. "You three came back here after the king and queen banished you. We had drinks, a few laughs. I think we even hugged once. It was fine. Like I said, it was just a minor misunderstanding, a breakdown of communication. I don't even really do curses anymore."

"Really?" Etta challenges. I don't think Etta is all that impressed with Em's story. Her jaw is set, and her face is so still, it's like she's holding a razor blade on her tongue.

Obviously, this is all very one-sided and surely Em had been properly terrifying at that party. But in my opinion? The baby girl we had raised like a daughter was told explicitly not to touch a spinning wheel and then she did it anyways. It was a simple enough request. It's not like we told her to stay away from water. I'm inclined to believe Em's version, at least most of it anyways.

"Yes, *really*, Merriweather." Em sighs. She draws her wand up and down the length of her body and the lovely pantsuit disappears only to be replaced with a silk caftan that's such a deep purple, it almost looks black. "In fact, I've changed. Quite a bit. In the mortal realm, I'm a life coach. A *very successful* life coach. I'm famous. I've sold millions of books. I've even been offered a talk show, which I'm considering. It's just that the marketplace is so saturated right now. I'm not sure that it's the right time." Em polishes her nails on her caftan and then looks at them admiringly.

"People come to you for advice and then they give you money?" I don't bother to hide my surprise.

"Yes, because I'm an immortal being who knows everything and believes in tough love. That's pretty much the definition of a Life Coach."

Em stands and the three of us stand as well, although I'm not sure why. It's not like *Em* is a queen. "Look, I could give you all some excuse like I'm tired or I've got work to do. Truth is, I just want to be alone. Why don't you tell me why you've come and don't try to say it was for some story that no one even remembers anymore."

As far I am I'm concerned, any information we uncover about our history, about magic and our relationship with other fairies, including Maleficent, is invaluable. But Em is smart. Too smart. There's no way we are going to be able to trick her into helping us. She'll see right through whatever coy tale we offer up. The situation requires honesty, so I decide to show our hand.

"Okay, first of all, I was wondering if it's possible that the curse maker . . . curser? I don't know the right terminology. But could they put a kind of . . . ominously terrifying shadow creature to keep us in line . . . *inside* the curse?"

"Yes," Em responds without missing a beat.

"Can this thing hurt us? Even though it's a shadow?" Etta rushes in with my next question.

"Probably."

"I feel like I should tell you that there is something like that chasing us." I stop and think about my words. "Not chasing us, but following us for sure, in a menacing way. But so far, I'm the only one who's seen it. My sisters have not seen it. Yet."

"Okay."

Maleficent had just talked for the better part of an hour non-stop and *now* she decides to be taciturn.

"Em," Ana prods.

"Well, it's hardly surprising that you're the cause of this, Flora, because you can be a total pain in the ass. What do you want me to tell you?"

"I don't know, but maybe put a protection spell on us or something? Stop rolling your eyes and making us drag information out of you. We're in real danger here, you know? We've got to find our wands, pronto." I don't bother to defend myself against her comments. *I'm* the pain in the ass? Ha! It's classic projection.

"I don't know what this thing is so I wouldn't know how to protect you from it. You wouldn't walk into a drugstore and say, 'I'm sick, give me something' and expect the pharmacist to know the proper medicine you need."

Etta steps forward, around the table. "That is exactly what you do."

Maleficent shrugs indifferently. "Whatever. I don't know how human medicine works. The short answer—since you insist on being so brazenly impatient—is that you three are fairies and you can't die. I don't know the magical make-up of this shadow, so I can't create a spell to banish it. Worst case scenario, you get disemboweled or possibly sent to another dimension. The Baby could die, but there's literally millions of babies. I wouldn't worry too much about it. Is that it? Is that why you came all the way here?"

For a split second I imagine leaping across the space between us and wrapping my hands around Em's swan-like neck. I can see myself tackling her to the floor and smashing her head into the carpet again and again with a perverse kind of glee.

Instead, I take a beat.

I may not be able to die but Maleficent has just provided me with a list of terrible scenarios that I don't want to find myself in. I let Longshadow go and focus on the bigger issue.

"No," I respond curtly. "Merriweather had her wand examined by Justy Bluehorn. There's nothing wrong with it. It's sleeping, apparently. He suggested that we ask an Oracle. The Oracle of a Thousand Eyes, to be precise. He thought she would be able to see where the other two wands are hidden so they can all wake up together. As you probably know, the Oracle lives in the mortal realm. Justy wouldn't take us there. I was hoping . . . we were hoping you could." My request is filled with equal parts sincerity and resolve. I don't remember Maleficent, but I think I know how to read her. She abhors weakness. I am required to walk that fine line between deference and authority.

"Why didn't he just open a door?" Em demands.

"He said he didn't want to get involved. He was concerned." I walk closer to Em with my hands clutched together. I'm not willing to vocalize the possible consequences of aiding us. Why bother? She knows well enough and I'm not eager to highlight them. "I think he felt like this was something you were already a part of since you came to our house and told us who we were. I get the sense that he's not the type of fairy who's willing to ummm . . ."

"Stick his neck out?" Em growls. "Put himself in harm's way for a friend?"

Maleficent opens her mouth as if to say something and then closes it again. She has a look swimming around in her brown eyes that I've never seen on her before. It's not concern or fear, which I'm grateful for. Her lids open and close slowly, catlike and then narrow ever so slightly. I instinctively take a step back. Em's usual indifference is gone. Her face has vacated any notion of vanity or pride. There's an electric darkness that sweeps through Em's irises.

She's...*angry.*

And then just as quickly, the rage drains from her eyes and she's back to her old self. I try to guess at what made her so furious. Maybe she hated the idea of Justy wanting her to take a risk that he wasn't willing to take himself, but I don't think it's that. I actually think that Em was angry *for* us.

And then it dawns on me with stunning clarity that Maleficent is rude, mean, and possibly (probably) homicidal but she is also loyal. All of this bluster is part of her act. It's a schtick. *She cares.*

"Very well," Em begins walking and we are forced to follow. "We'll open a door first thing in the morning and you all can stay here tonight."

Etta tugs at my sweater and Ana looks uneasily toward the kitchen. "That's a really nice offer Em but, you know, we have Baby and everything. We don't even have a fresh change of clothes."

"Nonsense," Em declares. "I can provide everything you need. Go ahead, grab the baby." We just stand there, frozen. I think we're each wondering how to gratefully decline Em's offer. This is, after all, a woman who when provoked had threatened a newborn's life, as a dragon. We're in her good graces, for now, but young as I am, I still understand that she's as fickle as she is mercurial. Em shakes her head in frustration and sails toward the kitchen where she grabs the pram and drags it out into the living room. "Now look, I don't have the patience or the inclination to try and figure out where exactly your house is from here. Nor do I want to have to fold a litany of steps to get you back here in the morning. I told you what happened with Princess Breeder Rose, sorry Briar Rose or Aurora or whatever stupid thing she called herself. I've offered to help when others can't or won't. What's it going to take for you three to relax and realize that I'm on your side?

It's no surprise to me when Ana that steps forward. Sweet Ana, whose long legs practically gallop to Em in two strides. She takes Em's hands and Maleficent looks at them as if they're covered in grease or spit.

"You're right. Sorry for being so weird. It's a very generous offer, thank you," Ana tells her earnestly.

Em pulls her hand away and flashes the briefest of smiles. "You're drunk but I appreciate the sentiment and I'm going to pretend that you're speaking for the rest of your sisters." Em takes hold of Baby's pram once again.

"You don't have to do that," I offer. "I know you don't like kids." I go for the handle of the carriage, but Em swats my hand away.

"It's asleep. I know where we're going, and you don't. You don't remember this house. Fauna, talk sense into your sister. She's twitchy and nervous. It's making her more unattractive than she already is."

Instinctually, I twist a loose curl in my strawberry blond hair. I decide to ignore Maleficent's jab at the way I look because it's likely that every being in any realm is unattractive compared to her. For a supernatural being who can change her appearance on a whim, Em seems unusually obsessed with appearances. It's not like she was born with that face. It's a lie—a trick, an invention of her own mind.

We walk past a massive stone fireplace where a giant portrait of Em wearing nothing but a sable fur coat and a throat full of diamonds is hanging above.

It's so shameless that I look away, even though I feel the eyes of the portrait burrowing into my back.

A long walkway runs the length of the open living area. There are several black lacquered doorways and one overly large aubergine one at the very end of the hall that I assume must be the master bedroom.

Em takes her wand and playfully taps at one of the black doors five or six times and then she swings it open. Inside are three well-appointed beds, complete with silken shams and velvet throws. My bed is ballerina pink. Etta's bed is cobalt blue, and Ana's is a rich emerald green. Atop each one is a pair of matching pajamas. To Maleficent's credit, there is a wicker bassinette between my bed and Ana's.

"Here you are, have a good sleep, and for the love of all that is mighty, *do not* knock on my door. Giacomo will get you anything you require in the morning, and I will let you know when I'm ready to begin the day. 'Night, 'night." Em slams the door and the three of us are left alone in a room that has been magically prepared for us, by a fairy who may or may not like us and who, on occasion, will turn into a dragon.

"I can't believe . . . are we prisoners?" Etta begins but I put a finger up to my lips.

"Shhh," I hush. "Em was nice enough to let us stay here and it would be rude to start complaining, so let's change out of these clothes and get into bed." I give Etta a stern look, a warning look. Em had admitted that very night that she had spied on us when we were in the shack living as mortals to raise the spoiled princess. I feel like it would be a rookie move to just assume she won't do the same now. Just because Em acts like she's bored by us doesn't mean that she actually is.

I slip on the light cotton pj's, go to the bathroom, and get into bed. I have no idea what time it is. It could be 10:00 p.m. or 2:30 in the morning. I don't feel all that tired, but I have to get some rest. I'm going to need to be at the top of my game tomorrow with the Oracle.

I miss my own bed, the softness of it and the way my pillow fits perfectly under my neck. I miss the sounds of our house, water rushing through pipes and squirrels running in the gutters. In the fresh sheets that really do smell like sunshine and with Em's tacit protection, I *should* feel perfectly safe.

I can hear the steady, constant breathing of my sisters, who somehow managed to fall straight to sleep. Above my head, there's a line of small rectangular windows that sit upon the wall, one after the other, like teeth. The moon, or at least an approximation of the moon, with its soft and silvery light, slips in.

I watch as a long shadow stretches along the wall. The shadow twists and turns unnaturally. Suddenly, I feel a massive weight on my chest and my heart begins to race like the wings of a little bird.

It can't be . . .

Longshadow can't have found me here! Not in this place with the fearsome Maleficent who nobody seems to like but everyone respects or fears or both. The shadow looms on the wall stretching grotesquely in perverse and unnatural shapes.

I want to call out to Etta and Ana, but they are sleeping so soundly that not a sheet has rustled, nor a quilt been tussled or thrown. They look like dolls, tucked away and put to bed by a child. I'm not sure it matters anyways because my voice has been snatched away by the Longshadow as if it was nothing, as if my screams wouldn't matter anyhow.

Terrified, I bring the covers up over my head and hate myself for it. I should be protecting Baby and my sisters from whatever that thing is. I can actually feel the shadow as it inches its way towards me, bringing a rage in its wake that's so intense it makes my entire body buzz and hum. I catch a whiff of a scent as well—leather and cedar mixed with something foul, something awful enough to bring bile to my throat.

I scrunch up my eyes and words tumble out of my mouth. I might be praying. I might be reciting a poem I'm remembering as Lo Smith from the seventh grade. The shadow hovers above the linen I am tucked under. The dark behind my clenched lids grows darker. I hold my breath.

1 . . .
2 . . .
3 . . . 3 . . . 3 . . .

And then . . . just like that...it is gone. It flies from the room and out the window.

I throw the blankets off and try to get my heartbeat back to its normal rhythm. My breath is quick and fast and loud enough to wake Ana. Under normal circumstances, Etta would also awaken but she's too exhausted.

"What is it?" my sister asks gently. "Did you have a bad dream? Oh no, is it Baby?" She whips around to look inside the bassinette.

"It was Longshadow," I manage in one breathy screech.

Ana straightens. I can see the look of concern in the faint light. "Are you sure? It's not that I don't believe you but we're all so tired and we've been through so much. Maybe you were just dreaming."

"It wasn't a dream," I hiss. "It was here in this room. It's definitely connected to this friggin' curse. It's like an evil, see-through pit bull. I think it's going to do everything it can to make sure we're too scared to figure this out."

"Well," Ana sits down beside me on the bed. "Pitbulls aren't evil. They're actually really sweet dogs. They're only aggressive if they're abused by their masters. Maybe we should think of Longshadow that way? You know, like it's a *neutral* thing, but the curse giver—or maker or whatever the term is—turned it bad. Maybe we can turn it good? By showing it compassion and being gentle with it."

"Are you out of your mind?" I whisper in a snarl. "This isn't the actual real world! The Undervale is an insane Fun House that is *not* fun! Longshadow doesn't talk. You can't pet it or offer it treats. It's magic. It gets near you, and it smothers you and squeezes your heart. I'm not talking in metaphors. I'm saying that it actually feels like icy fingers." I have my hand like a fist and I'm shaking it at her.

"We should tell Maleficent then," Ana concedes.

"Oh, okay, why don't you go down the hall and wake her up and inform her that the Longshadow she didn't give a crap about actually showed up here."

Ana frowns. "Uhhh . . . no . . . I don't think that would be good."

"Why not? What's the worst that could happen? I mean, what's a little evisceration? Giacomo is great at laundry. He can get out all the stains. Come on! March on down the hall and let her know that she's not the bad ass she thinks she is because Longshadow got in *her* house. You don't think she has some sort of magical security system? **It got past her**! Maybe then she'll understand how dangerous it is!

And stop gaslighting me into thinking that I'm being a drama queen over nothing."

Ana grabs my forearm. Her nails press into my bare skin leaving dents, like tiny bite marks. "Stop it," my sister tells me firmly. "You need to rest because you are absolutely raving right now. This is not about Em." Ana removes her hand and places it, this time with tenderness, on my shoulder. "I believe you. I believe there is something following us and that it's related to the curse and that it could hurt us."

"You do?" I ask, relieved.

"Between the three of us, you're the most . . . I don't know . . . observant? Sensitive? You pick up on things that go right by Etta and me. It's why you take such good pictures. The next time you sense or see this Longshadow thing, you have to find a way to—"

"You think I should fight it?" This alarms me. I don't want to combat the nefarious shadow monster. And didn't my sister just say that I should attempt to be gentle with it?

"No," Ana assures me. "You have to find a way to get past whatever it's making you feel so that you can do something proactive."

"It's not that easy, believe me. But let's say I could, what would proactive even look like when it comes to Longshadow."

"Us," Ana smiles. "Me and Etta. The next time this shadow comes for you, you won't have to face it alone. It'll be three against one. Curse or no curse, that Longshadow doesn't stand a chance."

- 11 -

"Now, you must remember that in the mortal realm, time is tedious. You can't play with the hours in the slightest, you can't have any fun with them at all," Em tells us the next morning. "Here in The Undervale, we can freeze time, stop time, and fold it up like a pipe cleaner but with humans, it runs in a singular, predictable direction. And I suppose if you want to get technical, there are *some* rules about time that are fixed for fairies as well. We can't go back and undo a mistake for example. Time won't budge for us with an intention like that."

"But what if we just wanted to go back in time," Ana wonders brightly, "like to the Regency era for example, we could do that?"

"Why would you want to do that?" Em looks at my sister with utter disgust on her flawless, make-up-free face. "They didn't have running water back then. No one brushed their teeth. People smelled. *So bad*. Like, you can't even imagine." Maleficent shudders and purses her lips.

"We don't have any magic. So, it's not like we could zip-zap time into submission anyhow." Etta's observation says bluntly.

"Yeah, this feels a lot like a sci-fi thing," I interrupt, trying to lighten the mood. "I love science fiction, but I don't really understand how it applies to this situation."

We had gotten up relatively early. A new change of clothes had been hanging in the closet for each of us. Giacomo had made breakfast and Etta had glared at him balefully the entire time. Em did not make an appearance until much later in the morning.

Now, she's standing in front of one of the black doors along the hallway. She's in an onyx-colored cashmere robe and bare feet. I notice annoyingly that even her feet are perfect. Her toes aren't too long or too short and they're painted a deep raspberry color. Em has all the grace and ease of a dancer, without any of the wear and tear that a life of rigorous discipline puts upon a body.

"You don't need to understand it, Flora. That part isn't necessary. Also unnecessary is you admitting you're into science fiction," Em says meanly. "All you need to know is that I can calibrate this doorway to enter the mortal realm at any time I choose. Now, you three have been gone for five years. When you break the curse, you can go back to the exact second you were last seen, because you haven't yet inhabited those days in the mortal dimension. I think it's best if we open the door to the current date on Earth. Just make sure that when you return to your human lives after this is ordeal is over to *come back here* to The Undervale for the same period of time you end up spending there today. You can't be there twice, you, see?"

I don't see. I don't get it at all. I had put my hair up in a loose bun on the top of my head. I cup the bulge with my palm, hoping this riddle of time will somehow be captured in my hand and seep down into my brain. I suppose that Em is right. It doesn't matter so much that I don't understand it now. I would, once we get our memories back.

"Okay, yeah, sure," I tell her as I refocus my thoughts. "So, what should we know about this Oracle? Is she nice? Are we friends with her? Does she have any hobbies or anything that we can soften her up a bit with before we ask her for help?"

"Does she have any phobias?" Etta pushes me to the side and places herself in front of Maleficent. She has to crane her neck to look Em in the eye. "Does she have any pets that look like pets but are actually monsters? Is she good at fighting with her fists? I assume she would defend herself that way in the mortal realm because fairies are secret there."

Em looks at us blankly. She then holds out her cup and Giacomo, in a perfectly orchestrated maneuver, takes it from her hands as he makes his way down the hallway to her room. "Merriweather, I appreciate your bloodthirsty enthusiasm but no, you should not try to engage in fisticuffs under any circumstance and no, she's not nice. Oracles are never nice. They're awful. They refuse to speak plainly. It's a game they enjoy playing- to confound and confuse as many people and fairies as possible while still telling the truth. Then they all get together to see how many dreams they managed to crush and lives they've ruined that week. They even give out prizes."

"Why are we even bothering to go then!" Etta screeches. "If this Oracle is just going to mess with us and leave us worse off than we are now, then we should try something else. There has to be some other way."

"There is no other way," I say firmly as much to myself as to my sisters. "Our wands are missing, and we need someone who was created to find misplaced things to help us. She's the only one with that kind of power so we're just going to have to take our chances."

"Yes, and as long as you memorize every single word she says, I can decipher them. The Oracles think they're so clever. I'm really going to enjoy beating her at her own game," Em says, openly giggling conspiratorially. "Now take this," she says giving Ana a silver heart-shaped locket.

"Oh! this is pretty." Ana is clearly impressed. "Is it magical? Is it really old? Did it belong to someone famous?"

"No," Em tells her bluntly. "I found it in a junk drawer. I think that one of my less financially gifted suitors gave it to me a century ago. He probably bought it at a five and dime, but don't let her know that. Hold it with reverence. Let her believe it's something precious. In fact, tell her you stole it from me. That will make her want it even more. Now, are you ready?"

We nod our heads in unison. Etta's in charge of the pram; Ana, the bribe; and I'll do all the talking. "The door will open in Savannah, Georgia. The Oracle of a Thousand Eyes spends every afternoon between 2:00 p.m. and 4:00 p.m. receiving supplicants in Crawford Square. Be courteous, of course, but firm. Don't let her bully you. Here we go." Em draws four semi-circles on the black door which leaves a trail of purple light as her movements progress. After that, she sketches two vertical lines and then six quick horizontal ones. Em turns the doorknob and lets it swing open.

Whatever trepidation I'm feeling, whatever notion I have that I'm not strong enough for this challenge, I mentally push away. I am both a fairy and a girl. I am at the very least two things but probably a hundred more.

A person never really knows what they are capable of until they are asked to do something which might result in abject failure. It's not the thought of succeeding in this task that keeps my head held high.

It's the very opposite.

I know that I might fail. And if I don't fail outright, odds are, I will say something I can't take back. I might ask for the wrong thing. There's a chance I'll hold my body in a such a way that my elbows or wrists will bend in an offensive manner.

Who will I have to become to keep going? An artist? A liar? A rebel? A thief? I know I can be all these things because I am certain that I have been them before. I need to try and remember those versions of myself and I'm hoping that the intensity and the danger that awaits us on a park bench in Savannah will bring those memories close to the surface. So, I keep my chin up and slip into what remains of my courage like a coat with only slightly tarnished buttons.

We saunter through the door with bluster. It seems that none of us are about to show weakness today. I take note of where Em has dropped us off—behind a grand, white mansion. Later, after we talk to the Oracle, I will press a brass key against the brick. That's the signal for Maleficent to open up the door again. I grab my camera from my tote bag and take pictures as an extra precaution. The Oracle could put yet another curse on us. She could send us across town, across the country; she could even send us to another country. When my thumb presses down on the shutter, the whirring click is soothing enough to quell these racing thoughts.

I snap off a few pictures of the park. The weather is lovely if a little on the humid side, and there are plenty of people wandering around, tourists mostly, and who could blame them? It's gorgeous and the air here is sultry. Spanish moss dips and sways from the trees forming a canopy; we are sheltered entirely beneath a leafy umbrella. The low-hanging moss is butter yellow and sea glass green. The curl in it winds around every branch and I imagine it must be what a mermaid's hair looks like. Savannah feels more like a fairyland than the actual fairyland I've seen so far.

The gazebo is right in the middle of the small square. It isn't overly fanciful, just a painted white structure with a metal roof but it is pretty. I can't quite see inside, but I do clock a few people in line on the low brick steps that lead to its center. We casually move the pram behind the last person in line who happens to be an older woman with an extremely high updo and shockingly pink lipstick. I can tell she's not a fairy. Though again, I'm quite sure how. There is a discernable difference between fairies and humans, and the only thing I can pin it on is the way humans seem to stand, as if the ground is tugging at them. The woman furtively glances at the three of us and then at the pram. She lifts a single, badly drawn-in eyebrow with disdain and turns away.

I respond with a nasty glare of my own. She must think one of us is Baby's mother. But so what? Who is she to judge? I want to tell her there's no moral ground here, not in a line to see a supernatural Oracle who may or may not actually have a thousand eyes. I wonder for a moment if all mortals are such hypocrites. Then again, Em likes to talk about how wonderful she is and she's the rudest person I've ever met. Maybe everyone is two faced—even me and Ana and Etta. We're here to *cheat and lie* to an Oracle.

Ana is less comfortable under this mealy-eyed woman's scrutiny. She takes Baby out and grabs one of her blankets, marching purposely toward a stretch of green. This que we're in could take a while and it's probably a good idea for Baby to have some time rolling around on the grass and staring up at the scraps of sky peeking out from the leaves.

Etta plants herself between me and Ana. As the tiniest of us, it's curious how Etta consistently designates herself as sentry. I'm used to this, so I just stare ahead, trying to get a glimpse of the Oracle, a task which is made difficult by the disappointed woman in front of me whose hair is blocking my view.

A young man comes scurrying down the steps, wiping a tear from his eye. The line moves forward. After about ten minutes or so, a middle-aged couple walks past after their audience with the Oracle. The woman clutches at the man's hand. Both have smiles on their faces, but I can't tell if they are the happy ones, or the kind you wear when you know you've done everything you could but find yourself fatefully at the end of a very long road.

Finally, it's time for the woman in front of us to go. I *really* want to hear what she wants, but I decide to be the bigger person and give her some privacy. I keep to the second step and turn my back and look at Ana. I gesture to her that it's time to pack up Baby. Etta also motions with her hands that it's almost our turn and Ana scrambles to gather Baby's things.

After a few moments, we're all there, waiting, together. The woman's voice rises.

"What do you mean a shallow pool with infinite depth? What is that? That doesn't help me!" We collectively grin in a way that I'm not ashamed to admit is petty as hell. The rude, big-haired woman pushes past us in a huff, and we approach.

The Oracle is gray. Her hair is gray; her skin is thin and the color of smoke that wafts from burning paper. Her dress is slate, and her lace cardigan is gunmetal silver. She's wearing large, round sunglasses that take up most of her face, and she is sitting very casually on a black bench. There are empty benches on either side and room enough for at least one of us to sit beside her, but we make an unspoken choice to stand together.

"Well, well, well," the Oracle cackles. "If it isn't the triplets. Never thought I'd see you three. Never thought you'd deign to ask *anyone* for help." The Oracle's voice crackles and rasps like she's trying to catch her breath, but I know she isn't sick. Fairies don't get sick, and they don't get old.

"It's good to see you," I say softly.

"I doubt that. Your lot don't tend to associate with my kind so cut the bullshit. And why don't you address me proper like? Show a lady some respect."

"Alright," I clear my throat. I'll have to wing it now. Is there some kind of a tradition here? I silently curse Em for not mentioning something so obvious. "Greetings to you, Oracle of a Thousand Eyes. We've come respectfully to seek your guidance."

"No need to get high and mighty now. Just call me by my name." The Oracle juts her neck forward and gives us a snaggle-toothed grin.

"I have no idea what your name is. I'm sorry," I confess.

"Oh, stop it. You know my name is Judy," the Oracle puffs.

"Sorry, yeah. Judy, we've come to..."

"Who's Judy? That's not my name. You know well and good that my name is Bernice."

I grit my teeth and exhale one long breath. Deference is not going to cut it. "What's a name?" I say offhandedly. "I go by Lo Smith here. A name is nothing more than a collection of sounds. I don't care about my name or yours. Someone stole my wand, and Fauna's too. We'd like you to look for them . . . with your eyes."

The Oracle's face moves into a sinister grin. Her lips don't spread so much as turn over on themselves. She cocks her head sideways and then stares at the baby carriage malevolently. "All right. If you give me the baby. I'll tell you where your wands are. I'll tell you free and clear."

"I'll only say this once, Oracle," I bend down to get closer and hiss. Etta pulls out her wand. "You will not mention that baby again. You won't look at her. You won't even think about her. The baby is off limits. And if you even mention to anyone that we have a baby, it will be the greatest regret of your life."

The Oracle slowly chuckles like a bleating goat. "You think you can just come here and threaten me, Flora? I don't like threats, not one bit."

"I don't know what you're talking about," I say innocently. "I came to make a deal. A deal that is proportionate to the favor we are asking. If you can tell us where our wands are, then you can have this necklace that Fauna stole from Maleficent's bedroom, right out from under her nose. She kept it beneath her pillow. I don't know what it does or where it's from, but it must mean a lot to her."

Ana whips out the piece of jewelry and the Oracle jumps with shocking agility and tries to snatch it away. Ana cleverly moves her hand just in time. "You'll get the necklace *after* you give us the answers we're looking for," I taunt.

Ana leaves the necklace dangling there, just beyond the Oracle's reach. The Oracle keeps her hands at her side, but she juts out her neck and sniffs at my sister's offering. "Hmph," the Oracle says as she sits back on the bench. "It certainly has her stench."

"Do we have a bargain?" I ask confidently.

"And just what do you think Maleficent will do to you when she's figured out you've stolen from her with only the one wand between you? Can't think that will go over well," the Oracle observes.

"Oh, she'll forgive us in a thousand years or so. She always does," I tell her smoothly. "Besides, once you give us the information we need, we'll find our wands. You know as well as anyone that we've never been afraid of Maleficent," I boast.

"Can't understand how you lost your wands in the first place," the Oracle comments slyly.

"Well, I can't understand how that's any of your business," I shoot back. "We don't sit in a nice safe park all day, do we? We're out *there*… in every corner of the world *and* in The Undervale with all manner of dangerous folk, doing dangerous things."

I keep my mouth shut after that. If I speak again, I know I'll lose the ground I've gained because of my rambling.

"Hmph. Let's say I agree to your terms and then let's say that you don't like the answers you hear. Then what? I've already got a list of enemies as long as my arm. I don't need the likes of Merriweather Bloomshade coming after me because I couldn't help her sisters out of a mess that was none of my making."

I can't help but curl my lip. I'm the one doing the negotiating here. I'm the one being all brash and threatening. Why is she bringing my sister into this?

"I know the rules, Oracle," Etta says sharply. "I'm well aware of how to play the game. I don't expect a straight answer, but I do expect an honest one. As long as you give us that, I'll have no quarrel with you."

"Very well, I accept your bargain," the Oracle says haltingly. "But know this: if Maleficent comes here asking about you three or the necklace, I will sell you out faster than a water tank in the Sahara. Though I'll admit to *wanting* a thing that old cow covets, it ain't worth incurring her wrath if it comes down to it. She's a mean one."

"Deal," I agree with a strained nod. I had told the Oracle that I wasn't afraid of Em, which is mostly true. I realize now that when it comes to fairies, almost everything was just mostly true or half a lie with a lick of certainty.

"This is a complicated and taxing request you're asking for. I hope you understand that."

"We've already made the deal, Oracle. Don't go looking for extras," I warn.

The old woman's nose twitches. "I'm no welcher." I don't believe her. I am sure the Oracle is the very definition of a welcher. She'll try to slip around our bargain and slide through even the tiniest of loopholes.

I will not let her do that.

"I'll be needing a very special set of eyes," the Oracle proclaims with unnecessary drama, as if suddenly she's an actor in a play and the entire park is her stage. She drags her wand from a holster hiding inside her cardigan. "They hurt something fierce, so don't expect me to linger. I won't repeat myself. You get what you get."

"Fine," I tell her icily.

The Oracle holds out her wand with one hand and with the other, she pulls out a glass bowl from underneath her feet and places it in her lap. Ana makes a slight gagging sound and I silence her with a harsh glance. Inside the oversized bowl are dozens maybe even hundreds of eyes. Actually…there are probably a thousand- hence the name. There are Human eyes and horses' eyes. Beetle eyes and salamander eyes and eyes that are diamond shaped and some that are like embers in a fire. The Oracle waves her wand over the bowl as she removes her sunglasses.

I watch with both revulsion and fascination at the sunken, empty sockets in the Oracle's gray face. Two eyes roll over inside the glass and begin to rise. They are as black as onyx, apart from the pupils which flash like repeating lightning strikes. The eyeballs float up and then crash into her face with a jolt hard enough to make the Oracle blanch.

The gray woman becomes even paler, but she sits up as straight as a pin, like the clouds above us have gone fishing and hooked her scalp.

"One wand is hidden where bodies press orange and red with careening noise to wake the dead. Yes, yes, that's just the door. The wand lies beyond something more. There are prisons and there are cages. Your wand is resting with all that rages."

I scramble to remember each word precisely, but then I relax a little when I see that clever Ana, has a small notebook out and is scribbling furiously away with the necklace dangling from her mouth.

"The second wand—" the Oracle takes a deep breath in, and I can tell that it pains her to do so. *"The second wand—"* the Oracle stutters, her voice softens, flickering in agony, *"it sleeps where there is no path, where there is no sky, where the thicket opened and ate your pride. Black dog. Devil dog. Demon in the sand. Your wand lies in a lie, in the dark, in the deep, in the shadow land."*

The Oracle's eyes pop out of the sockets with a sickening ooze. They quickly dive back down into the bowl and the Oracle replaces her sunglasses with shaking hands then places her hands on her thighs, palms open, as if they had been burned. Ana gently puts Em's locket into one of them and steps quickly away.

I have a hundred questions, but as Etta said, we know the rules of the game. Perhaps the Oracle knows for certain where the wands are or perhaps the eyes can see but the Oracle can't, and all the magic does is slip words into her mouth.

"Thank you," I tell her sincerely.

"You three," the Oracle says roughly. She taps her wand in the air and suddenly, there's a glass of water in her hands which she drinks greedily. "I have known you for eons. You've never once asked for my help. And in truth, even though I don't have much use for the Bloomshades, none of you have ever been unkind to me or mine, so I'll tell you this for free. Don't turn your back, girls, not for one minute. You are being watched . . . and not by me."

- 12 -

Em wears a very particular look on her face when she is concentrating. Her brow furrows intensely enough that if she had wrinkles, they would crack across her forehead. Her mouth opens ever so slightly, and her lips bow as if she's exhaling smoke instead of air. We're sitting at the table once again. Giacomo has provided us with coffee and Em is dressed in cashmere leggings and a voluminous purple sweater which looks as cozy and warm as a blanket.

"I can't yet wrap my head around the puzzle of the second wand," she admits with an exasperated tone.

"All that stuff about dogs and pride," Ana offers, "what even eats pride? I know I'm a little bit vain—I'll admit that much—but my sisters? Etta will wear the same outfit three days in a row, and Lo doesn't even wear make-up and she never uses any product in her hair which she absolutely should because we all know it's her best feature."

"First of all, rude," I clap back, "and secondly, it's a metaphor. Obviously."

"Yes," Em agrees while looking at Etta and me critically. "We'll get back to that one. It's the first riddle that makes more sense."

I take a sip of my coffee. Em was positively gleeful that the Oracle had taken the bait and exchanged information for a tacky bauble she didn't even care about. She had been decidedly less vocal about the notion that three of us are being watched. I repeated my concerns about Longshadow, but since neither one of my sisters could corroborate my claim, she dismissed it as a typical example of my paranoia.

The thing about Longshadow is, the more you try to explain it, the crazier it sounds. I decide against trying to convince her.

"Bodies press, careening noise to wake the dead," Etta says thoughtfully. "Could it be a graveyard?"

Em throws her an imperious look. "A graveyard? This is The Undervale. There are no graveyards here. I have half a mind to ask Giacomo to bring me a kitchen knife so that I can slice your throat open, Merriweather."

"Em!" I bleat. The color drains from Etta's already pale face.

"Well, how else am I supposed to prove that we're *immortal?* I keep telling you all, but, it doesn't seem to sink in. Clearly you three need a practical demonstration. And while Merriweather's wound heals, she wouldn't be able to talk, which I think we can all agree would be a real bonus."

"Try to cut me, Em," Etta warns pulling out her wand. "I might not be able to do magic stuff, but I can punch you in the face and shove this wand right up your ass."

"You say that as if it wouldn't be enjoyable, but . . ." Em begins

"No, please, please, don't finish that thought. Let's just concentrate on the problem. There will be no cutting or slicing or shoving. Okay?" I referee. Not for nothing, I notice that Ana looks far more intrigued than I believe is appropriate.

"Fine. Let me lay it out for you again: We've got no more use for a cemetery in The Undervale than we would a tax collector. We don't die! Em raises her fists and shakes them. "This isn't going to work unless you three start thinking like the rest of us. Your fear will be your undoing."

"We aren't afraid of dying," I go ahead and speak for my sisters. I haven't asked, but I'm guessing we all feel the same. "If we're afraid of anything, it's being trapped here, in this place where nothing makes sense and people change their faces on a whim and where we have no memories. We've already lost our lives—dozens of lives, maybe even hundreds."

I don't mention that I am also afraid of being trapped with Longshadow and no way to defend me or my sisters against it. . . I'm afraid that eventually, if I don't get my wand or my magic back, that Longshadow will be all I think about and every minute will be dark and every second will be cold and I will never, ever, feel safe again.

I don't say this because Em has about as much empathy as a mushroom. She doesn't need to know how worried I am, none of them do. I keep these fears to myself. I hold them in the sinew between my ribs.

Em sits back on her chair and crosses her legs. She smiles slowly, forlornly. "I must admit that there is a small part of me—a very small part, mind you—that envies your situation. Stop seeing it as such a burden," she suggests firmly. "Choose a different way of framing this. Consider it a rebirth of sorts. There are many things that I'd give anything to forget." Em stares at the wall, her eyes focus on a single point as though that invisible speck is as wide and cavernous as a desolate mountain range, as if the memories in question have momentarily escaped the mysterious mental vault an immortal uses to trap such things in.

"Yay!" Baby bounces up and down on Ana's knee and her laughter is enough to shake Em loose from the past.

"But" Em says almost wistfully, "the price would be far too high. Anyhow, the Oracle said, 'careening noise and bodies pressed together.' Think about it? Picture it—what do you see? Not bones, surely."

We sit in silence for a moment or two. I close my eyes and focus. Are there trains in The Undervale? They would be unnecessary, obviously, but fairies seem to have a hankering for nostalgia. I imagine tweed suits and fedoras, ladies in nylons with battered valises. A packed platform, the wailing whistle of an arriving train. I suppose the locomotive would have to be red or orange which if I think about it, are perfectly normal colors for a steam train, even a modern train, like one of those bullet ones- they could be red.

"A dance!" Ana says suddenly all aflutter. "The noise is music and the bodies pressed together is just a bunch of people on the dance floor."

"Exactly," Em agrees triumphantly. "You three will have to go a ball."

I can't help but slump my chair.

I liked my train idea.

"When is the next ball? A hundred years from now or something?" I ask dubiously.

"Don't be ridiculous." Em is being dismissive. *Again.* She draws her wand out from behind her shoulder as if she's plucking a feather off a pair of wings. I notice how each fairy keeps their wand close, in holders and holsters strapped to their body. Even Etta has placed her sleeping one within reaching distance. "This is The Undervale, there's a ball every single night, so," Em says efficiently as she sketches the shape of a square in the air. "Tonight's ball is . . . of course, this clinches it…The Ball Of Burning Crimson—there's your red and orange. Which makes sense given the season. Oh," Em's whines. "It's at Whifflecliff House, ugghhhh, *that place.*"

"But" Etta wonders out loud, "it's not autumn here. Not in your neighborhood. It's got to be a hundred degrees outside."

"Why are you saying that like I don't know where my own house is?" Em rolls her eyes. "Even humans get to live in whatever season that suits them. You think people are wearing mittens in Hawaii? I hate the cold. It makes my nose itch."

"Are we actually making small talk about the weather?" I break in. "It's autumn. Great. Now, what's wrong with Whifflecliff House? You made a noise after you told us. You grunted."

"I did not," Maleficent stares me down, her pupils split like a cat, like two sharp knives.

"Okay, fine. You didn't grunt. You gave us no reaction at all," I tell her sarcastically. "What is so bad about this place? Who lives there?"

Em scratches her head with a single nail. I can hear the muffle and scrape against her skull. "Many people live there. Fairy Manor Houses are ancient and full of predictable snobs. There's quite an elaborate royal family in The Undervale. Which makes no sense because really, everyone is related to everybody here."

"Like princes and duchesses? Fairies with titles?" I ask in alarm. Great. Now there's something *else* we have to keep in mind. What if we address some earl or viscount inappropriately and we don't get the answers we need because we unknowingly curtsied to the wrong fairy?

"Who even cares? That's not the issue," Ana says as Baby grips her fingers.

"It's totally the issue," I counter. "Think about it."

"Royalty?" Ana trills. "When everyone can do magic? No, I agree with Em—it's silly. The real problem is that we don't have anything to wear to a fancy ball."

"You don't?" Em feigns surprise. "How shocking."

"Ana," I utter, almost beneath my breath. I want to smack my head on the table.

"I'm not against wearing a nice dress," Etta chimes in. "But no corsets. I don't care how fancy the ball is."

"The clothes *are not* the thing!" I yelp.

All three of them turn their heads in my direction.

"Actually, they are," Maleficent contradicts. "There's nothing for it. You need a fairy godmother."

"No, we don't," Etta sputters. "Just wave your wand over us and put us in stupid dresses with bows and ribbons if you have to, but no corsets." My sister holds out her flat hand like a crossing guard, like she could actually stop Em from putting us in whatever outfits she wanted to. "We don't need to involve anyone else."

Maleficent cracks her spine and leans back in her chair, pushing her palms into the table. "I am very busy. I have a book to write, and I promised Giacomo I would watch him rake the gravel in the garden. He's really proud about how uniform and flat he can make it. It's really quite adorable."

"You don't have three seconds to wave your wand around and put us in something appropriate for tonight? Seriously?" I'm can feel my face begin to flush with anger.

"Stop being so petulant, Flora. It's exhausting," Em stands and shakes out her hair. "There are rules and silly little regulations which are so inane that I stopped attending. It's been almost two centuries since I've even been to a ball. You have to dress for the theme and if you don't get it absolutely spot on, the fairies in attendance get uppity; they may not even let you inside. A proper fairy godmother knows exactly how to game the system. She'll be aware of all the lame bits and pieces of protocol you'll need to know and the exact boring shades of whatever you'll have to wear. In this instance, my help might be a hindrance and *will you stop looking at me in that way, Flora.* I'm not your mother. I can't just fix every little problem that comes your way."

"Well, can you at least tell us where to find a fairy godmother then? Or would that take too much time away from you bossing people around, either in print or your own garden."

Em's pupil's return to the inhuman horizontal dagger slant. This time though, each sharp point begins to simmer violet. "That's it! Really. I'm this close . . ." Maleficent shows us her thumb and index finger with only a tiny space between.

I'm smart enough not to ask *how* close.

Em whips up. Her purple sweater billows around her like a rain cloud as she walks toward the front door. We hastily collect our things (and Baby's) so that we can follow her.

Ana is giving me a dirty look. I suppose I *may* have pushed things a little too far. But if Em would just act normal, then I could too.

Was my little barb really enough to throw us out now? Where would we even go?

Em is waiting with the door already open, and a single hand perched imperiously on her hip. "A fairy can only be expected to deal with so much, even a magnanimous and overly generous fairy like me. You three have tested my patience to its limit. *My* patience, which is well-known for being infinite. And if something terrible happens, I know I'm the one who's going to be blamed even though it would clearly be your fault. So, you need to leave. Now."

"Em," Ana pouts. "Please don't be mad at us."

"Can you stop mentioning feelings? It's so over-the-top mortal that I'm embarrassed for you. I said I would help, and I will. All the top-rate fairy godmothers and fathers live mostly in the mortal realm where people know how to be grateful for the aid and advice they're given. But I don't have the energy to start making a bunch of calls to see who's available at a moment's notice because you three were dumb enough to let yourselves be cursed. I will fold enough steps to take you to Nannette—that's Ninny to her friends—Ninny Goldendash's place. She lives in the village and she's semi-retired, so she'll probably be there. If she's not, ask someone else's help for a change. Do. Not. Come. Back."

"Maleficent," I begin with genuine contrition. I'm so relieved that she's willing to stand by us, even if her brand of support is unconventional. "I'm sorry for snapping at you. It was rude. But, if you could just put yourself in our shoes and try to imagine how scary this is, then maybe you could understand why I'm being so . . ."

"Snarky," Ana offers.

"Difficult and shitty," Etta says at the same time.

Em looks down disparagingly at my running shoes. "Empathy is a skill that I have yet to master. Do yourself a favor, Flora, let Fauna do the talking. You can't help yourself from whinging, and Merriweather is downright combative." Em flicks and swirls her wand and then pushes us out the door without even saying goodbye. I chide myself for letting my frustration and fear get the better of me. All I can do now is hope that this other fairy will be a bit more understanding, and that while we're gone, Em will figure out the last riddle of the wand. Although (and I would never admit this to my sisters) thanks to my big mouth, I doubt very much that Maleficent will spend even one second thinking about our predicament now.

- 13 -

The steps between the yellow lacquer of Em's door and the Village in The Undervale roll sideways and undulate forward like an invisible suspension bridge with no handrails. We unfurl ourselves onto the pavement awkwardly. Like all three of us are trying to get off a moving trolley car.

The building in front of us is shabby and surprisingly forlorn. The faded sign reads "Ninny's Laundrette," though I have to scrunch my eyes to make out the letters.

"I don't care what Em said," Ana announces as she checks on Baby, who's happily sitting up in her pram. "I don't want to be in charge. These fairies are slippery. Every word they say feels like a trap and then I get insecure. You should keep taking the lead, Lo. You've gotten us this far."

"You just told Em I was difficult and shitty," I point out.

"I said you were snarky. Etta said the other stuff."

"I did," Etta admits "But only because I didn't want Maleficent to think she was being ganged up on. We needed her help, and you *were* being kind of an asshole, though it was totally justified. Em gets off on baiting people. It's called *strategy*." Etta is wearing a jean jacket and she's gripping the edges of her cuffs so all I can see are the crescent tips of her light blue nail polish. Em had said her sister was combative, which is not exactly true. More than anything, Etta is just wary, which we need in this place. But her wariness can come across as paranoia or straight-up insulting when my sister feels anxious. Etta probably isn't the best one to talk to this newest fairy we're about to meet.

"Alright," I say as I put my hands on the metal door handle. I pull it open, and we shuffle inside, dragging Baby's pram behind us. "Hmmm," I comment with a frown. The lights overhead are fluorescent. A few of them pop on and off with a buzzing sound. The tall windows are covered in steam, blocking our view of outside. There are four rows of ancient-looking, turquoise-colored washers and dryers. Almost all of them are going. The room is filled with the lilting whizz of quiet motors and the clicking and clacking of tin drums spinning.

One fairy, a teenager like us, in a black turtleneck and round sunglasses is sitting at a rickety table reading a book. Another fairy, elderly and Black with loud plaid pants, is sitting in a chair directly opposite a dryer. His legs are spread casually, in the way that only men can manage without looking peevish. He stares at the clothes falling over themselves in the dryer, his brown eyes following each tumble.

I'm about to ask the man where we might find Ninny when the godmother herself swans through a curtain of beads.

"Oh well. *Oh my!* Flora, Fauna, and Merriweather! As I live and breathe!" Ninny wastes no time in gathering us up in her corpulent arms to give us a big squeeze. She smells like laundry, like the detergent racing through the pipes of each machine but also, of something else, peppermint and a spice I can't quite put my finger on.

She's a big woman. Everything on her seems disproportionately large. She's tall, taller even than Ana and wide enough to hold us all in her arms easily. The flowers on her kaftan are the size of dinner plates and as vivid as unripened limes. Her wrists are as thick as Etta's entire neck. Ninny's lips are painted an unrepentant red, and her hair, as white as pageant queen's teeth, sits atop her head in a mass of curls that are so high it *has* to be a wig.

"I haven't seen y'all in a month of Silkendays!" Ninny quite literally declares. Ninny's Southern accent is so thick every vowel is twice the length it should be.

"I don't get it," Etta says innocently enough as she looks around. "Can't you just do the laundry with magic? Isn't that the way it works here?"

The teenager at the table snickers and Ninny, in turn, gives us an odd look. She may have narrowed her eyes, but they are so big I can't properly tell. "What in the world are y'all talking about? You know how much I love the sound of these machines. It soothes the soul, and the smell! It's heaven. Why would you ask me such a thing, Merriweather? You were one of my *very first* customers."

"Ummm," I quickly jump in. "Yeah, about that, is there some place that we could talk in private?" The man watching the dryer glances in our direction, and the teenager grumbles something under his breath.

"Well, this is all very mysterious," Ninny says with a cheeky shrug. "Come on now," she gestures with her giant hands. "Let's go up into my apartment and sit a spell. Once we're settled, you can tell me all about your latest escapade."

Ninny walks with a lumbering gate, as if her kneecaps are made of marbles. It takes focus for me to maintain a neutral expression. I worry that we're broadcasting our predicament like a neon sign. Ninny looks back at us and purses her lips as she climbs up the few steps that lead to her living quarters.

Ana takes Baby out of the carriage and slings her over her narrow hips. "Yay! Yay!" Baby squeals excitedly as soon as we enter because on every shelf, on every table, hanging from the ceiling and standing in front of the windows are dozens of bird cages. Some are small and some are big enough to fit a whole family of birds. A few are gilded;

others are silver. There are rustic wooden coops, and some have bars painted in bright, tropical colors that are as skinny as pins.

"There's a lot of birds in here, Ninny," I comment nervously. It's the understatement of the year, maybe even the century, given where we are. There are so many that I don't think I get anywhere near an accurant count. The number of feathered pets in Ninny's apartment is not normal. She's a bird hoarder, if that's an actual thing.

"Don't be silly. They aren't *all* birds, not really." Without trying to be too obvious, I look in the cages and all I can see is feathers and wings which means that at least a few of her pets had started out as something else, and Ninny had changed them. *With magic.*

For a house full of birds, it's unnaturally quiet, save for a radio playing from another room. The creatures turn their heads to stare at the four of us. I can feel their beady little eyes on my skin, and I take an involuntary step backwards. Etta sees this and grabs my hand, pulling me closer to her.

Ninny sits down in a great big reclining chair. She drops her ample arms on the rests which are daintily covered in lace doilies. Ninny makes a waving gesture with her hand, signaling that we should sit down too, which we do, on a sofa with wide, scratchy, lemon-colored cushions.

Ninny tucks her chin and cocks her head slightly to the left before she says, "What in the Sam Hill has gotten into you three? Why are y'all acting so peculiar?" I clear my throat and look at Ninny, whose wrinkles are so deep around her mouth that I imagine for a brief second, half of my finger disappearing if I was to stick it into one the folds.

"It's a long story," I say as casually as I can. It's imperative that I come across as mature. I don't think of myself as a whiner, but Em's comments have made me insecure. "The short version is that someone here in The Undervale cursed us. They stole our wands and our memories." Ninny's hand flies to her open mouth as she gasps, but that doesn't stop me from continuing. "We went to see the Oracle of a

Thousand Eyes. We're pretty sure that one of our wands is in Whifflecliff House so we need your help to get us in there, get us ready and everything for the Ball tonight."

"Get you ready?" Ninny blinks. "I don't understand."

"We're asking for your help . . . professionally," hoping I don't sound overly desperate. "We need you to Fairy Godmother us, so that we're proper and we look like we belong there, because there's no way we can feel like we belong at a fancy fairy ball. We feel how we look and what we look like are seventeen-year-old girls who have never been anywhere special."

"I think technically, we—" Ana notes as she gestures at the specific bodies we are wearing, "have been to many of these balls, probably too many to count. We just don't remember them. And obviously never while we looked like this . . . these . . . girls."

Ninny closes her eyes for the briefest of moments and takes in a labored breath. "This must be real difficult for you ladies. I am *so* sorry."

I blink hard. Her empathy is unexpected. Her kindness is like a magic of its own, drawing tears from the corners of my eyes.

"Thank you," I tell her with real affection. "It has been difficult but mostly . . . disorienting. We know this isn't really us, but only rationally. Emotionally, I don't think any of us understand how we can be something else."

"Yes." Ninny's chin bobs up and down. "You must feel like the entire Undervale is like an upside-down cake. Take a look at me, why do think I look the way I do? I don't need to wear this body. There's no reason for me to be this old."

"Then, why do you?" Ana asks innocently and I'm glad because I'm curious too.

"Because I want to look how I feel," Ninny says softly. She rests her fingers beneath her dimpled chin and the air stills. The space we're in suddenly feels sacred. "Immortality is a road that keeps getting paved. And sure, the scenery changes once in a while but, it never really goes anywhere. You move forward, on momentum alone, but sadly there is never a destination. I am weary to the bone of this life. When I take a gander in the mirror, I want to see that. I think it would break my heart every day to see a bright-eyed girl with rosy cheeks; a girl who believes there are secrets left to learn and mysteries to uncover. That would be a lie. If I have to live this life, I don't think I could bear to do it as a liar."

Ninny's admission makes me feel deeply uncomfortable. She's talking to me like we're equals, like we're on that same road. I am not where she is. I am not bone weary. And I don't want to be an old lady. I would never choose to be an old lady.

"But you have a job," I counter reasonably. "You were created to help people, to make their dreams come true," I tell her earnestly. "Maybe if you lived in the mortal realm, doing that, it would be better. You would feel less ... *stuck* ..."

All she can do is offer me a sigh. "If you wear the mask long enough, it becomes the only face you recognize." Ninny shakes her head and the tower of curls sitting upon it wobbles slightly. "Good Lord, this is a morbid conversation. I apologize. I just can't believe y'all have to be so young. It's one hell of a curse." Ninny sweeps her head back and forth as if she's banishing those thoughts. "That sure is a cute little baby; what's her name?"

Ana looks at me nervously and I quickly jump in. Ninny had been remarkably honest with us when she didn't have to be. "We don't know her name, so we just call her Baby. Someone left her on our doorstep. Em said it was Baby's arrival that started unravelling the curse." I admit this because I don't think any of us need to be worried. Ninny's lonely and a little sad. I don't think she's the fatten-you-up-and-eat-you kind of fairy. My gut tells me to trust her, even if my brain is suspicious.

It's true, Ninny does have some birds that aren't really birds in her cages, I still don't think she's the type to hurt something or someone defenseless. Besides, as awful as Em is, she wouldn't send us here if Ninny was going to do something terrible.

Probably

"Who's Em?" Ninny asks while giving Baby a toothy smile.

"Maleficent," Etta says plainly.

"Maleficent, ha!" Ninny bellowed. "She's a scamp that one. If trouble was looking for a partner, she'd be the first one to invest. And she sent you here? To me?" We nod in unison and Baby giggles. "Can I hold her?" Ninny asks hopefully. Ana looks at Etta and me and bites her bottom lip. Em had said that Baby would be useful. We would never trade her or anything, but I can't see the harm in letting Ninny hold the little girl.

"Sure," I say as I scoop up Baby and plop her in Ninny's hefty lap.

"Well, aren't you the most precious thing!" Ninny coos and bounces Baby gently. "I do love babies. And the way they smell!" Ninny puts her nose into Baby's soft hair. "That is the best, better even than my washing machines. It's real sad that we can't have children of our own. I've looked after and loved so many babies. But babies grow into children and children turn into adults and then they . . ." Ninny trails off. "You girls must think I'm pitiful. I do apologize. I don't usually go on like this. It's just, well, I suppose I haven't had any real company in, well, I can't even properly say. Still, I can't imagine why Maleficent would send you here. You three are fairies, and therefore you are free to go to any ball in The Undervale."

"Yes, but we don't have our memories," Ana states quickly.

"We don't know the first thing about fancy parties here, or anywhere else," Etta acknowleges.

"Em—Maleficent—said that royalty would be in attendance and because of that, we would have to dress exactly right and that there were strict rules and if we didn't know them and follow them, then everyone would know the truth about us and if everyone knew that we didn't have our wands, that would be bad. *Very bad*," I gush.

"Hmph. I reckon Maleficent hasn't been to a Ball since, well, I don't rightly know. It's been hundreds of years," Ninny says with a grimace. "What Ball is it?"

"The Burning Crimson Ball," I answer.

"Well, that's downright silly, isn't it, Baby?" Ninny asks and then she puffs up her cheeks like a blowfish until Baby laughs. "The king and queen won't even be there. Besides, even though we don't like to admit it, the fairies have been influenced by the humans far more than we've influenced them. There's not so many rules anymore. You don't have to drink with your pinkie finger in the air or recite the Fourteen Oaths to the Dahlenia Grove or swear all ninety-six verses of fealty to the highest-ranking member of the royal family. Balls these days ain't got no class and no use for tradition. All you need is a dress and even then, folks here have gotten real liberal with that notion too. I can't think why she'd send you to me. Could she really be so out of touch with our world now? Even more than I am? Ha!" Ninny chortles at Baby who reaches up to grasp at Ninny's generous nose.

My eyes sweep the pokey apartment, at all the birds who should be singing or chirping but aren't. They are perched inside their cages, staring at us in silent judgment. There's a solitary chipped teacup beside Ninny's enormous chair and a dog-eared romance novel spread open at her feet.

The radio coming from the unseen room isn't playing any sort of happy tune or even a melancholy one. It's just a droning voice, the news or possibly a weather report, and I assume that this is Ninny's idea of company when she's not working in her launderette. I guess after a couple thousand years, you might get tired of entertaining. I can see how friendship might become exhausting when you've lived for eons on your own, even though that really is the thing you need most of all.

Em knew exactly what she was doing when she sent us to Ninny, and it wasn't because she was busy or annoyed with us. Well, she probably *was* annoyed, but she wanted us right here in this room with Ninny Goldendash who spends far too many days alone in that sunken chair with her silent birds.

Even though I'm a triplet, I do know what loneliness tastes like. It's bitter; it makes my cheeks hollow, and it never quite leaves my tongue. The feeling remains, just the barest dash of it, flavoring everything I put in my mouth, including and most especially my words.

"Well, you know Maleficent," I say coyly. "She gets bored so easily. I think she's sick of us. I know it's asking a lot, I'm sure you're very busy here with your business and all. But would you consider helping us? Dressing us? And Baby too, of course, she should have something pretty to wear."

Ninny gasps, clutching Baby to her. "You absolutely cannot take a human to Whifflecliff House. It's not safe!" Ninny implores as she shakes her head vigorously. "There are . . . *things* in that house . . . are you sure you don't want to wait for Maleficent to change her mind? It would be better for y'all if she accompanied you."

"Why?" Etta asks with alarm. "Will you please tell us what is so dangerous about a house? What things exactly?"

"In order to answer that question, I'd have to explain this entire world to you and by the time I did that, Baby here would be as old as you girls now. It's complicated. The Undervale is as dark as it is beautiful."

"The thing is though, without our wands or our memories, we don't even *know* the difference between good and bad. Something that looks harmless could in fact be extremely dangerous," I explain.

"And something that looks terrifying could actually be sweet and cute," Ana continues.

"It's best if you just pretend we're mortals, Ninny. How would you explain Whifflecliff House to humans? Is it terrible?"

"Not all of it," Ninny admits. "Some of it is real pretty. And I suppose nothing too awful can happen, considering you most certainly are neither human nor mortal, even if you think you are. Taking that into account, I will help you on one condition," Ninny says firmly.

"Yeah? What's that?" Etta asks skeptically.

"This is an innocent child. A truly human child. She cannot, under any circumstances go to that Ball. Baby can stay here with me. You can pick her up after the party, or even tomorrow."

"Oh I don't think . . ." Ana begins but I cut her off. I know why Ana is being so skeptical. Ninny is a stranger, but if Whifflecliff House is even remotely dangerous, then Baby needs to stay here.

"That would actually be great, thank you. And much safer for Baby. Besides, she can't be up all night." I can see Ana's face twitch out of the corner of my eye, but I ignore it. Maybe Ana can't look past all the creepy birdcages, but I know that Ninny is one of the good ones and obviously Em knows it too, which would make it *two* very thoughtful reasons now for why she made us come here. "So, you can make us presentable? And then all we have to do is walk in? We don't need a special invitation or anything?"

"Oh no, Sugar, those are only for the balls that the king and queen attend. And they don't go out so much anymore. The Burning Crimson Ball is all about the season so it's not as informal as a Summer Ball, but it's less stuffy than a spring one. All you need are pretty dresses, big smiles, and don't drink anything that is actually on fire. You'll lose an entire week to that particular cocktail."

"That's it?" Etta asks dubiously.

Ninny looks at Baby and gives her a big, broad smile. "Well, I reckon that whoever did this to you, though I can't for the life of me imagine who would, they want you to be muddled and confused. They're getting a sick kind of pleasure from your terror. Don't give them the satisfaction. Be brave. Be bold. The way you've got to think about it is that whatever happens, whatever you see there, will just become another story…eventually." Ninny reaches over and puts a hand on my knee "In the end, we're all just a collection of stories, you remember that. Now, stand up."

We stand and Ninny asks each of us to step forward and turn. She gives us a thorough inspection, craning her neck and eyeing us carefully. "Alright, here we go." Ninny slowly pulls her wand from a narrow pocket at her side. Ninny's wand, like her name, is golden. At the hilt is a tiny bird. She whooshes the wand around the us, leaving a trail of filigree flakes. The sparkling flecks transform our clothes as they land and settle.

When I see my sister's transformation, I cannot get my mouth to close. It becomes a door with a broken hinge. It takes everything I have not to burst into a fit of laughter. The only thing that stops me is the awareness that more than likely, I am wearing something similar.

Ana's eyes widen in shock. Etta grimaces. I make sure to warn them with a look before they can say anything. We asked for Ninny's help, and she has given it generously.

It's glaringly obvious, even to me, who doesn't really know much about these things, that taste is relative, and unfortunately, sweet Ninny doesn't have very much of it.

But…

Shit…

Em might think it's okay to exist in a constant state of rudeness but I refuse to be influenced by her bad behavior. We are not going to offer a single word of complaint.

Etta's gown has a satin blue bodice. The sleeves, which poof out like two marshmallows, are as bright red as the petticoat underneath. The dress is so wide that it looks like it's trying to swallow her. Etta's short platinum hair is swept off her face and she's wearing a garland of crimson dahlias. There's a collection of tiny scarlet maple leaves stuck around her eyes and over the bridge of her nose like a mask.

Ana is also wearing a mask like this, except hers is brown and bronze with jeweled acorn-shaped studs. Her dress is just as puffy as Etta's, maybe even more so; though instead of satin, it's mostly green velvet, apart from the orange sleeves which are just a bunch of silk scarves that are hanging all the way down her arms. Ana's hair is pulled back so severely I'm sure it must be painful. Her crown is a glittering combination of nuts and berries.

I take a deep and very courageous inhale and look down. My dress is by far the biggest *and* widest. Most of it is burgundy silk, apart from the bottom, where appliqued, amber-colored flames adorn the hem. Although my dress is sleeveless, it has a train that's at least five feet long. I touch my hair and find that it's in a style very similar to Ninny's. Ninny isn't wearing a tiara though. My fingers outline the edges of the contraption on my head, and I can tell it has the same flame motif as the dress. I touch my eyes and cheeks and my hand comes away sticky and covered in scarlet sparkles.

"It's not a real tattoo," Ninny assures me. "Just a temporary one. It is the Burning Crimson Ball and as least one of you should honor the bonfire," she says with a wink. "Don't y'all look precious! And glamorous! Like movie stars. Now wait a minute." Ninny disappears into the back room and emerges with a polaroid camera. "Smile!" she tells us. We manage three stiff grins. "Oh! I love this! I'm gonna frame it. Baby, you see how pretty they are?"

"Yay!" Baby claps and waves her fist.

"Do you love it?" Ninny asks hopefully.

Em had said it that very first day.

Fairies lie.

I am forced to embrace what I suppose is my true nature. "We really do. They are gorgeous dresses, thank you. We probably should be going," I suggest before Ninny can take another barrage of pictures. "What time does it start?"

"It started at dusk; don't worry about arriving too early and don't worry about Baby either. We're going to have a great time. I'll give her a bath and you can leave her bottles and such here. I can even read her a story or two. We'll be as happy as two ticks on a fat dog."

"I don't doubt it for a minute. She really likes you." This at least is true. Baby has taken a real shine to Ninny. "And you won't tell anyone about us, or Baby, right?" I ask, flashing on the odd patrons in the launderette.

"Oh Lord, no. Fairy godmother/child confidentiality. I wouldn't dream of it. Now y'all better scoot. Those dresses will turn back into your own clothes at midnight."

"Oh, really?" I try to hide my relief.

"Rules are rules. I suppose you need me to fold the steps to get you there?"

"If you wouldn't mind," I ask hopefully- although there's an actual lump of dread inside my chest because of this thing that is calling itself a dress and the event that is making me wear it.

"Not a problem at all; it's part of the service. I'm just happy you came to me," Ninny says with a smile so big that it takes up most of her face. I clutch the woman's hand and give it a squeeze.

"I'm glad too, Ninny." and I am. She's nutty and a little maudlin, but Ninny Goldendash is the perfect fairy godmother.

- 14 -

Maybe it's because of the dozens of burning torches floating along the drive- ablaze with fires that scorch a rainbow of colors leaping at least ten feet in the air. Possibly, it's the house- though no one in their right mind would call it that. This is a palace, with wings that stretch out so far in both directions I can't even tell where the building ends.

It also might be the lights reflected on the limestone, all shades of copper, titian, and ruby so that the Manor looks like it's partly engulfed in flames. The most likely reason is that we're about to attend a Fairy Ball. We're understandably equal parts distracted, thrilled, and terrified.

Because of all of these things, I don't notice the other guests, or what they are wearing. I saw them walking up the long path lined with giant trees, but I hadn't really *looked*. It's not until the doors of the Manor house swing open at our approach, assaulting our ears with such bass-heavy dance music, that I *finally* see the other attendees. My sisters and I stop short.

"This is not a Ball," Ana howls over the noise. "This is a Party with a capital P! And we look like Ukrainian nesting dolls from the 70s or when a little girl draws a picture of an imaginary princess using every single one of her crayons or..." Before Ana can continue what I'm sure will be a doozy of a rant, we're swept along by a crowd of people out of the entrance hall and then pushed into the main ballroom.

I'd been expecting an orchestra and waltzing, men in tails and top hats and women dressed, well, in proper dresses.

That is not what is happening here. Some girls are in dresses, of a sort, but they are outrageous affairs, with sleek feathers, body-conscious sequins, and decadent fascinators that spark and burn in glorious colors atop their heads. Some of the guys are in dresses too, but most are in suits- though the suits themselves range in every color from canary yellow to fire engine red. Not only are they *not* wearing ties, but the majority of them aren't also even wearing shirts.

The room is dark, cavernous even, and lit by strobes that roar into life and then turn off abruptly, morphing into black lights so that everyone and everything is neon. Smack in the center of the dance floor is a massive tree, at least twenty feet high. The leaves are all the brilliant hues of the season except they sparkle and gleam as if they are made of precious gems. A subtle blaze scorches all around, turning the foliage into a spectacular, roaring halo.

The air smells of myrrh and bonfires, and the music is so loud that my back teeth are rattling. I try to take a step forward, but someone is stepping on my absurdly long train. I yank it away and pick it up in my arms. The weight of it and the sheer amount of people in the room make my face flush. I can feel my entire body start to sweat. I pat my forehead with the back of my hand.

A striking woman walks past me. She is Asian, and her black hair is put up elaborately in a mass of waves and tucks like the most elegant of geishas. She's wearing a rich cardinal-colored kimono of a kind, although it hugs every inch of her gorgeous figure and is fastened to show ample cleavage and then again just slightly above her thighs. It settles and flows behind her like a peacock tail. She's with a dazzling man wearing nothing but orange-colored tuxedo pants. His bare, broad chest is adorned with a moving tattoo. An autumn branch crawls along his collar bone and every two or three seconds, a single leaf falls to join a pile that litters his navel.

The woman looks at us, furrows her brow, and looks again.

"Fauna?" she asks incredulously. Ana smiles back, but I know it's not a genuine one. She is not happy to be in the dreaded green and orange scarf-sleeved dress. She seems even less happy to be recognized. "Lapis, look, it's Fauna and her sisters! I just can't believe it. *Lapis!*" The woman says as she gives the man a smack on the arm. One of the leaves on his glistening chest falls from the branch obediently.

"I have eyes, Igni. I can see. Hello, Fauna, Flora, and you too, Merriweather. Happy Burning Crimson," Lapis says dully. His gaze flicks over us and then lazily around the room.

"Your outfits are so … retro. It's precious. Isn't it precious, Lapis?"

Lapis smirks. "It's something," he says reluctantly.

Inexplicably, I feel tears begin to well in my eyes. I don't think for one minute that Ninny had deliberately tried to make us look like fools. Our fairy godmother had been so proud of her work with the dresses. And she had intimated that it had been quite a while since she'd attended a Ball. After all we've been through—the curse, Longshadow, amnesia…so much…but it's this, being called out by a mean-spirited woman about something as silly as my dress that threatens to turn me into a puddle.

"Oh these," Ana yells over the music. "We thought it would be fun. You know … that we would be so fashion-backward that it would actually be fashion-forward. It was such a good idea … in theory. But I'm afraid our little experiment failed." She says as she looks down at her dress forlornly. I am in total awe at the absolute showmanship of my sister's performance.

"Yes," Igni sighs with a curled lip.

"But Igni!" Ana screeches with sudden enthusiasm. "You have such excellent taste. I've always thought you dressed so well."

"You have?" Igni feigns surprise. "Me?"

"Completely. How about *you p*ut us in something you think would look good. Surprise us! I know you can make us look amazing," Ana grabs both of the fairy's hands as if this stranger is her dearest friend.

"Well, I might have some ideas. I'm not sure," Igni declares demurely looking at Lapis who already seems bored with the conversation.

"Oh, please Igni," I cajole. "That way, if anyone compliments us tonight, we can tell them that it was all you."

Igni stands up a little straighter and puffs her chest ever so slightly. "Of course, my style is no match for yours, Fauna, but I suppose I could try . . ." Her words trail off, but she grabs her wand from some unseen place on her person so fast that it looks like sleight of hand. She waves it a few times over us and we are transformed. *Truly.* Transformed.

Etta's tiny frame is placed into a silhouette that is perfect for her. The dress is a strapless, teal fit-and-flare. The silk is adorned with tiny sequined marigolds that explode like a firework cascade every time Etta moves.

Fauna's lithe body is swathed in a hunter-green lace cat suit. There are swirls of darker velvet around her chest and lower torso as if a painter has taken a brush to her body to cover only what is absolutely necessary. Igni has spelled her hair up into an elaborate topknot.

I look down at my own burgundy dress. It seems quite plain at first, a simple column, and then I notice a hint of bare shoulders and something else. My eyes widen in alarm. Did Igni set me on fire? I brace for searing pain, but none comes.

"That cape is incredible," Ana says with genuine wonder. "It actually looks like it's burning, but the flames are pink and red. How clever, Igni."

"Thank you," she says demurely. "I was thinking of doing something similar, but I was afraid it might be too obvious. On me, of course," she laughs throatily. "On you, Flora, it's just right."

I'm pretty sure that Igni has just insulted me, but at least now the three of us look don't look completely out of place. Or maybe we do, but in a wholly different way.

"Yeah, I mean, yes, the illusion is really umm... innovative. Thank you so much, Igni. I'll make sure to tell every person I see tonight that this was your idea."

Igni grits her teeth through a thin-lipped smile. "No need. Just enjoy it. Come along, Lapis."

It looks like Etta is also about to say thanks, but they vanish in the crowd before she can open her mouth all the way.

"Well, that's something," Ana says smoothing her hands over the lace on her tummy. "We're like, modern fairies now ... I mean ... I think we are? These outfits are *so* good."

"Quick thinking, sis," Etta says as she gives her dress a little twirl.

"It was," I agree. "You knew just what to say. Still, it doesn't matter much what we look like if the Oracle was being literal. What if the wand is somewhere in this room? There must be a thousand people in here and I can barely see. How can we possibly find it?"

"We're just going to have to wait until the crowd thins out a bit," Ana says while bopping her head. "Which is fine with me. Let's dance, all of us."

"No way," Etta says firmly. "Too many people. But I do see a buffet in the far corner over there. I might grab something to eat."

"What about you. Lo?" Ana grabs my hand. "You'll dance with me, won't you?"

"Ha!" I snort. "You're wearing a unitard. I can barely walk in this dress, let alone dance. You go ahead. I doubt anyone will notice. Plenty of people are out there on their own. I'll watch from here."

Without needing further encouragement, Etta and Ana go their separate ways. I crane my neck to make sure Etta makes it to the food table. I can't see much from my vantage, but I watch as my sister gets on her tippy toes to reach up and pluck a biscuit from a golden macaroon tower. Etta's hands flutter in the air like two startled sparrows as she walks around the massive banquet table. Etta's standards are very high and so I'm happy to see my grumbly sibling so obviously thrilled.

As for Ana, her joy is unmistakable and unfettered. She shimmies and glides and bounces her head to the beat of the music. My sister is liberated.

I feel exposed and gawked at.

I'm sure Igni's dress is getting tighter, though it's probably just a reaction to the swarm of people breathing all the air that's meant for me. I close my eyes and take a labored, shallow inhale. I'm prepared to give my sisters a few moments of reckless abandon while I maintain my vigil. That's what it is to be a sister; it's as much about sacrifice as it is about companionship.

A man walks past me, catching my eye. Instinctively, I look away. When he walks past again, I can feel him staring and my hand begins to tremble. Why is this person leering? Finally, after a third pass, he stops.

"Flora? Is it you?" He asks in a tone that's both intimate and playful.

There's no point in denying it. Fairies lie about many things, but we can't very well lie about who we are when we're standing in front of someone who's probably known us for a thousand years.

"Yes, it's me," I say curtly, hoping not to encourage him.

"Oh." His reaction verges on desperate and then he actually pulls me into his arms. "What a relief!"

My heart begins to hammer. Whoever he is, I have to get away from him. His arms feel like a vice and there's something about the way he smells; it isn't wrong or bad, just uncomfortably familiar. It hits me suddenly, like a slap to the face. He smells of leather and pine, not exactly- but similar to Longshadow when it found me in Em's room. There is no way that it can be a coincidence.

I pull away from him and put my hand across my chest, on the fabric of the stupid dress as I try to catch my breath.

"I don't know you," I admit carefully as I take a step back.

"Flora, I realize it's been a few decades but that's hardly fair." He's not an old man, not really but if I had been human, he'd be old enough to be my father. He isn't dressed as ostentatiously as many, though I wouldn't call his maroon velvet suit conservative by any standards. And why does his outfit match mine so perfectly? Was that Igni's doing? Or has he been watching me the whole time?

"This dress was a bad idea. It's very uncomfortable, so I'd just like to stand here on my own if you don't mind," I say sharply.

The man looks visibly distressed. "If you're playing a game, I don't think it's a very funny one."

"I'm not playing anything." I whip my head around trying to get my sisters' attention but they're too distracted.

"Well then, you're being spiteful." He is clearly offended. "We loved one another for a hundred and fifty years. I love you still. Why are you being so dismissive?"

"Wait . . . what?" My seventeen-year-old instincts claw through my terror. "One hundred and fifty years? That's impossible. You're so old!"

A bubble of laughter escapes the man's mouth. He pulls his wand from a holster underneath his jacket. He waves it over himself and slowly, his face changes. He still looks like the same man—his hair is still dark and clipped short on the sides, though the salt and pepper vanishes as do the lines around his hazel eyes. He grows leaner and instead of a maroon suit, now he's wearing a pair of burgundy jeans and a plain black t-shirt with running shoes. He looks just a little bit older than me.

"There, is that better? Why are you so young? What's going on?" He goes to touch my elbow and I reflexively snatch it away. The man, now a boy really, gives me a stung look.

I bite at my lip. This person could be the one who cursed us. He's doing a very convincing job acting like he's confused but I know that's all it might be ... *an act.* Why does he smell like the shadow? Why do I instinctively recoil at his touch? If we really had been together for a century and a half (the very thought of which makes my heart lurch with a feeling that I can't even name) and he loves me still (my heart crouches and rolls again at that thought too) then maybe he's trying to settle some kind of score. This boy could *be* the shadow, always watching, waiting for me to be alone.

Of course, I can't be sure. I'm not sure of anything, especially not at this Ball where the music is so loud my ears feel like they might be bleeding. I need proof. I need ... my sisters.

"Flora?" The boy's face gets very serious suddenly. "You're scaring me now. Are you in some kind of trouble? Let's go someplace quiet so we can talk."

The last thing on Earth, or The Undervale or where ever we are... I want is to be alone with this boy. But if he's the one responsible for all of this, well, I don't have many options. I have to confront him, but at least I won't have to do it alone.

"Yes actually," I yelp over the din. "I would like to talk somewhere without this racket. I need to get my sisters though, okay? Don't go anywhere. Wait here." I hold out a single finger, then I hobble over to Ana on the dancefloor. I try to explain, but the music's too loud. Instead, I give Ana a desperate look and yank at her arm. Ana reluctantly follows behind me as I meet up with Etta who's still picking over the food table.

The music is way too loud for a proper conversation, but I corral them into a corner and bring us all into a huddle, muffling the bass with our bodies.

"There's a boy here," I begin. "He says he knows me, that we used to be together, for a really long time."

"What?" Ana exclaims. "Like an ex-boyfriend? Or maybe even husband! Do fairies get married? They must, right?"

I groan loudly enough for her to hear. "Forget about that! Why are you thinking about marriage? Who cares? There is a guy that's being overly familiar with me, and I don't trust him. I think maybe he's the one who cursed us."

Ana sucks in her breath and Etta manages to pull us all even closer. "Why do you think that? What did he say to you?"

"He didn't say anything." I squirm. "I just get a feeling ... and he kind of smells like Longshadow."

"Longshadow has a smell?" Ana yells.

"You never said anything about a smell!" Etta roars even louder.

"Again! Not the point!" I throw up my hands in frustration. "Yes, it has weird Christmas tree scent but there's leather too ... I don't know ... maybe it doesn't. Maybe that part is my brain going haywire. I could be wrong about this boy, who by the way was old when I started talking to him and then he turned himself into our age. It's shady."

"Or not," Ana counters. "Fairies change their faces and ages like we change the channels on TV. You probably made him feel self-conscious. He probably picked up on how skeeved out you were."

"Okay," I huff. "I could be wrong. He could be harmless. But ... he's really concerned about how I am. *Too* concerned, like he's angling for me to admit something."

"Well, maybe he just wants to help," Ana argues, "if you two were together for a really long time ..." My sister trails off.

"Maybe she broke his heart, and he wants to get back at her," Etta says quickly, mirroring my own paranoid thoughts.

Obviously, I'm going to have to take charge, because my sisters didn't see the boy and they don't seem to understand the importance of what's happening here. They're too busy trying to prove how romantic *or* psychotic he may be. "Here's what's going to happen," I say sharply and with as much authority as I can without being too bossy. "He said he wanted to go somewhere quiet to talk and I then I told him I had to get you two. So, once we get him alone- Etta, you take his wand off him."

"Me?" Etta screeches. "Why me?"

"Because you're the smallest and he won't expect you to be so aggressive."

"Have you met me?" Etta asks with a fair bit of sarcasm.

"You are emotionally aggressive, but not physically intimidating," I tell her reasonably.

Etta sucks her teeth loud enough for me to hear the crack over the din of the party. "I wonder how intimidated you'll feel after I punch you in the mouth."

"Stop," Ana hisses. "You *are very* tough, but people don't see that when they look at you. It's an advantage."

"Exactly," I nod my head. "That's what I meant. This boy . . . or whoever he is, has his wand tucked into a holster on his jeans like a gunslinger. It should be easy enough for you to snatch," I tell my sister practically.

"And if I can't and he turns us all into toads or something? What then?" Etta asks crossly.

"Well then, we know for sure that he's an enemy," I rationalize. "If he's a friend, then he'll understand."

"That won't prove anything!" Etta tries to reason. "What if he's just playing along to watch us squirm?"

"I think this is a very stupid plan," Ana pouts. "Why would he curse *all of us* if he was just mad at you? If we turn on him like a pack of wolves, we might be getting rid of the only person in this place who could actually help us."

"It's worth the risk," I counter. "If this really is the fairy who took our wands and our memories, then this could be our chance to confront him. And to be honest I don't care if he turns me into a toad or a goat or an armchair. At least I'd know what I really am. I feel like I'm losing my mind," I admit.

"Fine," Ana says as she begins to break away. "Let's try it your way if you're that desperate."

I don't really care if Ana thinks I'm desperate or if Etta thinks that too, because it's true, *I am*. More and more I feel like a piece of soft wood being whittled away by the knife that is The Undervale. I want an end to it and this boy could be responsible. For everything.

- 15 -

We walk slowly, because that's all my dress will permit. The boy is waiting patiently right where I had asked him to. His face brightens when he sees my sisters.

"Merriweather! You look so beautiful and Fauna of course; that outfit is smashing." I give the boy a funny look. No one uses the word smashing, at least not in this century.

"You wanted to talk?" I lean in and yell close to his ear. The boy nods his head and begins to push his way through the crowd making sure to look back every once in a while, worried I suppose that he might lose us.

The boy takes us to the main entrance of the Manor where there's a very grand staircase with a curling banister that sprawls up either side of the foyer. He begins to climb the stairs to the right, and we dutifully follow him. I was already sweating, given the dress's compression against my skin and now here's another battle. There's no way that I can lift my leg high enough to manage the large steps.

I pull the fabric all the way up to the middle of my thighs and start to walk...sort of..I'm doing a kind of hobbling penguin dance. The situation might be embarrassing if this was the kind of Ball that I had *thought* it was going to be, but Ana had called. This is a blow out.

No one cares about my stupid dress or that it's now just under the crease of my bum. I even have to side-step several couples groping one another on the stairs which makes me turn away and stumble even more. I'm no prude but their ardor seems exceptionally excessive and I have to assume they are getting off on being watched.

This boy I'm following up these ridiculously high steps told me we had been a couple. So, logically I know I'm not a virgin, but I can't remember sex. Even the word -as it floats from my brain and squats on my tongue feels awkward. Those three letters lodge between my teeth and stick there, niggling at me. All of this unbound passion flying around would have made me blush if my cheeks weren't already beet red from the heat and the sheer exhaustion of trying to breathe in my outfit.

The boy leads us down a hallway until he stops in front of a set of ornately carved white and gold gilded doors. He turns the knob and gestures for us to walk through. I catch Etta's eye. As Etta slips by him, she lifts his wand out of the holster with astonishing swiftness and gives him a good push through the doors. Ana rushes to close and lock them.

The boy whips his head around where his empty holster is lodged. He makes a complete circle like a dog chasing its own tail.

"What are you doing?" He exclaims more out of shock than anger. "Merriweather! Give back my wand! I told you, Flora, I don't think this is even remotely funny. If this is some kind of a prank, then I have to say that I've seen seven-year-old humans with more imagination." The boy holds out his hand and then straightens his arm until its rigid, expecting that Etta will give it back.

She doesn't.

"I really must insist," he says with more urgency.

I ignore his pleas and take in our surroundings instead. Although the room is not as vast as the library in the Village, it's very large. There are more books in the myriad of bookshelves than I could ever hope to count. There are also several comfy looking couches with seat cushions as high as my entire forearm, silken rugs, and a roaring fireplace that's so big, I'm pretty sure that all four of us could comfortably stand inside of it.

That being said, I've really had enough of fire. I struggle a bit with the fiddly hook of the cape but finally, I manage to wrestle it away from my shoulders. I kick it off me and the illusion continues burning like a cotton candy bonfire on the rug.

"This is not a prank," I say finally and then, I get an inspired idea. "It's a test. Events have transpired recently which have forced my sisters and I to make sure, uhh . . ." At this point, I'm scrambling. "To make sure that *we* are not the ones being pranked. Right, Fauna?"

"Uh huh," Ana says to the floor. She's a terrible liar. I should have asked Etta.

The young man finally puts his arm down only to close his eyes in frustration. His full lips purse for a moment until he eventually says, "Fine. This is nuts but go ahead."

"What is your name?" I ask hesitantly.

The boy stares at me blankly. He puts both his hands on his hips and his body grows as taught as piano wire. "Foxglove . . . but no one calls me that. It's Fox, Fox Pikepyre."

"And what do you do here in The Undervale? What's your special gift?" I question, while trying to sound as if this is all business when really, I have no idea what I'm going to say until the very moment a sentence leaves my lips.

"What do I do?" Fox laughs meanly. "Okay... Here we go again. Right back where we started. Back at you having a go at me and blaming my job for coming between us. You can be so unbelievably passive-aggressive, Flora." I have no idea how to respond. All I can do is look at him sheepishly. Fox shakes his head in obvious frustration. "You know that I'm a Siphon Administrator. I make sure that all the magic flows where it's supposed to between here and the mortal realm. You know this because we have literally had five hundred arguments about it. Anything else?"

"Yeah, where do you live in The Undervale and where's your house in the mortal realm?" I rush, determined not to react to what is clearly *a situation* between us. So far, Fox doesn't seem all that menacing, and he doesn't appear to be guilty of anything other than annoyance which, all things considered, he has a perfect right to be.

Fairies lie, Lo.

"What do you mean, where do I live? I live here! At Whifflecliff Manor. I've always lived here, and I've never had a house in the mortal realm," Fox snorts. "As you are well aware because 487 of our 500 arguments centered on that very topic."

"Oh, so you live in *this* house?"

Very suspicious. I throw my sisters a quick "told you so look" though neither one reacts. Now that I've got the thread, I intend to unravel it all until he slips up or admits to the truth.

I try and fail to take a full breath before I continue: "You live in this house so it stands to reason that you must know all the secret hiding places? The obscure vaults and hush-hush bolt holes? All the little nooks and crannies that no one else would know so that maybe you could hide something precious?"

"That's it," Fox announces curtly. Without warning, he snatches the wand out of Etta's hand faster than she has time to react. He puts it securely back into his holster and gives it a pat. "Enough. All of you, sit down, right now and tell me what the hell is going on. Have the three of you lost your minds? Has someone cursed you into lunacy?"

The room goes perfectly still except for the fire roaring in the mantle.

Fox used the C word.

He knows.

The dress is squeezing the air out of my lungs. I'm afraid I'm going to faint.

"Wait," Fox says as he scrutinizes each of us carefully. Whatever anger he was carrying drains quickly away. "*Has* someone actually cursed you?"

"Oh please," I manage to say between labored breaths. "You can stop now. It's obviously you. *You* cursed us! We went to see the Oracle of a Thousand Eyes. She told us that one of our wands was hidden in this house—your house. And you also happen to be my ex-boyfriend *and* you smell like the creepy shadow."

I rearrange my spine. I try to get as straight as possible in the hope that my shoulders will take some of the pressure off my waist—and also so that I look the way I absolutely do not feel, like I'm in charge, like I have some kind of authority here. "Now, we might not have any magic but there are three of us and only one of you and we can get to you faster than you can get to your wand, I can promise you that." I tell him in a voice that I wish was much louder. I just can't take in enough air.

Fox gingerly holds up his hands, the way you would approach an animal in distress. "You are quite mistaken, Flora, about all of it. Obviously, you three are scared and upset. If it would make you feel more comfortable to discuss this without me being in possession of my wand, you are free to take it."

I am not about to trust this boy who was a middle-aged man just a few minutes ago and whose name, ridiculously, is Fox.

"All right." I dive in quickly and retrieve his wand. "I will. I'll keep it and you'll tell us the truth right now or I'll break it in half. I swear. If you've done this to us, I'm going to make you pay for it." I am suddenly trembling. My mouth has gone dry. Ana approaches me slowly and closes her own hand over mine, over the one that's holding Fox's wand.

"It's okay, Lo. Just breathe," she coos. "I'll hold onto it if you want."

I pull my hand away by way of an answer. I want to scream. I claw at the fabric circling my abdomen. "It's this dress!" I pant. "I just want it to be off me. It's suffocating me. Is there a zipper or something? Tell me there's a zipper." Ana runs her hand along my back and down my sides.

"I'm sorry, Lo. No zipper. No hooks or buttons either. I suppose they just expect you to zap yourself out of it." Ana tries to console me, but I push her away. I'm not about to let this Fox person see me crumble. Not now.

Fox walks carefully over to the sofa and sits down, but he keeps his palms up and stretches his arms out. He could be surrendering. He could be waiting for an embrace. I look at the negative space he has made with his body and wonder for a moment what it might contain. Love? Contempt? Fury? Maybe there is nothing there at all, just oxygen and history.

"Flora, I do live here but so do about a hundred other fairies. This place, like so many Palaces and Manors in The Undervale are vital to both realms and must be maintained," he explains softly. "And I'll admit to knowing many secrets about this particular residence, but I'm hardly the only one who does. Has someone really cursed you? And your wands are gone? As in, *stolen?*"

My fist jumps to my mouth because I'm afraid I might start sobbing and for some stupid reason I think my hand will be enough to keep this sudden flood of emotion back and it sort of works although I probably look like I'm choking.

I had been so sure that Fox was responsible for this nightmare, but looking at him now, I'm not sure of anything. He seems genuinely worried. My breathing starts to sound like a needle skipping on a record player, quick and ragged. "Flora, please," Fox pleads. "I want to help you, but I can't do that until you tell me what's happened. You can trust me. You have my wand and I'm completely at your mercy. You know how rare it is for us to leave ourselves so vulnerable."

"We've already told you that our wands are missing. It's not like *we* could curse *you*," I argue.

"No, but you could destroy my wand and then what would I do?" Fox manages a smile.

"Are you really trying to say that in the entire history of The Undervale, no one has ever lost their wand? Or been tricked out of it?" Etta asks thoughtfully. I glance over at my sister who looks quite doll-like in her silk dress with the exploding marigolds. It is an excellent question. Surely there must be a way to replace a wand. If I've learned anything over the past couple of days, it's that fairies are not infallible.

"It's possible," Fox shrugs. "But I can't think of a single time that it's happened, until now. Then again, it's not exactly the kind of thing that a fairy is likely to admit to. So, will one of you please tell me what's going on?"

There is something inside of me, some hidden beautiful thing that makes me want to bend for this boy. I'm being naïve; I know I am. I have no recollection of my past. I can't remember a very long lifetime which must have had its fair share of disappointments and cruelty. But who I am now? Lo Smith? *She's* never felt those things, so I'm not nearly cynical enough to distrust him completely. I find myself looking down at my feet so that he can't read my face.

"I'll tell you," Ana says finally.

"Ana," Etta's voice is ripe with warning.

"He didn't curse us. It's in his eyes. He's not capable. Can't you two see that? Just look at him."

I don't want to look. I can barely trust myself, let alone this stranger who claims over a century of affection. If Ana wants to make the rest of the decisions tonight, that's fine with me. I'm exhausted.

Ana sits down on a couch opposite Fox and explains the whole story from start to finish. I grip the boy's wand tightly, running my thumb along its smooth black surface. I know I should give it back but, I feel safer with it in my hand. Not because I'm afraid he'll do something to us if he has it again, but because the weight of it in my palm is oddly reassuring.

When our tale is over, Fox leans back into the couch. He says nothing for a moment or two and I glance at him just long enough to see that he is very obviously ruminating over our dilemma.

"First of all," he says finally, "I agree with Maleficent's interpretation of the wand's location. It's got to be here. Somewhere." His words are a measured mix of melancholy and reluctance.

"Why do you sound like that then?" Etta asks. She's not sitting on the couch but has chosen instead to stand behind Ana. "Like you're a funeral director? Isn't that good news? Shouldn't we be happy that the wand is here?"

"No one has told you why The Undervale exists, right? I doubt Maleficent would bother, and Justy Bluehorn proved particularly cowardly, which is disappointing. I expected better from him. And Ninny, well, she's lovely but she isn't so great with the Big Picture kind of stuff," Fox points out.

Now is the moment.

I'm going to have to choose.

My body suddenly takes the lead; my limbs seem to know what my cautious reasoning can't concede. My posture relaxes as much as it can anyways, considering what my torso is bound in. And even though I hate to admit needing anyone, least of all this stranger, we do. We need him.

"Here," I say as I hand Fox's wand back to him. "I would sit down but that would be impossible. Literally."

Fox takes the wand gratefully and makes a little flick with his wrist. Immediately, I can feel my lungs expand. Somehow, he has loosened the dress and even added a few slits so I can take a seat, which I do, beside Ana. I clutch my hand to my chest and take one blessedly deep inhale.

"Flora." Fox leans over, inching across the distance between us. "You don't know me and that is . . . well . . . it's actually shocking how much that hurts. But I know you. You aren't a confrontational person, except maybe when you're bickering with Merriweather." Fox chuckles softly. "When something happens, you prefer to take a step back and either let the situation resolve itself or you circle around again and deal with who or whatever it is when emotions have cooled. That's why I cannot imagine why anyone would want to curse you . . . any of you. Merriweather, you've always been kind of a loner, preferring the mortal realm to this one and Fauna, everyone loves you. You don't have enemies and believe me, I would know. Gossip is currency in The Undervale and that's why this all so baffling."

"Well," I concede, "I suppose that's good to know. But now that you mention The Undervale, how *does* it work and could there be a connection between how it functions and what happened to us? Is that possible?

Fox's left eye twitches unnaturally, almost like a tic. He bites at his top lip. I can tell that he's wondering how much to tell us, or even possibly to tell us anything at all.

After rubbing his hands down his jeans as if his palms are sweating (I don't think uncursed fairies sweat), he begins to talk:

"This is going to get very confusing. Okay, all three of you feel like you're mortal, right? Prior to Baby showing up on your doorstep, you thought you were just normal teenage girls."

"Correct," Etta answers efficiently.

"You have no memories and no concept of what it means to be a fairy or what The Undervale is."

"That's not a question," I point out. "We've told you what happened. We aren't hiding anything. Ana even mentioned the scary Longshadow. We've left that baby you mentioned so casually with a fairy godmother who seems cool but who could also turn her into a bird, so from now on, let's just move forward with the assumption that we don't know anything about our lives before the curse or the mysteries of The Undervale, okay?"

"I'm just making sure," Fox says rather sternly. "I have to- because there's a lot. The Undervale is complicated and if you had even a single memory of something—anything—it would make it easier."

"Well, we don't," Etta clucks. "Just pretend that we're exactly who we think we are-mortal teenage girls." I glance over at my sister who just offered Fox a great bit of advice, though I think she did it by accident.

"Fine." Fox shakes his head either in sympathy or frustration but likely a combination of both. "If you did remember me, you would know that I don't curse people. Ever. No exceptions. My consciousness or—my brain if we're talking human here—it just doesn't operate in that way. I'm an engineer. I'm not concerned with petty squabbles or intrigue of any kind. The only reason I'm at this Ball is because it's in my home. But this place is not just a home or a Palace. It's something much more."

"What do you mean?" I ask, though I'm not sure I like where this is going.

"All right, how can I put this?" Fox taps a finger on his mouth lightly. "Mortals are responsible for all magic here in The Undervale. Each human being is like a star going supernova, burning bright and then extinguishing forever. The energy they create while burning is so incredible and so intense that it powers our world."

"But" I shake my head in disbelief, "*they* don't have any magic. They're just people and some do live extraordinary lives—"

"Like Marie Curie or RuPaul," Ana interrupts earnestly.

"Right," I continue, cutting her off quickly before she gathers momentum. "But most of them—billions of them—are just regular. They have mortgages and jobs and traffic and middle school ... ordinary is a best-case scenario. A lot of mortals, most actually, really struggle. There's famine, poverty, war ... but no magic."

"Yes, the life of each individual is filled with a rich tapestry of experiences!" Fox says with an excitement that feels inappropriate. "Humans are complex and very powerful. Every emotion they feel expends energy and that energy is flung from them with all the intensity of well, like I said, a collapsing star. Some of it remains in their world but there is so much, too much really, to exist in their realm without causing a tremendous amount of chaos, and so it finds its way here and we harness it. We use it like fuel."

Fox looks at me expectantly as I try to process this tidal wave of information. I wonder…do feelings have an actual shape? They *can* be heavy. Intellectually, an emotion can push and pull; it can weigh you down or buoy you up. But could I hold sadness in my arms? Is happiness a thing I can wrap up like a package and slip into my pocket? Even if I could, how does a thought translate into something real? That I can eat or wear or walk on?

"We can't use every single emotion, obviously." Fox says very matter-of-factly.

"Why not?" Etta asks brusquely. "Why can't every emotion be used if they're all just batteries for The Undervale? Most human beings don't even know what they are really feeling half the time anyways."

"That's the thing, *exactly*." Fox says as if we finally understand. I watch his shoulders slump visibly when he gauges the look on our faces and realizes we are still lost. "Right, well, we don't operate on pain and suffering here. I mean, *we aren't supposed to* because it's so unstable, but personally, I think that whoever cursed you, must have tapped into some of that to create your current situation."

"I know you think that what you're saying sounds perfectly reasonable, Fox, but you're not making much sense to us. Sorry," Ana tells him gently.

"Okay, okay," Fox thinks for a moment. "Take an emotion like anger, in the context of an abusive relationship. The anger that the abuser expends is dark and twisted. When it gets here to The Undervale, we can't get rid of it, because you can't destroy energy- so we lock it away. We put it in a vault- different vaults depending on the exact magnitude and depth and, and..." Fox is struggling. I can see it on his face—his eyebrows are knit together and his hands are moving faster than his lips, "and the texture of that emotion, the true essence of it. Now, when the person being abused finally realizes that they are worth something precious, and they come to understand that they deserve to be happy, well, the anger that *they* eventually feel—the anger that motivates them to change their life—well, that *is* anger that we can use because it's righteous and justified. We take that and we process it and it's either stored for a specific need or it's immediately recycled back to our wands, or the infrastructure needed to keep the lights on in The Undervale, so to speak."

My mouth curves into a slow smile. "So, what you're saying is that the fairy realm is really just a sort of rainbow-colored sparkly garbage dump that some people—like you—have to go in and sort through ... like, pick out all the shit and grime and filth of humanity to find what you think is good and noble."

"Ha!" Fox blurts, "yes, I suppose in a way it is."

"That sounds like a very subjective job," Etta remarks.

I agree with my sister but, it's too big an idea, too overwhelming right now to dive deeper into it. We need to stick to our mission. "And how is Whifflecliff Manor connected to this system, and could that connection be the reason our wands are here?"

"Well, there are vaults and storage facilities on the grounds. Human emotions are scattered in hundreds of Manors, Courts, and Palaces all over The Undervale. Personally, I don't think it has to do with magic or the power grid. My best guess is that this is *my home* and perhaps whomever cursed you assumed you'd never come here, hoping that things were still acrimonious between us."

"Are they?" I wonder what a bad breakup even looks like in The Undervale. My guess is, pretty awful.

"No, it took a little while- I'm not going to lie. But we made our peace with one another and the situation." Fox says with sincerity. "However, unlike most fairies, we kept things private. I have a feeling that whoever cursed you was counting on pettiness, betting that I would never help you, because you'd never find a wand here on your own. There are a lot of places that your nemesis could have hidden it . . . hundreds, if I'm being honest," Fox tells us sympathetically.

"Great," Etta sighs deeply.

"Now, now don't get discouraged," Fox says as brightly. "Just let me think for a minute. If I wanted to hide a wand, where would I do that? Well, there's Miss Curio's Cabinet. It's a sort of locker for enchanted items we give to humans and then after they die, the ownership reverts back to us. But Miss Curio is a meticulous record keeper. Nothing gets past her. She would know if a wand was concealed in her sanctum. She would have felt it. And since she hates when things aren't in their proper place, it's probably not there."

"Unless she was the one who cursed us," I throw out.

"Oh no, no." Fox waves his hand in opposition. "She hasn't left her post in half a millennium. I'm not sure that you've ever even met her. The ideal place would be the Sea of a Billion Tears but that's in Thistledown Palace, I mean, that's where I would stash it, but the wand is in *this* manor..." Fox taps a single finger on his chin. "The Hall of Stone Regrets, that's a possibility."

"I gotta say… the fairy realm is a real downer," Etta observes with a sniff. "Isn't there a Room Of Happy Laughter? Or a Lounge Of Dancing Kittens?"

"Of course. There are repositories like that," Fox tells her almost dismissively. "But given what Fauna told me about where you found the first wand, I'd wager that whoever did this to you isn't going to make retrieving the others a fun or easy experience."

"Unfortunately," I admit, "I think you're right. So, what other awful places can you think of that are here in the house?"

"There's the Mermaids' Waystation and it does connect via a duct to the Sea of a Billion Tears but mermaids, although technically fairies, don't associate with fairies like us if they can help it. They're snobs really."

"Yeah," Etta drawls, "I can see that."

"Well, I can't," Ana looks back at Etta with a frown. "I think it would be lovely to meet a mermaid. Their tails would be so beautiful, and they would glide through the water like dolphins."

"Do us all a favor, Fauna." Fox leans in and nods his head. "If you do meet a mermaid, don't *ever* compare them to a dolphin. Alright, there's the Chamber of Tattered Tarots but that's just a room full of cards really. Once a Tarot Deck has been worn out, it slips into The Undervale. They have a way of arranging themselves in the most delicate of structures and although there is a rather unsettled feel about the room, it wouldn't be much of a trial to search. I think we can scratch that one off the list."

"Sure," I nod as if Fox's observations are completely reasonable. As if a room full of forlorn tarot cards that prop themselves up on their own is normal and not even worth considering. I bring a thumb up to my mouth and bite at a hangnail. I catch Fox watching me. It unnerves me that he must know this is one of my bad habits and I force my hand back to my lap.

"There's the Closet of Agonies," Fox suggests.

"Oh wow," Ana's eyes grow wide. "What horrible thing is that?"

"It's actually not as bad as it sounds. It's an odd place really. It's a proper closet with heaps upon heaps of little shards and scraps of fabric. Every human has a best day and a worst day and somehow, a little fragment of whatever that person is wearing on both those days ends up in The Undervale. Those scraps are rewoven into bolts of fabric, paper and yarn that we use in both realms. They become very powerful pieces of magic."

I snort loud enough to make Ana give me a light smack. "Sorry. It's just . . . that makes no sense. I can sort of understand why a little chunk of clothing from someone's absolute best day would find its way here . . . sort of. But if you can't use bad stuff, why would the clothes from their worst day end up here too?"

"Because people are remarkable. Because even when the most terrible things happen—things that force them to believe life isn't worth living, that all there is to their world is suffering—eventually, more often than makes any sense at all, people find a way to carry on. And that awful thing, whatever it was, can turn into hope and strength and a kind of grace. For example, a woman finds out that she can never bear children of her own and then she adopts a baby that would otherwise grow up motherless. That moment when her doctor gave her the news felt like the most terrible day of her life, but time always changes the color and weight of a fabric like that. It never looks the same as the day it arrives."

"I love that example. There are so many ways to be a mom. The Closet is probably a very good place to hide the wand," Ana notes. "I mean, if there's just endless piles of material everywhere and they're already separated. Clawing through the Terrible, Horrible, No Good, Very Bad Day fabric would be unpleasant, but doable."

"Yes, in theory." Fox tilts his head from one side to the other as he considers it. "But they aren't organized into good and bad. It doesn't work that way. There's a lot of joy mingling with that sadness and pain. Like humans, it's messy and complicated. Whoever did this to you, they want to terrorize you. They want to make you feel wretched. I don't think it's as simple as finding something in a good hiding spot. I think it would be more."

"Well," I sigh, grateful at the very least that I can sigh, that the dress isn't suffocating me. "The Hall of Stone Regrets, that sounds pretty miserable. Any other spots we can look forward to enduring?"

"The Strong Room of Stolen Seconds—that place is very intense, and the Mine of Whispered Secrets is extremely dark."

"Dark because it's a mine or because it's bad?" I ask hesitantly.

"Both. It's worth investigating, certainly, but I suggest we leave it till last. There's no point in going down there unless we absolutely have to. We'll start with the Hall of Stone Regrets." Fox nods his head assertively and gets up off the couch.

"Now?" I stand too, though I'm not sure why. It must have been a reflex because as much as I want to find the wand, I'm in no hurry to experience any of the rooms that Fox has mentioned. They all sound equally horrendous. "Shouldn't we wait for the party to be over?"

"Why?" Fox asks, looking confused. "The revelry won't be anywhere near where we're going, I can assure you."

I remain on my feet even though what I really want to do is go back and flop down on Fox's extremely comfortable sofa. I run my tongue over my lips which feel tender and chapped from all the biting and licking I've done to them. I hate this. I don't want to go to any rooms or caverns with names that involve Agony or Tears.

Sisters ... they always know.

I feel Ana grab one of my hands and Etta tugs on the other as if to say, we're scared too, but we've got this. I smile at them gratefully. We really don't have a choice. What we do have are loyal sisters who will stand beside each other no matter what. Despite everything else that's happened or is about to happen, I know how lucky I am to have them. I'm ready to start looking.

- 16 -

We follow Fox down a vast carpeted hallway as thick and lush as red velvet cake. He thrusts open a door, and we trudge down a single floor on a spiral staircase. Fox opens yet another door with a key that's half as long as a table leg with a bow as thick as my fist. He pulled it out from his pocket with what I assume must be magic, like Hermione Granger's purse or Mary Poppins's carpet bag.

The keys keep coming and it's door after door, four of them in all. We creep across a small corridor, dimly lit by tiny floating globes. I try to imagine how big this place is, but I can't get my head around it. It occurs to me that in another lifetime, when I was properly Flora Bloomshade, I would have known my way around the Manor. I would have spent time here with Fox. I might have had keys of my own. My heart turns over like the starter on a rickety outer board engine—flooding and stalling and sputtering, unable (or more likely unwilling) to catch the spark.

Another set of stairs ends abruptly in front of a tall metal door with golden studs and silver bolts. It's so big and wide that a stampede of elephants would surely fit through with room to spare. I suppose it makes sense, as much as anything does in this place. Fox had said our first stop (and hopefully only stop) was a Hall. Halls are generous spaces. People go to concerts at Halls and receptions and charity functions too.

I know for a fact that this particular Hall will not be like a concert.

Fox pulls at the latch. The doors swing wide open, and I gasp, bringing a hand to my chest as if I'm some sort of delicate Southern Belle. Which I am not. *At all.* But I can't help it. This isn't just a Hall; it's a warehouse, two warehouses. The space is so cavernous, I feel like a little mouse.

"What *is this*, Fox?" Etta asks dubiously as she walks over and points to a plinth about half her height. Atop the plinth is a marble statue which looms over my tiny sister. The alabaster stonework is that of a girl but it looks...odd. Her carved eyes are contemplative, and her slim fingers are lifted above her mouth as if she's just about to say something but is too afraid to speak. "She looks so real," Etta trails off as she stares at the thousands of similar statues in various heights around the room. "They all do."

I gulp as I take a step backwards. "Fox . . . oh my God . . . Were these actual people?" I ask in horror. "Did you turn them to stone!?"

"What?" Fox's hazel eyes narrow. Ana, Etta, and I instinctively form a tight knot with our hands and arms. "No. Of course not! How could you think I would do something like that?"

"Because I don't know you and this is your house and these—whatever these are—are so disturbing that I feel like I might throw up!" I exclaim dramatically.

"I agree, they *are* disturbing, but it's not what you think." Fox steps toward us and we collectively lean back. "There is a lot of pain in this Hall, which is why I suggested we come here. It's not comfortable to be around these things. It makes my skin crawl too, but isn't that the point?"

"Why do they look so life-like though?" Finally, my voice is sounding stronger now. I'm getting over the shock of them, which is very different than being used to them. That is never going to happen.

"They aren't people exactly. I mean . . . This is frustrating." Fox balls his fists and releases them quickly. "When a human being is faced with a crisis or conflict, they have three universal reactions: fight, flight, or freeze. There are times when doing nothing—or 'freezing'—is the most evolved solution. I would even go so far as to say that if more humans made the decision to not react, their realm would be filled with far less strife." Fox strides over to a shorter statue of a young boy. His eyes are covered by the crook of his elbow and his shoulders are hunched up and slightly turned, as if he's shielding his body.

Fox rubs his thumb over the boy's carved toes. "However, sometimes, these instances of inaction are so traumatic, so filled with grief and shame that they morph into a sort of shellshock. And then, that actual moment hardens around the human, creating such a powerful impression—a mold, if you will—that it turns into a physical manifestation of the experience, which in turn creates these statues. The people represented here, for all intents and purposes, are trapped in this choice, even if it was the only one available to them, and in the mortal realm, they are still unable to move past it."

"So, they aren't alive inside the stone? You're sure this isn't actually a real person?" I dare to walk a little closer to another statue of a tall, thin man with his head bowed. "You couldn't wave your wand over them and unfreeze them?"

"Absolutely not," Fox declares in such an offended tone that I'm guessing even to suggest such a thing is unseemly. "We are merely guardians of this process, because the most interesting thing about the Hall of Stone Regrets is not the sculptures. It's that the inventory changes every day. A statue might be here for a dozen years and then suddenly . . . poof! It's gone. The mortal has finally been able to move forward past that moment. Or they die and death brings them the peace they weren't granted in life."

"That's sad," Ana says as she rolls her neck to examine a statue woefully. "At least the dying part."

"Yes, it is sad," Fox agrees. "But as I said, humans are complicated, and they aren't given much time to process these moments because their lives are so short compared to ours. I am humbled every single time I watch a statue disappear and I always hold out hope they were able to do it in their lifetime." Fox sighs contemplatively. "Anyhow, there are a great many statutes in the Hall. We should split up and start looking for the wand immediately. Try not to focus on the sculptures themselves, particularly on their faces. It can be very disconcerting. Focus instead on the bases and the plinths. Look for any evidence that they've been tampered with or any unusual seams that might lead to hidden compartments." Fox gives each of us a quadrant to search and strict instructions to meet him at the front doors in two hours.

I'm not thrilled with the idea of separating from Ana and Etta, but Fox has a point. There are thousands of frozen figures in the hall, and we need to be smart with our time. The giant space is unnervingly quiet. I hear not only my own footsteps- the clickity clack of my heels on the slate floor, but the echoes of my sisters' shoes as well.

The stillness is to be expected. The statues loom in their ominous state of petrification but the air too, is like a vacuum. There's not a mote of dust or a speck of dirt. My fingers reach and begin to explore the bases of the statues. They dance along every edge and corner hoping to find something more extraordinary than the pieces they are holding up. Out of habit, I inspect my hands after each plinth, expecting a grimy film but they are always immaculately clean.

Fox warned me not to look at them, which let's be honest, was a tacit invitation to do so. I'm not much of a rule breaker but I am extremely curious. Once I glance up at the folds of sock that have slipped halfway down a smooth and flawless alabaster calf, there's no going back. The figures are a grotesque menagerie of despair. Some reach, some crouch, and others blanche. Though their eyes are colorless and carved, they retain their expressions of panic and sorrow.

After a short while, I start to feel like I'm carrying their weight with me, as if I have collected each of the mammoth pieces and strapped them on my back. My shoulders hunch and I have to steady myself with one base and use its momentum to push me to the next one. I make a meticulous search of each one I come across, despite the ever-increasing pain pushing into my spine, but there is no hidden wand.

By the time I'm close to finishing my section, I am desperate to run. It's not just the hopeless energy that radiates off each statue, which is enough on its own to keep me in tears. It's something much worse. I feel like I'm being watched, which given the circumstance isn't all that surprising. There are tens of thousands of eyes in the Hall. But the intensity of the gaze I feel crawling up and down my arms is far more sinister than that of fixed stone.

I know it the moment Longshadow is here.

I make a perfect circle with my lips and exhale slowly until the air in my lungs is gone. I am standing in the middle of a testament to suffering. My fear isn't special. My circumstance, though unique, could be much worse as the evidence all around me attests to it.

And in the midst of all this pain and hopelessness, I find a kind of clarity. After I had seen the shadow that day in the woods, ever since I had let my curious nature take the lead and snapped its photo, something shook loose; it's just taken me a while to feel it. Capturing Longshadow on film has given me an advantage. If the creature has been spying on me for years without me knowing or even realizing, well, the jig is up. There's still a chance that Longshadow has nothing to do with the curse at all, that it's just some strange being of The Undervale, some malformed and perverted mortal echo that wasn't trapped in one of Fox's vaults. But I doubt it.

Whatever it is, I will not let it trap me like one of these statues. I will run or I will fight, but I will not hide under the covers again like

I did at Maleficent's. Longshadow doesn't get to dictate the movement of my limbs any longer.

Although I am quite self-satisfied by this new-found moxie, it has nothing to do with why I am here in the first place. Sadly, the four of us meet up at the appointed time but we are all empty-handed. There is no wand here.

I should be exhausted; we should all be dead on our feet, but I feel an abundance of energy. And by the lively look of the rest of the search party, it must be the same for them. I don't ask because my ignorance is becoming embarrassing, but I suspect that the hosts of the Ball have spiked the air with some kind of magical adrenaline so they can keep partying through till the morning. I feel entirely too alert and there's no way it's natural. I only have to look at Etta for further proof. Etta should be catatonic by now.

I don't like the idea that I've been drugged. Well, that's not entirely true. I don't really care if the fairies have a way of boosting our energy and keeping us all alert and awake. What I take offense to is not being given the choice. More and more I'm being herded into a single direction without any kind of say as to where I'm going or why. I know without a doubt that Flora Bloomshade would never let anything like that happen, but I am not Flora, not yet. I'm only Lo Smith and Lo, even as determined as savvy as she is, has very little power. Instead of feeling ashamed of this loss, I decide to embrace my powerlessness, because it's the only thing apart from the love of my sisters that I know to be absolutely true. Maybe acknowledging the loss of my power is the only way I can find it again.

I refuse to be like these statues of pain and misfortune. I'm well aware that everything is on the line and even though I might want to, I cannot afford to freeze.

- 17 -

"Well, that was a bust," Fox chuckles. "Get it? Because the wand wasn't there and the statues . . ." Fox's voice trails off. We're in no mood for humor and given that we're teenagers, it's not like we'd think Fox's Dad jokes are funny. To his credit, Fox just shrugs it off. "Right, well, I suggest we move on to the Strong Room then."

He guides us out the door, up four more floors, and across a wide mezzanine. The vibrating thrum of the bass from the party makes the portraits that hang on the walls bounce up and down. I fight the urge to straighten them as I pass, even though it makes my fingers fidget and pulls my ears toward my shoulders in irritation.

We are shepherded to yet another staircase; this one is much narrower. We can only go down in a single file and my bare shoulders brush up against the plaster ever so slightly. Fox takes us through another doorway which leads to a shabby looking hall.

I stare at Fox's back. I can't imagine that he and I had shared not just one but two lifetimes together. We had squabbled, probably over silly things like what to have for dinner or what color to paint a wall. We had given each other thousands of kisses. We had embraced and cuddled. We had shared a bed. I can't wrap my head around it, just as I'm sure Fox is finding it difficult to accept that to me, he is a stranger.

I am beginning to realize that in The Undervale, not only are many things possible, but many things are also true at the same time. There's never a single side of the story or an absolute color, which is probably true for the mortal realm as well, though on a much smaller scale.

Fox approaches a door that is small and squat. The wood is painted in vertical black and white stripes. He doesn't knock or ring a bell. He just walks right through and motions for us to do the same. Inside, a woman sits at a tidy desk and although her hair is a riot of rainbow colors, it's pinned severely back in place. Her hooded eyes are so brown that they are almost black and her nose so hooked that the tip of it ends at the top of her pursed lips. When she sees Fox enter, she scrambles to her feet. She's a tiny thing with thin wrists and a long neck that looks disproportionate to the rest of her slight frame.

"Good evening, Miss Speckledove," Fox says pleasantly. "I see you've decided to skip the party."

"I'm sorry, Your Grace. You know I don't go in for that sort of thing but if you would like me in the ballroom, I can go right away." Miss Speckledove's voice is both raspy and high and she flaps her arms nervously.

"Your Grace? Why is she calling you 'Grace'?" I'm bewildered.

"Some of us don't feel comfortable taking liberties, Miss Bloomshade," the woman declares snootily. "Some of us believe in protocol and tradition."

"What is she talking about, Fox? What's going on?" I demand. Miss Speckledove shoots me a look of outrage.

"Well I . . ." Fox stammers. "I didn't think it was so important. I am, first and foremost, a siphon administrator but I am also the Duke of Pikepyre. I didn't tell you because you were already so freaked out when you realized that I lived here, I figured that my title would just complicate things even more."

"Well, yeah," I shoot back, "but when we finally understood, you could have said something. *You lied.*"

"I didn't lie."

I fold my arms, one over the other and look him up and down. "A lie of omission is still a lie. You don't think it was worth mentioning that the reason this is your house is because you're the boss of everyone? That this entire place belongs to you and you're not just a tenant?" Fox gulps. "It *is* yours, right? Because a duke is just below a prince."

Actually, I have no idea if this is true. I am basing this solely on TV shows and bodice-ripping books. In The Undervale, every other fairy could be a duke. *I* could be a duke.

"I see that you are just as impertinent as ever, Miss Bloomshade," squawks the lady with the giant rainbow hair.

"Don't say another word about my sister, lady," Etta warns with her wand out. Miss Speckledove's tiny nostrils flair but sure enough, she leans away from Etta.

It's mean spirited, but I'm getting a kick out of watching Etta make that annoying prig of a fairy squirm.

"Technically, yes, as much as a Manor can actually belong to anyone. But this house is literally alive. I'm a guardian, not an owner. You can't really own a dwelling in The Undervale. It would be like keeping a slave."

"Which we don't do anymore, thanks to you and your modern politics," Miss Speckledove says directly to me in a voice that's as pinched as a puckered seam.

Well, *that's* interesting.

Slaves.

Obviously, Maleficent didn't get the memo, but if I stopped human trafficking in The Undervale, *that* could have gotten me cursed. Easily.

"I think you're probably a terrible person," Ana tells Miss Speckledove gruffly. Gruff for Ana anyhow. Etta looks like she's about to rip out the woman's throat.

"I'm not a person, I'm a fairy," she shoots back snootily.

"Let's just get back on track. Fox, come on. You know our . . ." I sneak a peek at Miss Speckledove, "predicament. You asked us to trust you and we did. How are we supposed to believe anything you say now?" There is a tense but silent exchange between us, filled with a history that I can't understand, and that Fox holds close. It's disorienting to us both.

"I don't think it really matters, Lo," Ana finally says in a gentle tone. "He never said he wasn't a Duke and given that he is one, he's probably the perfect person to be . . . taking us on this tour," she says deftly, well aware of our audience. "Let it go."

I tut softly. I guess it's not such a terrible transgression. And I had just been thinking about how more than one thing can be true at the same time. Fox is my ex-boyfriend *and* a Duke. There could be worse situations.

"Fine, let's just look for the—" I turn my head to glance at Miss Speckledove who has her arms perched on her hips and a very unpleasant look on her face. "The thing that we're looking for."

"Yes," Fox plays along. "Excellent idea. Miss Speckledove, we'll be going in now."

"Oh no, sir!" The woman practically bounds around her desk. "It's almost midnight. You wouldn't want to be in there at midnight, sir. I've spent over two thousand years training myself to withstand it. It would be most unpleasant for you." I notice how Miss Speckledove's concern doesn't seem to extend to me or my sisters.

"We're not here for a casual stroll. Hopefully, we'll conclude our business before the clocks strike. Thank you, Miss Speckledove." Fox grabs Ana's arm and pulls her toward the small arch. Etta and I follow despite Miss Speckledove's frenzied objections.

When I dip inside, I'm amazed to see that the space is the size of a supermarket. It even has aisles- though there aren't any cans of tomato soup or lightbulbs here. There aren't any shelves at all. Instead, each aisle is separated by floor-to-ceiling walls and on every surface of every wall, is a clock.

There are cuckoo clocks and digital clocks, moon-faced nursery clocks and sleek chrome clocks with hands as sharp as needlepoints. The sound is tremendous. Each clock is set to the same precise second and they all tick together in perfect synchronicity. I've never heard anything like it. My body begins to shudder with each tick-tock heartbeat that pounds with the intensity of an earthquake.

"What is this place?" I ask in wonder. "I know what you've called it- but is that what it is exactly? Just stolen seconds?"

"Yes, in a way," Fox says with a sudden strain in his voice. He begins to search the clocks on the wall in a frenzied rush. "Time is a human construct and fairies aren't bound to its earthly limits, but we must work inside its perimeters. Fairies will often gift humans more time—an hour, a day, sometimes years even. But those moments aren't really ours to give, per se." Fox moves to a different clock, this one is gold and has a band of rubies and emeralds imbedded on its face. He begins to circle the tiny, jeweled masterpiece with his hands, searching, I suppose, for the wand. "So, we sort of borrow the time from here."

"But where is here?" I'm starting to get frustrated. The ticking is invading my bones, rattling my organs. I try and fail to muffle the sound by plugging my ears.

"I really wish you would stop asking questions and help me look. We should all spread out, as we did in the Hall. We haven't got much time."

"Just wait." I step in front of him. "In case we get trapped here, in case something happens, I think my sisters and I should know exactly where these clocks come from."

"Very well," Fox offers reluctantly as he runs a hand through his luxurious brown hair. "Fairies will often punish despicable humans by stealing time from them. Every chunk of time they steal becomes a clock. When a fairy wants to gift time to a mortal, this is where they get it from, from one of these clocks."

"So, it's just bad people then? That the fairies steal from?" Ana asks hopefully.

"Of course not," Etta answers in a snit. "Haven't you learned *anything* by being around these ... these people? Any human that does the smallest little thing could be seen as an insult to a fairy. A person who cuts them off in their car. A person who talks inside a movie theater. It doesn't take much, does it, Fox?"

"You seem to know an awful lot about fairies for a person who claims to be a seventeen-year-old mortal girl," Fox snaps back.

"I don't know anything besides what I've seen, and I've seen quite a bit since Maleficent told us the truth," Etta tells him imperiously.

"I don't interact very often with humans," Fox tells her plainly. "And I'm certainly not going to be held accountable for what other fairies do. That isn't my job. My job is to oversee fairies like Miss Speckledove and she oversees the maintenance of the clocks. Now please, we must hurry."

"Of course, your Grace, I apologize for not moving as fast as you want me to," Etta counters icily.

"Stop it, Etta," I warn. "Fox is right. He can't control what other fairies do any more than we could control Maleficent." At that, Fox laughs outright. Etta raises an eyebrow, unconvinced, but the only thing I can afford to care about is checking the clocks, despite all the racket they are making.

"There are sixteen rows which is convenient because there are four of us," Fox remarks. "I'll take the first four rows and Flora; you take the next and so on. I'm not trying to be all high and mighty, Etta, but we really need to move." Before my sister can get another jab in, Fox runs to the farthest end of the room. I take my cue from him and follow quickly. Etta and Ana march off to their assigned rows and begin to search.

Midnight looms, and despite Miss Speckledove's dire warnings, I have no idea what this means or what will happen.

Typical.

Threats and omens are dished out like candy in The Undervale, but real consequences are always less forthcoming. With an eye on the time, I start to look. Luckily, each clock is mounted with an easily accessible ring and hook. There's a ladder on wheels along each wall that I take to with gusto.

I make a study of the first four or five clocks. I'm impressed by the craftsmanship and practically hypnotized by the enormous size of the jewels that adorn the more ornate ones. Thankfully, the novelty wears off in short order and eventually, all the clocks start to look the same. I realize it's easier to pick up each one, give it a shake, and then move on to the next as opposed to examining the faces for hidden seams or compartments. The wand would rattle. Even if the fairy who hid it has changed its size and shape, it would still be an object that doesn't belong.

I get through one aisle and then another. I make it all the way to the third aisle until I notice that it's almost midnight. I replace a square bronze clock gently as I watch the hands move. There are only five more seconds to go. I quickly grab the next clock; it's relatively small and made of wood. The numbers are hand-painted in bright turquoise. Miss Speckledove was just trying to scare us. There are a few cuckoo clocks here, so what if they all chirp at once?

Tick. Tick. Tick.

Miss Speckledove and her two thousand years of training. What kind of a person manages to work something like that into a conversation unless they are doing the whole humble brag thing?

Tick. Tick. ..

At precisely twelve, the clocks go off. The sound is so shocking and intense that I stumble off the ladder. The small wooden clock crashes onto the floor, exploding with tiny copper lights that look like a plume of glittering persimmon fruit flies.

There are chimes and beeps and cuckoos and sirens. I am sideways on the ground. The tiles bounce up with each chime and pound into my temple. I drag my knees up to my chest and cover my eardrums with the flat of my hands. The careening wail goes on and on. The noise changes the air. It is so dense and so spectacularly deafening that it invades my nose and mouth all the way to my lungs, filling them with the viscous, cloying howls of the midnight clocks.

I tremble and sweat and get up on all fours because I think I'm going to be sick. I brace myself for it and then mercifully, the room goes silent. I'm panting when I put my forehead on the cool slate of the tiles that are now mercifully still. The keening has stopped but only technically. My ears are ringing like I've been hurled from a percussive blast. I can hear something above the clambering in my head but it's garbled nonsense.

I feel a slight tap on the shoulder. I look up and see that it's Fox. His mouth is moving, and I struggle to understand. All I can do is point at my ears and wince. Fox nods his head back and forth encouragingly and gestures toward the aisles. He holds up his pointer finger, which I'm guessing means he only has one more aisle to search.

"Okay!" I scream and wave him off with my hand. I should probably check on my sisters but that will only waste time and I am desperate to get out of here. I don't know if that nightmare was just a midnight thing, or an hourly occurrence and I don't have it in me to find out. I drag myself up to standing.

At least there's one thing to be grateful for—I'm back in my street clothes. Both Ninny and Igni's glamour has worn off and I have never been so thrilled to be in jeans. I race from one clock to the next, shaking each one with increasingly furious speeds. I sense through my palms, hoping that I will feel a vibration or rattle on my skin.

I despise this room. The clocks . . . they are devils. Miss Speckledove is obviously in league with the wretched things. The woman is a snob and a sycophant. She had been so venomous toward me that I wouldn't be surprised at all if Miss Speckledove herself had cast the curse, especially if she blames me for ending slavery in The Undervale. Does she have it in her? This wild, imaginative curse with tentacles attached to every inch of our lives? She might. She's obviously in love with Fox and she hates me. She's also had thousands of years to plot and plan and scheme.

I shake the last of my clocks with renewed vigor, determined to catch the wily Miss Speckledove out, but infuriatingly, there is nothing. I climb down the ladder and race to the entrance. Fox's hands are empty as are Etta's. When Ana finally arrives, she does so without a wand and my heart sinks. I was certain this was the place.

I make sure my sisters are all right via pantomime. They're okay but like me, can barely hear. Even though the sound is finally draining out of my ears, I worry that it will never truly go away, that it will somehow remain, hovering in every quiet moment. I'm afraid that I will never truly know the utter beauty of silence again.

When we walk past Miss Speckledove, she's all aflutter. The rainbow-haired fairy clutches at Fox's bicep and lets loose a litany of words that gush out of her thin lips. He tries to assure her, albeit very loudly, that he's fine but she doesn't want to let him go. Her pleading face, her cloying hands . . . without even thinking, I push her back, pressing my fingers into the sharp angles of her collar bones. I do not speak, and my sisters are silent too. My hands are itching, flexing and unflexing.

I want to do something else.

I *would* have done something else had I been able to grab what my arms are reaching for. My wand is a phantom limb.

All I can do is look at her so intently and with such ferocity that Miss Speckledove actually flinches. I may or may not be royal, but I am definitely a triplet and as far as anyone else knows, it isn't wise to get on the wrong side of the Bloomshade sisters because we are blood related in a place where beings are made and not born.

Even I know that blood is a powerful thing.

Fox walks out the door as does Etta and Ana, but I remain. I give Miss Speckledove a final, steely look before leaving. When Miss Speckledove is sure that Fox is out of eyesight, she returns my glare, but it lacks the moral vigor of my own.

Definitely a suspect.

Fox leads us briskly away to the stairwell. No one says a word. The echo of the clocks are dimming but they are still in my head. He probably wants to get us as far away as possible and I'm in perfect agreement. We walk down a single flight and then through a door which leads us back into a far corner of the party.

This time, I barely register the music. It's nothing compared to what I'd just heard. I do notice the revelers making way for Fox. The crowd splits in the middle like soft paper torn in half. Some of the guests bow or curtsey. Fox gives them a benevolent nod but remains purposely strident across the room.

Begrudgingly, I've got to admit that Ana had been right. Fox is the best person to help us in our quest. I can't help but find this fact in and of itself to be highly suspect. Then again, since Em laid the truth on us, I find pretty much everything to be suspect. I'm becoming a conspiracy nut. Is that even possible? I'm way too young to be pathologically paranoid, except that I'm not young at all. My face is a lie, and my memories are false. I get a sudden pang of jealously when I watch the other fairies dancing with such absolute abandon. I wish I could say it's the curse that has me wound so tightly but I know it isn't. Ana had danced like that. I don't think I have it in me. Maybe I am and always will be the sort of person who can never just let it all go.

Ana is an optimist. Etta a realist who leans towards the negative. They are at opposite poles of a map that I'm not even on. Neither one of my sisters care about how others perceive these traits in them, but I am not as confident. I lug around a constant fear that I am being misunderstood or judged unfairly. Maybe this is why Longshadow is drawn to me and not them. It can sense how shallow I am, and that's what's been attracting it to me like a magnet. A shadow is a just a flicker after all. It has no depth and certainly no dimension.

I really hope that these negative thoughts I'm having about myself belong to Lo Smith and not Flora Bloomshade. Flora Bloomshade has to be infinitely cooler and way less self-conscious than Lo Smith. Flora has magic! She's thousands of years old! Her ex-boyfriend is a super hot Duke fairy with a big fat job and an even bigger house!

I want to go on imaging what I'm going to be like when I get back to my real self, but it's hard to focus on anything right now when my eardrums are still ringing from ten thousand bells. I swivel my head and decide that I should just concentrate on where Fox is taking us. It is too late, or . . . too early for this kind of self-reflection. We end up kitty corner to another door in the ballroom.

We had spent the past few hours searching in places that were more nightmarish than *actual* nightmares. Now Fox is taking us somewhere else, somewhere he had saved as a last resort. For a brief second, I consider bolting. I think about running home and getting into my bed, not to sleep. I don't think I'll be able to sleep for a week. I just want refuge, even if it's only for what remains of the night. My ears are aching, and my head feels heavy.

But . . .

Ana is on Fox's heels like a dog with a bone and Etta has reached across and touched her wand dozens of times already and that's just this evening alone. I can't let my sisters down. And so, even though a knot of increasing dread and worry worms its way around my gut, I keep going to whatever horror is coming next.

- 18 -

"Sorry about this!" Fox yells.

I lean over his shoulder and try to see what he's apologizing for. We're in a small room with a door at the end of it. I grit my teeth at what I think could be behind it. I take Ana's hand as Fox opens it and what I see is . . . nothing . . . just a room with another door. Fox moves to it swiftly, opens it, and again, we're in *another* small anteroom with yet another door. I know it's not some kind of fairy trick because each room we enter is different. Some are smaller, others a bit larger. One is shocking pink, and another has wallpaper with tiny woodland skeletons in various tableaus that are creepy and fascinating. Altogether, we go through eleven doors until finally we hit a stairwell. I move forward, towards the steps, but Fox gently places his index finger on the top of my wrist to stop me.

"First of all, is everyone all right?" he asks loudly, but he isn't screaming, and I can hear him clearly. At least there's that.

"I wouldn't say I was all right," Etta snaps. "I wouldn't go so far as to say that."

"No," I respond curtly, "you wouldn't say anything remotely positive, would you? For once I wish you would just lighten up."

"I'm just supposed to say that everything is fine when that stupid room with the clocks nearly gave me brain damage? Is that what you want?" Etta yelps.

Ana immediately gets in between us. "Etta, things are bad enough. Please don't make them worse by giving everyone attitude." I smirk with righteousness until Ana turns on me. "And Lo, you need to give Etta a break. She's allowed to feel however she wants. You can't police our feelings." Etta chuckles but stops when Ana pokes her in the shoulder.

"I am going to assume by that exchange that no one was hurt too badly? Obviously, the pain lingers but are you three okay to move on?" Fox asks but, the *way* he does makes me cringe a little. We're being silly. We're being teenagers. And I'm afraid that the younger we seem, the less information Fox is likely to give to us. "We're okay," I tell him resolutely. "That was quite an experience. But honestly? I can't believe you didn't get us out of there before midnight. We could have just come back ... you know ... after the clocks went off and resumed the search."

Fox lets out a breath making a noise that's somewhere between a sneer and a groan. "Well, since honesty is the word of the day, I must admit that I had no idea it would be so bad. I'm ashamed. The Strong Room is in my purview, and I *should* have known. But Miss Speckledove has a flair for the dramatic and I always assumed that she was exaggerating about the intensity of the clocks as a way of puffing up her own importance, which was not very nice of me. That poor woman has had to deal with that room day after day and I've been so dismissive of her. I plan to correct that and find her an adequate assistant."

"Well, that's... good?" I respond tentatively. Miss Speckledove's mean little eyes and harsh words are the last thing I want to think about. "I say we just leave the whole clock thing in the past where it belongs. I can see why you thought it might be there, even without the chimes—it's an awfull place...all that non-stop ticking, ugghh. But the wand wasn't there so, let's just move on." I go to walk down the dark staircase and once again, Fox stops me.

"This place," Fox gestures to the steps, "it's not like the other two. The Mine of Whispered Secrets is, well . . ." Fox rubs his temples with his thumb and forefinger and exhales loudly.

"I think the word Whisper being in its name it is already a bonus at this point," I say trying to lighten the mood with a chuckle. "You know . . . because of the other room . . . with all the clocks and the big booooooooongs . . . ." I stretch my fingers out, jazz hands doing fireworks. Fox stares at me bleakly.

"Come on," I nudge, trying to stay positive. "Okay, secrets . . . whispers . . . let me guess. It's a cavernous chamber where all the secrets that every human has ever kept in the history of humanity is stored. Is that what it is? Is that it?"

I'm smiling. I do not know why I'm smiling.

"Not quite. Secrets aren't necessarily bad. Let's say you love someone, but you don't say anything; you don't tell them because you're afraid of being rejected. That's a common enough experience and the secret eventually fades and becomes a memory—a little sad, but harmless. Now let's say you're a grown man and the person you're in love with is a nine-year-old girl. That's a different kind of secret altogether and **that** is the sort that we lock away in the Mine."

"Gross," I take a sharp inhale and pull my sisters in close. I stare at the door. I *want* to say that thoughts are only thoughts. That a person can think a thousand awful, terrible things a day and it doesn't necessarily mean anything.

Thoughts are not the same as secrets.

A thought is a passing fancy, a flurry of an idea that scurries away when something more interesting comes along. A secret is something you hold close. It's something you wear like a pair of gloves. It touches everything that you do. I keep secrets. I can't remember exactly what they are, but I know I have them. Everyone does.

I want to give this speech to my sisters, but I won't. I *don't*, because this is The Undervale and everything that I think is right, might be wrong- *or* whatever I think is right, is right in the wrong kind of way.

"Lo," Ana mutters fearfully.

"It's all right," I murmur as I pat her arm. Etta has gone silent and rigid. "So, inside this room, the Secrets whisper? Is that what they do? They say things?" I manage to ask.

Fox grimaces ever so slightly. For a moment, I think that he might reach out to me. He opens his body towards me and then he turns abruptly away. I had made it quite clear that I don't want him to touch me. Had I been too hasty? There is something about the way he's looking at me that seems familiar, that makes me feel like falling into him.

I absolutely cannot do that. I have to be strong now. For my sisters.

"Secrets are solitary things," Fox tells us softly. "They exist alone in their humans' minds. And these kinds of secrets, these unspeakable laments, they gather momentum as the keeper that's holding them gets closer to death. When the mortal dies, the secrets find their way here. The Undervale is like a magnet for them. The secrets believe they are finally free, and in a way, they are. They are free to find other secrets as dark and twisted as they are. They are free to seek company, which for them is a kind of paradise compared to the solitary confines of their human's guarded thoughts."

"You make it sound like they're alive," Etta says with alarm. "Like they have bodies or something. But that's impossible, even for here. A secret, no matter how terrible, is just a bunch of neurons firing in some-one's brain."

"That's not true, Etta," Fox corrects her gently. "In the mortal realm and right here in The Undervale, secrets hurt people all the time. Fairies and humans feel betrayed, cheated, bested, bruised . . . lied to," Fox looks at me and there is something in his eyes. Disappointment?

Sadness? Maybe even guilt. "But in the Mine," he continues, "one secret clings to another. One becomes two, two become ten, ten become a hundred, and the collective force of that many can be very dangerous indeed."

"Please stop," I plead gently. "We're already scared. The more you talk, the more the terrifying the idea of going down there is. Just tell us what what's going to happen down there. We need to know what to expect, that's all that really matters."

"I'm not trying scare you on purpose." Fox looks down at the stairs briefly and then back at us with a kind of sublime intensity. "I'm telling you this because I believe it will help you navigate the room. I'm giving you context so that when they speak to you, when you feel them, you'll know exactly what they are. There's a power in that. There's power in knowing what's true and what isn't. This *is* me, trying to prepare you."

"All right." I nod, steeling myself for what's about to happen. "So, we'll hear things and maybe feel things. What does the Mine look like? Is it completely dark? Do the Secrets have a shape? Are they strong enough to actually hurt us?" While I appreciated Fox's help, he's being a little too philosophical. I need practical.

"They don't have a physical form, so it's not like they could punch you," Fox warns, "but, they can envelop you. They can make you see things. You'll hear them certainly. You must ignore it. It is imperative that you focus on the task at hand. Don't stop. Don't listen and don't *ever* do what they say."

"I doubt that'll be an easy thing to do but practically . . ." Ana begins

"Ha!" Etta scoffs.

"*Practically,*" Ana says, ignoring Etta and I don't blame her. Sarcasm isn't going to help us in the place where we're going. "If someone hid one of our wands there," she asks frantically, "where would it be? Is it an actual mine with rocks and tunnels? How big is it? How long will we have to be down there?"

Fox exhales deeply. His full lips form a perfect circle and my stomach flutters and pulls until I look away from his mouth. "That's the one piece of good luck in all this. We call it the Mine because technically it's underground. But it is a single space. We'd never give the secrets anywhere to hide. And it's not even all that dark. The floor is packed earth over stone. We found that the dirt dampens the Secrets' strength. So, you should keep your heads down. Concentrate on the floor. If the wand is there, then it will be buried. I go into the Mine every year with a team to break up the larger masses of Secrets, but I don't look at the ground. I'm too focused on the swarms."

"This is dumb," Etta yanks herself away from her us. "This is the honestly the shittiest idea ever. You want to send us down into the scariest place in this freakshow of a house and look for something buried in the dirt? And what? Dig it out with our bare hands? That's crazy. It will never work."

"I am not sending you anywhere, Etta," Fox tells her sternly. "I'm going with you. Whatever you have to endure, I will endure it as well. Besides, the wand belongs to Lo or Ana. One of them will sense it. Even if it's sleeping in the dirt, if they get close enough, they'll feel it's power and hopefully that pull will be stronger than whatever the Secrets taunt you with." Etta shakes her head and rolls her eyes. "You've got your wand," Fox tells her bluntly. "You don't need to come with us if you don't want to. You can wait up here if you truly believe that this is an exercise in futility."

"As if I would let my sisters go down there without me." Etta scoops her platinum hair to the side of her face and promptly begins to walk down the stairs. "Let's go then. Come on!"

Etta stomps down the stone steps. She is angry, furious even, that Fox called her bluff. I can read her mood by the way she rigidly picks up each of her kneecaps and lands each foot with an indignant stomp. I want to tell her to calm down, that anger is the last thing she should be feeling as she's about to walk into a place like the Mine, but I know that if I do this, especially in front of Fox, I will only irritate my sister even more.

I descend the long stairwell that weaves and snakes its way down. The wooden steps are uneven, and they groan in warning when they take my weight. I'm not ready to face the Mine, just like I hadn't been ready to fold steps, see an Oracle, or take responsibility for Baby. I never thought of myself as particularly brave but now, I realize it's not so much bravery as it is momentum, of simply moving forward. Maybe that's all bravery is.

You take a step because you can't turn around, because there are no answers in the direction you've come from and no comfort in what you've left behind.

Maybe courage is just . . . *going*.

It's impossible to gauge the depth of our descent. I'll go down two steps and the actual stones beneath our feet will shift in another direction. We all turn, and then walk down twenty more. After a full ten minutes, we arrive at an average looking door. It is neither big nor small, sturdy looking or flimsy. It's the kind of door you see on a thousand houses—black, plain, and unremarkable.

"This is it," Fox tells us briefly. "Ready?"

"No," I answer honestly, "but open it up anyways." Fox nods tersely and turns the handle. Why are none of these places are locked up? Why is there no kind of security system, magical or otherwise if these vaults are so dangerous? If a Secret escapes, how would Fox even know? Admittedly, there's a lot about The Undervale I don't understand. It's more than likely that there *are* a dozen security measures in place that I can't even see. I suppose Fox wouldn't have to worry about someone breaking *in*. The real worry is that something will break *out*.

The door swings open. My muscles tense and I hold my breath without noticing. The Mine isn't a dark, dank space like I assumed it would be, at least there's that. The ceilings vault as high as a cathedral. The walls are painted with an aggressive and almost shocking white and there are dozens and dozens of iridescent globes hovering high in the air like chandeliers. The room is bright and spacious. I let go of a long breath in one steady exhale.

Fox takes my arm lightly but with authority. "I know it looks empty. It isn't." He makes me take a step, which instinctively, I fight against. "They'll know we're here now. Start looking!" he barks.

I pull myself away from him. Fox doesn't comment. He moves on to begin his search. Just when I think that he must have been exaggerating, that regardless of the terrible Secrets lurking in the space, they couldn't be that bad, the first Secret hits me. Not physically, nothing touches me.

Thankfully.

But a string of vile words claw their way into my ear canal.

As he lay dying, my heart leapt just as his was giving out. He tried to call out my name, but I just stood there watching. Waiting. We both knew that I could have saved him, but he was as infantile as he was rich. Did he really think I loved him? Ahhhh yes . . . there it is . . . the realization. He's going to die knowing what an idiot he was. And I'm going to get everything.

I'm so shocked that I bring my hand up to my mouth. Could the voice be real? Could someone really have just stood there, happily, waiting for their husband to die?

I quickly manage a glance at Ana and Etta. They are stock still. Etta's mouth is cracked open slightly and Ana's shoulder is pressed up against her cheek. And then, a chorus of voices rush through my skull with the brutality of a hurricane . . .

I killed him. I wrung his scrawny neck.

I watched her starve herself to death. I kept telling her how beautiful and thin she looked. I pretended at the funeral that I was shocked. I hated her.

I made sure he knew that he would never find anyone else. I told him he was useless and pathetic. I made sure he stayed with me.

I stole his life's work. I stole it and called it my own and he couldn't do a thing about it. He died with eighty-eight dollars to his name.

She never told me to stop. She never said no. The way I held her down excited her.

I hear a scream. I turn and see Etta crouching down, her face as white as the walls, gripping the sides of her head. "Ignore them!" I roar. Although really, it's more of a command to myself than my sisters. "Start looking at the ground. Keep your eyes down ... *move!*"

I take my own advice and begin scanning the packed earth on the floor. There are footprints in the deep soil. Maybe Etta had been right. Maybe this had been a stupid idea. How will we ever find a wand that's been buried here for years?

The Secrets continue hissing their twisted truths. As Fox had warned, some trickle into earshot like bait—nothing too terrible, just interesting enough to distract me, and then a swarm of them attack. All I can do is bat them around my head, but I'm not even sure it makes a difference. Etta is running as if she's being chased. Fox walks methodically, scouring the dirt beneath him. He seems very calm. But he's probably been to this room a thousand times. These Secrets, no matter how disturbing they are, aren't anything he hasn't heard before.

Before I can look down again, I notice a shadow on the far wall. I close my eyes right away, hoping it's a trick of the fairy lights. When I open them again, the shadow stretches like an elastic band.

"What is that?" Ana asks breathlessly, coming up behind me. "Fox, I thought you said these things don't have a shape. If they don't have a shape, then why is one on the wall there?" Ana points to the shadow in a frenzy and all four of us look at Longshadow.

It has come.

It has come *here*.

Or maybe it's come home. Maybe it was born here, in this vile Mine, with its disgusting Secrets. It would be a perfect breeding ground to make a creature like Longshadow.

"It's the thing!" I tell my sisters frantically. "It's *Longshadow*."

"What?" Ana asks, her voice echoing off the plaster.

"It's here?" Etta rushes. "With us? Here?" she reiterates.

"Stop looking up!" Fox practically snarls. "Please, please, just this once listen to me and keep your eyes on the ground."

My ex-boyfriend the duke seems wholly unconcerned with Longshadow being here in the most terrible and wicked part of his house. My thoughts flop over one another. I'm trying to arrange them in some kind of order. There needs to be discipline here. Priorities. The Shadow has revealed itself to my sisters. As much as I am relieved that they can understand what I've been going through, I also know this means it has gotten bolder, angrier . . . more desperate. This could be either good for us or very, very bad.

"Fox is right," I admit. "Longshadow followed us, but it doesn't have a wand and it's definitely not a Secret. We need to keep searching. Just . . . try to ignore it. Come on. Quickly! Look for bumps or cracks or whatever in the dirt." I hope I can take my own guidance. All my legs seem to want to do is run.

Ana marches over to me. Her face is pale. Her glorious hair is slick in the fairy light. She looks like an angel. "Longshadow shouldn't be here. I think this is very bad, Lo. It's so bad that we should go. Being around it feels worse than the Secrets. I am so, so sorry I didn't understand before, but I do now. Let's leave. We can ask around upstairs.

There are so many people upstairs . . . dancing people, *happy* people. They could come down here and help us. It would be safer; we would be safer."

"We cannot advertise our situation to the entire Undervale," I argue. "Besides, it's too dangerous . . . It wouldn't be fair to—" and then, just to prove my point, a tumble of Secrets assaults us both with enough force that we're shoved sideways. Although my ears are filled with the most horrid thoughts imaginable, I gather what's left of my courage and really look at the swarm.

It's very faint but I can see a flurry of letters and words jumbled together. They fade in and out, like messages written with breath on a window.

I grit my teeth in consternation. My fear is turning over into annoyance. These Secrets are hateful- like spiteful children, hissing and kicking.

But, most importantly . . . they aren't mine.

And they are nothing compared to the shadow that's gathering length, wrapping itself along all three walls so it can get close to me, growing in size to envelop me entirely.

"Ana," I say solemnly. "Listen to me, these Secrets don't mean anything to us. The horrible people who kept them are dead. These aren't ghosts, just remnants of awful histories that are none of our business. You don't need to be afraid of them. I will handle Longshadow. All you need to do is focus. Concentrate. Try to find our wands."

"I *can't* just ignore the Secrets." Ana's voice cracks. She's on the edge of tears. "They're too terrible. I feel like I'm going to be sick every time they speak to me."

"You don't have a choice," I tell her sternly. From the corner of my eye, I can see the shadow on the wall growing taller. "We will be stuck in The Undervale forever. We'll have to rely on people like Maleficent and Fox for everything. Don't you want your memory back more than you care about a bunch of stuff that didn't even happen to us?"

Ana dips her head ever so slightly. A single tear wells and falls down her cheek. Ana's whole body is trembling. "I don't think I can. I despise this house and all its weird and creepy rooms. It's like being trapped in a dream where you know you're asleep, but you can't wake yourself up no matter how hard you try."

I can feel the shadow reaching for me. Ana might think things are bad now, but it will be a hell of a lot worse if the shadow somehow gets to her. I position my body so that I'm firmly blocking the shadow's access to my sister. "Maybe Ana Smith is too afraid to go on," I say encouragingly, "but Fauna Bloomshade isn't. She isn't afraid of anything. She's marvelous. She's a writer and an actress with a string of fabulous lovers from one continent to the next. You've got to be her right now. Keep saying her name over and over again. Scream it if you need to and maybe the wand will find you."

The shadow is looming behind my shoulder. I can feel its icy stare. I turn Ana in the opposite direction and push her gently. "Go on," I goad. Ana tentatively takes a step forwards. "But Longshadow," she protests wildly.

"I'll deal with it . . . Go!"

Fauna Bloomshade
Fauna Bloomshade
Fauna Bloomshade

I suck my lips back towards my teeth in a scowl. When I turn to face the shadow, it lunges immediately. It wraps itself around my entire body the way a whip lashes a wooden post. I can't move, I can't even breathe. There's the same smell, though now I can tell that it is different than Fox's but not completely. The shadow's scent is more astringent and oddly brighter. It's strange. The shadow should smell foul, of rotten eggs and fish left in the sun. Why doesn't it stink? Why does it have such a slightly pleasing aroma?

"You're mine," the shadow whispers seductively. At the first rasp of its voice, the Secrets scatter. That can't be good, if the Secrets are afraid of it. "You belong to me, and I belong to you."

I am so scared.

But I am also beginning to feel something else—

fury

How dare this thing follow me here to this cavern of disgusting thoughts and urges? The curse is meant to punish me, well . . . aren't I being punished enough in this place?

And the audacity . . . the nerve of it! I don't *belong* to anyone. I'm not a thing to be owned or guarded or watched. But even as I think these thoughts, Longshadow eclipses them. It strangles my tenacity and resolve in its glacial grip, draining my will. The nearness of it makes me feel like I am less than nothing. I can't even open my mouth in protest.

"I found something!" Ana screams jubilantly. I manage to swivel my eyeballs enough to see Ana in a far corner hunched over on her knees. She begins to dig, and Fox runs over to join her. Etta meanwhile has come up on the other side of me.

"Fuck off!" she screams. "Get away! **Get away from my sister!**" I feel Etta fumble for my hand. It's clenched into a stiff fist and Etta, unable to pry it open, grabs my forearm with a frantic slap. The moment Etta manages to get a decent hold on me, the shadow retreats hastily. Although I'm terrified and shaken, I'm also so relieved that I begin to weep.

Longshadow doesn't seem to like its odds against more than one of us.

And this . . . this is a very powerful thing to know even though it cost me. Even though I thought it was going to rip out my heart.

It was worth it.

From here on out, all I have to do is make sure that we stick together- and I mean *together*- maybe even in the bathroom, until the curse is broken.

"Let's go, come on." Etta yanks me with such ferocity that I stumble forwards and trip. My sister quickly helps me recover and we both race over to Ana who is clawing her way furiously through the earth.

"It's here," she says rapturously. "I can feel it! It's singing, not a real song or anything . . . just music and it's loud enough to hear over the Secrets. Isn't that wonderful? Do you hear it too?" Ana is asking questions, though she doesn't care about the answers. She plunges her hand all the way down the hastily dug hole and when it emerges, she is holding a long, thin, jade wand. "I found it! I really did!"

In a split second, images and snapshots of memories pulse through my already racing veins. Just like when Etta found her wand, they are snippets, fragments, solitary sentences, and a collage of pictures that don't make any sense.

Keys jangling in an outstretched hand.
Bluebells
Lady's Slipper Orchids
Black water. Brackish water.

And then more images. Dozens. Hundreds.

I have no context for the events I'm seeing and since everyone is wearing different faces, I have no idea who is who or when is who or *where* is who. The images feel more like daydreams than actual experiences.

On another day, this might have brought me low. But today is different. I've survived so many emotional hurdles that I'm feeling positively Herculean. I've been threatened by the Shadow. I have heard the most vile and despicable things. I'd muddled through a deafening midnight in the Strong Room of Stolen Secrets, and I had seen, awful, terrible moments, frozen in the marble statues. My sisters and I have done something remarkable.

We survived.

Technically, yes, death was never on the table but, immortality still feels like a fable, like a made-up thing a mother might say to make her child less afraid. Forever is not a word I have accepted. Not yet. Every corner we turn, every door we open, every fairy we meet, brings a new and unique terror. I don't feel safe but still . . .

We survived.

It doesn't matter that my memory is unreliable. I'll get it back, just like I'll get *my* wand back. I only wish my sisters could understand how remarkable what we've just done really is, but they don't.

Ana's in tears, rattling and shaking her wand. Both Fox and Etta are trying to soothe her while rushing for the door. The Secrets are still screaming, and Ana is especially vulnerable.

As we climb slowly up the stairs, Ana's hysterics bounce off the narrow walls and stony nooks. I ask Fox why we can't magically ascend. Why there is no elevator to the Mine?

"The Secrets are especially volatile around magic and electricity," he says while holding Ana's arm. "Safer for everyone if we don't give them anything to get excited about." I'm not sure I like Fox being so familiar with my sister. I feel a pang of what I can only suppose is jealousy, which of course is ridiculous. I don't remember being with Fox. The boy I've just spent a few hours with hadn't even featured in the handful of memories the new wand had afforded me. Still, seeing them so comfortably entwined doesn't sit right with me. It feels off, like having to walk around all day with damp socks...annoying and unpleasant.

When we finally emerge and make our way through the several doors back to the ballroom, I'm not especially surprised to find the party still in full swing.

"It's the air," Fox confirms my earlier suspicion. "We spike it with a little something to keep everyone up for a full day and night. I think it's a monumentally silly idea. Even the best party in the world gets tiresome after a few hours but it's one of the few traditions we've kept here at the Manor. Still, we're not as young as we used to be," Fox says almost sadly.

"So, we couldn't sleep? Even if we went home right now and tried?" I ask without even bothering to hide my frustration. I would like to put the entire day behind me. I need some perspective and I'm practically aching for the routine of closing my eyes in the dark and opening them again in the morning.

"Sorry," Fox turns to me with genuine contrition on his face. Ana has stopped crying. Her eyes are puffy, and her lashes are clumped together. She looks even younger than her seventeen-year-old face. "But we can get some tea in the kitchen. It'll be quiet down there."

Tea? I think, *tea*? Really?

I don't want any tea. I'm not the friggin' Queen. I'm not even British and I'm certainly not some doddering old lady who sips out of a pretty little teacup without any magic in a world where magic seems to be the only thing that matters. We've done what we had come to do and now it's time to leave. I'm about to say as much when Ana puts a hand on Fox's chest. I raise my eyebrows.

"That would actually be great," Ana says breathlessly. "I just need … I need a minute to catch my breath. Is that okay with you two?"

Etta curls her lip by way of an answer, and I can't help but sigh. I don't know what it would be like to reunite with a wand that doesn't work, but I bet it's not great. Ana feels safe here and as much as it annoys me, Fox's presence seems to soothe my sister. Still, there's Baby to consider. Then again, it must be three or four in the morning. Ninny will probably be asleep, and Baby too. I suppose we'll have to wait it out at Whifflecliff Manor until daybreak anyhow.

"All right," I concede, though I don't even try to hide the churlish tone in my voice. "Tea it is."

- 19 -

I'm sick to death of stairs. I never want to see another set of stairs in my whole life. But Fox leads us to yet another stairwell and what am I going to do? Wait in the hallway? These steps are particularly wide and tiled with intricately detailed, hand-painted ceramic squares and diamonds.

A human catering staff is running up and down the levels with platters both empty and full. I fight the impulse to ask if they are prisoners, indentured servants, or actual employees. They can't be slaves because apparently, I had something to do with abolishing that. So, what are they? I have a list of questions as long as my arm, but I don't see much point in asking them. Fox might lie and even if the humans are here against their will, what am *I* going to do about it? I doubt Fox is the kind of fairy who gets off on seeing others suffer, but he might truly believe that a human is better off in The Undervale, and who knows? He could be right.

The kitchen is long and wide but, located deep enough within the bowels of the Manor that it's without windows. I can't help but wonder, again, what's the point? If everything can be done with the flick of a wand, then why do the fairies even need a kitchen, unless it's to make the humans feel more at ease? Or maybe some fairies enjoy cooking, like Etta does.

Given all of Miss Speckledove's bowing and scraping, another possible scenario is that the fairies feel more comfortable within a hierarchy. I don't understand why there would be royalty in the first place, if all fairies basically have the same amount of power and none of us were actually born, let alone bred, to be kings or queens. I suppose that if you have all the magic in the world and could do anything you wanted forever, it would be nice to know exactly where you fit. Fox is a duke. Miss Speckledove, a lowly supervisor. Both are extremely well-suited to their tasks and positions. So- this means that all fairies are equal, except they choose not to be equal at all.

The guesswork is giving me a headache. I'm in no position to try and understand how it actually works, much less why.

A human lady wearing a black uniform whizzes past me with a tray full of miniature hot dogs. Not just the wieners, but the buns too, with mustard and ketchup the width of tiny scraps of yarn. I manage to take three of them before the servers go all the way past, and I pop all of them sheepishly in my mouth. They taste amazing.

The black stove is as big and noisy as a truck. Dozens of copper pots and pans hang from the ceiling and a tall thin man who has his back to us is briskly stirring something in a massive pot. His chef's hat is askew and he's yelling profusely in French at his two assistants.

"Vite, vite!" The man barks at a small fairy who's got on apron stained with grease and what looks like cranberry sauce. "La crème sera prête dans trente seconds, où sont mes meringues?!"

The woman circles her wand and along the wooden island, six silver trays full of tiny butter-colored meringues suddenly appear. The chef inspects the meringues. He turns his hawk-like nose up just a fraction at the fairy's work. "Meh," he says, clearly unimpressed. "Ils sont tout blancs. Pourquoi ne peut te pas obtenir ces droit?" Chef throws up his hands to the heavens and the fairy looks like she might cry. "Juste verser la sauce." The fairy points her wand at the copper pot, and it lifts off the range and pours a creamy concoction over the meringues effortlessly.

"Hello, Chef," Fox says.

The man turns on his heels angrily until he sees who's addressing him. "Ah, Monsieur Le Duc! You are so young today!" he exclaims with great enthusiasm.

"The food has been delicious tonight. Well done," Fox declares benevolently. "Well done, all of you!" There's a murmur of thanks and a flurry of quick bows and curtsies "Is Mrs. Startwell in her sitting room?"

"I'm not sure, sir," the chef shrugs and pouts his thin lips. "I have been far too busy with the party."

"Very well, carry on," Fox tells them as he starts to walk down a wide corridor. "Chef is temperamental but he's the best cook in both realms. No matter how hard we try, magic just doesn't get it quite right," Fox whispers out of the side of his mouth.

"Well, of course not," Etta says grumpily. "There's a lot more to cooking than luck and magic. You can't take a shortcut and expect a masterpiece."

"Isn't that the truth," Fox agrees. He gets to a moss-colored door and gives it a brief knock.

"Come in!" a voice yells from the other side. Fox turns the brass handle and ushers us inside. A plump woman wearing a white, long-sleeved dress is sitting in a large wingback chair with her feet up. Her hair is braided in a crown around her head and her cheeks are flushed with color. "Hello, sir . . . Oh, and if it isn't Flora and her sisters!" The woman pops up and hugs me with such force I'm afraid she'll crack my ribs.

"Apologies for disturbing you, Mrs. Startwell. We just wanted a quiet place to talk, and your rooms are the most comfortable in the entire Manor. Do you mind? We can always go and sit at the servants table if you've had your fill of guests."

"Stuff and nonsense," Mrs. Startwell says dismissively. "I'll just go and make a pot of tea and bring it in. Then you girls can tell me what adventures you've been up to. It's been years."

"Thank you, Mrs. Startwell," I tell her as I look around. The room is cozy, with chintz-covered couches and little figurines of yorkie dogs decorating the various shelves. A fire crackles cheerily in the hearth. Because there's big copper ring of keys around Mrs. Startwell's ample waist, I assume she's the housekeeper at Whifflecliff Manor. My shoulders slump just thinking about what a massive responsibility that must be.

I'm also thinking that it puts Mrs. Startwell in an excellent position to sneak down undetected into the Mine of Whispered Secrets to hide a wand…

I suppose this is my life now. Every single person I meet is a suspect. This curse is turning me into an asshole.

"I must say," Fox announces to the small room with a toothy grin. "I haven't had an adventure like that in years." I throw him a baleful look and his grin disappears.

"I'm remembering stuff," Ana tells us somewhat fretfully, "but the memories don't make sense. It's like I'm watching a foreign film without the subtitles and trying to keep up."

"It's the same for me," Etta acknowledges. "Random things just keep popping into my head and I know they happened, but I don't know when or why and there aren't any emotions attached to what I'm seeing."

"Your memories are trickling back and that's a good thing. My theory is that the curse has scrambled them, encrypted them, if you will. Without the cypher, or in this case, Flora's wand, they're just going to look like a jumble of pictures."

I rub my fingers into my forehead with considerable pressure. I understand what Fox is saying and I agree. But my hands are reacting on their own, as if my fingerprints are the key and if I just press hard enough . . .

"Here we are," Mrs. Startwell returns with a golden tray. Her chirpy voice snaps me back to reality, or whatever this is. It doesn't feel real, not Whifflecliff Manor or this sitting room that could be in every single Jane Austen novel I've ever read. I glance down at the tea set and notice that it isn't very fancy; it's not anything I would associate with a Royal Manor. The pot is large and plain white. The cups have faded roses on them which makes me think that this must be the set she uses just for herself or close friends. "Chef was one step ahead and began preparing this as soon as you came to find me. We'll just give this a minute to steep, shall we?"

Mrs. Startwell sets the tray down on a high mahogany side table and lowered herself gently on a faithful wingback chair. "So, ladies, tell me. What have you been up to? I had heard there was quite a palava at your house?"

Ana smiles courteously and begins to speak. "Well actually, it's all been dreadful. We first noticed that something was off when Baby was left—"

Oh Ana, shut up please! I think to myself. I don't say this though. Instead, I point a single rigid finger in the air. "No," I tell my sister firmly. "There's no need to burden Mrs. Startwell with our problems. Mrs. Startwell," I say, managing a curt smile, "you must have been pre-paring for the Manor for weeks. I can't blame you for wanting a little respite down here. There are so many people in attendance, it's still wall-to-wall."

Ana glances at me sharply and then Fox does the same. Etta crosses her arms. The room is filled with an awkward silence.

"Flora," Fox says tersely. "Mrs. Startwell is a trusted friend. There's no need for secrets here."

I swivel my body around to face him directly. "There is every need. I'm sorry if you can't see that and I apologize Mrs. Startwell if

I've offended you, but this is a very private matter. I'm sure you understand."

"Of course, I do, dearie," Mrs. Startwell says without a trace of bitterness in her voice. "I do believe the humans have unduly influenced us in this regard. Not every story is meant to be shared. Not every opinion should be made available for public consumption. I blame everything on the social medium" Mrs. Startwell gets up once more and begins to pour the tea.

"I think you mean Social *Media*, Mrs. Startwell," Ana corrects jovially.

Fox is frowning and gives his head a few slow, disappointed shakes in my direction. I'm sure they all think I'm being a jerk right now but I don't know this woman, and I'm the only one of us left without a wand. It's obvious though, that Fox is taking my wariness personally. Maybe I'm just making things worse.

"Fox," I say to him gently. He looks up and his countenance softens. "I do appreciate everything you've done for us tonight. Truly. Thank you. We would have been lost, literally, without your help."

"You know I'd do anything for you, Flora, anything at all." I smile back at him, though the stature of my mouth is not broad or open. My smile is both contained and cautious. Duke Foxglove of Pikepyre is as handsome as any storybook prince and twice as amiable. He's everything I could ever want in a love interest, and *I am* interested but I am not entirely persuaded. There's too much history between us. His gestures are too intimate and every word he says is connected by an invisible string to some sort of promise that I don't understand.

We spend over an hour in Mrs. Startwell's cozy parlor. Fox is excellent at small talk. I'm guessing this has something to do with his Title. Then again, Ana is great at small talk too. Miss Speckledove had inferred that I wasn't good enough for the Duke, but that doesn't necessarily mean that me and my sisters aren't royal. It just means that we aren't duchesses or princesses. I'll ask someone, maybe Maleficent, although my instinct tells me not to. Power is important to Em. If we rank higher, I don't want to remind her.

Throughout the breezy conversation, I remain mostly silent. The Midnight clocks are still crouched behind my eardrums. My fingers tap along to what to remains of their steady rhythm.

It's exhausting.

I spend what's left of my patience on various attempts to dampen the sound, which only makes me seem more distracted and impatient. Etta offers her opinion only when they are discussing the food. It is only Ana, cradling her precious wand, who stokes the embers of the group's conversation.

Eventually, mercifully, it's time for us to go. The party is still in full swing. The shades have been drawn in the ballroom to keep the morning light far away. Fox happily folds the steps we need to get to Ninny Goldendash's launderette. Before we leave, I thank him once more and dare a kiss on his cheek.

No, I am not persuaded by Fox, not yet, but I'm eager to return once the curse is lifted. When I'm Flora Bloomshade again, I think that things will probably be very different between us and that is not an unwelcome thought at all.

- 20 -

By the time we get Baby home, it is mid-morning. We aren't tired but we are . . . tender. The Manor, and all of its assorted tragedies were given passage in each of us, and we brought back them back to the house because we didn't know how to let them go.

So, we retreat to our rooms- still close- but with enough space to process our experiences without the pressure of having to be brave or strong or bright and hopeful for the benefit of one another. We sulk and brood in our rooms. Etta takes Baby that night. We sleep and let our dreams shake loose the ghosts of the day before.

That short time we spend alone and quiet does the trick because the following day, we are all in better spirits. Etta cooks a big breakfast which we eat with genuine enthusiasm. After I have my fill of fluffy eggs and crisp bacon, I'm ready to share the perspective I had arrived at the night before.

"You know guys, this curse isn't just 'happening' to us anymore," I begin thoughtfully, "we aren't complete victims here. Whatever it throws at us, whatever it makes us endure, we've gotten through it. We look like total idiots most of the time, obviously, but we've been lucky, and maybe that's the point. Maybe luck is something we deserve, something that The Undervale has given to us."

"Ha," Etta chortles over her mug. "I'm not trying to start an argument, Lo, I'm really not; it's too early, and I'm only a quarter of the way through this coffee cup. But like, has it ever occurred to you that maybe . . . we did something awful, and we actually *deserve* this? And that the only reason we've gotten this far is so that whoever cursed us can finish us off in whatever remote, God-forsaken place the third wand is hidden in?"

"Etta!" Ana recoils in horror. Her hair is pinned delicately atop her head, and she's wearing a chartreuse Kimono with miniature roses embroidered on it. Yesterday, I had thought that she looked younger than seventeen. Today oddly, she looks older. "That is a terrible thing to say! You shouldn't even think it. We don't deserve this. We didn't do anything wrong. We aren't bad and now that I've been outside this house and talked to people in The Undervale, I know it for a fact. Whoever did this to us pilfered five whole years. They turned us into strangers. They stole our life and all our memories. Whoever did this to us is sick. Psycho."

"Maybe they are crazy," Etta concedes. "But that doesn't take away from the fact that this could have been their plan all along. Torture us for five years, send a baby in, watch us run around this city like morons and then get us to go to some secluded spot that, I dunno, exists only in the clouds, or between the pages of a book or some other imaginary place, and then turn us into bacteria or something and stick us in a petri dish. Forever."

"You are a super dark person," I tell my sister bluntly.

"I'm not actually," Etta argues. "I'm a realist."

"You're a pessimist," I counter.

"Enough. Geez, it's too early for this," Ana rolls her neck slowly.

"Alright, *fine*," I say with a defensive shrug. "Maybe there is some dastardly plan in the works. But my point here, is that we need to face whatever's coming. So what if we get turned into bacteria? Someone will come looking for us, either Maleficent or Foxglove or even that cute girl from the library." I give Ana a little wink. "I'm prepared to fight whatever this thing is, as long as we're together."

"But what about Baby?" Ana brings up fretfully. "What if it tries to hurt her?"

"I don't think we should rule Baby out as an operative," Etta remarks dubiously.

"Oh, stop. She can't even speak!" I shoot back instantly. I take a long steady breath to compose myself. "Baby isn't working for anyone. She's an unwitting pawn in this game, and it's up to us to protect her. She needs to stay by our side. I like Ninny. I think she's sweet but she's a little ... untethered. I'm not saying that she would hurt Baby, but I am saying that if we left Baby in her care for too long, she might, I dunno, forget about her or something. I know this quest of ours is dangerous, but we keep Baby with us. Agreed?"

"*Quest?*" Etta gives a laboriously hostile sniff. "Sure, yeah, okay.... Let me just get my Dungeons and Dragons book out, and you can roll the sixty-sided dice. Then, a scroll belonging to a Mage Elf will appear out of thin air inside a magical pouch full of answers about Baby."

"See?" I turn to Ana. "She's a pessimist and mean, *especially* mean today."

Etta shrugs. "Sorry. The word quest is just so extra."

"Well personally, I agree with you, Lo. Absolutely." Ana coos as she tickles Baby's double chin.

"And we're all on the same page that we don't play the victim, and we continue to be totally proactive in breaking the curse, even if it means we forge ahead *alone*. With no help." I'm not really asking, and by the look Etta is giving me, she knows it.

"Yes. *Fine*," Etta snaps. "It's not like we have much of a choice, do we? This baby cannot grow up locked inside this house. Maleficent told us we already tried that before with the bratty princess, and it didn't end well. So, yeah, we keep going, even if it means spending an eternity as a dot of ink on a page in an old dusty book that no one will ever find."

"Great. Now that we've figured that out, let's try and decipher the last part of the clue. Ana, can you read out the final few words the Oracle spoke, please? Maybe something will click because of our time in the Manor; we have more of our memories now and we also have another wand." I remark as finish off the rest of my coffee.

Ana clears her throat reluctantly and begins to read from the slip of paper she had hastily scrawled on during our visit to Savannah. "*It sleeps where there is no path, where there is no sky, where the thicket opened and ate your pride. Black dog. Devil dog. Demon in the sand. Your wand lies in a lie, in the dark, in the deep, in the shadow land.*"

"Hmmm . . . maybe we should start backwards, like, reverse engineer it," I suggest.

"Good idea," Etta agrees. "Especially since there's the bit about the shadow land and we have Longshadow following us. We're all a hundred percent certain that Longshadow is not a random being of The Undervale. We agree that it's connected to the curse, right?"

"Yes, ufortunately, I don't think it's just another bizzare part of The Undervale. It's definitely focused on us," I admit reluctantly. "But creepy stalker aside, doesn't *all* of The Undervale qualify as a shadow land? If we want to get technical, isn't it the darker echo of the mortal realm?"

"Good point," Ana says. Baby is bouncing on her knee, and she gives the child one of Etta's biscuits, making sure to lay down a large linen napkin around them both to avoid mess.

I take a moment to inhale deeply. "I feel pretty confident . . . *very* confident," I amend quickly, "that the wand is here, in The Undervale and not with the humans. What I don't know is if that's better or worse for us."

"The part where it says that the wand lies in a lie. That stands out. I think the Oracle was trying to say that someone we know is lying to us," Etta notes with dismay.

"Someone we know, yes." I'm thinking out loud now. "But that could also mean someone from our lives as Flora, Fauna, and Merriweather. Maybe it's someone we don't know now, as ourselves, so without our memories, there's no point on dwelling on that bit."

"Well, there is if it's Fox." Etta's back grows rigid. Her coffee cup is empty. My sister will be in fighting form now. "Didn't he seem just a little too nice? A little too accommodating? I mean *come on;* Ana's wand was in his house!"

"I like him," Ana says dreamily.

"You like everyone," Etta remarks, though not unkindly. "Lo, you have to admit, the whole thing yesterday felt very . . . I don't know . . . staged almost?"

I throw Etta a split second narrow eyed glare. "I don't have to admit anything actually. But I suppose . . . yes, there were times when I was skeptical." I take a small bite of toast. "But again, should we be focusing on that? If Fox wanted to hurt us, he had plenty of opportunities. Also, he helped us find the wand. He could have used his magic to steal it back and curse us again. Yes, he was enjoying the whole thing but not in a mustache-twirling villain sort of way. I think he's just bored. I think everyone here must get so bored that anything out of what they consider ordinary would be fun. I don't think he would have any been less enthusiastic if we were searching for a roll of dirty toilet paper or a giant ball of used gum."

"So, you trust him?" Etta asks imperiously while pulling her oversized teal robe around her even tighter.

"I wouldn't go that far," I admit. "But let's move on. This isn't about Fox. We should ignore all that nonsense about the dogs and the devils. I think they're probably metaphorical."

"Hold on a minute now." Ana leaps up, suddenly wide-eyed.

"Yay!" Baby squeals and claps at the same time.

"If we all believe that wand is here in The Undervale, then it would be moronic of us just to assume that those bits aren't real. If anything, they're probably *very* real. We need a plan to try to fight a dog that is possibly possessed by the devil, or an actual devil or *the* devil... you know what I mean." Ana is flustered. Baby seems thrilled by the excitement.

"Okay, well if it's a real monster that just looks like a dog...a bribe, like a *meat* bribe would not work," Etta says reasonably, as if she's really considering what kind of meat to bribe a demon dog with.

"It's not real, I'm telling you!" I clap back, exasperated. "It could be a fiend or a goblin or something, but it's not going to be an actual dog. It has hands, right?"

"The devil has hands; maybe the black dog is his companion. Everyone loves dogs. Even Satan needs a pal, probably more than most people if you think about it." Ana says as if that's a totally reasonable conclusion.

I groan quietly, hoping my sisters don't hear me. I'm trying my best to be patient and cooperative. "Look, whatever it is, we'll have to outwit it or outrun it. We don't have magic and we're not Navy Seals. Let's not worry about what we don't know." Why am I the only one of us who can be practical? "Let's focus instead on the only part that makes sense. The Oracle talks about a thicket. No path. No sky and a thicket. Once we ignore all the other stuff, it's obvious. The woods. My wand is hidden somewhere in the woods which is extremely problematic. We know that the streets rearrange themselves every day and we also know that there are at least forty-something days in what? A month? A season? Without our memories, we are completely screwed. The Undervale could be as big as Connecticut or the size of China, and since this is, you know, a *fairy* land, I bet there are more woodlands than neighborhoods and villages. What if the forests rearrange themselves like the streets? It would be like trying to find a needle in a stack of needles."

The table is silent as we process the dilemma. Only Baby's occasional mumblings pierce our thoughts.

Then Etta looks out the window and says, "I don't think so."

"What? That it's in the woods?" I ask tersely. I'm in no mood for one of Etta's arguments that are just for the sake of arguing.

"Oh no, I think it's in the woods all right." Etta draws herself up straighter. "I just think it's in *our* woods. Out back."

A chuckle kicks its way out of my closed mouth because of course, Etta is messing with me. When I see the serious look on my sister's face, I realize she isn't joking. My burst of laughter pops in the air and falls to the floor like a handful of beads.

"First of all, that would be a terrible place to hide it. It's way too obvious."

"More obvious than our very own attic?" Etta snarks. "Look, I love this house, probably more than the two of you. *My* wand was here. Ana loves to party and be social; the wand was hidden at a fancy Palace that we found during a *party*. You love the garden, Lo. You're always outside, taking pictures and raking or whatever it is you do out there. It makes an odd sort of sense. The person who cursed us is seriously screwing with us. He or she or *they* are making us hate the places where we feel safe, ruining all the sanctuaries that give us any kind of peace here in The Undervale. I don't know about you, but I'll never go up into that attic again. Ana, feel like going to a snazzy party tonight?"

"No way," Ana says adamantly.

"Well…Even if it was out there—" I fling my arm out ungracefully towards the back door, "we couldn't get to it. There's a barrier or something. I told you that I tried to investigate Longshadow, and something stopped me." My pulse instantly starts to race. My foot, buried in a thick wool sock, begins jiggling madly up and down. I had been prepared to explore all kinds of forested areas because I assumed there were all kinds of wilds in The Undervale: the humid, emerald brilliance of a rainforest; the barren, Joshua Tree-laden expanse near Maleficent's; the brush and bracken among giant sequoias and redwoods. I hadn't, not even once, thought about our own tame back yard.

"It does make sense though," Ana says with conviction. "And it's not like we would need a map. I do remember it out there. I mean, Ana Smith has childhood memories of days we spent in those woods. Isn't that so weird? I wonder if they're real?"

"I have memories like that too," Etta is even more confident. "It's almost like the curse couldn't quite erase them, so they changed them instead. It's not like we ever built forts. We've never been children but, I remember doing it."

I hunch my shoulders up. "I know. It seems so real. It's just . . . ummm…" I take my thick strawberry curls and wind them atop my head so tightly that my temples immediately start to pound. Logically, I know that both my sisters are making perfect sense. Emotionally, there is something visceral warning me away from those woods.

Longshadow

"I'm telling you guys. We cannot *physically* get in there." Personally, I'm all kinds of relieved about this. And I'm dumbfounded that my siblings are more afraid of a dumb dog that's probably just a morbid signpost or a flaming tree stump than *Longshadow*.

"The last time you tried," Etta begins rationally, "you were alone. We made it out of the front door *together*. Maybe we just need to go into the back woods holding hands or something. And there's Baby," Etta jerks her head slightly towards the infant. "Who may or may not be a spy but still, she might be a necessary ingredient. You're the one who's always saying that as long as we have one another, we can face anything."

I'd love to know where Etta has suddenly picked up this new attitude of solidarity. I'm the one who's supposed to spur us on. Ana provides peppy moral support, and Etta grumbles, even though there are more times than I'd like to admit that her grumblings are salient.

"What's going on?" Etta must sense my hesitation. "Why don't you want to go back there?"

"Are you worried about Longshadow?" Ana gently places her hand in mine.

"Not completely," I tell them honestly. "No more than I usually am. It's just that, I don't want to. The idea of those woods kinda makes me want to throw up." I turn my head away as I feel the inevitability of tears.

"That's it!" Etta proclaims as she stands up suddenly. "That seals the deal. If you don't want to go, then we are definitely going. The curse is jumbling your brain. The wand is out there. And also, I hate to say this, but we need to find Longshadow."

"Oh no," I shake my head vigorously. "We need to do the exact opposite. We need to stay away from it."

Ana looks at me. Her wide eyes blink sadly. "Lo. I know you don't want to hear it, but it's got to be said. Your wand is in the woods. Longshadow is in the woods . . ."

"Only sometimes!" I yelp. "Only when it's not following us literally everywhere we go!"

"Stop, Lo. You're smarter than that. If I had made this curse, if it was me, I wouldn't just use Longshadow to keep us in it. I would give that shadow your wand because it's the thing the scares you the most and the thing you absolutely do not want to face."

Baby claps and snorts but even her cheery nature can't lighten the weight of my sister's words. I dip my head. "Lo?" Ana asks gently, "Are you okay?"

I chew on my lip because I think she's right.

I *know* she's right.

"Lo!" Etta barks and my head whips up.

"Yes. Okay. We'll find Longshadow and we'll find a way, somehow, to make it give me my wand or force it to play charades so that it gives up the wand's location."

"Charades!" Ana snorts. "That would be funny." Etta and I throw her a grim look. "And also very terrifying. Whew. Scary."

Etta has already moved on. "Great. It's decided then. Let's start getting dressed and packing up for Baby." Etta stomps over to the fridge and begins to pull things out.

"You want to go right now?" My tongue is sticking to the roof of my mouth. At first, I want water and then, oddly, Justy's Moonshine. Maybe not that oddly. Alcohol seems completely appropriate right now. I don't understand what this is. I rifle through all the mixed-up, torn-apart emotions that are raging through me and find that I'm not fast enough to catch one to examine it. It isn't just fear. I know it's something else. Something that I can't name and my entire body flexes and clenches in frustration.

"We should go as soon as possible," Ana says reasonably. "We need our magic. We need to be able to defend ourselves properly, not just for our sake but for Baby's. What do you want to do, sit here and watch TV when you know your wand is out there? We can't do that."

"At the very least, I think we should tell Em that we're going, you know, just to be on the safe side," I say.

"You're stalling," Etta hollers from the kitchen.

"It doesn't matter if you're stalling," Ana says, slinging Baby over her other hip. "It's okay to be scared. I'm scared. Just think how strong we'll be when we get your wand back. Nothing will be able to hurt us, and you *should* call Em. I think it's a very responsible idea."

Ana makes her way up the stairs and leaves me alone at the table. I'm tempted to remind my sisters that five years ago, we had our wands and that hadn't stopped the curse. And honestly? If there was even the slightest possibility that they could locate my wand without me being there, I would tell my sisters to go without me, *that's* how afraid I am of my own backyard and Longshadow; Sisters United be damned.

I sigh heavily and my whole body droops. I know I have to go. It's either that or remain Lo Smith for all eternity and while that's not an entirely unappealing notion, the thought of being seventeen forever doesn't sit right. I'm not a vampire in one of Ana's movies.

I shuffle over to the antique phone and dial Em's number. After eleven rings, Maleficent picks up.

"What is it with you girls and wake-up calls?" the voice on the other end of the telephone barks. I grimace even though Em doesn't sound at all groggy. I doubt she'd been sleeping.

"Who are you talking to?" Etta hollers from the kitchen. "Did you call Em? You should be getting ready!"

"Stop ordering me around!" I yell.

"If you don't stop screaming," Em threatens, "I will hang up on you. Are you trying to blow my eardrums out?"

I wind the curls of the telephone cord through unsteady fingers. "Sorry, yeah, I just thought I'd give you an update."

"Could you possibly change your tone while doing so?" Em asks meanly. "You have a particularly unpleasant voice even when you aren't screeching."

"What? No…I can't change my voice. I just thought you'd like to know that we found Fauna's wand at the Ball. You could have warned me, by the way, about Foxglove."

"Who?" Em asks curtly.

"Foxglove Pikepyre, the Duke of Whifflecliff and my former boyfriend of a hundred and fifty years? You could have told me."

"Why would I have done that?" Em's voice is more ambivalent than offended. "I don't think about who you date. Your love life is about as exciting as a turtle's. You can't expect me to remember something so boring."

I know Em is lying. I don't think she's a completely terrible person, but I do think that there's a part of Em, possibly a huge one, that enjoys making people feel uncomfortable. "All right, fine," I surrender. There's just no point. "We believe that we deciphered the last of the Oracle's clues. We're pretty sure my wand is in our forest."

Silence.

"And by our, I mean the woods behind our backyard."

Silence.

"Em! Did you hear me?" I snip.

"Yes, I heard you. I'm not hard of hearing despite your best attempts earlier when you were wailing at your sister like a banshee."

"I was not." If Em thinks that was loud, she should hear some of the *actual* fights my sisters and I get into. Coyotes are more dulcet. "Anyhow, we are going out into the woods. It's gonna be dangerous for us. I just thought I would tell you."

"This isn't some passive-aggressive way of getting me to join you, is it? Because I am not trampling through the forest. I hate the outdoors." I pull the phone away from my ear and stare at it, baffled.

"No, of course I don't expect you to come. I just thought I would tell you in case you don't hear from us for another five years. The woods out back will be our last known location." Em sighs deeply through the receiver. "It's a safety precaution," I try to explain.

"Okay. Got it. Good luck then!" And then the line goes dead. All I can do is hang up and shake my head. I start heading up the stairs. Em had been particularly abrupt, even for her. Maybe she's upset that we hadn't asked her about the last clue. Maybe she's a bit miffed we didn't need her to figure it out. It would be just like Em to be annoyed at something like that.

I stare at my open closet and wonder what I should wear. I know now that the seasons here are an illusion. When I walk outside, the air will read my skin. It might look like autumn, but if I were to put on nothing more than a light summer dress, I wouldn't get cold. I would never get cold, or hot. I suppose it's one of the bonuses of living here but it still feels like cheating.

With that in mind, I choose a t-shirt and pair it with a soft blush and ivory-colored Fair Isle sweater. I pull on a pair of well-worn jeans that have a darker denim patch on one of the back pockets, as if they've been mended. These little things always turn me around. Did the curse do this? Did I? Did I love these jeans so much however long ago that

I didn't trust magic to fix them? The rules of magic are so strange here. You can make tea magically, but it won't taste as good as if you steep it and make it yourself. Magic will do the laundry, but there isn't a spell to make it smell as good as if you hang it out in the sun.

I look at the wool socks on my feet and wonder if they are too heavy. Would magic have given me the right answer about them? Could magic have told me if they were necessary? I'm thinking like a human. If I had magic, I could change the weather. I could change my shoes. I flex my toes inside the wool ... Shit. I could probably change my feet. I could turn myself into a sled dog or a marathon runner. I know it isn't healthy to dwell on, but I can't help thinking what a disadvantage we're at and at the same time, I also know that magic doesn't always make things better. How is that even possible?

Ultimately, I decide to leave the socks on and instead of my usual running shoes, I choose a pair of hiking boots that look properly worn in. I secure my hair in a long braid and stick a knit cap over my head.

I stare at my reflection in the small mirror attached to the inside door of my closet. I think, *who is this girl?* Like the weather, my face is a trick. In all likelihood, I probably didn't even choose it myself. The fairy who cursed us gave us our current faces and this has morphed into another kind of curse. I look so normal, so average. If you didn't know the truth about me, you'd never be able to tell from my rosy colored cheeks, or my tall, strapping frame, or the smattering of happy freckles on my nose that there is something seriously wrong. In that moment, I remember what Ninny Goldendash had said and I wish my own face reflected the anguish I feel. I want warts and scars and dry flaky skin. I want eyes thick with cataracts because there are shadows, and I might as well be blind for all the things I've seen in The Undervale and can't understand.

And I realize that in this, I *really am* like any other mortal girl. This feeling I'm experiencing is not unique. This wanting to look how I feel inside isn't special and there's a kind of comfort in this idea. I suppose it means I'm normal, except I am not normal at all. I am not a teenage girl.

Damn, I think to myself. This curse is working overtime.

I slowly close the closet door and make my way downstairs again. Etta had changed for today's outing with lightning speed because she has never in all her life thought about her clothes for more than 10 seconds. Now, she is laying provisions on the dining table.

"Ana will carry Baby's things in this sack," Etta says pointing at a hunter-green backpack. "We have bottles, formula, biscuits, diapers, three changes of clothes, and her blanket." Etta moves to another grouping on the table. "I'll carry basic provisions. We have enough food to last us three days, four if we ration. We'll all carry our own water. But we can't carry water for four days. Not without a pack mule. We've got to hope that there are freshwater streams we can use."

"*Or*" I offer, "we just focus on the fact that we aren't human, we live forever, and therefore no one is going to die of dehydration."

"Except for Baby," Ana rushes. "We'll have to find water for her." Ana is last to come down the stairs. No surprises there and also- no surprise that she looks like she's about to do a photo shoot for Ralph Lauren in her green heathered turtleneck sweater and fleece leggings.

"Okay, fine," Etta relents with a furrowed brow. She had forgotten; and I get it. It's not the sort of thing your brain just accepts straight away. Rationally, I know we are immortal. Emotionally, immortality is just a word we've all been throwing around without ever truly feeling its full weight. Etta starts barking orders again. "Lo, you are going to carry matches, a flashlight, a tarp, and first aid stuff. We might not be able to get killed, but we can be hurt. Even fairies bleed, and so we need to be prepared.

"All right," Ana says as she grabs her bag and deftly begins packing it with her one free hand. "I'll pack Baby's things but, don't forget her toy giraffe, Etta. She'll need something to soothe her in those big, dark woods, won't you, Baby?" Ana kisses the top of her head.

"Yay!" Baby says while kicking her little legs.

I start to pack up my own bright pink backpack. It must be mine because its pink, but it's so damned bright that when I look away, I can see it's outline hovering in the air.

Etta runs back and forth between the kitchen and the table, adding things and taking some things away. Ana and I make trips up and down the stairs for further items. Finally, when all three bags are kitted out fully, we stand back to admire our work.

"I don't want to jinx it, but I'm pretty sure we have everything we need," Etta says with satisfaction.

"Well, I'm not. We're thinking like mortals. I mean, yes, food and clothes and all that, but we need to be able to protect ourselves. We need weapons."

"What?" Ana's head whips around. "Like guns? We don't have any guns and even if we did, I wouldn't know how to use one."

"Not guns," I roll my eyes. "But we do have that baseball bat in the closet. We can take one of the knives from the kitchen, and I saw an old field hockey stick in one of those trunks up in the attic."

"You want me to just carry around a butcher's knife?" Etta puts both of her hands on her hips. She's decked out in jeans, a lightweight powder-blue hoodie with a denim vest over top. She looks like an extremely pissed off eleven-year-old. "What if I fall and stab myself accidentally? And honestly? I know I can be snarky as hell, but I don't think I could shove a knife into someone. Nope. I would just rather run away."

"First of all," I grumble, "wrap up the knife and secure it in your bag. Second of all, what makes you think we'll have a choice? Especially if we have Baby with us, we might not get a chance to run away. We could have no other option but to fight."

Etta moans and throws back her head in protest. Above all else though, my sister is practical. "Fine! But I don't like it. I can't believe you want me to take one of my Koji Hara knives outside. Do you have any idea how expensive those are? And what if I do have to stab some-one or that Devil Dog or the actual Devil? You realize I'll have to throw it away. I could never use it again." She stomps over to the kitchen and begins to rifle through drawers. I can still hear her talking to herself about steel and bloodstains as I climb all the way back upstairs to retrieve the field hockey stick.

In the attic, a shiver ripples down my spine. A few days ago, we had scoured this space for Etta's wand and ended up in a dilapidated, rotting room. A room so noxious that the smell of it lingers. It's a ghost of vapor that invades my nose and hunkers down in the back of my throat.

Even worse is that when I imagine the brush and bracken beyond our backyard, I find myself *longing* for that smelly, maggot-infested space. At least it was small.

I am far more worried about Longshadow than I'm letting on. Every single hair on my body stands on end when I think about being close to that monster. But we have to go and *that's* what really pisses me off. If I want my life back, if I want to protect Baby, if I want to remember who I am, then I must go into those woods. I have no choice.

I feel like I'm falling straight down into nothing. However ter-rible life is, a choice is something you can hold onto. If you have options, you have some measure of control. I don't have any of those things right now. My choices have been stripped away and there really isn't a word that's big or strong enough to describe this feeling.

Still, just because I have to, doesn't mean I *need to* go in there all "babe in the woods" (even though, yes, we are taking a baby into the woods). I grab the field hockey stick hastily and conclude that actually? I *could* hit a dog (if the dog was a red-eyed devil with needle-sharp teeth) but what am I supposed to do with a shadow? I can't hit it. Maybe we could shine a flashlight at it? I groan again as my fingers grip the wooden handle.

We're going to need a bigger light.

After we strap on our packs and arm ourselves as best as we can (the bigger light idea is great, but Em won't help and I don't know how to get a hold of Fox, who is the only fairy I would trust to provide us with magical back-up) it's time to go.

Ana is holding Baby in the carrier who is kicking both her feet furiously in excitement. We walk out the back door and make our way past the garden and the wildflowers to the entrance of the woods. The last time I stood on this very spot, my body had tacitly refused to go forward, and today, it feels the same. I try to take a step, but the mud is swallowing my boots. Though my knees are shaking, I can't make any other part of me move.

As if reading my mind, Etta and Ana slip their arms into mine. "Lo?" Ana says sweetly. "Walk." And even though it's the very last thing I want to do, even though I have the most tremendous urge to race back into the house and get into my bed and under the covers, somehow, I take one step forward, and then another, and then we are all suddenly inside the woods and I know that there is no going back.

- 21 -

It doesn't take me long at all to realize that my bravery has been rewarded with complete and total disorientation. Even if we had a map (if such a map existed), I wouldn't have known which direction to go in. My sisters are counting on me to *feel* my way toward the wand. Which is unfortunate because terror is chief among my emotions and the rest . . . the rest, I still haven't managed to decipher.

The woods are unnaturally dark. The sun can't or won't penetrate the canopy of oaks and maples. This is especially bad for us; not jsut because we can't see what's coming but also, and more importantly, shadows inhabit spaces without light. There are no trilling birdsongs, no musical chirping from unseen winged creatures. There are only the manic, predatory caws from ravens and crows.

The Oracle had said that the wand was hidden where there is no path. In a strategic, although also possibly such a dumb move, it's reserved for the worst kind of horror movies, the three of us veer from the small dirt clearing that leads away from our house. We know that if we follow it, it will take us through a series of hedges and bracken and twist itself open to a lovely meadow and past that, a swimming hole.

But we can't take the path. Instead, we push our way through the dense brush. Twigs snap beneath our feet and Ana's hand hovers over Baby's head protectively to keep the branches away. I can't make sense of the forest. At first, it's dirt, mud, and clusters of ancient-looking trees. After about a mile or so, the trees thin and the mulchy ground is replaced with waist-high grasses.

Buzzing flies add to the discordant symphony of the corvids. Etta isn't much of a talker on the best of days and I suppose Ana is staying quiet so I can focus.

I do try. I try so hard that my temples start to pound but I don't feel anything. There is no elusive tug or mysterious aura lingering in the distance.

Finally, after walking for almost two hours, Etta declares that we should stop and rest. We clear the tall grasses and find ourselves back in a denser collection of trees. These specimens are different than the ones close to our house. These are tall pines that creak and moan as the blustery autumn wind passes through them. Oddly, the air around us is still. Only the pines sway to gusts that we ourselves can't feel.

I scrunch my nose at the smell of the evergreens. It reminds me of Longshadow and makes my stomach roil. I don't want to accept it, but I have to assume it's a good sign. It probably means in some twisted sort of way that we are going in the right direction.

Etta had spied a fallen log, which is probably why she suggested that we stop here. We arrange ourselves on the moss-covered bark. Ana keeps sliding downward until eventually, she braves the damp earth to lean her back against a nearby tree which immediately stands still as she settles into it. I throw her a tarp from my pack to protect my sister's pants, which she gratefully accepts. Ana releases Baby from the harness and changes her diaper. Baby is now lying on her back, free to kick and grasp. This usually delights her but even though the child is gurgling, I can tell that Baby's sunny disposition is somewhat subdued, until we hear a loud, boisterous giggle escape from Baby's bowed lips.

We all look at Baby who has both hands above her head, palms out as if she's clutching at the sky. That's when we notice the tiny lights dancing around her. Ana leans in closer and then jerks her head back.

"Uhhh . . . guys?" she says in a tentative voice. More lights in various hues ranging from electric blue to shocking pink and gleaming gold begin to gather around us and I realize when I get close enough for a proper look, that these are not lights at all but *fairies*—tiny, winged fairies with clothes made of spider webs and pansy leaves and woven grasses painted in swirling designs. These are the fairies that Em had told us about. The kind that I had always pictured before I knew I was a fairy myself.

"Flora!" squeals a wee little thing joyously. She's wearing an amber dress made of what looks to be dried tree sap.

"Fauna!" blurts a boy fairy who is mostly naked save for a little pair of shorts that have been cut from a pair of butterfly's wings. Even though he is tiny, barely two inches tall, his abdominal muscles are well-defined as are the ones hulking over his brown shoulders.

"Merriweather!" a third fairy screeches. She's wearing a robe of black feathers, or maybe it's just a single feather cut into pieces.

"You brought a baby, a *human* baby," yet another fairy observes.

"Yes, yes." Ana swats her hand gently away toward the fairies clustering around Baby.

"Of course, we knew you would come," the raven-feathered fairy says. "That shadow character must be stopped. Everything around that cabin has died! Shriveled up and gone to pot!"

"You've seen Longshadow?" My pulse quickens. It thumps so hard against my arteries that I can feel them move under my skin. My sisters and I exchange worried glances.

If Longshadow is bound up in *our* curse, why is it bothering these fairies? And what is this about a cabin? Shouldn't it just be living wherever we are? It's got real estate now?

Great. I have more questions than I did when I even started this 'Too Dangerous for Any Person with a Brain in Their Head Quest', and I had *a lot* of questions.

"We've seen it. Our eyes may be small, but they work perfectly well. Flora, you mustn't go there," the fairy in amber says solemnly. Her sweet little face is beset with worry, and she keeps touching her scarlet-colored collection of dozens of braids all pinned back in odd shapes. "That shadow is too dangerous for just the three of you to manage—"

Before I can ask them exactly how dangerous they believe Longshadow to be, the tiny fairies begin talking. Their sing-song voices crowd the air around us to capacity, making it impossible for me to get a word in edgewise.

"Especially with a human baby!" another one interrupts. "You should leave her here, with us."

"We do love babies," the fairy continues in a tone that makes me think her love of babies isn't really love at all, but something else. Something that isn't even close to being benevolent. "You must go back to town and get more Big'uns. You'll need a whole army to get rid of that monster. It screams you know, every night. It's horrible. It's absolute torture."

"Stuff and nonsense," the boy fairy says. "These three are powerful enough on their own. They don't need any help and we certainly don't need any more Big'uns trampling through our forest, stepping on our mushrooms and shaking our homes down around our ears." The fairy flies just a few inches from Ana's face. "How are you, Fauna? You look awfully lovely."

I give myself a moment to ponder the particulars of that relationship.

"They can't go. Not alone," another fairy whines.

After that, it is sheer chaos. The fairies argue and buzz and dart around the four of us so fast that I go cross-eyed.

Finally, I say, "Enough!" and the swarm immediately falls silent. All I can hear is the tiny hummingbird flutter of their wings. "Now, first things first, where is this cabin?"

"It's not a cabin, it's a shack. Four walls and a thatched roof."

"That's not true, Flora! It's huge! It's got at least ten rooms. The roof is made of tin."

"I wouldn't say it's huge," another fairy breaks in, "but it doesn't really look like a cabin; it's more of a cottage? There's a dead garden in the front of it, just rows and rows of massive brown stalks."

"It's like no cottage I've ever seen," one interjects sullenly. "It looks more like a privy if you want my opinion."

"All right," I exhale slowly, through my teeth. "First of all, you're sure the shadow creature actually lives there? It has an address?"

"Oh yes," the fairies nod and exclaim so earnestly that I'm willing to believe them on this one point. Longshadow has a lair, which maybe makes sense?

Well, no. It doesn't make sense, *obviously*. It's a killer shadow which shouldn't exist, but here we are.

"We don't need the descriptions," I bluster. This is in fact, a complete lie. I'd love a description but they're fairies—proper Tinker Bell fairies with fake-sounding accents which makes me think that they're probably more full of shit than the others, like their size has made them pissier. "Let's make it simple. Where is it? Can any of you agree on that?" I ask tersely. Of course, it is possible that Longshadow's dwelling could change itself every day, but I doubt it. I don't think these little fairies are toying with us to be mean or because they are secretly in league with Longshadow. I think they are contradicting one another because they are bored.

All fairies are bored.

"Oh yes, we know where it is," a voice says grumpily.

"It's about three hundred trees north and twenty trees west," another one breaks in.

"It is not!" the Raven fairy objects. "It's one hundred and thirty trees east and then sixty-eight trees north."

I groan and whip out my hand quickly. I grab the fairy closest to me and hold it fast in my palm. "Right!" I announce in the most intimidating tone I can muster. "We don't have time for this. I want the truth. Right Now. Or I'll squeeze this one till its guts come out of its mouth."

The winged fairies collectively gasp right along with my sisters. "I'll do it, I swear I will. So . . . one of you better start talking and if you even think about lying to me, I'll . . . I'll . . . come back here with Maleficent and she'll burn your little village to the ground!" More gasps and some of them even shriek. I don't like being this mean. It feels like I've swallowed a handful of gravel and now it's just sitting there, weighing down my stomach. But the situation calls for me to be bold and bossy and just a teeny bit evil. In other words, like a real fairy.

"It's about a quarter mile away," the amber one says angrily. "Walk east and then when you see a big redwood with a carving of the Green Man on its trunk, you turn north. There's no trail or anything. The house is sitting smack dab in the middle of a copse of fallen pines."

The blinking purple creature is squirming against my fingers, and I bring it right up to my face. "Have you actually seen this shadow?"

The stubborn fairy remains silent and sticks his tongue out at me.

"I've seen it," a surprisingly deep and accented voice says. This fairy looks older than the rest with snow-white hair and a little bow tie made out of braided dandelion petals. "But I'll not say a word about it until you let Talon Bitterdew down, you Big'un scoundrel."

"I will not," I respond, channeling my inner Maleficent. "You don't get to dictate terms to me. You'll tell me what I want to know, or my sisters will pluck the rest of you out of the air. For all I know," I spit, "all of you are the shadow! If enough of you move together and dim your light, it would look an awful lot like the thing we've seen, wouldn't it, Etta?"

"Absolutely," Etta purrs. I give Talon a little squeeze and the tiny fairy howls.

"All right, all right," the older fairy says. "I can see that this thing has got you well and truly spooked otherwise I can't imagine why you'd be treating us so poorly. We've all seen the shadow. It started off small–not much bigger than us, and I'd notice it out of the corner of my eye. I thought it were nothing really, maybe just a Dreamerfly or a Coral Hopper. And then it got bigger. It rolled around in the dirt and side-winded its way around the trees."

"What shape was it?" I ask quickly, "Was it in the shape of a person?"

"Not right away, no," the fairy says thoughtfully. "It were more like a ball. I was still thinking it were an animal. Then the house appeared, wand magic to be sure, and the shadow grew. It weren't in the shape of a man or beast at first but lately, it has taken on the form of a Big'un. It skulks around these parts, spying. And woe to you if you ever get caught in its wake. To find yourself in the shadow of a shadow is like wearing a crown whittled by icicles. It's a dark and twisted thing; you can feel the hate sliding into your pores."

"That is a weirdly specific description, but thank you?" I offer. "Still, you need to tell me what this thing is . . . not how it makes you feel or how it moves. If you know exactly what it is, we need to know." Now that they are speaking (relatively) plainly, I can feel some measure of resolve stir inside me. We're getting information, and in this case, information is power. The more we understand, the better chance we have. Talon has stopped fighting against me. The little man is just sitting in between my fingers, wearing a scowl.

"I told you it's a shadow, Flora Bloomshade, and you've said the very same. I'm not lying to you."

"Yes, but nothing here in The Undervale is ever what it seems exactly," I argue. "If it was just a shadow, it couldn't touch you, let alone watch you, and it certainly wouldn't be able to make you feel like you're wearing an ice cube crown. Could it be some kind of demon? Could it be an actual monster?"

"There are no demons here, girl! Demons aren't real, as you well know. A demon is a nightmare invented by humans to remind them of the evil they're capable of. And what is a monster? One man's monster is another man's pet elephant. It's all in the looking."

"No one should keep an elephant for a pet," Ana says with a pout.

"Agreed. Also? That's not much of an answer," Etta tells the fairy impatiently.

"Well, that's all the answer you're going to get from me or any of us," he squawks indignantly, straightening his little yellow bow tie. "I have no idea what kind of creatures the Big'uns keep in their fancy palaces and pretty castles. I don't know what that thing is beyond what I can see. It looks like a shadow. That it doesn't act like a shadow, well, that I wouldn't ken."

I realize that by holding Talon hostage, I am in fact, acting like a monster myself. I release him, and he repays my onslaught of conscience by giving me a swift kick on my thumb before fluttering away.

The tiny fairies begin to gather around us, their wings flapping furiously, making a sound like wind hitting a loose sail. The fairy who at first had been so excited to see me, flies right up to my face, with a look of consternation.

"You shouldn't go around threatening us," she warns. "Just because we're small doesn't mean we're harmless."

"Well, you're not harmless enough to deal with the shadow, are you?" I clap back angrily, leaping to my feet. The fairy backs up and then they all swarm around me as I stand, turning my skin into a riot of colors even in the dim light. "How many of you are there exactly? Hundreds? Thousands? It's not like *you* sent an army to dispatch that thing. It seems to me you just fly around and complain about it. And now, me and my sisters and a little tiny baby have to go and get rid of it. I threatened you because you were acting like jerks. You were deliberately trying to confuse us, and believe me," I point my finger at them, "today is not the day you wanna do the folksy cryptic thing."

I'm so mad that it feels dangerous. I'm downright enraged and I don't get it. I've been in far more annoying situations these past few days. Even Em, who's supposed to be our friend, has been far ruder than the itty-bitty fairy brigade.

I guess I've had my fill.

I've reached my limit.

And to be fair, these pretty little things, these wide-eyed wisps in gossamer gowns and ivy breeches *are* spiteful. They know way more than they are letting on. They might see me as a "Big'un" but it's not like with the flick of their teeny wands, they couldn't grow as tall as they wanted.

Longshadow lives in *their* forest. And they're just waiting? For me and my sisters or some other band of regular-sized fairies to deal with it? They're either the most entitled community I've ever met or the wimpiest. Maybe both.

Without my memories, I'm adrift. In The Undervale, everyone is a fairy so, why don't we all get along? Why all the lying? Why can't we just trust one another? Big or small, queen or scullery maid, Earth Scorcher or Wish Granter, we're all the same.

I resent my isolation with vigor. I shouldn't have to feel so scared and bewildered. No matter how many times I turn this situation over in my brain, I cannot understand why *my* fight isn't *every* fairy's fight. And of course, more than that, I can't even begin to grasp why one of my own would have done this to me.

None of it is fair, but Em had said on the very first day that nothing is fair in this world or any other. I could, in theory, just remain in this flustered state of inequity. I could clench my fists and gnash my teeth at the injustice of it all but that won't get my wand back. The Undervale doesn't care that I'm a victim and so I will have to do all the caring—in private and in the dark, where everyone, fairy and human alike, goes to nurse their tender wounds.

The fairies fly off in a frenzy. I had basically told them to go away, and off they went without another word, encouraging or otherwise. All of them that is but the handsome young man with the muscles. He kisses Ana on the cheek with his tiny lips which must feel like being nuzzled by a field mouse. And then he flitters off too.

"At least we know where to go now," I say, though my voice has all the burnish of an old piece of scrap metal.

"That's *only* if they were telling the truth," Etta huffs. "Of all the fairies we've met, they're the worst. They somehow managed to be pretentious while sucking up to us at the same time. What do they even do out here? They don't have electricity or telephones or buildings."

"Oh, hush up, Etta," Ana scolds while getting Baby back in her harness. "Who knows what they do? They could have a very elaborate and advanced society. Just because they choose to keep to themselves doesn't makes them ignorant or backward." Ana pulls on the straps of the carrier to secure Baby properly. "Sometimes, with the two of you, it feels like being stuck between the tide and a wave. You're always crashing into people, Etta, and Lo, you're relentless." Ana stands, taking the blanket and tarp with her. "If you had been a little nicer, more patient, we could have maybe gotten somewhere with them. Instead, you basically threatened murder. What's the matter with you? How could you have been so mean?"

Ana throws the tarp at my feet, and I whip it up off the ground ferociously. I fold the piece of plastic tersely, into more quarters than necessary and stuff it into my pack. I pause, letting a single breath leave my body in one long, exhausted push.

"You're right," I admit reluctantly. "I was being mean. But I don't like it here. Don't you feel how wrong it is? They enchanted you, Ana. They fooled you because they look so cute and innocent.

"That is not true," Ana argues. "They only fooled me for like, thirty-six seconds, *max*. It's just that I don't like to see anyone being bullied. And you were being a bully."

"Well," Etta interrupts, "if Lo hadn't done it, I would have. And you can swear up and down that you weren't taken in by the Hello Kitty of it all, but you were. And that's what they count on, so I say bravo to Lo, because she saw through that twee bullshit. She wasn't being a bully. She was doing what was necessary."

"Etta, thank you," I tell my sister genuinely. "But Ana does kind of have a point. I was being a bully, but only because we could have spent an entire week being nice to them and it would have been the same back and forth made of moon dust and metaphor confetti. We needed answers and we needed them quickly. I did what I had to."

"Also? Those are the kind of fairies that steal babies, Ana," Etta says in prim solidarity. "They're the ones that humans are so scared of."

"That's ridiculous," Ana waves her baseball bat in dismissal, but her hand goes rigid on Baby's back. "How would you even know that?"

"I read," Etta tells her indignantly. "I know you all think I don't, but I do. And I've been reading every book at our house that I thought might have to do with fairies, even if it only mentioned the word fairy on a single page."

A fleeting look of disbelief passes between me and Ana. It isn't so much that Etta was reading something other than a cookbook which was odd, but not out of the realm of possibility. It's that Etta is an extremely practical person but not necessarily resourceful. She generally tends to rely on us to come up with the more academic solutions to a problem.

"Well, I'm glad you did that. But it doesn't matter anymore." Ana points out dismissively. "They've gone and now we're alone. I hope you're happy with that."

"I am, actually," I tell her with my head held high. I begin to walk with purposeful strides in the direction that the elder fairy had given to us. Of course, given our circumstance, I'm not happy. I am, at the very least, less angry. But if I know anything, it's that it is always better when it's just the three of us. We grumble and bicker and nip at each other like puppies, but my sisters are everything to me.

A tingle of terror races down my spine when I consider the alternative. What if I had to go through this alone? What if I didn't have sisters? I was wrong before about not trusting anyone in The Undervale; there are two people beside me that I would trust with my life. I hear a voice in my head telling me it's vital to remember this the next time I feel like everything is hopeless. I don't know if it's Third-Eye fairy mysticism or the invisible threads that weave all siblings together, regardless of magic.

I don't have very long to dwell on this idea because the cranky fairy who spoke with the lilting voice had been telling the truth about this one thing at least. After less than twenty minutes, through a dense and dark hedge and a copse of evergreens that spread their trunks like giants raising their knuckles at the sky, the cabin appears, out of nowhere.

It is not spectacular but it's not a shack either. It doesn't look like a privy or a cottage. It's a simple log structure, rectangular in shape and big enough to claim more than one room.

There's a stone chimney but no smoke wafting out of it. There are plenty of windows, but they are dirty and covered in grime. The front door is red, the shade of a dangerous woman's lips . . . the color of blood. Trees spill out around the house on every side. They lay there, cracked and fallen, their leaves long gone as if the house had dropped from the sky with such a force that the ground buckled, and the earth plucked off its own skin so as not to be near such an unnatural thing.

My eyelids get stuck to my irises. I lose the ability to blink. I feel a kind of vertigo, as if I'm falling forward, as if the cabin is drinking me up through a straw. I lean on the field hockey stick to steady myself. I don't want to run away but I do get an overwhelming urge to hide. It's so amateur, all four of us just standing here out in the open. What if Longshadow is close? What if it can see out of the streaks in the windows? The problem is that there's nowhere to hide. Any tree that might have offered us cover has been destroyed. My body involuntarily shudders at the idea of being wrapped inside the shadow's icy embrace, of being smothered by its unending darkness.

If we lose, is that what will happen? Will Longhadow devour us like the music box? Will we be trapped and turned into frozen statues unable to move or fight or even see one another? Will a part of us end up in Fox's Hall of Stone Regrets? No. At least that wouldn't happen. The Manor deals with mortal emotions. We are immortal. This should be comforting but all it really means is that Longhadow can torture us … forever.

"I know **we have** to go in there," Ana says in a voice barely above a whisper, "but I have to point out, after consuming what is probably ten thousand hours of various forms of media these past five years, that it is a profoundly idiotic thing to do. Nothing good ever happens to young girls who wander into abandoned cabins in the woods. *Ever.*"

"We really don't have …" I begin stoically but Ana interrupts me and starts in on a list using her hand to further illustrate.

"Dateline, about a hundred podcasts, Morgan Freeman movies—what am I saying? *All movies*, anything Stephen King has ever written, the weird German shows on Netflix …"

"Okay," I whisper back with clenched teeth. "I get it. We all get it. It's a total friggin' cliché. Wait? why are you still watching those weird German shows on Netflix? They give you night terrors."

"Are you scolding me right now? Seriously?" Ana hisses.

"Oh my God, please shut up," Etta says with a weary sigh as her posture changes. I know this stance well. Her head flops down dramatically and her shoulders droop. She's chosen to cast herself as the downtrodden mother of half a dozen children who talk back and never clean up after themselves. "We need a plan. If we go in without a plan, we deserve every horrible thing that's definitely going to happen to us. Are we just supposed to march in there and start making demands? To a shadow?"

When I think about going into that house, like, actually moving my feet and walking toward it, I almost throw up. My mouth is dry, and my breathing is so shallow that I feel like I'm back in the dreaded ball gown that Igni stuffed me into. But then, suddenly, miraculously, my heart is struck like a match and a smoldering fire begins to burn away at my fear.

My wand is close.

I can feel it on my tongue, and it tastes like nickel and strawberries and Etta's hot chocolate laced with chili powder.

"That's exactly what we're going to do." I take a triumphant step toward the menacing, ramshackle cabin. "We're going to go in there and find my wand and once we do, *we're going to tear that shadow apart.*"

- 22 -

I march ahead, over the dead trees that are splayed on the forest floor like fallen angels, their green wings ripped open, their limbs brutally severed and hanging at impossible angles.

"Slow down," Ana whines as she puts an arm around Baby's body to try and brace her from the suddenly swift movement.

"Whoa, hold up, cowgirl," Etta hisses. "You can't just go in there. I told you; we need a plan. At the very least, we should try and look through the windows or something."

"My wand is close. I can feel it. So, get your knife out, Etta and keep up," I order without even bothering to look behind me. My focus is on that door. I walk up three small steps and onto what might have passed for a porch somewhere. The small space is only big enough for the rocking chair that's propped on it. The chair is covered in spider webs and worm rot. It looks like it would collapse even under Baby's weight, not that I'm willing to test the theory. I'm starting to feel very hot. and I give the collar of my sweater a tug.

I stare at the door for a couple seconds which gives my sisters ample time to catch up. There is something about that door. I don't know if it's the color—that particular shade of red—or the shape which oddly, is round when the rest of the house is so square. Maybe it's the way it shines, overly lacquered as if it's been licked by a zealous boy with no experience in kissing. It's not what I'd imagined. It doesn't look like the entrance to the lair of a creature who's been terrorizing and stalking us.

Longshadow is probably counting on this distraction, and I shake my head aggressively. I need to care less about the stupid door and more about opening it.

I put my hand on the knob and Ana jolts forward to stop me, covering her hand with mine. "The proximity of your wand has turned you into a weird ninja who doesn't know any kung fu moves."

"Ninjas would not be doing kung fu," Etta says bluntly.

Ana smacks her head with her palm. She's going to ignore Etta. So am I. "Have you lost your mind? Look at this place!" I can see Ana gesturing wildly out of my periphery. My eyes are fixed on the shiny, red gloss. "This is serial killer central! Actually, I take that back. Even a serial killer would be afraid to go in there."

"We can't go home, Ana," I protest. "Not without my wand."

"I'm not suggesting we go home," Ana says softly. "I'm suggesting that we just take a beat, approach with caution . . . We should take it slow, considering that we have no idea what's on the other side of that door and we have a little baby with us, okay?"

"Okay," I shrug my sister's hand off. I bring up the field hockey stick defensively, which isn't a plan—what's a stick going to do to a shadow? But it's a gesture that Ana needs to feel safe, so I give it to her. Etta holds out the butcher knife in a trembling fist. Ana lifts up the baseball bat and ducks a little. I gingerly turn the doorknob, and I'm a little disappointed that it's unlocked. I'm all riled up now. I was ready to knock it down in one swift, determined kick.

The door creaks as it swings open and I'm the first one to step slowly inside. It's everything I had expected it to be and at the same time nothing at all like I imagined. There are elements of the music box room where we had found Etta's wand. This shack is not a replica of our living room, thank God, but the furniture is mostly moldy and tattered. Many of the cushions have come unstuffed, leaving bits of foam and feathers spilled onto the filthy wood floor. Oddly, there is a single pristine chair. It's covered in a brocade with poppies so luminous that they almost look wet.

There is a kitchen, but it would be a stretch to label it as a working one. There's battered stove and a sink with more rust than porcelain. There are wood planks instead of counters and few uneven shelves. Platters and plates of maggot-infested food are piled on all these uneven surfaces. But…there's also a pretty bowl of shiny apples that are so inviting I'm almost tempted to take one, *almost*. Even without my memory, I know well enough that apples and magic are notoriously dangerous bedfellows.

There is so much white crockery shattered on the floor that it looks like packed snow. The shelves hold a motley crew of opened tin cans with blackened mold clinging to the edges and nests of hair and paper wrappers for rats or mice to make their dens. There is, like the bowl of apples, one neatly stacked pile of untouched dessert plates.

It's not until I see the pictures though, that I truly understand the depravity of Longshadow. They start in the narrow hallway that leads to the single bedroom. There are dozens upon dozens of pictures of me and my sisters smacked on the wall, each one punched with a rusty nail.

There's me, outside raking, and Etta standing in front of the fridge. There is Ana sitting in the bay window in her bedroom reading. They are stolen moments. They are snapshots that rip away at everything that makes me feel safe.

And they are also … just plain bizarre.

Some pictures are framed and focused so that we are clearly identifiable. In others, it's just a single earlobe, a wrist, or the curve of a neck. Some are so zoomed in, it's impossible to see anything but the blurry folds of our colored clothes.

Ana begins to cry silently. I try to keep myself steady. But there is no way to stand upright here. Each photo is a boot on my neck, grinding it into the ground, strangling me. We reach for each other and hold on.

We are trembling.

Etta of course, does not cry. Ana shudders and Baby, sensing her distress as babies do, begins to bleat and fuss.

I refuse to break down. Instead of feeling pain or fear, I deliberately corral my emotions, herding them into a more useful direction. I feed my anger, using this vile place as kindling to stoke and fan the flames as they rise to lick my ribcage.

"We have to find my wand," I say breathlessly. "And we have to hurry before it comes back. We need to search everywhere."

"Are you seeing what I'm seeing?" Ana shakes the baseball bat at the walls. "This thing has been watching us, studying us . . . it's a full-on stalker. It's a shadow that can take pictures and develop them. How is that even possible? Lo! Are you listening to me? Think about what I'm saying," she demands, almost furiously.

I don't think about it.

I stomp along the hall until I'm in what I suppose is the bedroom. I can feel my sisters behind me now, the heat and anxiety radiating off them. It's quiet. Too quiet. My ears attune to our collective breathing, shallow and labored as it is. I turn so that I'm facing the bed. It takes more willpower than I thought I was capable of not to react. The sheets are stained in disgustingly faded patches of yellow crusted puss. As if that wasn't bad enough, there's also the deep burgundy brown of old blood.

But the pillows are crisp and white and looked freshly laundered. This place makes no sense at all.

My eyes sweep the room. There are battered crates filled with books and I find this to be morbidly fascinating. What would a malevolent shadow creature even read? Turns out the Longshadow's tastes are surprisingly similar to ours. There are cookbooks and romance novels, photography books, coffee table-sized art books, and historical fiction. Maybe it's not so surprising. What better way to understand your prey?

I give myself five seconds to take it all in and then I start to move. I pick up the first crate and dump the contents on the filthy, wooden floor. I open the books, laying waste to their spines as I look for a hidden cutout big enough to hide my wand.

Etta and Ana also begin to search. Etta flips the bed over and her gag reflex takes over and she makes a retching sound that's pitiful enough to make me cringe. Thankfully, she doesn't actually throw up.

We ransack every inch of the bedroom and as we do, the inconsistencies become even more confusing. There are garments hanging in the closet, which is baffling. A shadow does not need clothing. Most of the flannel tops and t-shirts are covered with holes and rips and unidentifiable stains but there are a few items that look like they have just been purchased: a summer dress with little pink flowers and a handmade cardigan with red roses for buttons. There are jeans, pressed at the seams, hanging next to *another* pair covered in mud and grass stains and the rusty spread of caked blood.

The more I search, the less I understand. Did Longshadow build this place? Or rather ... *could* Longshadow have built this place? My gut tells me that it did. That it didn't just stumble upon this abandoned cabin and move in. The impossibility of both scenarios no longer rattles me. In The Undervale, it seems like nothing and everything is impossible.

All of this and still no wand. We move back down the oppressive hallway. Ana begins ripping the photos off the walls and in turn, I give the walls, a thin wood laminate, a hard knock with my field hockey stick to make sure there are no hidden compartments. Oftentimes, the stick goes right through, leaving a trail of pockmarks and the skittering feet of vermin fleeing their nests.

We make quick work of the living room. We let Ana have the one nice chair because she's carrying Baby even though I know the kind of dust we're kicking up in this foul place can't be good for her. Etta and I begin to eviscerate what's left of the couch. I move onto the old, boxy TV set. I gleefully kick it off a crate and watch it explode on the floor. I keep stomping until the back cracks open. I check to see for myself if the wand has been squirreled away in there. It hasn't been.

There is another makeshift plank shelf holding rows of VHS tapes and DVDs. The shelf isn't level. I don't even know how it's managed to stay on these walls that are soft with mold and rot.

Oddly, like the books, they are films that could have easily been found at our house. Maybe this is how the curse works, maybe this is how the "magical" appearance of new forms of entertainment happen. Does Longshadow collect these things in the mortal realm and then drop them off when we're sleeping? That theory makes my skin crawl because . . . *Shit.* Could Longshadow have been sneaking in all these years while we were sleeping and vulnerable? That thought leads to an increasingly dire one, one that is so perverse that it makes the muscles in my neck contract with such vigor that my entire body freezes. The actual content of all these bits and pieces of ephemera- Longshadow *knows* us.

It knows us very well.

It knows what we want. It knows what we like. All around the cabin is evidence that Longshadow isn't just stalking us, like Ana had said, but in its own foul way, is trying to please us, or maybe I'm being too generous. These comforting distractions we've been turning to inside the curse have mollified us into accepting our reality.

In the kitchen, my boots meet the broken dishes to make a sound like trampling on the shells of a thousand dead insects. There are dirty, grime-infested plates and bowls in the small sink, all covered with flies which plume when I get near them. There's also a copper pot, untouched and without even so much as a single smudge. A package of open chocolate chips lies on the rough counter, or at least I think it's chocolate chips . . .

Everywhere I turn, there is some new disgusting shrine to Longshadow's depravity mixed in with a single untouched simple pleasure that the three of us enjoy. As I search and burrow and put my hands inside things that make me gulp and gag, I feel the stirrings of panic start to take hold.

What is Longshadow?

When I focus on Longshadow, I sense a frisson of energy, along with a heightened feeling of despair, hovering around us. It isn't the same energy I felt in Whifflecliff Manor or Em's desert ranch house. It isn't magic per se, but it is magical. I don't know how I know this. Just like I don't know how my lungs expand with air or my eyes know when to blink. I just know. It's the truth.

Maybe it's because my wand is close...

I stop the ransacking entirely so that I can collect the disparate threads of my thoughts. Longshadow is not a fairy. That, I am sure of, especially since the little sprites in the forest had not identified it as such. It isn't a demon. A demon would be in Hell- or from Hell. I can just about wrap my head around the fact that there are two realms—fairy and mortal. I'm not mentally ready to accept that there are more realms...Heaven *and* Hell. Mortal *and* Fairy.

So, Longshadow isn't a fairy or a demon but -it isn't just a shadow either. Shadows can't touch you, let alone hurt you. There is something, right on the tip of my tongue. I *know* the answer. The curse is blocking it but it's inside of me, somewhere.

"Lo!" Etta reprimands, "this is hardly the time to take a break. You think our luck is going to hold out forever? Longshadow is going to come flying in here any minute."

"Peter Pan," I say suddenly. The words just explode from my mouth, a surprise to myself as much as my sisters.

"What? What does that mean?" Ana asks while bouncing Baby.

"In Peter Pan, Peter's shadow left Neverland on its own," I begin. "It's how he met Wendy in the first place; he was looking for his shadow. Tinker Bell was a fairy, and she was, *you know* . . . not to be mean but . . . kind of a prissy jerk, right? And teeny tiny, just like the ones we met in the forest today. In the end, Wendy had to sew Peter's shadow back on. That's how she got it to stick."

"Yes, but even if a fraction of that story is real," Etta protests, "Peter's shadow didn't *do* anything. It didn't have its own house of horrors and it didn't hurt anyone."

"I know that." I itch my forehead with the inside of my elbow. My hands aren't going anywhere near my face until I wash them. "The Hall of Stone Regrets turns life-changing moments into statues. Is it such a crazy leap to think that Longshadow is the *actual* shadow of the fairy who cursed us? I mean, maybe their anger was so intense that it broke away. Maybe it couldn't be contained and so it became the shadow of the anger? Isn't that possible?"

We all look at one another. The cabin, which had been so still, so unnaturally quiet, begins to fill and thicken with potential. Invisible plies of probabilities weave themselves together into strands which become rope which becomes a chain that I can almost hold on to.

Longshadow isn't a person or a monster; it's a *possession.*

Longshadow *belongs* to someone.

My mind begins to run full throttle . . . who? Who does it belong to?

Maleficent—the obvious choice because even though she is the coolest person I've ever met, she's also terrifying.

Foxglove Pikepyre—Ana's wand was in his Manor; He's my ex-boyfriend; He's suspiciously nice, and he makes me feel uncomfortable in ways that my teenage body does not understand.

Justy Bluehorn—has a shoe fetish, no judgment but it's incongruous to his general vibe. Also? He didn't want to help us, even when Ana asked with her biggest doe-eyed face.

Miss Speckledove—She hates me. Full stop. She may be in love with Fox. Scratch that, she is absolutely in love with Fox.

Ninny Goldendash—Most likely not? But the bird thing, that is hard to get past.

All the twee tiny fairies in the woods— Spite and Sprite are two words that are conspicuously similar. They only gave us useful information when I threatened to kill one of them, yet they claimed they needed our help. *And* they live here in the woods.

Just as I'm about to ask my sisters for their opinion, the door explodes open.

Etta was right.

Our luck has run out.

- 23 -

Longshadow looms in the doorway, which as far as I know, is the only way in or out of the cabin. A shadow is a curious thing, made of both light and the absence of light. I was so sure, down in the Mine that Longshadow was at least fifteen feet tall. Now that I'm in front of it, I'm shocked that we are the same height.

"Lo!" Ana screams and something startles inside me, like a chime of wrens that take to the sky. My senses roar into life. I will *not* be made into a statue like the ones in Fox's Hall. This moment will not define me. I have my sisters to protect and a baby who absolutely cannot be left in this creature's clutches.

I dodge right and the shadow does too. I move left and it apes me. I dare a long, full look at Longshadow, hoping to catch a glimpse of familiarity, a clue to its owner. In the gazing, I realize that its body is composed of more than mere darkness. It may well look like a shadow and move like one too but that isn't *all* it is.

Inside its center is a swirling mass. Longshadow undulates in waves. It is ink blooming in a violet ocean. It's a dozen hurricanes. It is clouds billowing and colliding into a disaster of storms without end.

I crouch low and use my feet to leap. I imagine I'm a tiger or some other ferocious canine. Longshadow does not expect this and I'm able to scramble around it and out the door.

"Come on, you bastard!" I taunt. "Come and get me!" I can only hope that Longshadow takes the bait and will give chase, allowing my sisters to get away. I run and I run *fast*, like my skin is made from the silken sails of cutters and my bones are nothing but loose twine. My feet skim over brown pine needles and I twist and hop over rocks that jut from the ground like slate spikes. I try not to think about Etta and Ana and Baby. Poor Baby. I pray that my sisters will be smart enough to leave me behind, if not for their own sake, then for Baby's.

I quickly turn my head to try and get a glimpse Longshadow. What I see is that it is looking less like a shadow and more like the outline of an actual person. Unfortunately, it is still ephemeral enough to glide over the bush and bracken of the forest with ease. That glimpse costs me- I trip and fall flat on my face. A rock cuts into my cheek and I can feel the blood dripping down, flowing into my mouth.

I realize with frustration that there is no possible way I can out-run it. It is a creature made for running and hunting and hounding down. At any time, it could have grown and enveloped me, but it's making a game out of it and relishing the chase.

I refuse to give that vile thing any kind of pleasure. I may not be able to die, but I'm certain Longshadow is contemplating a thousand ways to make me suffer. In a split moment, I decide to accept the pain, whatever it is. Nothing can be worse than living this half-life, this life without memory or magic. It's not even living. I am patterns and routines wrapped in terror. Am I supposed to spend eternity holding my breath? Waiting for Longshadow to . . . what? Devour me? Haunt me? Turn me into yet another person? I can't.

I don't want to do it anymore.

I stop short. It isn't exactly a clearing. But there's enough room for me to reach my hands out without touching any trees. Now that

I've made up my mind to do this, I realize that there will never be a perfect space for this confrontation. There isn't anywhere in The Undervale where I would have the advantage. Right here is as good as any other place.

I turn swiftly, angrily, and begin to run *towards* Longshadow and it does the same, matching me stride for stride, its arms pumping at the same speed.

I don't have a plan. I'm going on instinct alone. And my instincts are telling me that you cannot fight smoke. You can't bite air or punch into vapor. When we crash into each other, I half expect to emerge clearly out the other side of it.

That is not what happens.

Longshadow is as solid as a bag of bricks. The force of our collision takes my breath away and I grunt like a wild animal when we both land on the ground. Without hesitating, I go right for Longshadow's face and head. I pummel my fists into it and each time I do, it feels like I'm sliding through a fissure in an iceberg.

The tiny old man fairy had been honest about that too. As Longshadow engulfs me, my teeth begin to chatter like an endless, battered freight train. My skin loses its color going from pink to white to pale blue. The frigid temperature drills inside my joints, locking them in place, making it impossible for me to move.

Longshadow maneuvers itself to straddle me. I am beyond despair. The shadow is not simply cold, it is desolate. The loneliness it projects onto me is gut-wrenching. I feel like I haven't seen or talked to another soul for a thousand years but at the same time, it's also like I'm in the middle of a room with a hundred strange bodies pressed up so tight against me that I can't breathe. The thing I feel the most though surprises me and I don't understand it. None the less, it then hits me with a thundering smack.

Shame.

I'm ashamed. Why? I didn't ask for this Longshadow thing to choose me. I don't want its attention or its curse but here I am, just lying here, unable to fight it, too cold and frozen to even use the muscles in my mouth to tell it to get off me and go away.

Longshadow leans down close. My teeth are still chattering, and it clamps around my jaw with an icy hand. "It's time," Longshadow whispers. Its voice is the sound of an arctic wind gusting through a malnourished ribcage. It's the jangle of a locked door and the scrape of a fistful of nails along an airtight window. It is an awful, terrible noise and yet . . .

And yet . . .

I am listening. The noises it makes are as ugly and raw as a newborn rat. And like any newborn thing, it has its own kind of pull, regardless of how hideous it will grow up to become.

"It's time," Longshadow repeats. "It's time to remember."

"No!" I manage to scream, though I'm not sure how. I'm not even sure my mouth is open. I don't want this. Anything but this. "Please," I begin to sob. "Please don't. Please leave me alone."

Longshadow laughs perversely. The sound of its hissing and gurgling is enough to make me retch. "It's far too late for that. What did you think was going to happen?!" Longshadow suddenly screams in my face. Its breath is uniquely fowl- like a corpse frozen for a thousand years inside a block of ice suddenly exposed to heat. Each drop of melted water revealing the inevitable decay and putrefaction.

"You stupid, STUPID girl. This is all your fault."

And then Longshadow kisses me and my lips freeze, and every microscopic bit of oxygen is pulled from the cells in my blood. The day goes as black as the inside of the Longshadow's belly. It keeps its lips pressed against mine until they start to burn and it is what makes me finally remember.

It isn't the cold.

All along. It was how I burned. For him.

INTERLUDE

"Flora!" Aaron bellowed. "What is taking so long? It's not raining. I repeat, IT IS NOT RAINING! If we don't go now, babe, we're gonna miss out on the first nice day of spring that we've had. The sun is actually shining . . . Flora!"

Flora, who was up in her room grabbing a silk scarf for her hair, laughed at his enthusiasm. It was true, the weather forecast had predicted an entire afternoon of sun. Flora didn't need a scarf for any reason other than she imagined it might look glamorous. She had an image of herself traipsing through Ferrah Heath like a black and white film star who may or may not have tipped off the paparazzi.

She quickly tied the scarf around her shoulder-length red hair and raced down the stairs. Aaron was standing at the open front door with his arms crossed. "Okay, okay, I just need to find my keys!" Flora giggled.

She raced over to the small table in the front hall alcove. When she didn't see her silver keys sitting on top, she grimaced and quickly started ransacking the table's only drawer until she heard the jangle of metal on metal.

"Looking for these?" Aaron asked with a rather smug grin on his face.

Flora dropped her shoulders and smiled. "Very funny. I'm not running *that* late."

"Not at all," Aaron said smoothly. "And who am I to complain in the face of artistic genius? I'm just a lowly attorney while you . . . You're on the verge of winning a Pulitzer."

Flora walked over to him and snatched her keys from his hand. She laughed a little. Aaron was always poking fun at her. With anyone else, it might have come across as annoying or even patronizing but with him, the cheekiness was part of his charm. Flora had been alive for thousands of years. Her kind always liked it one of two ways: Fairies wanted deference or challenge when it came to mortals. For a while, deference was fun, then it got boring. A challenge was always more interesting.

And Aaron was very interesting. She had met him at one of Siobhan Shigeru's farm-to-table dinners at Siobhan's B&B called Broom and Board. Siobhan wasn't a fairy, and she wasn't exactly a witch (despite the tongue-and-cheek name of her business.) Siobhan was a member of a highly secretive order of women called the Jaen. Even after a millennium, Flora still didn't know what the Jaen were or where they got their power from, but their Avening Chapter ruled the town with efficiency, progress, and tolerance, which is why Flora and so many other magical beings chose Avening as their residence in the mortal realm. Each chapter had thirteen women (and there were chapters all over the world). They also had plenty of magic, but the Jaen had limits whereas she had no limits at all- as long as she had her wand.

Her wand.

As Flora was locking the door, she felt a tiny sliver of panic. She had been in such a rush that she had left her wand on the kitchen counter. Flora silently cursed her own negligence. She had been in her darkroom, developing prints for an upcoming show with her own two hands. Magic worked. It developed the pictures, but it left out some mysterious and crucial ingredient. The images were somehow less . . . Visceral? Dimensional? She couldn't pinpoint exactly what it was but when she used magic, her photos weren't good enough.

Flora wasn't sure if it was superstition, a habit, or sheer stubbornness, but she never brought her wand into the small darkroom where she relied solely on her own experience and artistic eye to coax the blank paper to bleed and roar the images to life. The two things felt mutually exclusive, which was silly, and she knew it. Even if it was superstition, she didn't want to jinx all the good luck she'd had as a photographer all these years by suddenly changing her own rules.

She didn't like to be too far away from her wand though; no fairy did. She thought briefly about going back to fetch it, but then she stole a glance at Aaron. His blue eyes regarded her with sheepish intensity and his hair, which was usually just unruly, looked positively Byronic. She didn't want to make him wait. It was as simple as that. There was a part of her that cringed a little to think that she, Flora Bloomshade, an immortal being with infinite knowledge and an eyewitness to all of history could so be anxious to please a human man she had just begun dating.

Undeniably, there was a part of her that was glad of it. She was happy about her lack of cynicism, that she was capable still of caring about pleasing anyone, let alone a human. She was only going to be gone for a couple of hours. Her wand would be safe, and she would get to experience a few thrilling moments of unpredictability. It kind of felt like the slow climb of a fast-moving roller coaster. Walking out into the Heath without her wand held the same frisson of excitement. There was no real danger but there was just enough exhilaration to get her blood pumping.

Flora's house was a cozy two bedroom that she had improved with magic over the course of a couple of centuries. From the outside, it looked like an English chocolate box of a cottage. Inside, it was bright and airy with clean modern lines and little clutter. It had a large rose garden in the front yard but in the back of her house was a lilting porch that needed replacing, a small patch of grass, and a wood gate that led out to the Heath. For all intents and purposes, her back yard was the forest. Aaron had suggested a picnic at Pond Meadow. Technically, the Heath belonged to every resident of Avening, but this little spot was a hidden gem. Few locals even knew of its existence. Aaron only knew about it because she had told him and he had been born in Avening, raised there too, but had only recently returned after the end of a disastrous marriage with the remarkable claim that Vancouver was not big enough for both he and his ex-wife. Flora could never love the way mortals did. Passion could not be sustained indefinitely, and even amiable companionship became something like melancholy after three hundred years or so.

Unlike so many other men, Aaron's emotions were broad. They spilled out of him without guile or embarrassment. She enjoyed the fact that he did not fold up his feelings into tiny, dollhouse envelopes, only to be unfolded when appropriate and even then, barely big enough to read properly. Flora liked the way he asked for what he needed and wanted instead of playing games. She thought it was rather heroic for a mortal. She also thought it was sweet and romantic, this gesture of a picnic, complete with a gingham blanket and a basket filled with wine and tiny sandwiches.

She led him through the tall evergreens that were generally more used to rain than snow in this part of the world. It had only snowed once that winter, though it had been far from a mild one. It had been wolfishly cold and damp and now that it was late March, she was happy to see the first signs of spring. Birds were chirping, Lady Slippers poked their tiny heads out of the ground. And while she was covered up with a sweater and light jacket, she didn't need gloves or mittens. Flora touched her scarf and hoped she didn't look silly, like she was trying too hard.

They talked little during the half-hour hike to Pond Meadow. It was mostly sighs and sideways looks between them. He held her hand and she brought his fingers up to her lips once or twice and kissed them. Her sisters believed this man was ordinary and didn't hesitate to tell her so. She tried to explain what it was about him, but they didn't understand. Aaron was after all, a human.

He was handsome but not overly so. He wasn't rich or famous. But he had something, some spark of power that Fauna and Merriweather couldn't see. Flora thought he was a conjuror in waiting, as if any moment he might pull a fistful of rubies from his pocket. His breathing changed the molecules of air around him, thinning them out so that his body moved with such ease and grace that gravity seemed like a theory that he didn't especially care for.

It had only been a couple of months and she had been cautious. Aaron said he liked that about her. He would tease her and call her Princess, yet he courted her accordingly with love notes tucked into the books she was reading, and flowers bundled with hemp left propped up on her doorstep. He didn't ask her too many personal questions, which she appreciated, as Flora disliked lying even though her survival depended on it in the mortal realm. Aaron made up for her reticence by talking openly about his own past. He had been adopted by a couple who never thought they could have children and then two years after his arrival, a miracle happened, and his mother gave birth to his sister. He never said implicitly that he felt like an interloper in his own family, but the way he told the story could leave no other impression. It wounded him, sometimes to the point of sullenness which she empathized with. He was an outsider and so was she.

Pond Meadow was a lovely spot in the summer. Tall grasses shot out from the marsh, like rows of green-headed pins. Flora often escaped the heat and swam alone in the cool water. In spring, the pond was high, and the banks were a mix of mud and clay with patches of moss slipping between mottled grass.

"This looks good," Aaron said as he surveyed a flat area about twenty yards from the water's mouth.

"Sure," Flora agreed. Aaron carefully laid the blanket down. He smoothed the fabric with his fine hands and straightened the corners. They took their boots off, and Aaron flicked the basket lid open and grabbed a bottle of red wine.

"So fancy," Flora jeered.

"What? You don't think I can pick out a nice bottle of wine?" Aaron laughed, though the laugh seemed to stick in his throat. It didn't come anywhere near his face.

"Of course, I do," Flora corrected herself quickly. "I just meant that this feels very . . . Luxurious, with the setting and all the preparations you made. You pulled out all the stops."

"You're worth it," Aaron told her adoringly. "I've never met anyone like you." Flora chuckled to herself and looked down. It was cheating. *Of course*, he had never met anyone like her. She was a fairy. Aaron uncorked the bottle with ease and poured them each a generous serving in a stemless wine glass.

Flora took a sip and smiled. In truth, she didn't like red wine all that much, but she would never dream of saying so after all the trouble he went through. "This is really nice," she told him warmly.

"Come here," he said simultaneously scooting close to her and pulling at her coat. He kissed her long and deep. He tasted wonderfully of the spices from the wine, and he smelled like Christmas plums and evergreen boughs. He touched the side of her face and then with more urgency, kissed her harder, his tongue exploding into her mouth.

She pulled back but kept her hands on his cheeks. "Hey," she said softly, "are we in a hurry or something? Did you make plans for later?" Flora laughed a little nervously.

"No," he kissed her throat and her eyes. "Of course not. I only want to be right here with you." Aaron took the glass from her hands and placed it off the blanket. Flora watched it teeter but remain upright on the uneven grass. A tiny flicker of alarm went off in her mind. Aaron leaned back and put his own glass down, spinning it in the mud.

He reached for Flora again. "Just wait," she said lightly.

"For what?" Aaron asked greedily. "I've been waiting for this since the day I met you. I've been a good boy. I've done all the right things. I've bought you dinners. I've brought you flowers. I've written you poetry—"

"That was Pablo Neruda," Flora ribbed gently.

"Whatever," he told her as got closer. "I did this whole picnic thing. I even made the sandwiches myself. Stop playing coy, Flora. I get it. You're not a slut. I respect you, so come here."

Flora was still considering his words when he pounced. Had she been playing coy? She didn't think she had been playing anything. She had only been trying to get to know him. Flora balked at the word slut. There was no such thing. Slut was a word meant to put girls in their place. Flora was no girl; she wasn't even human.

Aaron was now fully on top of her, groping her breasts through her sweater. "Stop," she said. She was sure she said this. She must have told him to stop because Aaron was a nice man, and he would never continue if he thought she had reservations. She had to admit that maybe she didn't say no. It was possible she didn't tell him to stop because truthfully, she was in shock, and her body had folded in on itself completely like a giant, flesh-colored greeting card.

She mentally reached for her wand a dozen times and the more she thrashed, the more he seemed to believe she was excited. She cursed her own stupidity. What was she thinking to not have brought her wand? She had witnessed an eon of men. Men who kept women eternally pregnant. Men who kept their daughters uneducated, who denied them the right to vote or own property. Men who believed that females were inherently inferior, dumber, more emotional, only useful for marriage and cooking and cleaning and lying on top of. Flora had seen all this, and she had been silly enough to believe that it had changed but the changes had only started happening in this century. How could a few liberal ideas overturn a hundred generations of programming? She had gone out to the woods, alone, with this man. This was her fault. All of it, even if she did say no.

Flora stopped moving entirely. Every minute he was on top of her, he became bigger, taller, heavier. She didn't see the point in pushing him away. She knew he wasn't paying attention to her anymore and just the thought of pleading flooded her with even more shame. Aaron pulled her pants down just far enough to get her legs apart and that's when she broke in two.

She heard a voice in her mind say, *it's best that you go away for this part*, and so that's what she did. She closed her eyes and tried to imagine she was somewhere else, but the pain and the humiliation was a tether. Flora couldn't get very far at all. She could just about picture Pond Meadow in the summer. The heat licking her back. Her palms brushing over the stalks.

This body she had on, this one she was wearing now, was relatively new. It was so new that she was physically still a virgin. Aaron never took off a single item of clothing, not even his jacket. He didn't even bother to kiss her. He covered her entire face with his hand and pushed it away as if now the way she looked was offensive.

Eventually, she managed to unshackle enough of her mind to imagine July. Yes... She imagined that it was July, and she was inside the Pond. Alone. With the minnows skittering across her bare feet. She turned over and exposed her bare skin to the sun . . .

But...

Her body knew.

Her body knew that this was a lie.

Her body told her that the moon was drowning, and that Aaron's current would pull her under for good. He thrust inside of her, and the entirety of his skin became sandpaper—scraping, scratching, burning, and still . . . Flora didn't move. Tears surrendered from her eyes, either from the pain or the shame. She dug her nails into her palms, but they were too short to break the skin which disappointed her. Flora wanted to feel a different kind of hurt, one that she alone was responsible for causing.

Apparently, Flora wasn't a fighter. She had thought she was and *that* was the thing. She would have challenged anyone who had said that she wouldn't have fought back. But here, now, she knew the dirty truth of it. She was not a fighter at all. She was magical. Flora had magic and when you have magic, you never really lose. What did that make her? A fake? A fable? A pretender . . .

Why wasn't she scratching his eyes out and screaming? She should have screamed bloody murder, but Aaron had stolen her voice, and she was only partly in her skin anyways. And what would she say to him or anyone that might have rescued her? This was her boyfriend. He liked her and she liked him. He might even love her. This might be what love looks like to him. She left her wand at home. She kissed him. She took his wine. She still liked him. Aaron wasn't a rapist even though he was raping her right now. He couldn't be.

It didn't take all day. The sun didn't set and rise again but it felt that long. It was probably a few minutes, hundreds of seconds, maybe a thousand, and then he grunted. He sounded like a sick dog. His legs and torso shuddered, and he dropped fully on top of her. Then he propped himself up on his elbow and kissed her nose.

"That was amazing," he told her earnestly.

Flora opened her mouth. She was sure she was going to finally scream and call him terrible, awful names or at the very least ask him why, why had he done that? She would have happily shared her bed with him if he had taken it slow . . . If he had just . . . *Asked.*

But the only thing that escaped her throat was a bit of strangled air. Aaron reached over for a paper napkin to wipe himself off. That's when he noticed the blood. "What is this? Are you on your period? You could have said something."

Aaron's query shocked her vocal cords into action though admittedly, the action was meek. "No, no. This body has never done that before."

Aaron raised an eyebrow. "This body? Why are you talking in the third person?" He looked between Flora's legs and his lip curled just a little. "Are you a virgin? Seriously? How is that even possible? You told me you were twenty-nine."

Flora reached for a napkin of her own. She did not look as she wiped herself down. "Am I not allowed to be a virgin?"

"That's a stupid question," Aaron laughed throatily. Flora saw all the way to his molars. "Of course, you're allowed. In fact, it's kind of sweet. I just wish you had told me. I don't want you thinking this thing between us is more serious than it is."

Impossibly, Flora's heart sank. YES. She had thought it was serious. Last week he had hidden a note in her pocket that said, "You steal the air from my lungs." They talked every night before they went to sleep. She had stopped drinking coffee for him because he couldn't tolerate caffeine. She gave up coffee! You don't do that for a casual fling. He had just been inside her. Was that all he wanted? It seemed like a lot of effort to expend for something that was relatively easy to get, especially from her. She'd been too cowardly to even put up a fight.

"It's getting cold; we should probably head back," Aaron told her abruptly. Flora nodded her head and did up her pants. Aaron stood and when he looked at the blanket, he groaned dramatically. "This blanket is my mom's. It belonged to my grandmother, and you got blood all over it." Flora was on her knees. She bent her head to examine the stain. There was more there than just blood.

"Sorry," she mumbled.

"Well, you can wash it. I don't know how to get stains like that out and my mother will disown me."

"Okay," she said, though she had no idea why. Nothing was okay. Flora didn't understand what was going on. She knew that logically, she should be feeling something, but it was as if she had been emptied out, like a bucket bailing a leaking boat or a week's old garbage can. She was hollow and exhausted.

"I'll take all this stuff," Aaron told her kindly. "You just carry the blanket." Flora nodded her head, and he led her out of the forest. Every once in a while, he would touch her back and Flora made sure not to wince because she was afraid. This was Aaron when he was being nice. She didn't want to see the version where he was upset. She kept her hands in her pockets so that he couldn't see them tremble.

He walked her to her door and kissed her on the cheek. "I had a really good time, Flora. Sorry about the whole virgin thing."

"Uh huh," she responded numbly.

"What?" Aaron's neck jerked back. "You didn't have a good time?"

"No, I did, thank you." Flora managed what looked like a smile, but really, it was only her face cracking in two.

"All right, I'll call you tomorrow." Aaron turned his back and walked away. For him, it was like any other goodbye. His stride was broad, and his head was held high. Flora pulled her keys out of her jacket with trembling fingers. Once she was inside her house, she raced to the kitchen counter and grabbed her wand. She pulled it close and rubbed its smooth wood surface along her face.

Flora zapped the blanket with magic to clean it but she then she folded it carefully herself and laid it on the back of one of her chairs. Later, she couldn't believe she had done that.

She slowly climbed up the stairs, leaving footprints that were half mud and half water in her wake. Flora spent an hour in the shower and when she got out, she used magic to burn the clothes she had been wearing.

She bundled up in sweats and climbed into bed. Her sisters found her there four days later. For four days she hadn't moved. She did not sleep or eat. She just kept replaying what happened at Pond Meadow over and over again in her mind. She had gotten it so wrong. If only she could go back! If only she had brought her wand or found her voice. If only she had told him no more firmly . . . But she had done none of those things. The list of things she should have done grew into the hundreds.

"Why are you in bed, Lo? Are you feeling a bit down?" Fauna carefully bent herself around Flora in the bed, resting her chin on her sister's shoulder.

"What's going on?" Merriweather demanded. "We haven't been able to get ahold of you for days. Would it have killed you to answer a message?"

Flora sat up. She didn't think she'd be able to tell them. She was so embarrassed. She'd been so irresponsible and now she had made them sick with worry.

"Spill it," Merriweather warned. "Or I'll pull whatever it is out of your head with my wand." Flora shuddered. She knew her sister wasn't bluffing, and she also knew she couldn't take another invasion of her body.

Slowly, carefully, she told them the entire story.

In turn, Fauna and Merriweather's fury made the entire house shake. A thunderstorm cracked in the sky above. Flora's bed began to rumble as if she was sitting in a hot rod with a chrome engine and pipes as fat and wide as an organ's.

"I'm going to kill him," Merriweather said matter-of-factly.

"No," Flora scrambled. "He doesn't deserve to die. It was my fault too. I went out into the woods without my wand. I'm not even sure I told him to stop. I was leading him on for months. Yes, he was inappropriate, absolutely. But I could have stopped him if I'd just been smarter. I apologized to him. I said thank you. So you see . . ."

"Now you listen to me," Fauna took her sister's hands and pulled them into her chest, close to her heart. "I'll admit, we shouldn't go anywhere without our wands for a million reasons that don't have anything to do with what happened out there but he's a monster. You trusted him. He violated you. He ra—"

"Don't say it," Flora snapped. "Don't you say the word. I'll be fine. I just need time."

And so, her sisters gave Flora space. They punished Aaron, though they did not kill him, and still, Flora did not leave her bed. Spring turned to summer. Flora's camera gathered dust and her darkroom grew great looping cobwebs that hung down from the tiny ceiling like macabre party decorations. Every day they would visit her and every day she would assure them that she was to blame and that once she had forgiven herself, all would be well again. Fauna and Merriweather tried a hundred, *a thousand* different ways to explain to Flora that what happened was absolutely nowhere near her fault but Flora either could not or would not listen.

The heat of summer heightened and cooled. Fauna considered it a victory when Flora showered and even more of a victory when she left her bed. By the time September came, Flora managed to get dressed but she would not leave the house. She clutched her wand like a life preserver. She slept with it in her closed fist. Flora knew that something was wrong with her. She knew enough time had passed and that she should've moved on. She also knew that this happened to humans all the time and they didn't have the luxury of hiding away in their houses for months on end. They had to go to work or school. They had to pay bills and cook for their children. Flora came to the confounding conclusion that for all her power and magic, she was not as strong-willed or resilient as the mortals. Being a fairy had softened and coddled her. It had made her entitled and given her a delicate constitution.

That's why, on one blistery October day, Flora was sitting on the couch, dressed and washed and wearing a new body. When her sisters walked through the door, they looked at her curiously. "Sit down," she told them calmly. "I have a plan . . ."

- 24 -

Longshadow breathes a heavy, menacing sigh into my ear. "Yes," it purrs. "You remember now." I feel myself go slack, just like that day in the woods. All my limbs are dead weight. My flesh is a bag of discarded offal, full of tongues and livers.

I had replayed that spring day at Pond Meadow for months. It looped in my mind. It was the only thing I saw and the only thing I thought about. I tried changing bodies. I went through a dozen before I realized that it only made things worse. My mind couldn't escape that day and to wear a different face made the whole experience seem even more complicated.

I needed the resolve of mortality. I needed to feel as humans felt—that there was only a finite amount of time to work through trauma. For fairies, time is inconsequential. I didn't want to wait a millennium to feel normal again. There *was* a way to process the assault in my mind, but I lacked the tools I needed to do it and more importantly, I did not truly understand the nature of urgency. As Flora Bloomshade I looked at the future and saw only years and years of pain.

I brave a long hard gaze into Longshadow and had a sickening realization that it isn't Aaron. It's not a monster. It is a collection of deferred trauma. *My* deferred trauma. It took years of thinking and believing absolutely that I was a human for me to finally understand that you can't just dismiss pain like an unwanted child. That child will always return angry and full of vitriol with fantasies of revenge. A child cares nothing for logic. A child is not concerned with why it was unwanted. It is concerned only with being abandoned. In its fury, it wants is to hurt others as much as it has been hurt.

By using my magic, I had tried to take a shortcut. But the young woman on the blanket that belonged to Aaron's mother was *raped*. There are no short-cuts to getting over that violation. It was all right for me to freeze that day, just like I'm frozen now. It was okay that I did not know how to fight back against such a shocking betrayal. And it *was* a betrayal.

I lift my head and stare into the heart of Longshadow. Here is my anger. Here is all my bitterness and hate. It swirls around like a thousand purple pinwheels. Longshadow's shape can barely contain each revolution; it swells in agony to accommodate my rage. As Flora, it was easier to blame myself than feel the weight of this savagery. It was easier to believe that this all could have been prevented if I had just made different choices.

I have to own that a small part of that is true.

A very *small* part.

As wise as I was, *as I am*, I had missed all the signs that pointed directly at Aaron's true character. Signs that in hindsight are glaringly obvious to me now. But had I? Really? Or had I chosen to ignore them because I liked him so much? I wandered into the woods alone with a man I did not know very well thinking that I didn't have any power of my own, - without my wand. But I had plenty. I am thousands of years old. I have seen empires rise and fall. I have watched kingdoms devour other kingdoms. Even as Lo Smith, with no magic at all, without a single memory, I have power. So, to recuse myself completely of responsibility would mean I'd have to deny that I had any power at all.

Still...

Still . . .

Etta and Ana come crashing through the bushes. Etta's out first, pumping her little arms and legs and biting down on her lip with such outrage I'm afraid she'll need stitches. Ana follows quickly after. She has the baseball bat out, and she's protecting Baby with her other hand which is wrapped around the carrier with the tenacious grip of a Python.

"Stop! Stop!" I scream and my sisters skitter along the mud. Their breathing is rapid and their postures rigid and flexed.

Longshadow hisses at them and then turns its attention back to me. It has no eyes for me to look into. It cannot see the truth. It has no heart for forgiveness and no fingers to count the number of people who love it.

But *I do.*

I let the tension rise in my joints as the swell and clamoring music of my very own magic roars through my ears. It is a song that's telling me what to do. I reclaim the use of my body and in one swift and determined motion, I shove my hand into Longshadow's center and find my wand inside the icy depths. If I had known that my pain would have birthed such a monster, I would have made a different choice. And by that same admission, if I had known what Aaron would go on to do to me that day, I would never have gone with him; I wouldn't have spent one minute with him. But I had felt such affection for the man that I had let my defenses drop as easily as a silk robe falls off a bare shoulder. It cost me dearly, but had Aaron been a good person, the reward would have been extraordinary.

This is the gamble we take, fairy and mortal alike, when it comes to allowing ourselves to be seen from every angle, for letting another person run their fingers over the grooves and ridges of our true nature like braille. This kind of exposure offers so many opportunities to be hurt. However, there is a 100% chance that we will never love or be loved if we choose the alternative, if we lock ourselves away and wrap ourselves in so many layers that we can never be touched or read or seen. Longshadow stole our wands and hid them in places that were as ugly and terrible as I felt about myself when *I* cast the curse.

"It wasn't your fault," I whisper.

"It wasn't your fault," I say again, and Longshadow grows lighter, less dense. The pressure on my bones lessens. "No one will ever hurt you like that again. Let go."

Longshadow shudders as it shrinks. I don't know if I'm willing it to disappear or if it and I are finally accepting the truth. Probably both. I grip the wand tighter. "*Let go,*" I plead and then, I pull. I yank my hand out of its arctic reach and the shadow moans. It's not a howl of pain or a growl of danger. It's the low and steady wail of relief. Longshadow spins inside itself, growing smaller and smaller until it's just a speck that floats up and away. I know the Shadow will never completely disappear. I will always have to contend with the day at Pond Meadow, but it will never grow any bigger than a mote of dust, and though it will always hover on the periphery, the shadow will never truly hurt me again.

I roll over in the mud and clasp my wand to my chest as my memories come flooding back in a torrential rush.

1,2, 3 . . . 4

That awful gingham blanket.

A castle with slate turrets that Fauna has turned emerald green.

A singing girl. A silly girl. A sad girl. A mortal girl.

Purple fire.

Steel. Bullets. Swords. Tanks. Airplanes. Shelter. A spell I weave to make them all less afraid.

Fox. Fox and me. Fox and his ridiculous Manor with so many rooms we can't count them. Fox's hand and the crestfallen look in his eyes when I let go of it.

Wind. Water. Ocean. Ships. Streets that twist and move.

Roses. Roses are red and sometimes pink. I always make them pink.

Etta stomps over to where I'm lying and crouches down over me. "Never again," she barks. "That's the last time I ever let you curse me, and if you even think about asking, for whatever reason, I'll curse you. I'll turn you into a toilet seat or a slug. I mean it, Flora, ***Never. Ever.*** Again."

- 25 -

"Giacomo!" Em hollers. "Giacomo, what are you doing? Why are you not here?" Maleficent tuns her head tersely toward us and shakes it. "It's like he deliberately goes to the other end of the house when he knows I'll be needing him. Giacomo!"

Finally, Giacomo appears at the door, though door isn't quite the right word for the exit to Em's backyard patio. It's more like a window, several tall windows that fan outward breaking up Em's wall like a row of bronze turnstiles.

Giacomo regards her laconically. "Finally, what on earth were you doing?" she demands.

"The laundry," he responds with attitude. Em must really have a soft spot for this one.

"Well, stop it. Stay in the kitchen. We're going to need drinks. A lot of drinks. **Are you raising your eyebrows at me**?" Giacomo shrugs slightly. "I can't with you today, just bring us another round and then another after that until I tell you to stop." Giacomo turns on his heels and retreats. Em sighs dramatically.

The four of us are sitting at a teak table on her deck, which has a spectacular view of The Undervale's desert. It's all brush and cacti. There are a few other houses but apart from that, it is so open it's as if the land has taken in a giant breath in and then exhaled the vista clean. The sun has dipped and now swells on the horizon. Baby is mercifully asleep in her pram. I had conjured and charmed a little pink parasol to protect her precious face and tiny body from the afternoon glare. The rest of us have plenty of shade under Em's wide umbrella which is the size of a car.

"I don't understand why you didn't call me," Em throws up her hands, and her long nails glint in the light. "Not at first, of course, because you know how uncomfortable tears and sweatpants make me, but after a couple months, you should have sent for me. Did you think I was incapable of helping you? Did you really imagine you were the first fairy that a mortal had hurt . . . in that way?" Her voice trails off. Actually, I did think I was the first. I couldn't imagine another fairy being so unguarded with a mortal, let alone Maleficent.

Maleficent?

That's a conversation worth having, but not now. Maybe not ever, unless she's the one to bring it up.

"I wasn't thinking properly, Em, and let's be honest. You have many wonderful qualities, but empathy is . . . well . . . you know . . . I couldn't deal with you being angry with me and I assumed you would be."

Em glares and squints her eyes in disapproval. "Well, I wouldn't have been. Not deliberately anyways." My sisters and I give each other the briefest of knowing looks. It seems Em is always trying *to not* be awful.

Her success rate is worrisome at the best of times.

"And this Aaron person, why didn't you just kill him? Slowly. It beggars' belief that you let him live."

"We aren't murderers. We don't just kill people," Ana says indignantly. She's still wearing Ana Smith's face. She has the same wide eyes, like two perfect circles of cut green velvet. But, unlike the Ana before we got our wands back, her hair is set like it's been blown out by a professional and her Kelly green silk dress with its high frilly collar and billowy sleeves looks like it was tailor made for her by the best couturier in Paris.

"What are you talking about?" Etta snarls. Etta looks exactly the same. "Of course we kill people. We've fought on the right side of every significant war the humans have ever waged."

"That's different," Ana puffs out her chest. "That was war, not murder."

"It felt a lot like murder, just saying," Etta sits back in her chair.

"Yes, yes," Em waves her hand dismissively. "Bang, bang, stab, stab, we've all gone to war, usually as men of course. But I'd like to know how you punished this disgusting creature."

"It was actually quite a lot of work," Etta says as she straightens her back and preens as she pats at her short hair. "First, we had to remove the memory of his existence from every person who had ever known him, who had ever met him, who had even heard of him. *That* was a time suck. But of course, we didn't remove *his* memories. Then we turned him into a young lady and left him in a country with very poor health care and no regard at all for women's rights. He's in a really bad place, emotionally—I just checked on him. It's incredibly gratifying."

"Oh, *that is* good," Em said with a chipper smile. "It works on so many levels. Flora, you must feel like justice has been served."

My sister's elaborate vengeance didn't make much of a difference back then and it still doesn't now. My face, which is still Lo Smith's face, is neutral. I've smoothed out and straightened my unruly hair. Instead of a t-shirt, I'm wearing a crisp linen blouse and a very expensive watch. "I don't think he's worth wasting a single thought on. Emotions are energy, especially in this place. It's enough that I know he won't hurt another girl the way he hurt me."

"Ahh yes," Em nods. "The shadow creature. You three must understand now, how remarkable it was that you were able to create it, Flora. Fairies can't create in that way. We can conjure illusions of people, golems, changelings, and what not- but a sentient being? I've never heard of such a thing."

Giacomo walks out onto the deck holding a large tray and an obscenely oversized pitcher. He sets the tray down with a clang and clears his throat. "Very funny, Giacomo. I suppose you want me to pour our martinis out of this inappropriate vessel like its beer?"

"Hmph," is all he gives her before disappearing into the house.

"That wretched servant," Em clucks irksomely. "I'd turn him into a lizard but then he wouldn't have any hands, would he?" She says this with a sly smile.

"Well, my theory is that Longshadow was born because we were, for all intents and purposes, human, in a magical place." I'm changing the subject. Em could go on for hours about her servants. "Humans create monsters like Longshadow every minute of the day. We have dungeons and mines and vaults full of them. It's one of the main reasons that The Undervale even exists."

"Yes, but you aren't human, darling," Em snaps. "And the curse itself! I understand that you were traumatized, Flora. You weren't in your right mind, but you two—" she points her finger at Etta and Ana "—You went along with it. Your idiocy leaves me speechless. I can't even remember the last time I was speechless." Em taps her chin with her finger. "It might have been the invention of the Internet maybe? Or when the humans started throwing acid on denim and wearing it? *That* was mind-boggling."

"We ran out of options," Ana declares with a shake of her head.

"Flora was becoming a ghost," Etta tells her plainly. "She was in so much pain. It's not exactly like we volunteered with gusto, *believe me*. It was more like we went along with it."

Em glares spitefully at us and pours herself a martini. She brings the pitcher up high and lets the liquid fall slowly, annoyingly, into the glass. "That doesn't even make any sense." Em is clearly irritated. "You didn't erase the memory for good, did you? Why would you think that things would be any different once she recovered it?"

"Because" I say as I grab a glass of my own. "I needed to believe that I was mortal. I needed to become human so that I could really heal, or at least, that was my logic at the time. Fairies…we never get sick. We never get hurt. We don't die. Time doesn't mean anything to us. A fairy doesn't know what to do when something terrible happens because nothing *really* terrible ever happens. Humans understand how to survive in a way that fairies don't- because fairies are never afraid, not completely, not wholly. And *human* women? They're always afraid. Afraid of walking home alone, of empty parking garages and vans with dark windows and leaving their drinks unattended. And yet, they survive, even when the worst things happen. You know why?" I ask rhetorically while pouring myself a healthy drink. "A girl is born knowing how to flinch. All humans instinctively understand that pain is part of life. And most mortals—not all, but most—persevere because they have experience recovering. When they get hurt, the pain passes because time actually moves for them. *That's* what I needed. I needed to believe that time was finite. I needed to gain that experience with authentic, genuine feelings. And I knew that if my sisters didn't go along with it, they wouldn't leave me be. Not in the condition I was in."

Maleficent puts her drink down and looks at me intently. "You hold humans in far too high a regard, Flora."

"And you have let magic spoil you in ways that you don't even understand," I shoot back. Etta and Ana instinctively lean away from the table as Maleficent stares at me with a look so cold, it's meant to break someone apart.

Not me though.

I was never that fragile. I wish I had remembered that.

She taps her long nails on the wood table and electricity hisses in the air. Smoke and copper spread across my tastebuds. Then Em opens her mouth and laughs. Etta and Ana exhale audibly.

"You're still not yourself, old friend," Em purrs. "Even you have to admit that much."

"None of us are our old selves," Ana jumps in quickly. "I have *all* my memories. I remember my entire life as Fauna Bloomshade, but somehow, I still feel like I'm Ana Smith- like a seventeen-year-old girl. It's the oddest thing."

"Well, I imagine that's because you went for so long without using your wands and believing that you really were just girls." Em shrugs casually and takes a drink. If she had been offended at my barb, she has either gotten over it or she is storing the insult to use against me at a later time.

"I don't really mind," Etta says softly. "Etta is a pretty cool gal. She's feisty, like Merriweather, to be sure, but she worries less about things. She's less anxious."

"And Ana is less concerned with attention," Ana proclaims innocently. All three of us look at her with a frown. "No, I mean obviously, Ana likes to be noticed but unlike Fauna, Ana does more things that make her happy. She doesn't care as much what other people think of her."

"And Lo is okay," I say with a smile. "Flora couldn't understand how she let that day happen. How she gave up so much power—her *real* power, not her magic—to that awful man. Lo understands that he was a manipulative asshole. Lo knows that Flora's only crime was trusting the wrong person and maybe, not listening to her instincts. It was not her or . . . my fault. *It wasn't my fault;* it was his and I'm going to be all right."

"Wait." Em drains what's left in her glass. "Are you three trying to tell me that you are going to remain in those bodies, as those teenage girls? Seriously?"

"It's not so much about the way we look as how we feel," I try to explain. "We feel like humans who know that they are really fairies, as opposed to fairies who are pretending to be human. Obviously, at some point, we won't feel like teenagers, but it takes a while for mortals. I don't think they feel like adults until they're like, thirty."

"Some of them never feel like adults," Etta corrects me.

Maleficent's hands jut out. The elegant bones on her wrists swivels back and forth. "So, this is a choice. A deliberate, actual choice to wear these very young, very unremarkable bodies." Not a question. Not even an observation. Em is making a judgment.

"As Lo Smith, I'm extremely remarkable," I counter. "Regardless of our height or weight or skin color—the number of freckles we have, the size of our feet, the length of our legs and eyelashes—my sisters and I are and always will be extremely remarkable."

"And humble," Maleficent chuckles to herself.

I shrug. "It was more of a philosophical, bigger picture kind of thing."

"If you're going to start with the whole 'you go, girl!' finger snapping, I will throw up on the table. I will actually retch, right here. It's adorable you still think that our appearances don't matter but save it. I'm not buying what you're selling. The world—mortal, fairy, other—it doesn't work that way."

"And I think it's sad that you're still so obsessed with the way a thing looks on the outside," Etta backs me up. "We've literally worn a thousand faces and I have had the most remarkable experiences, really deep and meaningful journeys, when my appearance was nothing special on the surface. That's all it is. Surface."

"Especially since it's all so subjective," I push. "You told us about how and why we beefed way back when," I begin and Em's body language changes immediately.

Maleficent closes her eyes and then bows her head as she starts to cackle. "You three were hideous old ladies—sometimes big, sometimes wispy, which was so confusing, and you had the hats? Remember?" Em lifts her arms over her head and brings her fingers together like she's playing charades. "The pointy ones that looked like pylons."

"I liked those hats," Ana frowns. "They had these cute little veils on them, and they matched our capes."

"Right, as I was saying," I interject before Ana goes on a sartorial walk down memory lane that could take an hour, two hours . . . more if she keeps drinking. "What you didn't say when you were regaling us with your extraordinary version of events was that at the time, your face was shaped like a giant...fox?" I phrase this as a question because I'm not sure what animal she was using for inspiration. "And you had these black . . . I don't know if it was a head piece or a wig or if they were real horns coming out of your head? But for sure, your face and I guess your whole body was green. Chartreuse is probably a better description. Anyhow, you looked like a Martian."

"Avant-garde, ever heard of it?" Maleficent hisses. "Alexander McQueen would go on to copy that whole aesthetic centuries later. You've probably never heard of him but ask Fauna. I was a trailblazer. It was a *Look*."

"Was it though?" I ask with a grimace.

Em practically growls. "What difference does it make? Honestly. I really couldn't care less if you want to be in those bodies for a thousand years, and I don't want to argue because I'm so much better at it than you, it becomes tedious. Let's squash that, okay? Because there's one thing that's been bothering me." Em has shifted gears so quickly; I don't have time to respond to the insult. I want to tell her that I'm not a lawyer so who cares about my rhetoric skills? But the window has passed. *She is good.*

"Not bothering exactly, because honestly, I don't care all that much. I suppose it's more like...*wondering*. Did you have some kind of fail-safe? After five years, you got some poor mortal to bring a baby to your door so that the curse could start to unravel? Because I have to say, the baby thing was not necessary. Or was saddling yourself with a snotty kid another part of your punishment and self-loathing?"

"What? Y—yes," I stutter. "I mean no. I mean . . . there was a fail-safe. The curse was supposed to fade on its own in two decades. I didn't hide the wands, you know. I buried them in our backyard. It was Longshadow who hid them. Maybe to protect me? By putting them in places it thought I'd be too scared to go into or maybe as a way of getting me to confront what happened. Without the Oracle, we never would have found them."

"I think we're all aware of how close we came to losing our wands, thanks," Etta notes bitterly. I can't exactly blame my sister for being annoyed. Ana and I had coerced her into going along with the plan. Longshadow was never part of the agreement. I clear my throat. It really doesn't matter. We have our wands and now there's a much more pressing concern.

"That's why we came here today." I put my elbows on the table and lean forward. "We all sort of assumed that you stole Baby, that you figured the presence of such an innocent mortal would bend the curse's will."

"You what?" Em gapes.

"We understand, Mal," Ana tells her kindly, using her own personal pet name for Em. "We didn't know what was going on. We thought we were teenagers and you probably assumed that we would judge you too harshly, that we wouldn't understand about the kidnapping, which to be fair, we probably would have done. We would have thought you were a horrible fairy person."

"We know now," I lower my tone to sound thoroughly empathetic, "that you were just doing whatever you could to make things right. But it's time; Baby needs to go back to her parents."

Em's face freezes as if someone has slapped her. Then her lips curve upwards and she breaks into a hearty laugh. "I didn't take that baby!" Em is laughing hysterically. She'll stop for a minute, look at Baby, and then start up again. When she sees that we are most definitely not laughing, she calms down and wipes the tears from her eyes. "God, you threaten to kill a baby *one* time . . ."

"Em," I roll my eyes and try to reason with her over the intermittent whoops of laughter that she can't seem to quell. "All we're saying is that we don't care if you stole her. It's kind of sweet, but we need to give her back."

Maleficent stops laughing abruptly. She stares at the three of us wildly. "You really think . . .? *I* didn't take her! I hate babies, you know that." Em downs the martini in a single, effortless gulp. "I can barely stand the fact that she's in my house right now. Babies are wearisome and they smell bad, and they are entirely too fragile. I promise you; it wasn't me."

I look at Ana and Etta, confused. "If it wasn't you then . . ." I wonder out loud.

"Well, who else did you tell about this curse of yours?" Em demands.

"No one!" I screech. "The only people that knew were the three of us. You two didn't say anything, did you?" I ask my sisters.

"Of course not," Ana promises.

"As if I would ever admit to my friends that I would willingly turn myself into an amnestic seventeen-year-old for twenty years," Etta scoffs. "The answer is no. I definitely did not tell anyone."

I stand up and walk over to Baby who has just woken up and is now happily gurgling in her pram. I swoop her into my arms and Baby smiles as she reaches for my hair.

"I don't understand." I put my hand over Baby's fist to stop her from yanking too hard. I would happily raise Baby as my own. I love children but I would never deprive a child of its family. If Baby is an orphan or a foundling, well, that's a different story. But if she is, then who would have known to bring her to The Undervale?

"Looks like you have another mystery to solve," Em chuckles sarcastically. "At least you have your memories and your magic this time."

My sisters and I exchange worried looks. We'll have to get to the bottom of this quickly. It's not like the old days when fairies could just take any baby they wanted to. The queen has rules and more than likely, the three of us are in breach of them.

"Oh no," I say softly as I pull Baby closer to me.

"Yay!" Baby says, not to contradict but because it's the only word she knows.

I catch my sisters' eyes. We don't need to say anything. After so many thousands of years, we have a code of blinking lids, chin tilts, tapping fingers, and bitten lips. After deciphering each other's faces, it looks like we're all in agreement. Any plans we may have had for re-entry into our fairy lives would have to wait. Baby needs us. We have to take her home.

EPILOGUE

Ninny Goldendash sits in one of her ample aluminum chairs. She runs her long nails over the fraying bits of woven plastic that were once brightly covered in checks and stripes along the arm rest and bucket. After fifty years, their colors have dimmed to anemic reds, washed out blues, and forlorn yellows.

She watches the clothes in the tumble dry fall over one another again and again. The ancient turquoise machine has a rhythm all its own and its contents are trapped in a cyclical waltz. 1,2,3 ... 1,2,3 ... 1,2,3 ... Ninny's body sways, keeping time with the dryer.

The bells that hang above the front door slam into one another, announcing the patron's frenzied arrival. She feels him behind her, though she doesn't bother to turn her head.

"Ninny—" the voice begins.

"*Not here* for heaven's sake." Ninny pushes herself up from the chair and peels her dress away from the back of her knees that have grown sticky in the launderette's humidity. "Anyone passing by could see you. You want to get caught? You aching to spend some time in Her Majesty's dungeon?"

"Stop being so paranoid," he tells her flatly. This is a new face he's wearing. At least he'd been smart enough to do that much.

Everyone in The Undervale knows him, but it always takes a second for fairy sight to kick in, for the residents to see past the glamours and to the truth of who they really are. He must have been counting on this delay. Still, he is very bundled up, with a long black coat and the brim of a featherless fedora pulled right down to his brows. "No one's looking. No one even suspects."

"Not yet," Ninny corrects him. "Come on." She gestures, as she walks to the back of the store and the entrance of her private quarters. She hears him on the steps. He is light on his feet where she is considerably more deliberate. Her slippers heft down into the floorboards and each stair groans just a fraction beneath her weight.

She thinks for a moment about what to do next. She knew that he was bound to come, eventually. Ninny isn't up for a fight, and she has lived for too many years to be lectured. Setting the tone, she drops herself into the large armchair that squats in living room and leans back. He chooses to remain standing, and this decision alone gives her a preview to his mood.

"I can't believe how short-sighted you were, how reckless," he hisses. "You took her! What were you thinking? That she wouldn't be missed?"

"I was thinking that we can't wait any longer. That the situation is becoming untenable, and we cannot do this without them. Yes, I took a risk, but it paid off. The curse is broken." Ninny's casual drawl is gone- replaced with sharp vowels and cutting consonants. She doesn't want to argue, but she's ready to defend her decision.

"The Bloomshades have been parading her all around The Undervale. Someone is going to say something and we're going to get caught, either by the Royal Guard or those . . . those people in the mortal realm."

Ninny sniffs apathetically. "They aren't really people though, are they? That's the whole point."

"You know what I mean," the man says as he furiously shoves his hands into the pockets of his wool coat.

"No," Ninny shook her head defiantly, "I don't. This is a time-sensitive problem. How can you not see that?"

All the birds in all their various cages collectively swivel their heads around to stare at the man with their small, black and beady eyes. She watches him straighten and roll his shoulders. He is trying to get comfortable beneath their gaze. A single side of Ninny's mouth turns up. Half a smile. Her old friend will not find a moment of comfort under her pets' steely and judgmental gaze.

"People are getting hurt. *Children*. It's alarming to me that you think this isn't urgent," Ninny continues to argue.

"Children are always getting hurt. It's one of the many disgusting things that happen in the mortal realm," he whips back.

Ninny grips the fat armrests until the whites of her enormous knuckles turn into five luminous ridges. "Not these children. They need us and we need the Bloomshade sisters. I'm not going to apologize."

"Well, you should!" the man counters. "That's the least you could do considering that you made a decision without so much as a word to me that affects both of us, all of us really, including the Bloomshades."

"You're whining," she tells him flatly and he winces. Ninny's not sure if it's her harsh tone or the glare of her birds that makes him look so uncomfortable. "What's done is done. They have the baby, and they will guard her with their lives. More than that, they're going to want to figure out where she came from. When those girls learn about that place, when they find out the truth, do you really think that they'll wish we waited?"

"Uhhh," the man considers what to say. With Ninny, it's always best to know *exactly* what to say.

But before he gets the chance to continue, Ninny keeps going. "Were you gonna do it? Twenty years from now- "Were you planning on bein' the one to tell the Bloomshades that we could have prevented this mess from going any further, but we waited because it was dangerous? Because we may have tipped our hand? You know how they feel about kids. They aren't like other fairies in that regard."

He thinks about her words for a moment and then bows his head. The only thing Ninny can see is the black brim of his hat. "No. I wouldn't have volunteered for that particular conversation. But now that they have the baby, we should go to Flora, Fauna, and Merriweather and tell them straight away. We need to let them know so that they can prepare. You *are* going to tell them, right? They need ample warning."

Ninny chortles. "I won't need to tell them. They'll figure it out faster than I could confess to my part in breaking Flora's curse. All they need to know is *where* I got the baby, not who delivered her. I'd rather not distract them with how I interfered in their very strange personal business."

"Ninny . . ." he says cheekily, as he looks her in the eye. "Are you afraid? Of the Bloomshade girls?""

"You're damned right I'm afraid. And you should be too. That's the point. When they find out where that baby came from, nothing and no one will be able to contain their rage. The Bloomshades may well be the only ones who are powerful enough to stop this."

"But the queen—"

"Screw the queen. She *knows*. She knows about all of it, and she won't do a damn thing because of politics." Ninny was getting worked up now. She felt the ire rise from her toes and shoot up her wide calves and into her heaving bosom. "Those girls are gonna have to contend with her too and you know what that means."

"What? No," he yelps. This is not what he signed up for. Treason? Sedition? Maybe the rumors are true. Maybe Ninny Goldendash has lost her mind. "*Contend* with her? You mean fight her? The queen?"

"She calls herself that, but she ain't never been much of a ruler. I reckon that one of the Bloomshade gals should take over The

Undervale." Ninny's drawl is back and thicker than ever. Her eyes have gone wide and wild. "They're gonna have to, if they want to stop what's been goin' on." Ninny leans forward. The chair rumbles beneath her frame. Her massive hairdo tilts to one side. Swinging around her neck on a thick gold chain, her wand begins to crackle and glow. "It's perfect…The Bloomshade sisters will fix everything. No more queen, no more of that nasty business in the mortal realm." Ninny's grin is wide and full of unspoken plans. "Two birds. One stone."

ACKNOWLEDGEMENTS

This is a book about a lot of things but the foundation of it is built on sisterhood. I have the greatest, funniest, most loving and supportive girlfriends all over the world- from Reykjavik to New York to California, all the way to Hawaii. These women know when to break out the wine and the emergency Kaftans- perfect for crying, belly laughing, dancing and watching episodes of Star Gate (or other similar 90's campy sci fi). Blood may be thicker than water but who hikes up to see a glorious bloodfall? Who soaks in geothermal pools of blood? Vampires? I guess? I'm almost positive I don't know any vampires (at least the bloodsucking variety at any rate.)

I'll take the water thanks.

I could not have written this book or any other without their support in every definition of the word. They have my deepest gratitude.

I also want to thank my husband Matt, who graciously and lovingly gives me the time and space I need to work. My father, David Foster who is my loudest and most fervent cheerleader and fan. Finally, I would like to thank my children who have endless patience and grace when I am deep into work mode. I often get lost in these worlds I build. My kids always know where to put the breadcrumb trail so I can find my way to them, to the real world, back home.

ABOUT THE AUTHOR

Born in Victoria, British Columbia, Amy Skylark Foster is an award-winning songwriter and author. As a musician, she has collaborated with and written songs for Michael Buble, Beyoncé and Solange Knowles, Cher, Andrea Bocelli and Blake Shelton. She is also very involved in the fiber community as a knitter, crocheter, yarn dyer and weaver. She has her own yarn label and spends time in the wilds of Iceland on various sheep farms. Amy slip casts ceramic pieces and loves experimenting with glazes that almost always never explode in her kiln. Most of the year, Amy lives with her husband Matt and son Vaughn in Portland, Oregon. She has two adult daughters, Mikaela and Eva who are off pursuing their dreams. Amy spends her summers in Akureryi, Iceland- a magical place where there are definitely elves, trolls *and* fairies.